SAGEBRUSH
SEDITION

SAGEBRUSH SEDITION

A Novel by

WARREN STUCKI

SUNSTONE
PRESS

SANTA FE

Sunstone books may be purchased for educational, business, or sales promotional use. For information please write: Special Markets Department, Sunstone Press, P.O. Box 2321, Santa Fe, New Mexico 87504-2321.

Book design I Vicki Ahl ═══════ Cover design I Elizabeth Stucki
Body type I Franklin Gothic Book ═══════ Display type I Melbourne
Printed on acid free paper

Library of Congress Cataloging-in-Publication Data

Stucki, Warren J., 1946-
    Sagebrush sedition / by Warren Stucki.
        p. cm.
    ISBN 978-0-86534-631-4 (softcover : alk. paper)
    1. Grand Staircase-Escalante National Monument (Utah)–Fiction. I. Title.
    PS3619.T84S24 2008
    813'.6–dc22

                            2008017614

WWW.SUNSTONEPRESS.COM
SUNSTONE PRESS / POST OFFICE BOX 2321 / SANTA FE, NM 87504-2321 /USA
(505) 988-4418 / ORDERS ONLY (800) 243-5644 / FAX (505) 988-1025

This book is dedicated to the Grand Staircase/Escalante National Monument itself and all the people involved in its creation, both for and against. It is an immense, a wild and an amazing place.

ACKNOWLEDGEMENTS

QUINN GRIFFIN

for his time and help in understanding the rancher's point of view.

MONUMENT MANAGER DAVID HUNSAKER

for his time and help in understanding the Bureau of Land Management's point of view.

SHERIFF LAMONT SMITH

for his help in understanding the county's point of view and showing me the lay to the land.

LINDA STUCKI

my wife, who as usual was tireless in going through the book several times, ferreting out story flaws, grammar, spelling and punctuation.

LIZ STUCKI

my niece, for her time and talent in creating the book cover and the monument map.

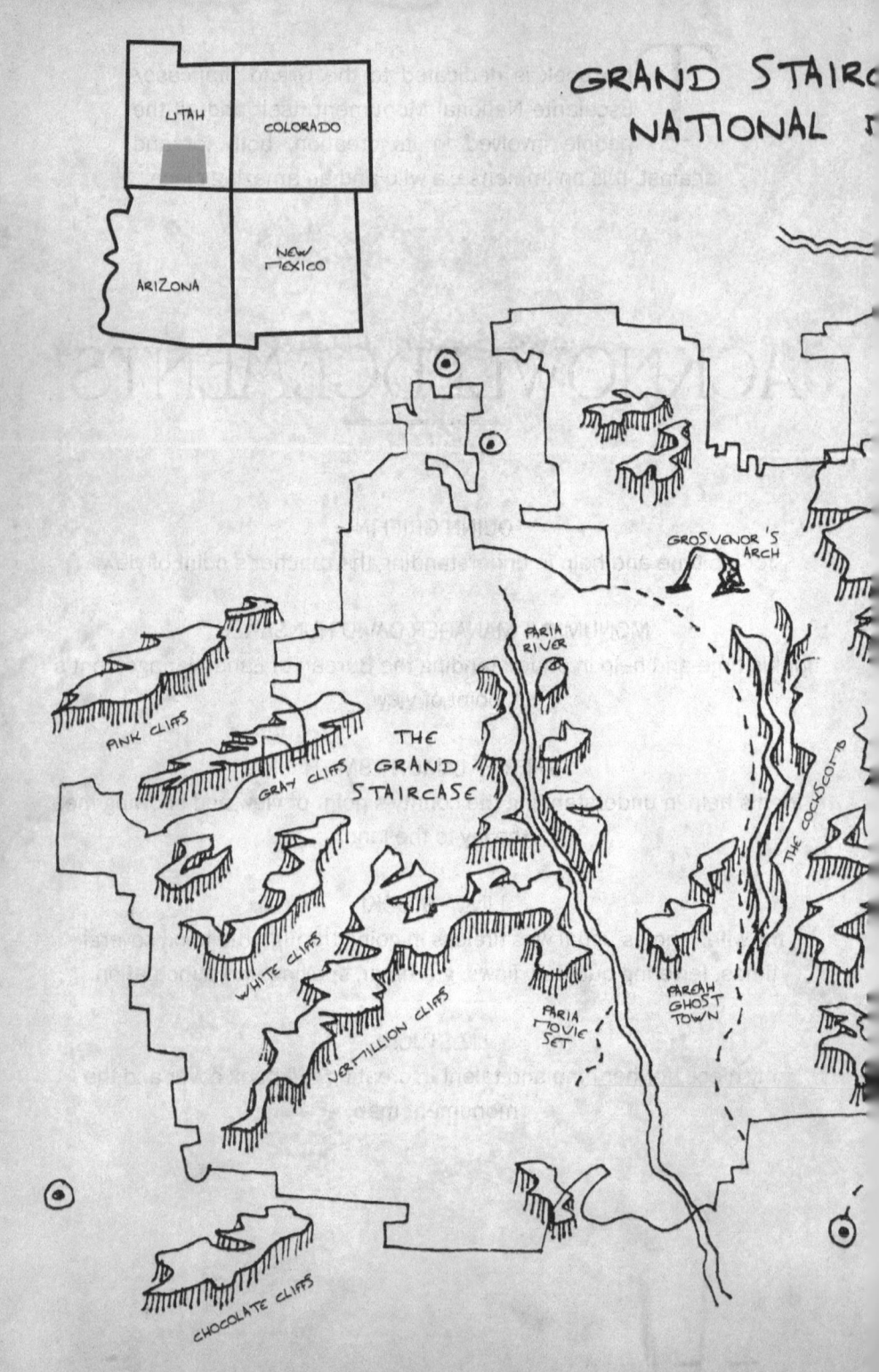

PROLOGUE

Outside El Tovar Lodge, Grand Canyon National Park, Arizona

September 18, 1996

12:10 P.M. Mountain Standard Time

THE PRESIDENT OF THE UNITED STATES:

Thank you very much, ladies and gentlemen. Thank you for being here and for being in such good spirits. Thank you, God, for letting the sun come out. This is a sunny day - we ought to have a sunny day for a sunny day.

Thank you, Rob Arnberger, for the work you do here at Grand Canyon National Park and for your participation; to all of our distinguished guests. I want to say a special word of thanks to my good friend, Governor Roy Romer from Colorado. And then you, Secretary Bruce Babbitt, for your long, consistent, devoted efforts on behalf of America's natural heritage. (Applause.)

I also want to thank the Harvey High School Choir and the students and the faculty from the Grand Canyon Unified School who are here. (Applause.) Where are you all? Thank you. (Applause.) I think this ought to qualify as an excused absence. (Laughter.) Or maybe even a field trip.

I want to thank all of our tribal leaders who are here and, indeed, all of the Native Americans who are here. We are following in your footsteps and honoring your ethic today. (Applause.)

I want to say a special word of thanks to my longtime friend, Norma Matheson. Norma and her late husband, Scott, became great friends of Hillary's and mine when we served together as governors. After Scott passed away, Norma honored me by asking me to come to Utah to speak at a dinner in his honor for a foundation set up in his memory. I never was with Scott Matheson, I never even talked to him on the phone that I did not feel I was in the presence of a great man. Both of them are truly wonderful human beings. And I am grateful for her presence here today and for her commitment. (Applause.)

And finally, I want to thank—more strongly than I can ever convey to you—the Vice President for his passion, his commitment, his vision, and his sheer knowledge of environmental and natural heritage issues. It has become a treasure for the United States and I have mined it frequently for four years. (Applause.)

I remember when I was trying to decide what sort of person I wanted to ask to run with me for Vice President and I made up my mind I wanted somebody who was smarter than I was—that left a large field to pick from—(Laughter)—someone who was philosophically in tune with me, someone who would work like crazy, and someone who knew things I didn't know. And I read Earth in the Balance, and I realized it was a profoundly important book by someone who knew things I wanted to learn. And we have learned a lot and done a lot together over the last four years. Very few things we have done will have a more positive, lasting effect than this, and it will always have Al Gore's signature as well. And I thank him for what he has done. (Applause.)

Ladies and gentlemen, the first time I ever came to the Grand Canyon was also in nineteen seventy-one in the summer. And one of the happiest memories of my entire life was when, for some fluky reason, even in the summertime, I found a place on a rock overlooking the Grand Canyon where I was all alone. And for two hours I sat and I lay down on that rock and I watched the sunset. And I watched the colors change layer after layer after layer for two hours. I could have sat there for two days if the sun had just taken a little longer to set. (Laughter.)

And even today, twenty-five years later, in hectic, crazy times, in lonely, painful times, my mind drifts back to those two hours that I was alone on that rock watching the sunset over this Canyon. And it will be with me till the day I die. I want more of those sights to be with all Americans for all time to come. (Applause.)

As all of you know, today we are keeping the faith with the future. I'm about to sign a proclamation that will establish the Grand Staircase-Escalante National Monument. (Applause.) Why are we doing this? Well, if you look at the Grand Canyon behind me, it seems impossible to think that anyone would want to touch it. But in the past there have been those who wanted to build on the Canyon, to blast it, to dam it. Fortunately, these plans were stopped by far-sighted Americans who saw that the Grand Canyon was a national treasure, a gift from God that could not be improved upon.

The fact that we stand here is due, in large part, to the Antiquities Act of nineteen-o-six. The law gives the President the authority to protect federal lands of extraordinary cultural, historic and scientific value, and in nineteen-o-eight that's just what Theodore Roosevelt did when he protected the Grand Canyon.

Since then, several Presidents of both parties, Republicans and Democrats, have worked to preserve places that we now take for granted as part of our own unchanging heritage: Bryce Canyon, Zion, Glacier Bay, Olympic, Grand Teton. These places many of you have been to, and I've been to many of them myself. I thank goodness that the Antiquities Act was on the books and that Presidents, without regard to party, used it to protect them for all of us and for generations to come. (Applause.)

Today, we add a new name to that list: the Grand Staircase-Escalante National Monument. Seventy miles to the north of here in Utah lies some of the most remarkable land in the world. We will set aside one million seven hundred acres of it. (Applause.)

On this site, on this remarkable site, God's handiwork is everywhere in the natural beauty of the Escalante Canyons and in the Kaiparowits Plateau, in the rock formations that show layer by layer billions of years of geology, in the fossil record of dinosaurs and other prehistoric life, in the remains of ancient American civilizations like the Anasazi Indians.

Though the United States has changed and Utah has grown, prospered and diversified, the land in the Utah monument remains much as it did when Mormon pioneers made their way to the Red Canyons in the high desert in the late 1800s. Its uniquely American landscape is now one of the most isolated places in the lower forty-eight states. In protecting it, we live up to our obligation to preserve our natural heritage. We are saying very simply, our parents and grandparents saved the Grand Canyon for us; today, we will save the Grand Escalante Canyons and the Kaiparowits Plateaus of Utah for our children. (Applause.)

Sometimes progress is measured in mastering frontiers, but sometimes we just measure progress in protecting frontiers for our children and all children to come. Let me make a few things about this proclamation clear. First, it applies only to federal lands—lands that belong already to the American people. Second, under the proclamation, families will be able to use this canyon as they always have—the land will remain open for multiple uses including hunting, fishing, hiking, camping and grazing. Third, the proclamation makes no federal water rights claims.

Fourth, while the Grand Staircase-Escalante will be open for many activities, I am concerned about a large coal mine proposed for the area. Mining jobs are good jobs, and mining is important to our national economy and to our national security. But we can't have mines everywhere, and we shouldn't have mines that threaten our national treasures. (Applause.)

That is why I am so pleased that PacifiCorp has followed the example set by Crown Butte New World Mine in Yellowstone. PacifiCorp has agreed to trade its lease to mine coal on these lands for better, more appropriate sites outside the monument area. I hope that Andalex, a foreign company, will follow PacifiCorp's example and work with us to find a way to pursue its mining operations elsewhere. (Applause.)

Now, let me also say a word to the people of Utah. Mining revenues from federal and state lands help to support your schools. I know the children of Utah have a big stake in school lands located within the boundaries of the monument that I am designating today. In the past these scattered school lands have never generated significant revenues for the Utah school trust. That's why Governor Scott Matheson, one of the greatest public figures in the history of Utah, asked the Congress to authorize the exchange of non-revenue producing lands for other federal lands that can actually provide revenue for the school trust.

Finally, I was able to sign legislation to accomplish that goal in nineteen ninety-three. And I will now use my office to accelerate the exchange process. I have directed Secretary Babbitt to consult with Governor Leavitt, Congressman Orton, Senators Bennett and Hatch to form an exchange working group to respond promptly to all exchange requests and other issues submitted by the state and to resolve reasonable differences in valuation in favor of the school trust. By taking these steps, we can both protect the natural heritage of Utah's children and ensure them a quality educational heritage. (Applause.)

I will say again, creating this national monument should not and will not come at the expense of Utah's children. Today is also the beginning of a unique three-year process during which the Bureau of Land Management will work with state and local governments, Congressman Orton and the Senators and other interests to set up a land management process that will be good for the people of Utah and good for Americans. And I know a lot of you will want to be involved in that and to be heard as well.

Let us always remember, the Grand Staircase-Escalante is for our children. For our children, we have worked hard to make sure that we have a clean safe environment, as the Vice President said. I appreciate what he said about the Yellowstone, the Mojave Desert, the Everglades, the work we have done all across this country to try to preserve our natural heritage and clean up our environment. I hope that we can once again pursue that as an American priority without regard to party or politics or election seasons. We all have the same stake in our common future. (Applause.)

If you'll permit me a personal note, another one, it was sixty-three years ago that a great Democrat first proposed that we create a national monument in Utah's Canyonlands. His name was Harold Ickes. He was Franklin Roosevelt's Interior Secretary. And I'm sorry he never got a chance to see that his dream would become a reality, but I'm very glad that his son and namesake is my Deputy Chief of Staff and is here today. (Applause.)

And it was thirty years before that, ninety-three years ago, that a great Republican President, Theodore Roosevelt, said we should make the Grand Canyon a national monument. In nineteen-o-three, Teddy Roosevelt came to this place and said a few words from the rim of the Canyon I'd like to share with you as we close today: "Leave the Grand Canyon as it is. You cannot improve upon it. What you can do is keep it for your children, your children's children, and all who come after you. We have gotten past the stage when we are pardoned if we treat any part of our country as something to be skinned for. The use of the present generation, whether it is the forest, the water, the scenery—whatever it is, handle it so that your children's children will get the benefit of it."

It was President Roosevelt's wisdom and vision that launched the Progressive Era and prepared our nation for the twentieth century. Today we must do the same for the twenty-first century. I have talked a lot about building a bridge of possibility to that twenty-first century, by meeting our challenges and protecting our values. Today the Grand Staircase-Escalante National Monument becomes a pillar in our bridge to tomorrow.

Thank you and God bless you all. (Applause.)

End 12:27 P.M. Mountain Standard Time

1

PRESIDENT WILLIAM JEFFERSON CLINTON

It is a rare gift—the subtle inflection, the deep resonance, the rolling modulation, the impeccable timing. With just the intimacy of his voice, he massages coarse unrefined noise into fine polished oratory, much like rare wine transforms an ordinary supper into a regal meal. Add to this the engaging warmth of his southern drawl, often spiced with random dashes of self-deprecating humor, and even the weakest of arguments often prevail with no more muscle than his matchless style.

A modern Demosthenes, some would readily compare him to William Jennings Bryan, some with John Fitzgerald Kennedy, while others would eagerly canonize him right alongside the immortal Abraham Lincoln.

"Someone ought'a kill that sum-bitch!" Bucky Lee Eakins snorted as he snapped off the radio then turned to face the others, his gray stubbled face pinched with disgust. Positioning a gob of tobacco juice on his ochre stained tongue, he spat through a quarter-inch gap in his yellowed incisors at a plastic spittoon bucket. Missed.

"Well, that might be a little harsh—"

"—Jesus," Bucky Lee exclaimed, cutting off Douglas "Roper" Rehnquist, "they'se already own two-thirds the goddamn state."

"But he—"

"—he didn't even have the guts to give that speech in Utah," Bucky interrupted again. "Even Teddy Roosevelt, when he deed'icated the Grand Canyon, did it at the goddamn Grand Canyon. That sum-bitch is at least a hundurd and fifty miles away. What a chicken shit," Lee concluded, again expectorating. Again missing. On the rough-hewn plank floor, a puddle capped with mustard foam was beginning to circle the plastic bucket like a frothy moat.

"There's a fine line between discretion and cowardice," Douglas "Roper" Rehnquist volunteered, unhooking his boot heels from the lower rung of the kitchen bar stool. Standing, he stretched out his lanky frame, popping several vertebrae. "He's afraid if he sets foot in Utah, some crazy redneck, like you Bucky, will shoot him."

"Wouldn't mind it." Lee shrugged as he heaved a two-gallon galvanized steel-mixing tub and set it on the counter with a metallic thud. "Wouldn't mind it one damn bit. He's nothin' but a hippie, a womanizer and a draft-dodger. Went to England instead of Nam, you know."

"Oxford—University College, I think, but he didn't inhale," Douglas "Roper" chuckled, subconsciously rubbing his right hand over the stump where his left index finger used to be.

"Yeah, he's a regular pillar of salt." Lee spat again.

"What's that supposed to mean—a pillar of salt?" Ruby Nez asked, not trying to hide her disgust, from her perch on the other kitchen barstool. "You talking about a pillar-of-the-community or Sodom and Gomorrah?"

"Neither. Don't think for a minute this won't affect you, Rube," Lee said, positioning a hand-crank cast-iron meat grinder over the mixing tub and securely screwing it down to the counter lip. The manufacturer's label, TSM, was prominently stamped on the side wall of the hamper. "Nothin' better than these old TSM grinders. Can't break 'em with a sledge hammer."

"What's TSM stand for?" Roper asked idly.

"The Sausage Maker, what'da ya think?" Bucky countered. Once the grinder was securely fastened to the counter, he looked up at Ruby, frowned, scratched his whiskered chin then continued with his original train of thought. "And this heer is one time your looks ain't gonna help ya none, Rubles. Don't mean a damn thing to them BLM boys. They'se asexual."

"Asexual?" Roper Rehnquist asked, arching an eyebrow.

"I've earned everything I've got. Looks had nothin' to do with it," Ruby snapped, her fine features turning flinty hard as black obsidian.

"Don't hurt none your second husband happened to up and die and leave youse that bottomland on the Escalante and that allotment on the fifty."

"That ranch was losing money till he married me, and that's a fact."

"Never did quite figure out how he died," Bucky commented, "somethin' strange about it."

"Died in a hunting accident," Ruby said unflinching. "Nothin' strange bout it at all."

"Only they never found the shooter or the gun."

"They found the bullet, a thirty/thirty. You have a thirty/thirty, don't you?"

"Yeah, an I'm a purdy damn good shot too. Won me some shootin' contests in my time," Bucky asserted, then reached in a counter drawer, pulling out three soiled, blue-ribboned metals, each bearing the inscription, first place. Proudly, he displayed them on the counter.

"They don't say they were for shootin'," Ruby contended.

"They don't say they weren't, neither," Bucky retorted.

"So, you do admit to owning a thirty/thirty." Roper suppressed a smile as he got directly in front of Bucky's face and argued, trying to sound like a prosecuting attorney.

"Everyone does," Lee smirked, pulling a hind quarter of venison from his propane refrigerator. "There's more thirty/thirtys in the state of Utah than cell phones." He paused momentarily as he plunked the meat down on the counter with a thud then looked over at Ruby. "Probably doesn't matter what everyone's been a sayin'?"

"Bucky, you best not go there," Doug Roper Rehnquist cautioned.

"Yeah—yeah, no point in closing the barn door if'n the horses have gout."

"Bucky," Ruby answered, gritting her teeth, "most of the time I have no idea what the hell you're talking about."

"Well, all I'm a sayin', is let them sleepin' dogs die. 'Specially them mean sum-bitches."

"He had his good side," Ruby replied defensively.

"Shore he did, Rube," Bucky said sarcastically, "and so did Ted Bundy. But, all I'm sayin', is all you ranchers is goin' a be in a world of hurt by this here tree hugger."

"He just got done saying there would be grazing," Ruby contended testily.

"Yeah, for now." Lee cut off a small chunk of meat, stuffed it in the grinder and began cranking. "That's just to get the monument in place with the least amount of ruckus. Once things settle down, how long do youse think Gore and his flower-sniffers is goin' to let youse desecrate them holy lands with your stinkin', shittin' cows? Hell, far as they're concerned, them bovines are worse'n them friggin' four-wheelers."

"Nothing worse than ATVs," Roper confirmed.

"Well, I'm not sayin' I'm trustin' 'em," Ruby said.

"I'd be just as worried about the Grand Canyon Trust buying up all the permits," Roper argued. "I'll be darned if I can figure out where they get all their money."

"That's pretty strong language, college-boy," Lee mocked.

"Well, they just bought that big ranch outside of Moab and another on the Arizona Strip," Roper declared, "so they're getting their money from somewhere."

"Bleedin' heart liberals back east, and the Sierra Club," Lee growled. He now had a respectable mound of ground meat, looking like a pile of extruded red worms, impossibly tangled in the bottom of the bowl. "And Robert Redford."

"Why Redford?"

"If'n they have their way, you'll all be a turning in your cowboy boots, chaps and Stetsons for fancy lace-up boots, 'luminum walkin' sticks and Spandex. Shit, he has some nerve callin' hisself a Utahn."

"Who?" Roper asked.

"Robert 'where-the-red-fern-don't-grow' Redford!" Lee spat out the words, followed by another errant attempt at the bucket. "Who'd ya think?"

"I don't think he's so bad," Doug Roper declared, "he means well. But, I suspect your little operation here is goin' to suffer more than Ruby and me."

"I'll be fine," Bucky Lee said, twisting off the top of his can of Skoal. "I'se gone and got myself diversified, like them Wall Street boys."

"Diversified?" Ruby asked.

"I'se got a new line," Bucky said, putting a pinch between his tongue and cheek, then went back to his meat. "Don't youse worry none about me. Soon I'll be making six figures and youse guys will be comin' to me beggin' for a loan and of course I'll say no."

"That'll be the day," Ruby muttered.

"How you going to make that kind of money?" Roper asked.

"Confidential," Bucky Lee said. "Like they say in the marines, don't show, don't kill.

"As usual," Ruby declared, "you're all mixed up."

"You'll see," Bucky Lee insisted, "All I can tell you it has something to do with rocks."

"Rocks!" Ruby exclaimed. "Are you crazy?"

"Clinton definitely said there would be no mining," Roper insisted.

"These ain't just any rocks," Lee explained. "These are rare and there's no mining and that's the beauty of it and that's all I'm goin' to say about that."

"If I were you, I'd be more worried about the BLM closing down some of my old but profitable businesses," Roper said.

"What'a youse mean?" Lee asked, as he sliced off another hunk of venison and continued cranking the grinder.

"Hell, Bucky," Ruby cut it. "Even before the Monument, what you were doing here was illegal."

"What'a youse talkin' bout?" Bucky placed meat-flecked hands on his hips, feigning shock.

"I doubt this will come as a surprise, but there's laws against selling illegal hides and pelts," Roper answered.

"I don't sell nothin' but what I'se got government permits for. There ain't no law agin trappin' an I know, there ain't no law agin making deer sausage or salami any more'n there's a law agin you makin' that awful homemade wine of yours, Rube."

"You're right," Ruby agreed. "But there is a law against poaching and you can't sell wild game in Utah and you can't transport it across state lines either."

"I don't do neither," Lee declared brashly, wiping his hands on his Levis. He finally had the mixing tub two-thirds full of ground meat. "I make meat products for my own use and when I do occasionally do a little retailin', I just charge a small processin' fee, no charge at all for the meat. You know, for my time and the pork filler. Nobody gives me free pig meat."

"Some might call that splitting legal hairs," Roper concluded as he looked over Lee's shoulder, eyeing the tub.

"Or some might just call it plain bullshit," Ruby said.

"You can't make bulls out'a bullshit," Bucky replied.

"Jesus," Ruby said, crossing herself in the traditional Catholic way. "Just once, I wish you'd make some sense."

"Well it's no more bullshit than those cougar hides you bring in for me to sell. I suppose you got a permit for all them?"

"I thought you just sold your own trappings," Roper said, breaking into a disarming grin that seemed to instantly expunge the sadness from his eyes and fill the empty hollows of his cheeks.

"I have a right to protect my calves," Ruby retorted quickly, ignoring Roper.

"Is that what you call it?" Lee sneered. "It's just fortunate, I guess, that one cat hide brings youse more money than a whole yearlin' calf on the hoof."

Plainly irritated, Ruby turned and stomped away, weaving around clumps of floor debris. A half dozen rapid steps and she was clear across the one room cabin, another half dozen and she was quickly back.

"If it's so risky, why do you fence them? And why is it you always have fresh sausage meat year around?"

"I have my sources," Lee said, unperturbed. Deftly he cut a slab of pork loin and began pushing it in the hopper with one hand and grinding with the other. "You need to add a third of pork, venison doesn't have enough fat."

"It's September eighteenth," Ruby persisted, "a full month before hunting season. How is it you've got fresh venison?"

"Like I said, I got my sources. Hell, Rube, you're part Injun. You of all people ought'ta know not everyone needs a huntin' license."

"I'm a quarter Cherokee, you know the Trail of Tears. Not related to the local Indians."

"The trail of what? Well anyway, that's almost like being part Injun."

Ruby shook her head in disbelief then added, "so the Utes just give you their meat?"

"More like sell it. Navajos too." The mixing vessel was now full and Lee used a large manual mixer to blend the ground pork and venison. "Looks good, huh?" he said, smiling through his stained picket-fence teeth.

"So the Indians sell you their deer meat," Roper said thoughtfully. "But when you retail, you just charge for processing and not for the meat. Sounds like you'd need an extra high processing fee just to break even."

"S'mantics," Lee said, adding some sage and red pepper, "word games. I'll fry up some fresh and let youse try it. S'on sale to my friends, youse know."

"Yeah, I'll bet it is," Ruby snickered.

"Just need to add my secret spices," Bucky divulged as he retrieved a Mason jar from the cabinet directly behind him. Opening the jar, he took a pinch of what appeared to be a mixture of various kinds of dried leaves, pulverized them by rolling back and forth in his palms then sprinkled the flakes on the ground meat.

"Smells like sage," Roper suggested.

"No, it smells more like sagebrush and after a good rain," Ruby declared, as the piquant musky odor diffused through the cabin.

Suddenly the over head lights flickered off then came back on for a moment then abruptly went dead.

"Generator's outta gas," Bucky announced as he pulled a gas can from the cabinet under the sink. "This won't take but a minute."

Bucky disappeared out the kitchen door and five minutes later the lights flickered back on. Bucky reappeared at the door then went back to his sausage bowl.

"Well, I've gotta be going, anyhow," Roper said. "Cows won't move themselves."

"Are you moving them off the Fifty down to the Bench already?" Ruby asked.

"Nah, just moving them from my East Spring pasture to my Tank Springs pasture," Roper explained. "You know, BLM makes me rotate every two months."

"Seems awful early," Ruby insisted, looking puzzled, "I'm not rotating mine for at least another month."

"Yeah, but with the drought, my feed's mostly gone," Roper answered. "Your pasture probably is in better shape."

"Brisco ask you to move early?" Ruby asked suspiciously.

"Nah," Roper replied. "Feed's just gone. Cow's can't eat dirt."

"This is way early," Ruby persisted. "You're going to run out of winter pasture way before spring."

"Just have to sell some early." Roper shrugged.

"Who's this guy, Brisco?" Bucky interrupted, mashing the sausage into patties and grabbing a frying pan out of the sink. "I'll cook youse up a batch."

"He's the new head of the BLM," Ruby replied," and he's a she—Judith Brisco. She took over for Egan."

"Can't say that I'm sorry," Roper said, sitting back down on the stool again. "Didn't much like Jon Egan. Never knew where he stood."

"Well," Lee said, dropping meat patties into the sizzling hot skillet. "This is just the beginning, mark my words. First they'll ask you to move early, then they'll ask you to voluntarily drop allotments, then they'll just seize 'em. Be just like the little Battle of the Bighorn."

"Nobody asked me to move," Roper replied, a hint of irritation laced his voice, "and I'm not moving all three hundred and fifty. Anyway, I don't see any similarity to the Little Bighorn."

"If they restrict my allotment, I won't be able to make it." Ruby frowned and removed her black Stetson, then untied the red-checkered bandana that bound her coal-black hair. "Not the way beef prices are droppin'."

"You an Roper ought'ta go on and join up outfits—less overhead and youse are across-the-fence neighbors anyway," Bucky advised. "R and R ranching, sounds good."

"Well, it's a bit more complicated than that," Ruby said, still fussing with her hair.

"Not that complicated. Youse two are already shackin' up anyway, ain't you?" Bucky Lee sneered.

"No!" Roper blushed, quickly averting his copper blue eyes to the smudged fireplace at the far end of the disheveled room. The rancid aroma of hot grease and frying sausage permeated the room, making the cabin feel, in spite of the clutter, a little more homey.

"Can't believe you're such a prude," Lee smirked as he forked sausages onto a paper plate. Almost instantly, a grease halo appeared on the plate encircling each patty. "Youse ain't no saint, even if ya don't cuss and yer old man was a Mormon Bishop."

"Whether we are or not, is no business of yours," Ruby cut in fiercely.

"Bucky, I've never claimed to be like my father."

"Youse absolutely right," Lee smirked, "and youse certainly ain't. He was a real cowman. Here, try some of this, Rube." He offered her the paper plate. "Use your fingers—I ain't washin' no dishes."

Not waiting to be invited, Roper plucked a hot patty out of the frying pan then quickly tossed it from one hand to another while it cooled. Gingerly, he took a bite. "Hot!" he wheezed, hurriedly sucking in cold air. After a moment he continued, "you know the one I feel sorry for is Angus Macdonald."

"You mean that stumpy Englishman?" Bucky asked as he wolfed down a sausage.

"With a name like that," Roper scoffed. "No, not English, Scottish. He's about as English as haggis."

"What's the difference?" Bucky asked. "Either way he's a limey."

"Scotland was settled by the Picts and the Scotti in the north and Angles and Britons in the south," Roper answered matter-of-factly. "England, on the other hand, was settled by various invaders including the Kelts, Romans, Angles, Saxons and the Normans. That's the difference between them, that and about a thousand years of war."

"Jesus, college-boy, that's a hell-uv-a-lot more than I wanted to know," Bucky growled.

"I was just trying to explain."

"It don't do no good showin' off heer. Nobody's impressed," Bucky said sourly, "an if'n youse was so good at college, why din't you stay?"

"No good jobs for English history/literature majors," Roper said, staring down at his now leathery hands and again massaging the finger stub. Certainly, they were not the hands of an English history professor. "And I couldn't stand being cooped up."

"Well anyway, what about Angus?" Ruby interrupted. Suddenly, she seemed interested.

"Din't you date him for a while?" Bucky asked

"It was nothing," Ruby declared. "Just sat with him a couple times at the bar."

"That's not what I heer'd," Bucky said. "I heer'd he was sweet on ya and still is, and youse just up and dumped him."

"No," Ruby protested, shaking her head, "we were always just friends."

"They'se say he had it bad." Bucky turned off the gas on the stove. "They'se say he used to follow youse everywhere. A regular midnight stalker."

"No," Ruby insisted again, firmly. "We were then and still are, just friends."

"Well it don't matter. What about Macdonald, anyway?" Bucky Lee asked Roper. "What's he got to do with this heer daisy-pickin' liberal's folly?"

"He owns Highland Mining and Mineral. They're just a small outfit, not like PacifiCorp or Andalex. Really don't think he has other assets other than his Kaiparowits coal leases."

"Well then he's just plain dead in the water," Lee said flatly.

"I suppose, like a canoe without a paddle," Ruby said sarcastically.

"No, more like a mallard swimmin' next to an aviary," Bucky said.

"It's not just us and Angus goin' to be affected," Roper continued. "What about loggers, hunting guides and prospectors? All of them will be affected."

"Your president made it clear there would be no minin', prospectin' or loggin'," Lee said. "An who knows for sure bout huntin'. What a prick!"

"I didn't vote for him," Roper asserted. "But I do feel bad for Angus. He's a nice guy."

Stone-faced, Ruby concentrated on her sausage and didn't comment.

"Nice guys always get the shaft," Lee said, his face immobile.

"That's why I'se constantly worried about myself."

"Yeah, I worry about that too," Roper said dryly.

"What'll he do?" Ruby ignored Lee, as she gingerly forked another patty.

"I suspect he'll have to move, or find another way to make a living," Roper answered, shaking his head. "Maybe I'll teach him to cowboy."

"Like I said, somebody ought'a shoot that sum-bitch."

"Who—Angus?" Ruby asked.

"No, pay attention. The Pres."

"I hope you're kidding," Roper said, standing, looking for something on which to wipe his greasy hands. Finding nothing he used rumpled newspaper stacked on the edge of the filthy Formica counter.

"I never joke about my's good ideas."

"Guess that means you never joke," Roper said grinning.

"You'd never get within a hundred miles of him," Ruby asserted. "Maybe you could kill him with voodoo or telepathy. Or your stupid parables."

"Killin' his representatives would be like killin' him—"

"—Jeez," Roper cut in. "Let's change the subject. You're starting to spook me."

Ruby stood up and tossed her empty plate into the already full wastebasket. They all watched as it bounced off the heap, then glided to the floor.

"Bucky," Ruby groaned. "Why don't you clean up this dump?"

"Why?" Lee shrugged as he dumped the grease from the frying pan into an empty Pork-and-Beans can, then he tossed the frying pan back into the cluttered sink. "You want to take some home? Custom sausage is hard to find. 'Specially this good stuff—five bucks a pound."

"Processing fee?" Roper asked sarcastically.

"I'll take a couple pounds," Ruby said, a hint of embarrassment in her voice. She glanced over at Roper and shrugged. "Well, I'm getting damn tired of hamburger with my eggs."

"Oh, what the heck," Roper sighed. "Give me a couple of pounds too."

Dividing the sausage into roughly two portions, Bucky Lee wrapped each with wax paper then he snatched the faded newspaper from the counter and double-wrapped, taping both bundles securely with duct-tape.

While watching Bucky, Ruby struggled to retie her hair. Giving up, she stuffed the red bandana into her Levi's pocket and replaced the black Stetson over her tousled head. Mesmerized, Roper watched these antics out of the corner of his eye.

"Doug, you still planning on helping me with my brandin' day after tomorrow?" she asked, heading for the door.

"If'n they'se not branded by the time they'se six months, they becomes property of the county," Bucky said.

"Really?" Roper said sarcastically.

"Anyway, they're not six months yet," Ruby said. "And nobody enforces that law. How can they, it's Fifty Mile Mountain."

"Like I said, I've got to move my cows to my Tank pasture that morning. Can we get yours done in the afternoon?"

"Only got about twenty head, but at four to five months, it'll be a rodeo," Ruby smiled. "Tell you what, I'll give you a hand moving your cows, if you'll help me in the afternoon."

"Deal." Roper grinned.

As they stepped for the door, Bucky gave Ruby and Roper their packages.

"How'd you know this is two pounds?" Roper asked skeptically, "you weigh it?"

"Nah, I can just tell," Bucky muttered. "Bin in this business too long."

"Well, we'll be seein' you." Roper nodded to Bucky as he ducked through the door.

"I mean it, we really shouldn't let him git away with this horse shit," Bucky mumbled at Roper's back.

"What?" Ruby asked, looking sharply at Bucky as she took her parcel.

"We should do somethin' to stop him."

Roper stopped in mid-stride and turned around again.

"For hell's sake, stop who?" Ruby pushed on by.

"Whose the hell we bin talkin' bout?" Lee demanded, a drop of spittle stuck in the gutter of his chin.

"Stoppin' it now is like stopping a train after the caboose has already passed," Ruby declared backing down the walkway. "But if you figure out a way, let me know."

"There's nothing we can do," Roper insisted, his brow furrowed. "It was done perfectly legal. He invoked the Antiquities Act. "

"Antiquities Act, my ass! This is about as legal as my marriage, or my divorce for that matter," Lee hissed through the cleft of his clenched teeth. "An it's immoral. Only in the west does the federal government own this much land. It wasn't supposed to be that way. When territories become states the federal government is supposed to give back all federal lands to the state. That's the way it was in Texas and back east. That's the way it was everywhere exceptin' here in the west. Did ya know the federal government owns more'n sixty percent of this goddamn state?" Lee paused for a breath. "Youse gotta figure somethin' out college-boy, or we'll all be gatherin' our belongin's, like dust bowl refugees of the Great Depression, and jumpin' trains or road-hitchin'. Either way, we'll be out of heer a beggin' for jobs."

"John Steinbeck revisited, huh?" Roper said.

"Who?" Bucky glared back.

"Forget it. There's nothing we can do, not now—not now in nineteen ninety-six," Roper said firmly. "Like I said, the Antiquities Act makes it all legal."

"We're startin' to get a group together," Bucky said confidentially, pausing to fire a wad at the bucket, again hitting high on the sidewall. The yellow slime stuck momentarily then slowly slid to the floor. "Informally, of course. Either one of you interested?"

"Nah, I don't think so," Roper said, shaking his head and scowling.

"Youse think about it, Roper. How bout youse, Rube?"

"When you get things organized and decide what you're all about," Ruby said hesitantly, "let me know. Then I'll decide if I'm interested."

"I'll tell youse two right now, might don't make right and legal don't mean eagle, " Bucky Lee snarled.

"Christ Almighty!" Ruby crossed herself again then stared incredulously at Bucky for a moment. She started to say something, abruptly changed her mind, pivoted on the heel of her boot and quickly stomped away.

"Who put a burr under her saddle?" Bucky asked, feigning offense.

"Sometimes you just have that effect on people," Roper smiled, shaking his head.

"Like the prophets of old, I'se just tell it as it is," Bucky Lee replied, staring at Roper with bleary eyes. "This heer ain't no popularity contest."

"Well then, Bucky," Roper said testily, raising everted palms skyward in an apparent show of frustration. "What's your answer?"

"All I'm sayin' is it's time to stand up and be confounded. Somebody's gotta take back this country from them friggin', bleedin' heart liberals."

2

One Year Later

THE GRAND STAIRCASE

Well over fifty-five hundred feet in total elevation, the cliffs of Utah's plateau land are towering, rangy and distinctively colored. It is, in fact, the various rock hues that have inspired each tier's popular name.

Commencing with the rim of the Grand Canyon and rising ever higher and higher in a northward progression is a great system of cliffs sometimes christened in western geology, the Great Staircase. In geological time, the oldest cliffs form the basal strata and the youngest, the crest or the crown. At the lowest echelon, sits the desert-edged Chocolate Cliffs; the second terrace, the brilliant Vermillion Cliffs; third, coursing ever upward in a step-like manner, are the chalky White Cliffs; the next landing, the steely Gray Cliffs; and the pinnacle, the lofty Pink Cliffs, alpine cap of the Aquarius Plateau.

Certainly, such a regal staircase, so massive, so majestic may be tramped, traversed, or otherwise trekked across by mere mortals—but surely only Gods may glibly stride up and down its colossal steps.

"What a great speech!" Sean Dunn O'Grady jumped to his feet, enthusiastically joining the erupting applause. With tears brimming and overflowing, he turned to the short, balding man on his right and shouted above the din, "Isn't he great? Best damn president since JFK!"

The thunderous applause continued and so did Sean. His hands ached, his palms turned a meaty red and his fingers felt like stiff wooden appendages, numbed from the paralytic pounding. But who cared? What a victory! What a day!

Just imagine, Sean Dunn O'Grady rubbing shoulders with congressmen, senators, cabinet secretaries, governors, top-level bureaucrats and a virtual who's who of the Intermountain business community. Everyone who was anyone was here, that is everyone except the conspicuously absent Utah political delegation. They considered it grandstanding, but to Sean it looked more like a grand display of sour grapes. The governor, both senators and both representatives, all republicans, as a show of solidarity in their displeasure, had snubbed the proceedings. What sore losers. Who needs them? Who cares?

But what an honor for the likes of Sean Dunn O'Grady. Never in his wildest dreams did he think he would be hobnobbing with these people, literally the de facto royalty of America. Nor did it matter that they mostly ignored him. What counted, he was here!

Looking around he grinned, his abundant freckles bunching at the corners of his mouth and surfing over the bridge of his nose. Without a doubt, from the looks of the attendees, he must have the smallest bank account of anyone. Being president of the Southern Utah Chapter of the Western Wilderness Alliance wasn't exactly a yellow brick road paved with blocks of gold bullion or landscaped with dollar trees. But he hadn't done it for the money. He would gladly trade trivial paper money for a righteous cause any day. Environmental crusades were his staff of life, his soul food, and that's what he did it for. Today was his payday, not some computer printed check. And this was one hell-uv-a-day.

When he'd first received the invitation, he had been ecstatic. It was so unexpected, not that he hadn't dreamed about it. The summons had to be the administration's way of thanking him for his part, however small, in bringing this mammoth project to fruition. And he had played a modest part. Perhaps, a bigger part than anyone had realized, but some things are better left unsaid, some stories simply cannot be told. By their very nature, some things are not to be openly applauded and are meant only for self-congratulations. His role was like that.

From his church days of another life and time, he knew pride was a sin, but even in those days it was always considered a minor sin. Now as a devout atheist, he really did not believe in retribution for transgressions, thank God for that, nor rewards for good works. He realized, of course, a certain code of ethics was necessary for society to survive and keep anarchy at bay, but he really didn't believe in sin, only crime, and of course crime was legislated by society as a firewall to deter chaos. But if a crime was committed and not witnessed, was it still a crime, philosophically speaking of course? Certainly that would be true of sins, if you believed in an omnipotent all-seeing God, but probably not of crime. Sin implied someone was watching and intimated future retribution. Crime on the other hand, suggested punishment by mortals. So, if someone committed murder and it was not witnessed and there was no evidence, it cannot be punished by mortals. Therefore, is it a crime? Or a sin? In essence, Sean rationalized, this was nearly the same question of a tree falling in the forest and no one hearing it.

Anyway, no one would be hurt by his momentary plunge into the narcissistic world of self-congratulations and self-backslapping. So for now, he would bask in the warm glow of the victory, gorge at the table of triumph, sleep in the bed of the conqueror. To the victor go all of the spoils, thank God, if not all of the adulation.

"So what do you think, Sean?"

"Huh—huh?" Sean mumbled, forcing his mind back to the present. "S—orry. Guess I was daydreaming."

"Do you want to be a part of it?" Monument manager Judith Brisco asked, trying to keep the irritation out of her voice, "or not?"

"I apologize," Sean said sheepishly. "Be part of what?"

"A part of this," Brisco trumpeted, arching her petite arm through the air with a grand flourish, "a part of the team."

"I was never very good at teams," Sean acknowledged, rubbing his eyes, then running forked fingers through coarse, shoulder-length, red hair. "What exactly would we be doing?"

"You really didn't hear a word I said," Brisco sighed, placing her hand on her slender hips. "I'm about to appoint an advisory team to take stock of what we've got, gather preliminary information before we formulate a comprehensive management plan. When a corporation buys a company, the first thing they do is take inventory—see what they've got, what needs to be fixed, what needs to be purchased, what needs to be sold and what needs to be changed.

"The first thing I need to know is what we've got. How many springs and rivers have dried up with the drought? What kind of shape the rangeland is in? How many cows are presently grazing on the allotments compared to what those same permits allow? And does the foliage justify such numbers? Are we overgrazing? Is natural grass being replaced by opportunistic weeds, like thistles, tumbleweeds, snake broom and rabbit brush? Is erosion a problem? How many deer do we have? How many elk? Is poaching a problem? How much private property is in the monument and who owns it? Are they being good stewards? How many mines are here and are they just paper mines, leases, or has some digging actually commenced? How many minor roads? Which ones can be closed? How bad a problem are the ATVs? It's a huge area, one million seven hundred thousand acres, and in short, I need to know what's going on in every last single acre.

"My management style is definitely hands on. I like to make informed, educated decisions and I like to be involved in every one of those decisions. In my jurisdiction, I definitely will not tolerate loose cannons," Brisco declared, her dark brown eyes glancing around for scowls of dissent. Fortunately, there were none.

Seated at a square oak conference room table were about a dozen men and women stuffed at various angles and inclines in their uncomfortable chairs, some slouching, some stiff with rapt attention, some resting their chins on their elbows and occasionally some dozing.

"My crack team, and it will be a crack team, will be a composite of BLM specialists, environmentalists, ranchers and recreational consumers," she continued. "So how about it, Sean, do you want to represent the environmentalists?"

Sean's mind had already started drifting.

It had been more than a year since that great speech and that equally great day, but none of the luster had faded. He could remember when he had started working on this project, more than ten years ago. At first, just trying to convince anyone outside of Utah that these canyons and plateaus had any real value had been a monumental task. In those early years, there were virtually no recreational backpackers, campers or sightseers in the Grand Staircase area. Other than Sean, the only other human creatures were cattlemen, Indians, hunters, miners, prospectors and the occasional fugitive from the law. Trying to convince people of the beauty of this land was like trying to convince the Cattleman's Association of the elegance of a Jackson Pollard painting.

Back then, alpine terrain seemed to be all the rage—camping, hiking or photographing lush green foliage with musical bubbling brooks and relaxing in cool mountain air. Very few people appreciated the beauty and solitude of the dry desolate deserts of the American West. To most, they were forbidden wastelands, God's forsaken earth, badlands, Satan's Strand, Hell's Kitchen and on and on. Why preserve them? Nobody wanted to go there anyway. Nobody wanted these lands. Certainly, not the state of Utah.

He was like a lone voice crying in the wilderness. No one listened, no one cared. As it says in the Gospel of Matthew, a prophet is never appreciated in his own land and certainly, Sean was not appreciated in his. Involuntarily, he grimaced. It was irritating, even downright embarrassing, that even after all these years he still unconsciously looked to the Bible for justification. It seemed one was never completely free of childhood indoctrination. Some atheist he'd turned out to be.

"Sean!" Brisco bellowed.

"Huh?" Sean stammered as he again jerked his mind back to the present. "I'm sorry, I didn't sleep very well last night."

"Obviously. In the short time I've known you," Brisco chastised, "it seems you do a lot of that. I can't imagine how you get anything done."

"I manage, but I admit, I've always been a dreamer—an idealist," Sean confessed. "But when needs be, I can roll up my sleeves and do the dirty work."

"I'll take your word for that," Brisco said. "Well then, while I've got your undivided attention, let me make this short and to the point. Do you want to be a member of my inventory team?"

"I'm really sorry," Sean said, trying to focus. "I was thinking about this last year. It has been truly amazing."

"Well, yes," Brisco said curtly, "but that's all past history now. We need to organize. There's work to be done. Do you, or do you not, want to be a part of this project?"

"Anything," Sean said softly, with a hint of reverence in his voice, "anything to do with the Grand Staircase/ Escalante National Monument, I want to be a part of."

"Good," Brisco said, reaching up to smooth her already immaculate auburn hair, "then it's settled. Ron, will you stand?"

Wearing the brown BLM field uniform, Ron Sparks stood up and grinned. He appeared to be in his fifties, robust with pent up energy, balding with gray hair swept back at the sides, accommodating blue eyes and wide grin.

"This is Ron Sparks," Brisco said. "He is the deputy monument manager and will handle a lot of the day-to-day operations of the park. His experience has all been BLM and he comes to us from the Idaho state office. Among other things, Ron will be in charge of the Citizen Advisory Committee and that group will report to him. Now Monty, will you stand?"

A middle-aged, slightly stooped, thin man also wearing the standard two-tone chocolate and beige uniform of the BLM with logo patches on both shoulders rose from the far end of the table and scowled silently at the group. He looked slightly emaciated and tired, and his skin had a fallow amber tinge, as often seen with cancer patients or people with cirrhosis of the liver. His eyes, however, were anything but cadaverous. A mahogany brown, they were alert, hard and mean.

"Monty Coleman," Brisco continued, "for now, will double as a law enforcement specialist and as range conservation officer. Hopefully soon, we'll be able to hire another range conservation specialist, so poor Monty won't have to do both. However, he does have vast experience in both areas. Also at our disposal from time-to-time, we will have a government hydrologist, a botanist, an archeologist, a paleontologist, a geologist, a zoologist, forest and range management specialists and a historian.

"Finally, Mr. Douglas Rehnquist, would you stand? Mr. Rehnquist is a local rancher with two permits in the monument both in the Fifty Mile Mountain area. He has consented to represent the ranchers and their interests. Would you like to say a few words, Doug?"

Roper stood up and eyed the group. Most of them looked back

at him with varying degrees of suspicion or indifference. He cleared his throat.

"My name is Douglas Rehnquist, but my friends call me Roper. I am a permitee on the Grand Staircase. Specifically I have two allotments, Lake Allotment on Fifty Mile Mountain and the Soda Springs Allotment, just to the east of Fifty Mile Mountain down on the desert and bordering the Glen Canyon National Recreation Area. I, for one, am happy about this new monument and see no reason we can't all make use of this tremendous resource together. All it takes is patience, a little give and take, and a little bit of mutual respect for each other's goals and dreams." Roper again looked around the table then sat down.

Abruptly Monty stood, a fierce scowl painted on his face, his thin lips stretched and blanched.

"Yes, Monty," Brisco acknowledged.

"Why him?" Monty asked. "That's like inviting the enemy to your flight briefing the night before the mission."

"I agree," Sean blurted out, suddenly wide awake and bristling, "it—it's like inviting a bear into your camp to help you fix dinner."

The smile disappeared from deputy manager Ron Sparks' face and the rest of the group looked stunned by the outbursts.

"Monty," Brisco chided, "you're not with the marines anymore and Sean you have a lot to learn about the fine art of diplomacy, though I must say it is nice to finally see you awake."

"Might just as well be up front with it," Monty snarled.

"And I don't like it neither, not one damn bit. I, for one, know what these ranchers have done to the land," Sean growled. "They've literally raped it."

"Let's remember," Ron Sparks grinned nervously. "The monument is designated as a multi-use park. If we manage it well, there should be enough room for everyone."

"Sean," Brisco interrupted, taking charge. "This is a new era. You and Monty and the ranchers are going to have to learn to get along. I know it's hard. Coming from the National Park Service, it's been an adjustment for me as well, but we'll learn together."

"But they—they've been damn poor stewards." Sean persisted. "And you know what Christ said about poor stewards."

"The range is in better shape now than it has been in the last fifty years," Roper said, "and I have old photographs to prove it."

"Enough!" Brisco said. "What we don't need is in-fighting. If we can't get along, how can we expect everyone else to. In this committee we will work out our differences like professionals and we will follow the guidelines as set forth by the administration—to a T."

Though he didn't show it, Sean was embarrassed by his biblical outburst. Goddamn it! What was wrong with him? Quoting the Bible. After all, he was an atheist now.

For a tense moment, the three combatants eyed each other suspiciously, then Brisco once again took charge. Using her most officious voice, she continued, "now let me take a moment to outline our strategy, how I envision the new committee will function."

Sean settled back in his chair and began to drift as Brisco droned on. Politics—yeah, he knew about politics. His whole life had been involved with politics, or at least political agendas. Over the years he'd learned one could only accomplish so much with politics then when things started to bog down, one had to resort to other less refined techniques. Covert methods. As he had become more involved with the environmental movement, it was in the other methods Sean had realized that he had a natural talent. Not that he didn't agree that politics were always the first step, but for sure it wasn't the only step. In his experience, political solutions were tedious, evasive and hard to come by. When the political effort was exhausted, that's when they always came looking for him.

However, thank God, he'd hiked practically every gorge in the red rock maze, ascended almost every juniper-peppered plateau, hiked all the colorful cliffs of the Grand Staircase and explored virtually every dusty valley where only rabbit brush, blue sage and black brush grew. Indeed, it was an enchanted land dotted with the occasional red sandstone arch, random shoulder-width slot canyons, sporadic phallic monoliths and the rare bizarre rock garden, uncanny in their resemblance to a moonscape. And as the *piéce de résistance*, the monument was a virtual treasure of Jurassic and Cretaceous fossils, anything and everything from massive dinosaurs to tiny trilobites.

But the Staircase could also be treacherous. With very little standing water on the entire park, just a random spring and an occasional seasonal creek, people could, and sometimes did die in this harsh land. Dehydration, starvation and snake bite in the summer—cold, snow and exposure in the winter, not to mention the rare gunshot wound, occasional skull or bone fractures from a fall, or the infrequent assault by a renegade cougar. However, perhaps, the biggest risk was becoming disoriented and lost. With few roads and even fewer marked trails, even with a map one could wander for days and never see a sign of civilization and never see another soul.

But what really irritated Sean were the ranchers. Rough and uneducated, they didn't act like they loved this land. Actually, at times, they behaved as if they hated it. To them, it was something to conquer or subdue, not to appreciate and preserve. And those cows! Those foul stinky, dirty beasts. They destroyed, trampled or gnawed everything from the fragile native grasses to the delicate desert rose. And then, they shit everywhere, including the hiking trails, pristine pure springs and the fragile riparian banks of the delicate Paria River.

Stubborn and possessive, deep down these ranchers actually believed this land belonged to them and not the American people. While vigorously trying to keep hikers and campers off the land, they would, at the same time, not move their cows from an allotment until it had been totally stripped of anything vital or green. Not even a prickly pear cactus or a quaking aspen sapling would be left unscathed. The situation was intolerable. Personally, and with God's help, he would drive them from all public lands.

That would not be easy, Sean knew. Even though this was government land, the BLM allotment leases were extremely hard to revoke. They were open-ended leases that could be inherited, passed from father to son, or sold to another rancher like any other commodity. That was why the Grand Canyon Trust was so effective. Rather than trying to force the ranchers off the land, they simply bought up their allotments at a fair price then put them in cold storage. Obviously, that was the preferable way to purge these leases, but unfortunately there was not an endless supply of money and some ranchers were more stubborn than greedy. They simply refused to sell.

The only thing worse than the cowboys were the miners. It seems they all had subscribed to General Sherman's scorched earth technique of mining, strip and burn. What this amounted to in Sean's estimation, was a legal destruction of the land. As with the ranchers, only one thing flourished after the miners were done, the ugly scars of erosion. That excavating arm of nature that systematically destroyed dismembered and disemboweled the land.

Over the years, even while still in college studying paleontology, Sean had visited Wilderness Alliance clubs across the west, constantly talking up the area. Slowly, almost imperceptibly at first, they had started to come, this time, his kind of people. People who appreciated the play of shadow and light across the sheer canyon walls, intricate but ephemeral patterns constantly changing with the arching sun. People who loved to just sit quietly and watch the amazing kaleidoscope of deepening colors of clouds as the sun slowly sank behind a square purple butte. People who relished crisp clean air, wild flowers, blue skies and the red silica sands. People who enjoyed photographing or painting wildlife, not shooting them, eating them, or skinning them for pelts. People who appreciated solitude and valued a chance for of introspection.

In the past, there were daunting times when Sean was convinced this day would never come. In those early days, no doubt about it, he had pushed the envelope, both morally and legally. But in some cases the ends did indeed justify the means. This monument, to Sean's way of thinking, was one of those cases.

This magnificent land deserved to be protected. Sometimes, he would sit quietly high on a plateau and look across at the grand vista with awe and reverence. At those times, he could almost understand why people assigned such beauty to God, though there wasn't any reason one could not have beauty without God. Beauty was a learned response, it was in the eye of the beholder, Sean reasoned, and not in the eye of some imagined God.

Sometimes he wished he still believed, even though he knew the idea of God was silly, invented by man's own insecurities. Other times, he wondered if the president was really a believer, or if he was just being politically expedient. Caving in and going to church because that's what the majority of Americans expected from their president. You didn't need much political savvy to know that translated into millions of votes. But after all, the president was a Rhode's Scholar and arguably, the most intelligent president we'd had since Jefferson. No way, Sean thought, that a man like him really believed in the naive concept of God.

As clearly as if it were happening today, Sean saw himself standing in the human line that snaked for at least a hundred yards, inching slowly forward to shake the president's hand. What an honor, it would be—to shake this great man's hand. Whenever he heard the back stabbing of the republican conservatives attacking this man, Sean turned livid. To his way of thinking, if Mount Rushmore was being sculpted today, William Jefferson Clinton's handsome profile would surely grace the mountain's face—though he really did not believe in defacing mountains in that way.

The only slightly disconcerting thing was, well—to be honest—was all the credit he had heaped on vice president Al Gore in the speech. Not that the vice president didn't deserve some of it, he had written a book and had always been a good friend of the environmentalists, but he had a knack for usurping credit, stealing the limelight, so to speak. Remember that internet fiasco? And certainly, Gore hadn't done all the leg work, the grunt work that Sean had. It had been Sean who had slugged it out in the trenches and fought the dirty little secret war. The war politicians, by inference gave their blessing, but didn't want to know the gory details so they could distance themselves. They had to keep their hands clean and reputations spotless so they could continue to captain us toward more lofty goals.

Not that Sean had expected the president to actually mention his name in the dedicatory speech, but it would have been—

"—So, will Monday be all right with you, Sean?"

"Huh? I'm sorry."

"For God's sake!" Brisco exploded, her small frame shaking. "Could you pay attention?"

"I said I was sorry," Sean snarled, his normally docile ruddy countenance now blazing bright crimson with anger.

"Can you start to work on my inventory project this Monday?"

"Yeah, I guess that will work for me. Monday'll do fine."

"Where do you want to meet, Ron?" Brisco asked the deputy manager.

"You can call me Sparky," Ron said as he faced the group with a smile. "How about the Escalante office?"

"Okay, then we'll meet on Monday," Brisco confirmed, "at the BLM office in Escalante, just on the east end of town. Any other questions?"

Slowly, Brisco surveyed the room. "I want you to know I take my mission as steward of this land very seriously. President Clinton put me—uh—us in charge of this fine monument and in twenty years, I want Americans, when planning their summer vacations, to mention the Grand Staircase in the same breath as the Grand Canyon, Yellowstone or Yosemite," she paused and looked them each in the eye.

"It's a big task and we will have our share of problems and maybe even a couple of setbacks, but let me assure you, I know we are up to the task. Someday this will be one fine national monument." She paused again for effect, gathering her papers. "Well then, I have one last question. Does anyone here play chess?"

"I beg your pardon?" Ron Sparks asked, not sure he'd heard her correctly.

Puzzled, the rest of the group stared blankly back at her.

"Does anyone here play chess?" Brisco repeated, glancing over the room. "When I'm not working, I like to play a little chess—for recreation. How about it, Sean?"

"Nah, I'm not much into games," Sean replied, "never held much fascination for me."

"Monty?"

"Never had the time."

Brisco looked over the room again. "Well then, let's adjour—."

"—I used to play a little," Roper said hesitantly.

"Excellent," Brisco said, pleased. "We'll have to arrange a game sometime. Well then, if there's nothing else, let's adjourn."

"Could I have you all stay for a couple minutes," Sparks grinned as Brisco got up and left, "and we'll go over specific assignments."

As he watched the manager leave, Sean couldn't help but wonder what was wrong with the monument the way it was. Briefly, Sean saw in his mind her vision, another Yellowstone or Yosemite with throngs of people, inundated lodges, congested hiking trails, trash littered roads, thick foul air and noisy traffic jams. It made him shutter.

Brisco had her agenda, he had his. For now, he would help, as long as their agendas ran parallel courses. But another Yosemite—no way!

3

THE CHOCOLATE CLIFFS

With its genesis roughly 240 million years ago in the early Triassic geological period, the Chocolate Cliffs are the granddaddy of the Staircase's terraces and form the first and lowest rung. Created from brown mud deposited on the fluvial plain of an immense pre-historic lake, the rocks produced are mudstone and siltstone and these stones, along with a thin layer of beige sandstone, make up the Moenkopi formation. As a signature feature of this layer, erosion occasionally exposes large sheets of fossilized ripple marks.

Capped by a mosaic of Shinarump Conglomerate, the Chocolate Cliffs are the oldest, least visible and most deeply buried of all the Staircase cliffs. Only on the very southern border of the Monument, east of Kanab, is a comparably short shelf of Chocolate Cliffs that erosion has unearthed for inspection.

Judith Brisco fought the unfamiliar knobs and ridges of the lumpy mattress, then rolled over and once again tried to go to sleep. God, how she hated these motel beds. In the lodging business, there seemed to an unwritten but almost universally adhered to code, furnish your rooms exclusively with stone-hard mattresses. Try as she might, Judith could think of only two possible explanations: one, long ago, someone must have decided that hard mattresses were good for the back and that theory was still popular today. If true, whoever that person was, had obviously never studied the normal spine curvature. No way was the spine straight as a board, so why should beds be? Two, hard mattresses were more cost effective. They were cheaper to manufacture or less likely to sag under body weight and hence would not need replacing as often. Regardless of the reason, Judith sighed, now one could hardly stay in any motel without sleeping, or at least trying to sleep, on a concrete slab.

At least her own bed was on the way, arriving today she hoped. She had rented a small one-story bungalow in the Ranchos section of Kanab. It was a wonderful house in a picturesque location just across the Kanab Creek and right smack up against the looming Vermillion Cliffs. This setting, up against the cliffs, was a constant reminder of why she was here. Here in this God forsaken little Mormon town without so much as a Wal-Mart, a Macy's, an opera house or even a movie theater. She was here to forge a national monument out of a mishmash of raw materials, whereas a little over a year ago there was none.

Ever since her arrival, she had been treated with courtesy and civility, but with a definite coolness. Not being Mormon, she had expected some minor cultural problems, but the one thing she had not foreseen, though in retrospect she should have, was the overwhelming public sentiment against the new monument. Naively, she would have suspected the citizens of southern Utah would have been happy. A new monument would instantly put them on every travel agency or tourist industry trade map and it goes without saying, the increased auto and bus traffic would be good for business. My God, it was not like they were throwing up six-story tenement housing or constructing a heavily-polluting manufacturing plant in the center of downtown Kanab.

If she lived to be a hundred, Judith would never understand westerners. It was almost as if they were a genetically similar but nonetheless a totally separate species, like the land mammals and porpoise, or the fish and shark. Somewhere along the evolutionary road, they had made a left turn from mainstream Homo sapiens. In general westerners were definitely independent, irascible, incongruous and contrary, with an inherited inbred paranoia for big government and bureaucrats. On the other hand, come Fourth of July, Memorial Day or Presidents' Day, they were almost universally very vocal flag-waving patriots. Unarguably, it was a schizophrenic position. They loved their country, but hated their government. However, one thing was for certain, westerners did consider President Clinton's creation of the monument a blatant federal government land grab. Of course, this was all nonsense. This was totally inconsistent with historical fact. Long before there was a monument, Mormons in Utah or even before there was a state of Utah, this land had been the possession of the federal government.

Specifically, she was getting plain damn tired of the sniveling argument that the western states had not been treated fairly, or at least consistently with the eastern states. Of course, they had not. No body said they had. The reason there was very little federal land in the eastern states is because they never had been federal territories. They were sovereign states first, then they banded together to become the United States. In the Midwest, territories on the road to statehood purchased or homesteaded their land, thereby acquiring it from the federal government. The same principal was applicable to the West but here, there was so much land nobody wanted, nobody claimed. The only land considered of any value was that associated with or adjacent to water, but a lot of lands were inaccessible and arid. Shamefully, even the federal government had tried to push some of this wasteland off on the American Indian, often creating reservations out the most barren sections of this land. But regardless of that, somebody had to be a caretaker of those lands and it fell by default to the federal government. And that scenario was also true of the one million seven hundred thousand acres now called the Grand Staircase/Escalante National Monument. The only federal land grab in the west was in their collective, overactive and paranoid imaginations.

Even after all arable land had been claimed, the federal government had magnanimously set aside large tracts of land adjacent to those sections claimed by early pioneers as state school trust lands. This was to make doubly sure in the future that western states would remain on equal footing with the other states.

This continuing undercurrent of animosity thoroughly astounded Judith. During the early years of her career, having spent some time at Big Bend National Park, she was used to disgruntled Texans idly talking sedition, mainly due to government regulations controlling the market price of domestic oil, but of course they never really meant it. Here in the West, she was not so sure.

Rolling over again, Judith pounded and repositioned her pillow, then wormed slowly across the bed, searching for that elusive comfortable spot. Why had she not asked for another pillow? Loudly she sighed in frustration. Until her furniture arrived, she was stuck in this over-priced, over-rated, but very uncomfortable motel. At least the lodging fare was not coming out of her pocket. The taxpayers were picking up the tab but in her estimation, they were getting more than a little ripped off.

She rolled again and stared at the white ceiling tiles. If she were honest, this bed was no worse than some of the places she'd slept in as a kid. Groaning, she closed here eyes. They, Judith and her Mother, had lived in some real dives back then. She remembered the time they were residing in the Washington DC area, just about the time her mother and father divorced. Before the divorce, they'd had a nice home. Her father, a career Marine officer, had been stationed at the Pentagon. Though she was only nine at the time, she still remembered how handsome he was in his royal blue and white dress uniform. Then came the big break up.

One night her mother and father had a particularly loud fight. Then he moved out. Sometime later she learned he had moved in with another woman. At first he came to see her frequently, then occasionally and finally not at all. For a while they continued to live in the Bethesda, Maryland house, but as finances became tighter, her mother sold the house and for the next few years they lived in various apartments in the DC area including some in very suspect neighborhoods and some with very uncomfortable beds.

During those early years, they would have perished had it not been for the assorted government relief programs for the poor and single parent families. Her father was supposed to pay child support and alimony, but the checks never came. Eventually, her mother obtained employment as a clerical at the Department of Interior. It was during the Kennedy administration and rightly or wrongly, her mother had always credited JFK as their savior.

It had just been the two of them, her and her mother. With almost no money, they never went to the movies or restaurants and her mother despised television. They spent the long empty days and evenings playing chess. Her mother was more than a fair player and it had been years before Judith could come even close to beating her.

Needless to say, Judith grew up appreciating government assistance programs, JFK and the entire Democratic Party. She never cared much for the wealthy, stingy, uncompassionate republicans. More, not less, government had been their savior. Judith, to no one's surprise, had become and remained a loyal democrat. In Utah, she thought ruefully, that was somewhat akin to being an African-American at a Klan rally.

As her mother struggled ever upward, tirelessly climbing the bureaucratic ladder, she taught Judith the pearls she had gleaned on the way. These are tough lessons, she had counseled young Judith, and if you want to survive, you best learn them. Point one, this is a man's world. Two, men view indecision in women as an overt sign of weakness. Three, men consider women's primary station in life in the bedroom, not in the work force. Four, you can never trust men. There's always a hidden agenda or an ulterior motive.

After graduating college, Georgetown University, with a degree in management, she followed her mother into Civil Service. Initially, she secured a job with the National Park service at Gettysburg. From there she moved a lot, but eventually worked her way out west, first at Mount Rushmore, then Big Bend, finally the crown jewel, Yellowstone. Slowly she learned agency politics and worked her way up the precarious, often treacherous, management ladder until she was named assistant superintendent at Crater Lake National Park.

Fortunately, the National Park Service was only marginally subject to the capricious winds of political rotation and even through republican administrations she continued to advance. However when Bill Clinton became president, he inexplicably began placing national monuments under the stewardship of the Bureau of Land Management. At first, being loyal to the Park Service, she considered this an egregious affront, but this attitude would soon change.

Then came the day, her moment in the sun, when President Clinton created the BLM Grand Staircase/Escalante National Monument and plucked her with all her park management skills from the National Park Service and put her in charge! She still glowed with pride at the memory. So far, that had been the crowning achievement of her life. In celebration, she and her mother had a quiet restaurant dinner highlighted with a bottle of champagne.

That had been over year ago and she'd spent the entire past year organizing. There had been hundreds of meetings and countless airplane flights from Washington DC to Utah trying to put together a team, come up with a preliminary management plan, devise a budget, and create an initial outline of how she envisioned the monument would grow in the future. Needless to say, it had been a stimulating and exciting experience.

Then harsh reality set in. She actually had to physically move to the monument, to Utah. After a month, in frustration she had written to her mother her general impressions of the West, small dusty towns, devoid of culture and manners, with no amenities and a hard to define feeling of hostility to authority. Add to all this, the unique oddity of Utah society, basically a one religion state with all social and cultural life centered around the Mormon Church, and sometimes she felt a foreigner in her own land. Sometimes, it was almost more than she could bear.

Then to heap dismay onto disappointment, she did not particularly find her new monument fascinating, breathtaking or even enchanting, at least not in the same way as Yellowstone, the Grand Canyon, or the majestic Yosemite. It was mainly just a remote tumbled landscape of black brush, sagebrush, junipers and pinions with flattop mesas, and occasional eroded hills that looked for all the world like a cheap copy of the South Dakota badlands. Yes, it was colorful, reds, whites, pinks and purples, but no green, at least not lush kelly green. It was dry and dusty with few mountain streams and even fewer lakes or ponds, but to its credit, it was one of the truly isolated places left in the forty-eight states. The Sierra Club and wilderness alliances loved it and wanted to keep it that way, but Judith envisioned something else. Something more refined, more polished, more developed. Some paved roads and some park lodges where you could get a good meal and a good bed. Certainly, not like this damn bed she was trying to sleep on tonight. Twisting over to her right side, she felt her lumbar spine groan as it sagged downward, trying to make contact with the hard slab.

Administration had made it clear, without question, the environmentalists were the people with the most political clout, the most money for campaign war chests and were the most politically correct in their view. Her job was to keep them happy. It didn't take long for her to realize that group wanted the monument to themselves. No multiple uses for them.

They didn't like cowboys and they certainly didn't want cows defecating all over their hiking trails, and deep down Judith had to admit, she agreed with them.

However, in his proclamation, President Clinton had clearly stated there would continue to be multiple uses for the Grand Staircase/Escalante National Monument. So for now, at least, she was stuck with that principle. That, of course, did not mean that all sides would not be tugging at her shirt, trying to increase their influence.

From her years in the National Park Service, she was well grounded in, and did not need to be converted to, the idea of conservation. That was the whole idea behind the Park Service. Fortunately there, they did not have to contend with the concept of multiple uses. But she was now with the BLM and to make the best of it and to try to appease the warring factions, she had formed this advisory committee. Not that she expected any real wisdom from it, but she knew it looked good and was definitely good PR.

Maybe, it had been a mistake to have Sean O'Grady represent the wilderness alliance. He was such an irritating hothead. It seems redheads always were. But it was more than that, he was also, perhaps, dangerous. Already she had heard the gossip, rumors of environmental terrorism before the monument was created, but perhaps that was just prattle. She had seen no actual evidence of any wrong doing. He had applied for the position of monument paleontologist, and as it turned out, they did need one. The monument was a literal treasure trove of fossils. Having him on the committee would serve a dual purpose. She could keep an eye on his environmental activities and evaluate him for the possible paleontology position.

Then there was Douglas Roper Rehnquist representing the other side. He was a likeable enough guy and seemed to be a well-respected member of the ranching community. Also from the way he spoke and the way he carried himself, he appeared to be quite articulate and probably some college education. Not your typical Utah cowboy and as a bonus, he did play chess! Perhaps the only chess player in all of Kane County, she thought. Though he was a native southern Utahn, he seemed sincere in his belief there had to be room for everyone. It was his belief, there would be an initial and difficult acclimation period, but we all could struggle through it and learn to work and live together. That was probably overly idealistic and more than likely he was just trying to protect his dying kingdom, making sure it was not his ox that was gored, but he seemed sincere. It was truly amazing to Judith, how accommodating people became when they realized they might very well be on the losing team.

Once again, monument manager Judith Brisco pounded her pillow trying to soften it then rolled on her back and stared at the ceiling. It would not be easy, but by God she would make a damn good monument in this god forsaken country.

Closing her eyes, she tried to let her mind wander aimlessly into directionless colorless oblivion. Then the phone rang. Without bothering to turn on the light, she rolled over and picked up the phone.

"Hello," she mumbled into the receiver.

"Judith, this is your mother."

"Oh, hi, Mom," Judith said without enthusiasm.

"Did I wake you?" Alise Brisco asked, her voice as raspy as sandpaper from her years of inhaling tobacco smoke.

"No Mom," Judith replied. "I can't sleep in motel beds.

"When you moving into your house?"

"Soon as my furniture arrives. Hopefully later today."

"Have you seen your new office?" Alise asked.

"Yeah, it's not much," Judith said. "They rented the old high school in the center of town and are remodeling it into offices. Someday, hopefully soon, they're supposed to start on a new visitor center, actually several."

"Several?"

"Yeah, unlike the National Park Service, the BLM is not going to put visitor centers in the monument itself. Instead, they're going to put them in border towns. Three are planned, one in Kanab, Big Water and Escalante."

"That seems like a monumental waste of money," Alise laughed hoarsely. "Monumental, do you get it?"

"Yes, Mother," Judith answered crossly.

"What do you think of the town?"

"It's not much. Tourist town. Maybe fifteen hundred people. No malls, no department stores and no theaters."

"Do they have an Episcopal Church?"

"No, the closest one is in St. George and that's eighty miles away," Judith said, "and that's just a small congregation. They just have Mormons out here, Mom."

"I know nothing about Mormons," Alise said, "except they don't drink and they're into polygamy."

"I don't think so, at least not the mainstream," Judith said. "But there is a polygamous community, Colorado City, about forty miles from here."

"I could never understand that," Alise insisted, not trying to hide her disgust, "being that subservient."

"Me neither. It's barbaric."

"Do you like your job?" Alise asked. "You sound depressed."

"I don't know, Mother," Judith sighed. "There's so much to do."

"Are you afraid you can't handle it?"

"Of course not, Mother," Judith declared, a little more stridently than she had planned.

"Then what is it?"

"Nothing and everything," Judith replied, "it's complicated. There's all these special interest groups. I've suddenly had to learn the fine art of political juggling."

"What groups?"

"Well, the two main ones are the cattlemen and the environmentalists. They can't seem to get along. In the Park Service we never had to deal with the ranchers, there weren't any."

"Well, remember the future of this country is with the environmentalists. Ranchers and beef are on their way out."

"I agree, Mother," Judith said. "But for now, I'm caught in the middle."

"Judith," Alise said, "be firm, decisive and take command. Indecision is always viewed as a sign of weakness, particularly among men."

"Okay, Mother, okay," Judith said curtly, silently waving her hands in exasperation.

"I'm just trying to help," Alise explained.

"Of course, Mother," Judith said. "When you coming out?"

"I'll give you a few months to get settled," Alise replied. "You found a man yet?"

"Oh, really Mother!" Judith raised her voice, but involuntarily looked down at her flat stomach. She still had a good figure. "You of all people asking me that."

"Well, they're mostly trouble anyway," Alise declared. "Have you at least found someone to play chess with?"

"No, not yet—maybe."

"Have you entered any tournaments yet?"

"Oh really, Mother," Judith said. "You don't know Kanab, Utah."

"Well," Alise insisted, "you'll lose your skills, but that'll give me more of a chance when I do come out."

"Right now, I don't have time," Judith replied curtly. "Got to go. I need to try and get some sleep tonight. Tomorrow, I've got one meeting after another."

After hanging up, Judith closed her eyes. What had she gotten her self into? She had one million seven hundred thousand acres with almost no facilities. No paved roads, very few gravel roads, no campgrounds, no visitor centers, no marked hiking trails, almost no water and no lodges. Then add to that, more bovines than tourists. What the hell was she thinking? Obviously, she had been flattered by being offered the top job and the pay increase was certainly a factor, but wasn't she a better fit with the National Park Service where they had already developed a system for preservation and visitation?

———

Roper didn't sleep well either. Somehow his stomach had transformed into a cauldron of hot bubbly acid, occasionally boiling over and rising up his tender esophagus. He had no one to blame but himself. Famished when he'd arrived home from the BLM meeting, he'd fried up some of Bucky's sausage. It was surprisingly good, but now he was paying for it. In one way or another, it seems with Bucky you always paid for things twice. Roper was nauseous, gaseous and his throat burned like he'd gulped battery acid. Getting out of bed, he took a couple of Pepcids then climbed back in and once again began tossing and re-tasting the sausage.

In lieu of sleep, his mind began resorting through the day. Roper didn't quite know what to make of the meeting tonight. On the surface, everyone was cordial enough, except for Monty Coleman and Sean O'Grady, but he had gotten the feeling he was just being tolerated and most of the group would be happier if he weren't there.

Also, he didn't quite know what to make of Judith Brisco. Superficially, she seemed to be pleasant enough and efficient, but not overly friendly. Obviously, she did possess leadership skills as illustrated by the way she handled the surly Monty Coleman and the hothead Sean O'Grady. On the surface, at least, she seemed fair.

To her credit, she was a chess player; being a chess player she couldn't be all bad. At that moment, Roper decided to play her. Probably he'd get slaughtered, but it wouldn't be the first time. A few years ago he was a fair player, but he hadn't played very much lately. Not much opportunity. While at Southern Utah University, he'd been a member of the chess club and once he'd even played a Russian Grand Master who was in town to speak at the university and ski at Brian Head. There had been nine of them in a big room, arranged in a large circle and each had brought his own chess board. Circulating from table to table, the Grand Master took only seconds to make a move then quickly moved to the next board. No, Roper hadn't beaten him, but he had lasted through eleven incredible, though constantly harried moves. Actually, he was he last one standing.

Games notwithstanding, there was no doubt about it, Brisco had a big job ahead of her and Roper for one, was certainly not envious. He wouldn't trade her jobs for an outright warranty deed to the Fifty. Undoubtedly, she had people coming at her from every direction, politicians, bureaucratic superiors, environmentalists, recreationists, ranchers, miners, hunters, loggers, not to mention the day-to-day problems of managing her own staff. And to top it off, she had a presidential mandate to create a national monument where there was none. No, she could have that job all to herself and in the meantime, not knowing her background or any ulterior motives, he decided to give her the benefit of the doubt.

However, on the other hand, he was pretty sure Sean and Monty were two characters on whom he'd best not turn his back. He couldn't quite put his finger on it, but he thought he might have known Sean from somewhere, another time or place, but the particulars escaped him. With his flaming red hair and cold hazel green eyes, he was a striking, though not a handsome man, one that if you'd met, you'd not likely forget. But try as he might, Roper couldn't remember. Maybe it was nothing.

Monty Coleman, however, he knew he'd never met, but he knew his kind, cold, calculating, amoral, the ends justify the means. In short, he was dangerous. As the range conservation officer, unfortunately Roper knew he would be dealing with him on a frequent basis. Hopefully, Brisco would soon hire another range con man, freeing Monty for full time law enforcement. That job appeared to be a better fit.

Again, Roper got up, this time sorting through his medicine drawer for some Tums. There were none, so he went to the kitchen and mixed himself a cocktail of cold water and baking soda. Just then the phone rang.

"Doug, is that you?" Ruby asked. She sounded far away and like she'd been crying.

"Are you all right?" Roper asked, concerned.

"Yeah," Ruby sniffled, sounding congested, "just had a bad night."

"Do you want me to come over? I can be there in an hour."

"No, it's okay, Doug, but it's nice to talk to someone."

"Do you want to tell me about it?"

"No, it's just a personal thing. But I'm going to take care of it," Ruby declared, her voice full of resolve.

"Can I help?"

"You are helping more than you know, just being my friend."

"Well, if you need anything," Roper insisted, "just let me know."

"I appreciate that. Did I wake you?" Ruby asked more brightly, an obvious effort to change the subject.

"Nope, got heartburn. Don't know if it's from Bucky's sausage or the meeting I attended tonight," Roper laughed, suppressing a burp.

"Didn't know you had a meeting."

"Yeah, monument manager Brisco asked me to represent the ranchers on an advisory committee she is setting up."

"Oh—did the ranchers ask you?"

"Did the ranchers, ask me what?"

"Did they ask you to represent them?"

"Well, no."

"Well then, don't take it for granted that you're representing them," Ruby said, then quickly added, "I'm sorry, Doug. I'm glad there's at least one rancher on that committee, but all I'm saying is the other ranchers may not like it."

"I just hope I can make a difference," Roper continued, somewhat defensive.

"I hope so too. Anyway, the other reason I called is to see if you were still planning on helping me tomorrow with the brandin'?"

"Yeah, if you'll help me move cows in the afternoon."

"Can do. Where do you want to meet?"

"On the Bench at the Cliff Trail," Roper answered, yawning.

"Thanks, Doug," Ruby said. "Sorry, about that comment."

"Forget it," Roper said, then turned to hang up the phone.

"And Doug," Ruby added, "sorry about calling so late."

Roper replaced the phone, gulped down the soda water, then crawled back in bed.

She is right, he thought as he rolled over. No one had elected him spokesman for the ranchers. Brisco had appointed him, probably because someone had recommended him as a person she could work with. But on the other hand, he sure hoped Brisco didn't think he would be a "yes" man. Whether the other ranchers realized this or not, he was there for only one purpose, to see that they got a fair shake as this monument progressed. If not handled right, this whole thing could blow up in their faces like a match in a grain silo.

Rolling over in the other direction, he pounded his pillow, like tenderizing sirloin steak. Though he could still taste that damn sausage, he was happy about one thing, Ruby had asked him to help her. It wasn't like he didn't have enough to do tomorrow, but the thought of spending the day with Ruby made him smile.

Roper rewound their conversation. She did seem upset about something tonight. He was flattered she had turned to him for moral support but in retrospect, she hadn't told him much. He was the first to admit he didn't know much about women, but in his meager experience when a woman became that upset it was usually over a man. Other than rumors about Angus Macdonald and possibly Skinner Jacobson, Roper really didn't know of any men in Ruby's life. But then again, he really didn't know much about her, other than he could easily tell she was a competent rancher, an expert horseman, and quite pleasant to look at.

Holding onto that very agreeable picture, he finally dosed off.

4

THE VERMILLION CLIFFS

The second step of the Grand Staircase, the Vermillion Cliffs, often over a thousand feet thick, is composed of three separate and distinct layers of primal Triassic rock.

Forming the bottom layer of this multi-tiered butte is the Chinle formation. Composed of Chinle shale and Shinarump conglomerate, it is 225 million years old and makes up the lighter strata near the base of the cliff.

The bulky red middle layer is composed of Wingate sandstone. Created approximately 200 million years ago, it was formed from huge prehistoric sand dunes that in time were buried by another layer and eventually ossified.

The top and capping layer is the darker Kayenta formation. Estimated to be 190 million years old, it is composed of siltstone spawned from an ancient lake during a more moderate climate and is characterized by its distinctive horizontal stratification.

In the whole scope of the Grand Staircase, the Vermillion Cliffs are the most prominent, the most easily viewed and make a spectacular backdrop for the city of Kanab.

Roper Rehnquist took a deep breath of fresh air as he looked around at the magnificent view. God, how he loved this way of life!

The pungent odor of burning calf hair, the popping sounds of a hot juniper fire heating a long-handled branding iron, the physical strain of wrestling a hundred and fifty-pound calf, the frantic bellowing of the animal being branded, the unique stench of the black tar unguent being slathered on the raw horn bed, the incomparable sight of lacy white clouds racing on a glacier blue sky, the musty fragrance of riding a horse through hip-high wet sagebrush, or just the very common sight of the rugged Utah hillsides flecked with moss green junipers now dressed with bluish round berries and the *coup de grâce*, the locker room aroma of dust and sweat, confirming an honest day's work. These were the things Roper had missed during his years of academia.

Absentmindedly, he gazed south in the direction of his BLM allotment. There was nowhere on earth quite like it. Fifty Mile Mountain was essentially a flattop mesa stretching for fifty miles. The entire southern tip, twenty miles or so, was his Lake allotment and comprised his summer range. In the late fall, he drove his cows off the mountain onto Fifty Mile Bench then after a month or so grazing there, he trailed them down onto desert floor. Here they would spend the winter. This area, his Soda Springs allotment, was more arid, but much warmer. Between the two allotments, he had about one hundred and fifty square miles, about half of that on Fifty Mile Mountain.

Geographically and geophysically, it was a big and difficult operation. Historically, the BLM had not allowed any road construction upon Fifty Mile Mountain and only minimal building construction. After years of haggling, they had permitted one corral on each allotment. Taking advantage of that window of opportunity, he and his father had built corrals, but also a small cabin on each allotment. With no roads up onto Fifty Mile Mountain, constructing that cabin had proved to be something of an ordeal. Everything, all building materials including nails, 2x4s, cement, windows, caulking, stove, sink, pipes and all furnishings had to be packed up by horse over a steep narrow trail that snaked directly up and over the face of the Straight Cliffs.

The Soda Springs cabin had not been a problem. With a spur road leading right to it from the Hole-in-the-Rock Road, those same building materials had simply been trucked in. Subsequently, the Soda Springs cabin was a little bigger and a much more comfortable compared to the mountain cabin. Over the years, the system had worked well. Depending on the season and where the cows were grazing, they always had shelter and a dry place to sleep.

Spring and fall, cattle moving time, were always a challenge. Considering the narrowness and pitch of Cliff Trail, all Roper could drive off the mountain at any one time was a small herd of about thirty to forty head. In the fall, he would gather cows in the corral at Lake Pasture until he had approximately forty head, then he would push them off the Straight Cliff Trail to the Bench then after a month of grazing there on to Soda Springs. He repeated this cycle until he had all three-hundred and fifty cows off the mountain. In the spring, he simply reversed the direction and drove the cows back onto the Fifty. All in all, he averaged about eighty or ninety nights a year in those two cabins.

Of course the wild ones never came off. For over a hundred years, ever since his granddaddy had started grazing the Fifty, there had been feral or wild cows. Originally, the wild ones had probably separated from his grandfather's herd, missed in the fall roundup due to the incredible ruggedness of the land. Now, however, they were basically a separate species. Any cowboy worth his salt could tell a wild cow at a glance. They were tall, rangy and weighed upwards of sixteen hundred pounds, sporting a full set of wicked horns like fine-honed curved sabers. Their eyes were wild and suspicious, and their attitude and posture were consistently confrontational. Without the assistance of man, they were born, reproduced and died. Darwin's system of natural selection had made them a fierce and violent breed that had somehow had managed to survive severe freezing winters, crippling droughts, deadly predators such as mountain lions and man, and they did this all on an impossibly rugged rangeland where they had to have the dexterity of a mountain goat just to get around.

Mostly, they kept to themselves over on the remote western lip of the mesa, adjacent to the wild horse allotment. In the winter, they would duck off the mesa top, just under the rim where it was more protected from the freezing wind and blowing snow. In summer, they would invariably return to the top of the mesa. They kept their gene pool fresh by occasionally enticing one of Roper's young heifers to join them. Also, those cows missed in the fall roundup would often end up joining the wild ones as a matter of survival. On her allotment, Ruby had managed to rope and brand a few wild ones, but she almost never got them off the Fifty to market. At first opportunity, they would break way and vanish back to the west side, often coaxing a young cow with them. There was no economic advantage to them at all, so they were tolerated because—well—because there was nothing else one could do.

Located just to the north and bordering his Lake allotment was Ruby's Mudhole allotment. Her winter range ran off the western side of the Fifty Mile Mountain into the Woolsey Arch area, on the opposite side of the mesa from Roper's. Even though Ruby had only one allotment, her total area was probably larger than Roper's two allotments. But her lease did not have as good pastures and possessed fewer springs. As a consequence, Ruby was only permitted to graze one hundred and eighty head compared to Roper's three hundred and fifty. As with Roper, the BLM had not allowed her roads and only one corral, and though she had been permitted a cabin, she had not yet constructed one and now with the new monument, undoubtedly the permit would be rescinded. In this area, ranching was a mammoth undertaking and almost an impossible task for one person. Roper had to admit he was amazed that Ruby had hung in, even after her husband had died. No doubt about it, the girl had some grit.

Yes, he did love this land. Even if he wasn't pushing cattle, he enjoyed simply riding his horse up on the Fifty and gazing out at the scenery. He considered that entertainment and preferable to an afternoon at the movies or a ball game.

However, not the least of these agreeable afternoon activities was watching Ruby Nez go about her work. As the old timers would say, she was mighty easy on the eyes. Though she did her best to dress as a common wrangler, some things were impossible to disguise. The view from atop his dun, General Stepper, was indeed splendid. Roper didn't mind one little bit taking a break and watching her go about her work.

As was her habit, Ruby always bound her raven black hair up with a red bandana, like the city gangs, though obviously she was not trying to imitate them. She then capped her head with a sweat-stained black felt Stetson. About her only concession to her well concealed, but ultimately insuppressible femininity, was a stunning Indian-crafted turquoise broach pinned to the right side of her hat band. Exposing a bit of black bra strap, her long-sleeved western shirt was ripped at the back, probably from ducking through strands of a barbwire fence. The oft-mended Levis were clean, wash-faded and pleasingly tight. Scuffed, dusty and worn thin at both the toes and heels, her fancy leather-tooled boots looked as if they wouldn't last out the year. She looked just about as far away as you can get from a fashion model, Roper thought chuckling to himself, though she would look damn good on just about any runway. Ruby was one of those women who looked good not because of her clothes, but in spite of them.

A lot of women are pretty in a world where beauty can be bought in a supermarket or salon, or purchased at a plastic surgeon's office for a price, but what impressed him about Ruby was her inner beauty, her physical strength, the way she managed her business, how she handled a horse or roped a calf. Though she had asked for his help, he couldn't help but feel she could have handled today's little operation fine by herself.

Here on the open range with no corrals or squeeze chutes, calves had to be individually roped and thrown to the ground with their right sides upturned. Not an easy task when you're dealing with a six-month-old, hundred and fifty pound, frantic and bawling calf fighting you every step of the way. No question about it, a corral would have made life much easier, but even after repeated requests, the BLM had steadfastly refused him or Ruby any further corrals or buildings, hence the branding on the open range.

Once on the ground, a glowing hot branding iron was plucked from the fire and slapped on the calf's side, searing a lazy N on the calf's hide. Then, while he was still on the ground, a Barnes dehorner was paced over the horn bud and the handles were suddenly forced apart, thereby pinching off the nubbin. Instantly, a spurt of blood would gush from the severed central artery. Quickly, the cowboy would then smother a thick layer of black tar unguent on the raw horn bed and with luck this usually controlled the hemorrhage. If not, the calves bled until the muscle in the arterial wall spontaneously contracted and the vessel clotted. Very seldom, if ever, did a calf die from horn bleeding.

Lastly, while they had them roped, all males were gelded. Roper had watched the old cowboys do this with their teeth, taking only a minute or so, but not with six-month-old calves. He personally had never got the hang of using his own incisors though he wouldn't admit that to the cynical old-timers. If the truth be told, he found the practice highly unsanitary and disgusting, preferring a sharp pocket knife instead.

Even though the testicles resided in separate compartments, if one made the incision in precisely the right place, over the midline scrotal septum, both could be removed through the single one-inch long incision. Leaving the spermatic chords untied and the wound open, always made Roper a bit nervous. But if you were not going to ligate the chords, then you damn well better not sew up the scrotum. Otherwise, the resulting hemorrhage with no accompanying drainage could make the scrotum swell to the size of a basketball in no time. In the past, Roper had seen that happen.

Though Roper worried about infection with an open draining scrotum, he wasn't about to argue with the way cowboys had been doing things for hundreds of years. Not only had they been doing it, but doing it with very few complications. And on the positive side, the sutureless technique was considerably easier, faster and cheaper.

Like so many other things in his life, Roper continued to follow tradition in favor of new techniques or modern science, strange behavior for an educated man. Not that he was opposed to science or progress, but he preferred an unpretentious lifestyle, simply taking the time to enjoy a sunset or the companionship of a neighbor's visit. Starting your day at 5:30 a.m. or 2:30 p.m., it was your choice as long as the work got done. To gaze at the majestic panorama of the jumbled, wind-carved canyonlands or the imposing solitary shaft of Chimney Rock or the strangely eroded toadstools called hoodoos and suddenly realize, this is my office.

This is the reason he had dropped out of school and moved back to Escalante though he knew the popular rumor circulating was that he couldn't cut it. Maybe they were right though God knows he'd tried. Unfortunately, his academic passion, English history and literature, was not very marketable, even with a master's degree. He had tried teaching, that was about all you could do with that particular degree, for two years as a graduate assistant at Southern Utah University. As home of the Utah Shakespearean Festival, SUU loved anything and everything English and they felt that his expertise in British history and literature would only add to the growing aura of authenticity of that Tony Award winning festival. But after a couple years, this Stratford-on-the-Desert seemed to lose some of its luster and seemed more than just a little incongruous, maybe even ridiculous. More and more, he longed for the life he knew as a kid.

His professors and colleagues had warned him that his ranching dreams were actually pipe dreams, nothing more than sandcastles precariously perched on the beach at high tide. As they pointed out, the family ranch was rapidly becoming extinct and nowadays cattle ranching was becoming almost as paradoxical as Shakespeare in the desert. Probably even more so and not half so likely to provide a livelihood, and certainly there was no associated benefit or retirement package. And now with Clinton creating this new monument—hell maybe they were right. Maybe he was a threatened species, just like the Desert Tortoise, the Mexican Spotted Owl or the Virgin River's Woundfin Minnow, but there was one glaring difference, he had no Endangered Species Act to protect him. More and more, he was beginning to feel most Americans were okay with letting his kind disappear. After all that era had been abundantly preserved in celluloid for the western movie channel and that was enough. Roper sighed and leaned on the saddle horn.

"Doug!" Ruby yelled. "I could use a little help."

Roper waved in acknowledgment then spurred General Stepper toward Ruby. She was kneeling on a bawling white-faced calf, but couldn't quite reach the branding iron. Reining in General Stepper, Roper jumped down and snatched the hot iron.

"From the amount of work you've done, I can tell you right now, you haven't earned much of that picnic lunch." Ruby grinned as she watched Roper apply the fiery iron. Instantly, the scintillating heat waves rose accompanied by the pungent odor of burning hair and the frantic bellowing of the young bull. He lunged against the ropes but with a knee on his chest, Ruby held him fast.

"What can I say," Roper shrugged with a grin, jumping back as Ruby released the calf. "Good help is hard to find."

"I saw another one head into that clump of cedars," Ruby said, pointing to her right.

"Me and Moses'll go flush him out," Roper said, his blue eyes following her gesture.

Effortlessly, he remounted General Stepper then clicked his tongue for his dog to join them. Moses, a spotted brown Catahoula Leopard hound from Louisiana, immediately took the lead, nose close to the ground, hunting for the smell of the calf.

For some years now, Roper had been using Catahoula Leopard hounds to help with the round up. They literally took the place of another wrangler and in some ways were better. They could sniff out cows in thickets so dense that normally Roper would ride right on by. Also, if asked, they would hold a cow or even a small herd at bay, confining them for hours while Roper went on to hunt for more cows. In a very real way, during roundup the dogs also provided the extra corral that he so desperately needed and had been denied.

Within minutes, Moses had located the calf, pushing it out of the dense undergrowth where Roper could throw a rope on him. It snapped taut and Stepper back-stepped, dragging the bellowing calf to Ruby. She quickly branded, castrated and dehorned him, all in less than ten minutes.

"Well, that about does it, thank God." Ruby crossed herself in the traditional Catholic way, then slapped the dust from her Levis. "Let's head up to the rim where we've got a view and some shade, then I guess I'll have me some lunch."

"Fine by me," Roper agreed. "I'm starved."

"Didn't hear me invite you." Ruby grinned.

"I'll tag along just in case you change your mind," Roper chuckled.

"Suit yourself," Ruby smiled, dark eyes flashing, "but I don't feed slackers."

"It's almost four," Roper said, consulting his watch. "Always thought lunches were supposed to be at noon. What kind of chicken outfit is this?"

"Quit your whining," Ruby said. "Lunch or dinner, what does it matter? From the amount of help you've been, you'll be lucky to get any."

Mounting, they worked their way over to the rim of Fifty Mile Mountain. Pausing briefly at an overlook, they soaked in the view. Immediately beneath them was the sheer gray face of the Straight Cliffs. Further below, the desert valley spread out like flood waters, flowing to the north and south, though not so much toward the east. That direction was blocked by a maze of red domes and ribboned walls that constituted the lower Escalante canyons and were actually part of the Glen Canyon National Recreation Area. To the far north was the town of Escalante and to the far south was the tumbled landscape of red Navajo sandstone that made up the basin of Lake Powell. Through this narrow arid valley snaked a serpentine gravel road, connecting Escalante with the Hole-in-the-Rock and subsequently to Lake Powell.

Ruby pulled a small ground tarp from her saddlebags, spreading it over the thick layer of pinion and juniper needles. While she retrieved the steak sandwiches and cold drinks, Roper stretched his wiry frame out on the tarp, resting his back against a downed pinion log. He couldn't imagine anything better, a picnic with Ruby Nez. Life was good.

"You want a beer or Coke?" Ruby asked, holding up both.

"Coke," Roper said, taking the can and popping the tab. He took a long swallow, then settled back on the canvas. "Ah, that hits the spot."

"You don't drink beer?"

"Nah, it's against the Word of Wisdom."

"And caffeine's not?" Ruby asked, gesturing toward the Coke.

"Well," Roper stammered. "I guess it's a matter of degree."

"So alcohol is a bigger sin than caffeine," Ruby said, as she finished unpacking the lunch and arranging it on the tarp.

"Something like that."

"Makes no sense to me," Ruby said bluntly, offering Roper a roast beef sandwich. "But then again, your religion never has."

"And Catholicism does?"

"Well, as least there's a direct line to St. Peter," Ruby replied.

"Doesn't matter that the line ran through miles of corruption, debauchery, plunder, murder and child molestation?"

"And Mormonism doesn't have any skeletons? Tell me about Mountain Meadows."

"That is a subject for a different time," Roper said. "How do you suppose the pioneers ever got their wagons through Hole-in-the-Rock?" Roper asked, changing the subject and gazing south at the barely visible bulwark of Navajo sandstone where the early Mormon pioneers had literally carved a wagon trail through solid rock.

"Hell, Doug, I don't know, that's why they call it Hole-in-the-Rock," Ruby answered sharply as she opened a beer. "I suppose, they just took a concrete saw and ripped a hole in the canyon wall, then parted the Colorado like the prophet Moses and walked across."

"Your sarcasm is duly noted, " Roper said, "but it still amazes me. They did all that back in eighteen seventy-nine."

"They wouldn't have had to do it at all if they would have just followed Father Escalante's route," Ruby said, then she broke out into a grin, "I'm just giving you a bad time. It was an amazing feat."

"I guess it's the history in me," Roper said then fell silent, munching on the sandwich, "but that sort of thing has always fascinated me."

"Why'd you really come back, Doug?" Ruby asked after a moment of silence. "You know what they're a sayin', don't you?"

"Yes, I know," Roper replied and took another bite. "I didn't get caught cheating on my doctorate and I didn't wash out. I got good grades and I was a fair teacher. Believe it or not, I just didn't like it—not like I do this," he said gesturing at the panorama before them.

"They say you were almost done."

"Depends on what you mean by done. Finished my masters and was about halfway through my doctorate." Roper stopped for a sip of Coke. "One hundred and ten hours a week between teaching and working on the thesis. Never seeing blue sky or breathing fresh air finally got to me. Then one day I had an epiphany."

"Like Joseph Smith?" Ruby said with a smile.

"Will you let me finish?"

She nodded.

"I finally decided, this is not for me. I'm not going to prepare one more lecture for unappreciative students, or write another superfluous paragraph on the Battle of Culloden and the futile Jacobite Rebellion."

"Is that what your thesis was about?"

"Yes. Of course, it's all been written about many times before, that's why I titled it, *A New Perspective, on the Battle of Culloden*, not that there was anything wrong with the old perspective. One day, I just realized that in the grand scheme of things, what I was doing didn't make a whole lot of difference. Did the world really need a new perspective on something that had happened over two hundred and fifty years ago? So I finished the semester, put the thesis in cold storage and came home."

"Your dad hadn't sold the ranch yet?"

"By then, he'd had a couple of offers, none very good. He was trying to hang on till he could sell at a fair price. Didn't want to just give it away."

"So'd you buy it from him?"

"I tried to, but he wouldn't hear of it. The compromise was I would take care of him and all his medical expenses," Roper said. "Ironically, he died three months later—prostate cancer. Never did get his money's worth for the place."

"I'm sorry, Doug," Ruby said softly. "You two were close?"

"He taught me everything—taught me to love all this," Roper whispered, a catch in his voice. "I guess he's the real reason I'm not a college professor."

"You may have been a good teacher," Ruby said, "but I'm glad you came back."

They ate in silence for another moment then Roper continued, "you never told me that you used to date Angus Macdonald."

"You never asked," Ruby replied. "Does it matter?"

"No, not really. What happened?"

"Nothing, really," Ruby answered and looked away, straightening the tarp. "It was never anything serious, at least not on my part."

"You still seeing him?"

"No!" Ruby snapped. "It just didn't seem right. There was a big cultural issue and of course, the age difference."

"Is he what had you so upset last night?

"No—no," Ruby stammered, turning a bit red. "I'm sorry about that, Doug."

"Not a problem for me. I just wish there was more I could do."

"Well," Ruby replied, taking a sip of beer, then changing the subject. "How many of my calves you think we missed?"

"I don't know, maybe three or four. Would've had less if I was a better roper," Roper replied, rubbing the stump of his missing finger.

"Been meaning to ask, what happened to your finger?"

"Nothing," Roper said, finishing the Coke and setting the bottle aside. "When I was twelve or so, I was calf roping at the little buckaroos rodeo. Caught my calf all right, but when I whipped the rope around the saddle horn, got my finger caught up in it. The horse then put on the brakes and the rope snapped taut with a hundred and fifty-pound calf hurling to a stop on the other end. Well, my finger just popped off—like an assassin using a piano wire."

"That's why they call you Roper?"

"Yeah," he said, fingering the stump. "I guess, it's what you might call a sarcastic nickname."

"Kids can be cruel."

"Well anyway, it stuck; it's not so bad."

Ruby sighed and stood up. "Well, we can't get 'em all, country's too damn rough."

"They may be a little bit wild, but they'll still be here when we come back in the spring."

"Any we leave now will join the wild ones."

"Yeah, I know what you mean," Roper said. "I got fifty head or more of the wild ones that hang out in those canyons over by Indian Gardens, you know, on the west side of the mesa."

"You ever try roundin' them up?"

"Next to impossible, herding cats is easier."

"I've got thirty or forty," Ruby stated, "big ones, mean ones. Can't get 'em off either, Lord knows I've tried. They're no damn good the way they are. Eat my grass. Been thinking about selling hunting permits."

"Like a deer hunt?"

"This would be a lot harder than hunting deer," Ruby said, shaking her head for emphasis, "straight up and down terrain and a hell-uv-a-lot more dangerous. When cornered, those wild bulls'll charge. Gore you or your horse. The only danger in deer hunting is some California greenhorn might shoot you or the possibility of getting lost."

"You're not serious?"

"I'm hurting, Doug," Ruby insisted, "and if I lose this allotment, I'm going to have to find some creative ways to make money."

"You'll be back here next fall," Roper contended, "mark my words."

"Yeah, maybe," Ruby said doubtfully, "but I honestly think they'll try and drive us out—if they can."

"They can't. Remember the proclamation said there would be grazing."

"Forget the damn proclamation. Proclamations can be amended. They do it all the time."

"Well, at least we'll have some input. Committee work starts on Monday. We're doing some preliminary leg work."

"Oh," Ruby said, failing to mask the displeasure in her voice. "I almost forgot."

"Somebody's got to work within the system."

"Well, put in a good word for me," Ruby said sarcastically. "Unlike you, if they ask me to remove my cattle from my allotment, I'll have no where to go, 'cept broke."

"Even though I have two allotments, they're both inside the monument. My perch is just as shaky as yours."

Ruby started to say something then changed her mind. Instead she began gathering the paper trash and empty cans.

"Hello, the camp!" Someone yelled from off to the left, on the other side of a thick stand of junipers. "Is that you Roper?"

"Yeah!" Roper hollered back. "Who's there? Skinner?"

"Yeah," Skinner Jacobson called back as his palomino gelding patiently worked around the thicket and through the waist high sagebrush. "Howdy, Rubles," he grinned. "You're looking might pretty as usual."

"Skinner," Ruby said, then nodding at the gelding she added, "nice horse."

"Best I can tell, there ain't no holes in her," Skinner agreed.

"You want a beer?" Ruby asked.

"Sure pretty lady." Skinner dismounted, grinned then stripped forward both ends of his mustache to a perfect point. "Unless'n you got somethin' harder?"

"Nope," Ruby answered, taking his reins and securing his horse. "It'll have to be beer."

"What you doing up here?" Roper asked, getting up to shake Skinner's hand. Lately, every time Roper saw Skinner he was amazed at how much he looked like the legendary General George Custer.

"Same as you. You seen any of my strays?"

"Nope," Roper said. "Don't usually get yours this far south. I often get a few of Ruby's 'cause we border, but I'll be moving my cattle to my Tank

Springs pasture. If I see any of yours, I'll let you know."

"A little early, ain't it?" Skinner asked, accepting the beer from Ruby. "Did that new Manager ask you to move?"

"No—there's not much feed left," Roper replied, shaking his head. "No point in grazing down to the roots, the grass won't come back."

"Trying to stay on their good side, huh?" Skinner said, then took a swig of beer and wiped his mouth with the back of his hand.

"No, not particularly," Roper continued, "but if we show them we're responsible range managers, maybe they'll pretty much leave us alone."

"Don't count on it, college boy," Skinner said.

"Well," Roper said undeterred, "you've got to admit it's a pretty bad drought. Haven't had more'n five inches all year."

"That's why they call this here place a desert," Skinner said, "it's supposed to be dry. But if'n I'd know'd the feed would go this fast, I would've raised more hay."

"Yeah," Ruby sighed, "but takes water for that too."

"Guess that leaves only one choice, take 'em to the auction in Salina and give 'em away," Skinner complained, shaking his shaggy blond head.

"Good luck, cause that's what you'll be doing," Ruby said. "With the price of beef now, you might as well just shoot 'em."

"With this drought, everyone's been selling," Roper said. "That drives the prices down."

"No shit, Cowboy," Skinner said, sneering. "Nothin' like stating the obvious."

"Also, beef's not selling like it used to," Ruby added.

"This here no red meat craze has nearly blow'd me away, " Skinner said. "People's acting like if'n they eat red meat today, they's goin' have a stroke or heart attack by tomorrow. It's all so much bullshit."

"Well, I'm open to suggestions," Roper said, everting his palms in a show of frustration. "What'll we do?"

"The only other option as far as I can tell," Ruby replied, "is bankruptcy."

"Let's not jump to conclusions," Roper said. "If we work with them, they will work with us. Nobody wants to ban ranching."

"Yeah, and Kim Basinger wants me real bad," Skinner replied.

"You got any better ideas?" Ruby asked.

"I've been talking to some of the other guys," Skinner said, lowering his voice and quickly looking around. "And they think we need to organize. Otherwise, they'll pick us off one by one. You know, divide and conquer."

"We are organized," Roper said. "It's called the Garfield/Kane Cattleman's Association."

"Nah, we was thinkin' of somethin' more discrete, more covert." Skinner stood up and looked Roper in the eye. "Somethin' whose actions are not so easily traced."

Roper evenly met Skinner's glance. "I flat don't like secret organizations."

"That so?" Skinner sneered. "What about that Mormon Church of yours? Talk about secret organizations."

"What are you talking about?" Roper asked, gritting his teeth.

"All right, that temple over there in St. George. Tell me what goes on in there."

"I can't discuss that."

"My point, 'zactly," Skinner grinned, again reshaping his moustache. "I'd think you'd be sore by now."

"Sore?" Roper asked, winkling his forehead.

"From all that pole fence sittin'. People say to me, that Roper ain't got no balls, but I tell 'em, yeah, he's got balls all right, just sore ones from being sit on."

Roper glared at Skinner for a moment and took a threatening step in his direction.

"Come on, you token cowboy" Skinner taunted, raising his fists. "I've waited for this a long time."

Instinctively, Roper also hoisted both fists, the left one looking a bit asymmetric with the index knuckle and finger gone.

"Consider this payback," Skinner snarled.

"Payback?"

"Payback for that bottomland your father stole from me," Skinner hissed, his face taut and his fists ready.

"I wouldn't exactly call outbidding, stealing," Roper replied, taking another step forward.

Swinging wildly, Skinner's right fist clipped Roper's chin. Roper staggered backward, but regained his balance. He then hooked with his left and as Skinner was ducking from that punch, he quickly jabbed with his right hand, solidly connecting with the side of Skinner's face.

Instantly, Ruby wedged between them. "This is not the time," she said firmly as she shoved them apart. "We've got real problems ahead and we don't need all this testosterone bullshit."

"This ain't over yet," Skinner said, pointing a finger at Roper, "not by a long shot.

"I'm not looking for a fight," Roper said. "Let's just forget it."

Skinner glared at Roper for a few seconds then turned to Ruby. "How about you, Rubles? You interested in our little group?"

Hesitating, Ruby gnawed at her lower lip. Alternately, she glanced at Skinner then at Roper, then back at Skinner again. Throwing up her hands, she walked toward her buckskin. Turning back she muttered, "maybe, I don't know. I've got to know more about it."

"Well, we're havin' a meetin' at Bucky Eakins cabin tomorrow night at eight. You ought'a come, Rubles." Skinner crushed his empty beer can with his boot heel. "In fact, I could pick you up and we could go together."

"I don't know about that, Skinner."

"I'll throw in a sit-down restaurant dinner at the Prospector's Inn."

"You know I don't have time for no sit-down dinners," Ruby replied gruffly. "But if I'm out in that area anyway, I might drop in. See what it's all about."

"I can't save myself for you forever, Rubles." Skinner flashed a full-toothed grin. "Not with all the other ladies after me."

"Yeah, I'm sure it's been tough on you," Ruby said, dead-panning.

"What about you, college boy?" Without warning, Skinner hurled the crushed beer can at Roper, bouncing it squarely off his chest. "Wouldn't hurt you none to hear both sides."

"Believe you me, I know both sides," Roper said, picking up the beer can and pitching it in Ruby's trash bag. "And there's got to be a better way."

"Like advisory committees?" Skinner snarled.

"Yeah, that for one."

"Well, you best be careful out there," Skinner warned, eyes narrowing. "You have no idea what you're getting in to."

5

THE WHITE CLIFFS

Running east to west, the third rung on the staircase, the White Cliffs, form an immense chain of sheer face-rock covering almost a hundred miles across southern Utah. One of nature's favored rocks to sculpt, it tends to fracture along vertical lines and is often etched into huge domes and sheer perpendicular walls or hollowed into alcoves and arches. The eroding, receding cliff line shows the distinctive wind blown layers, often resembling the huge primordial sand dunes from which they were born.

Undoubtedly one of the most visible formations in the area, the White Cliffs are composed of white to pink, coarse Jurassic sandstone appropriately christened Navajo sandstone. Created during an arid climate one hundred and eighty million years ago, the White Cliffs are three to six hundred foot sand drifts that were swept into the area by violent Jurassic winds and over the eons have slowly solidified.

I t was early, 7:30 a.m., when the teams departed the prefab, clay brown office in Escalante, Utah. Immediately splitting into assigned pairs, each squad had a different mission as commissioned by Deputy Manager Ron Sparks. The unlikely team of Douglas Roper Rehnquist and Sean Dunn O'Grady climbed in Sean's 1990 dusty, dented and rusted Toyota Landrover and headed out of town.

In silence, they drove east on State Road 12 through the tiny Mormon farming community of Henrieville, then onto equally small Cannonville. There, Sean turned due south on the paved Cottonwood Road, driving right on past the right hand fork of the Skutumpah Road. A little further down they passed the road to Kodachrome Basin on the left. At this point the blacktop abruptly ended, but the road continued on, now gravel, still proceeding roughly in a southerly direction.

Dust billowed and swirled from the back of the Landrover and sifted into the cab through Sean's cracked-open window as well as up from small fractures in the metal floorboard. The ongoing drought coupled with increasing tourist traffic had pulverized roadbed to fine clay powder. Roper rubbed his nose and stifled a sneeze then glanced at Sean, wondering if he dared suggest he close his window. In grim silence, Sean focused on the road.

At Grosvenor Arch, he turned from the main road, angling east on a two track lane, at times hard to see. Roper knew this track eventually led to the top of the seven thousand foot Kaiparowits Plateau. After another ten minutes, they descended down a precarious perpendicular canyon into a cavernous gorge aptly christened, the Gut. In places, the road was no more than a downward slanting rock shelf that had been carved into the solid sandstone wall, barely offering enough room for the Landrover to squeeze by. In lieu of a shoulder on the left, the terrain abruptly dropped straight off for a dizzying two to three hundred feet. Occasionally, when Sean bounced over imbedded gnarly roots or squeezed by table-sized rocks that a remote thunderstorm had washed onto the road, the outside tire would come perilously close to the edge.

Eventually they crossed the dry wash bed marking the nadir of the huge chasm then started up the other side. Fighting dust, hairpin curves and jolting over boulders, washboard, roots and potholes, they lurched up the fifteen percent grade, eventually leveling out on the far wall.

From here, the view was unparalleled. Appearing mostly steel-wool gray in color with splashes of creamy brown sandstone, the Kaiparowits Plateau stretched out far below them, dotted with a smattering of dwarf pinions and junipers. The plateau was upturned at the edges, like the rim of a saucer, with the western border being supported by the strange saw-toothed Cockscomb formation. The eastern border was shouldered up by the massive Straight Cliffs and to the far south Roper could see the blue-green gashes in the tabletop, marking the plateau's deepening network of drainage canyons. Wahweap Creek, Warm Creek, Last Chance Creek, Reese's Canyon, Navajo Canyon, Rodgers Canyon, Monday Canyon, Sunday

Canyon all emptied south into Lake Powell. Glancing through the window to the north, he could make out the long slender snaking arm of Headquarters Valley. Even though the trip here had been a bit like a roller coaster ride, Roper had to admit the view made the trip worth it.

The agenda for the day, as the ever genial Deputy Monument Manager Sparks had earlier briefed, was to drive to the top the Kaiparowits Plateau and see what was happening with the various coal leases. In principal at least, Andalex and PacifiCorp had agreed to sell their leases back to the U.S. government, removing all their mining equipment, but not so with Highland Mining & Mineral. Andalex and PacifiCorp leases were located on the southern rim of the plateau, close to the Burning Hills, whereas Highland's lease was right here on top, almost the geographic center of the huge plateau, in the Paradise Canyon area.

Apparently, Angus Macdonald, sole owner of Highland, had agreed to absolutely nothing and had in fact been recalcitrant and difficult to find. There had been no negotiations with him and none had been scheduled. Rumor had it he had been camping out somewhere on the Kaiparowits, probably near his lease, but no one from the BLM had been able to talk to him since that pivotal day, September eighteenth, the day the monument was created. Scuttlebutt had it however, that he was furious and did not want to talk or negotiate.

Sparky had instructed Sean and Roper to scout out the Plateau, particularly the Paradise Canyon area to make sure there had been no recent digging, and if they could find Macdonald, try to arrange a day for him to meet with Manager Brisco. After that, if there still was time, they were to inspect any ranching operations in the area. Specifically, check on the number of cows presently grazing and if the number was appropriate for the present poor range condition. With the drought, Sparky had needlessly reminded them, the land would not support nearly as many cows. Sean had snorted at this and Roper silently suspected one was probably too many for him.

Shifting uncomfortably in his seat, Roper glanced over at Sean. His freckled jaw was set and his green eyes focused straight ahead. To Roper, the complete lack of conversation was beginning to feel more than just a little strained.

"You ever hike up there to Grosvenor's Arch?" he finally asked.

"Of course," Sean replied curtly.

"Me too," Roper volunteered then waited, but there was no response from Sean. "Kinda makes you realize the monument is probably necessary—" More silence. "—to preserve God's handiwork," Roper's voice trailed off. He felt a bit foolish, like an old man with senile dementia talking to himself.

"God had nothing to do with it," Sean suddenly barked, startling Roper. He'd almost forgot he'd said anything.

"Well, all I'm saying—"

"—so anything beautiful is from God, anything ugly or repulsive is from Satan. Pretty naive stuff isn't it?" Sean hissed, still not looking at Roper.

"I was just trying to make conversat—"

"—Grosvenor's arch was created by the very natural forces of nature, wind, water and frost. You don't have to throw God into the mix. That's just another layer that's not needed."

"If you find a Rolex in the desert, you instinctively think it was made—"

"—don't give me that tired old watchmaker's crap. I don't see any machined parts lying around Grosvenor's," Sean declared as they bounced through another pothole, banging both their heads on the roof. "Do you?"

"Well no, not in that sense, but certainly the human body is pretty intricate. So complex, it makes you think there has to be a creator."

"Yeah, he created man in his own image, I remember. Yet, man eats, drinks, defecates, urinates and copulates like any other mammal. Maybe, your precious damn cows were also created in God's image."

"Maybe not the exact image," Roper said, "but if you've got a template that works—"

"—with a sledgehammer anyone can pound a square peg through a round hole."

"Well then, what do you believe?" Roper asked, immediately thinking he should have shut up. "I'm sure you've got a theory."

"Damn right, I do," Sean confirmed. "I believe Darwin got it right on the first try. The reason we eat drink and copulate like animals is because we are animals. I know that idea drives you creationists crazy. You prefer to distance yourselves from the animals, but if you take into consideration the track record of the human race, I'm sure the animals would like to distance themselves from us. However, despite their objections, we did descend from primates."

"That's is your opin—"

"—I'm not finished yet," Sean interrupted. "Eventually man developed the capacity for abstract thinking. With this newly acquired skill, he became capable of contemplating his own demise. Of course, this scared the hell out of him, so out of necessity he invented an antidote, something powerful enough to grant him eternal life. With a task this big, he needed a super power, a supreme being, so he created God. But eternal life is still a pretty big favor to ask of anyone, including God, so man developed an elaborate system to court God's favor. Hence, worship, religion and sacrifice were born. Now that's your real creation."

"This is getting us nowhere," Roper said, "you're certainly entitled to your opinion."

"And regardless of the absurdity, you are also entitled to yours," Sean snarled as he braked down for a curve.

Again, they rode in chilly silence. The road, resembling an obstacle course, darted up and down numerous dry washes and around countless S-curves, but in spite of the occasional assent, the trend was ever downward. Navigating off the steep bulwark of the Gut required all of Sean's attention. Finally, the road leveled off a bit as they crossed the almost barren stretch of Four Mile Bench and approached the pygmy forest of Dog Flat. Without comment, Sean abruptly turned south off the more well-traveled road onto a barely visible two-tire track.

"This is not the road to Paradise Canyon," Roper observed.

No answer.

"Paradise Canyon is the other—"

"—I know damn well," Sean blurted out, "where Paradise Canyon is."

"Then, may I ask, where we are going?"

"I just want to check on the Ruby Flat dig." Sean forced out the words, as if it took a great effort. "It'll only take a few minutes."

"An archeological dig?"

"Paleontology."

"Looking for what?"

"Dinosaurs."

"I didn't know you were interested in that," Roper said, arching an eyebrow.

"Got my bachelor's degree in paleontology," Sean answered, warming slightly. "At the time, there were no jobs. So I've never really worked in the field."

"I know what you mean, my degree's in English history and literature," Roper said, then added with obvious enthusiasm, "but I do love paleontology. I do a lot of reading."

"Periodically, I do some volunteer work," Sean continued. "With this new monument, I was hoping they might hire me as their paleontologist."

"Maybe they will," Roper said, bracing for an upcoming bump. "I didn't know there was a dig here on the Kaiparowits."

"There's several. This one was started a year or so ago by the University of Utah, before there was a monument, but now it's under the direction of the BLM. So far, it's been poorly funded and staffed, all from the university with almost no help from the BLM," Sean said. "Compared to its potential, not much is being done."

"Morrison formation?" Roper asked. "Like Vernal's Dinosaur National Monument?"

"Nah," Sean shook his head. "The whole Kaiparowits is Cretaceous. We're talking about the Straight Cliffs formation, seventy to ninety million years ago. Same formation that has all the coal."

"Then we're not talking Jurassic dinosaurs," Roper said. "Like Tyrannosaurus Rex or Stegosaurus?"

"No, but we're seeing their eventual successors, right before the dinosaurs disappeared," Sean explained, "not nearly as much is known about Cretaceous dinosaurs."

"So what species are we talking about?"

"The better known ones are the Parasaurolophus, the tubed duckbill dinosaur, and Theropods like Dasplotasaurus. He's a direct descendant of T-Rex."

"Have they found any of them here?" Roper asked, his eyes shining with fascination.

"We hope to," Sean replied. "They've been found in similar formations in Alberta, Canada and in New Mexico."

"Bet they would be almost priceless," Roper said, shaking his head in amazement.

"Don't know if it's true," Sean continued, "but I've heard of an intact Parasaurolophus bringing eight to nine hundred thousand dollars on the black market."

"Black market?" Roper asked, surprised. "I didn't know there was a black market for fossils."

"Actually," Sean said, slowing the Landrover to a stop, "there's a very active black market, mainly overseas, Europe or Japan. Wealthy private collectors or even some reputable museums buy fossils and are careful not to ask many questions."

"Surely, there's none of that going on here."

"On the contrary," Sean replied, opening his door. "In fact the BLM has a ten thousand dollar reward for information leading to the capture of any fossil thieves."

"It's that common?"

"Yeah, we've found a number of abandoned digs. Of course, we don't know for sure what they took, but sometimes we can get a good idea by what they left."

"What do you mean?"

"Sloppy excavation. Small bones overlooked and left behind. Sometimes we can extrapolate which fossil must have been removed."

"I'd think the monument would put a stop to that," Roper observed as he climbed out of the Landrover and joined Sean.

"Believe you me, they would like to," Sean replied. "There's just not enough personnel to patrol an area this big."

Turning, Sean started hiking down a fairly well worn footpath. "We have to walk from here. It's only about a quarter mile."

With Sean leading, they trudged along a serpentine trail that meandered over a thin layer of fine red soil, probably coming from the erosion of the Pink Cliffs. Though this layer was only two to three inches thick, it was unusual because it contrasted sharply with the surrounding rocks, an almond colored sandstone. This strata, however, was crimson red and was undoubtedly the reason this area was called Ruby Flats.

After about fifteen minutes of brisk hiking they arrived at the dig located on the east bank of a ten-foot deep arroyo. Through the years, sporadic floods had eroded away the Ruby colored sand and through the dishwater-white shale, leaving a gray flank of exposed Straight Cliffs formation. The entire site had been cordoned off into a half dozen roughly equal rectangles, each area tagged with a different colored flag.

Presently, there were three workers, two males and one female, all crowded into the very most easterly rectangle next to the crumbling bank. Oblivious to the approaching visitors, they were intently dusting, scratching, brushing and gently picking away at the overlying blanket of dirt and debris. The entire crew was from the University of Utah's paleontology department, his alma mater, Sean informed Roper as they approached, and he personally was acquainted with the team's leader, Professor Leonard Albright.

Dressed in khaki cargo pants and a denim shirt, the goateed Doctor Albright looked up and smiled when he saw Sean approaching.

"Ready to go to work?" he asked, standing up and offering a hand.

"Wish I could, Lanny," Sean responded, enthusiastically shaking the offered hand, "but the monument manager Brisco has got me tied up today."

"We surely could use a hand," Albright said, stroking his salt and pepper beard. "As usual, we're very short handed."

"Hi, I'm Doug Rehnquist." Roper stepped forward, deciding Sean wasn't going to introduce him.

"You Sean's assistant?" the professor asked, eyes twinkling mischievously.

"You got that right," Roper grinned back. "You must have a fair idea how much Sean likes cowboys."

"About as much as miners I suspect." Albright grinned.

"What you working on?" Sean asked, motioning toward the partially unearthed fossil.

"Not sure yet," Professor Albright said, removing his red Utah Ute's football cap and running his fingers through thick gray hair. "Think it's some kind of a Theropod, probably of the family Dromaeosaurus. In some ways, quite similar to the other Dasplotasaurus we've found, but this skull has protective plating. It's a bit smaller in size and has four toes."

"Sounds more like Velociraptor. They're Cretaceous," Sean suggested, "but perhaps a bit later than this dig."

"I thought raptors were Jurassic," Roper interrupted.

"Only in the movies," Sean snickered. "Only in Jurassic Park."

"You're right," Albright continued the original train of thought, "this is a bit like Velociraptor, only no S-curve to the spine and again there's that darn skull."

"So what do you think?" Sean asked.

"I'd rather not say," the Professor replied.

"Come on," Sean insisted. "You've aroused my curiosity, don't leave me hanging."

"Well," the Professor said, eyes shining with excitement, "I don't know for sure and it's certainly not official yet, but we may have discovered an entirely new species!"

"Wow—congratulations, Lanny," Sean exclaimed. "Lanosaurus does have a certain ring."

"Let's not start celebrating yet," Albright said. "There's a lot of hard work left and as I said, this is all preliminary."

"Mind if we take a closer look?" Roper asked, straining to get a look at the site.

"Not at all," Professor Albright replied. "Come on over and I'll show you our little baby."

For the next twenty minutes, Lanny Albright guided them around the periphery of his prized fossil, pointing out details, much of it too technical for Roper. Superficially, it didn't look like much more than a slab of chiseled rock, but Lanny was obviously ecstatic. According to the professor, it was an adult male, approximately eight to nine feet tall, with a disparate three digits on the arms and four on the toes, curveless cervical vertebra and a thick bony armor plate on top of a ten inch long skull. Though not directly involved, Roper couldn't help but get caught up in the excitement. Lanny's enthusiasm was infectious. Even as a rancher, he could understand why this kind of work could be appealing, even exhilarating.

"Well," Sean said at last, using his hand as a visor and eyeing the sun, "we'd better get going if we're going to check on those coal leases."

"Glad you dropped by," Albright said warmly. "And if you do get some free time—"

"—I'm pretty tied up for a month or so," Sean replied, "but after that."

"Don't forget come November we close the dig down for the winter."

"You going to be able to get this thing out of here by then?" Roper asked, as he climbed back over the rope of the cordoned area.

"Nah, not this year." The professor shook his graying head. "We want to remove it intact. That takes time."

"Well if not this year, you count on me for sure in the spring," Sean said, also retreating from the rectangle.

"If you don't think I'd be in the way," Roper offered. "I wouldn't mind giving you a hand come spring. I usually have a little down time after I get my cows moved to the summer pasture."

"You'd be welcome any time." Lanny Albright smiled, but Roper noted Sean's dark frown.

After expressing their appreciation to Professor Albright and his crew, Sean and Roper, hiked the fifteen minutes back to the Landrover. In silence, they climbed back in the SUV and after another ten minutes, they were back on to the main road, again heading toward Paradise Canyon.

"Thanks" Roper said, "I had no idea. That was really interesting."

Ignoring him, Sean didn't answer, focusing on the road.

Moody, Roper thought, then settled back and gazed out the side window at the slowly passing pygmy forest.

"Why you here, anyway?" Sean asked after a few minutes.

"What?" Roper had been watching the landscape and imagining what it look like when it had been populated with Cretaceous dinosaurs.

"Why you here, token cowboy?"

"That's the second time in two days," Roper replied, an edge to his voice, "that I've been called that." He gritted his teeth and looked down at his boots for a moment. "I guess I'm here 'cause I love this country and want what's best for it."

"Well, isn't that nice," Sean said sarcastically.

"Why the burr up your saddle?"

Sean thought for a moment then said. "You cowboys don't care for nothing but the bottom line. If you rape and pillage the land, that's okay 'cause your grandfather did it, it's your heritage, your sacred tradition. Dammit, from my point-of-view, the whole purpose of this monument is to get guys like you off this land."

"Surely, there's room enough for everyone," Roper said. "The concept of multiple use will work. Anyway, most government and independent studies show the range is in better shape now than it was fifty years ago."

"That's not saying much. That was the dust bowl era," Sean replied.

"Let's agree to disagree," Roper insisted, "and change the subject."

Sean was quiet for a few moments then asked tersely, "how much farther to Macdonald's leases?

"We're almost there, I think."

"Thank God," Sean growled, as he bounced the Landrover around another sharp turn.

Bang! A shot rang out from the immediate right—and close.

Instantly, Sean lost control. Veering violently to the right, the Landrover vaulted over the raised shoulder, was briefly airborne, then plunged straightaway into a solid juniper and abruptly came to a jarring stop. Sean and Roper were thrown head first into the windshield. Fortunately, Roper was restrained by his seatbelt so he only sustained a glancing blow, but Sean's belt was not buckled.

The force of the impact popped the passenger-side door open and the horn started to blare as Sean's chest came to rest against the steering wheel.

Momentarily dazed by the impact, Roper fought to remain conscious. He tried to focus. All he could see through the splintered windshield were crushed and broken juniper limbs. As he raised his head, he felt dizzy, disoriented and claustrophobic. Then, it occurred to him they had been shot! And whoever had done the shooting was probably still out there. They were totally exposed, hunkered down and waiting for the kill, like hand-fed pheasants on a game farm.

With some effort, Roper snapped open his seatbelt, ducked down on the seat and nudged Sean. "We better get going, we're sitting ducks."

No answer. Roper shook Sean again, harder, but still no response. The continued blaring of the horn was more than nerve-racking. Reaching up, Roper pulled Sean down on the seat then sliding on his belly he exited feet first out the open passenger's door, dragging Sean with him. With Sean's chest no longer pressing against the steering wheel, that god-awful racket of the blaring horn stopped.

Once on the ground, Roper quickly checked Sean. He had a bounding carotid pulse and was breathing deeply and regularly, but he had a nasty bruise and a growing hematoma on the right forehead. From the looks of it, Roper decided, Sean had sustained a concussion with its common sidekick, unconsciousness. That's the price you pay for not wearing seatbelts.

Staying low, Roper dragged Sean under the big juniper. With both the Landrover and the tree, they had some cover to the right, which is where the initial shot came from. On the left flank, however, they were totally exposed.

Leaving Sean under the tree, Roper looped around behind the SUV through a sloping gully with thick stands of junipers and rabbit brush. For ten minutes, he patiently circled, hoping to get behind their assailant. Ahead, Roper noted a small clearing.

Then suddenly, there he was, wearing a red and white checkered plaid shirt and crouching over a downed pinion log, his back to Roper. He had his gun trained on the Landrover.

Picking up a solid broken branch, Roper slowly advanced, taking care to place each step precisely where his boots would make no noise. Finally, he was close enough. Raising the club high above his head, he paused briefly, then started the club downward. Suddenly, he stopped, only inches from the tweed capped head.

"Angus?" he asked with uncertainty.

Whirling, the short, gray bearded man Immediately raised his rifle to his shoulder.

"For gods' sake, Angus!" Roper yelled, "it's me—Roper."

"Jesus, Mary, Mother of God," Angus exclaimed. "I almost kilt you."

"Are you out of your ever-lovin' mind?"

"I—I didn't know it twas you, laddie," Angus stuttered.

"Doesn't matter who it is, put that damn gun down," Roper ordered, relief flooding over his face like warm water from a shower. "What the heck are you trying to do with that thirty/thirty?"

"Did—did I kill the other laddie?" Angus asked.

"No. He'll be all right, I think," Roper replied, "but he's out cold and got a goose egg big as an apple. You'll be lucky if there's no skull fracture."

"I was just tryin' to warn him."

"Warn him about what?"

"To stay off me land."

"Angus, you know darn well this is public land."

"Aye, but it's my lease."

"We'll talk about that later," Roper said, again pushing the barrel of the gun aside. "We best get back and check on Sean"

"Who is it?" Angus asked, lowering the gun.

"You really lucked out this time, my friend. It's Sean Dunn O'Grady of the Wilderness Alliance."

"Should've kilt the lit'le son-of-a-bitch." Angus spat out the words.

"You'll be damn fortunate if he doesn't press charges," Roper said. "Come on, let's go and see if he's coming around."

"Okay laddie," Angus sighed reluctantly. "Let's give it a go."

Roper wrested the thirty/thirty from Angus and headed back to where he'd left Sean. Roper examined him again. His vital signs seemed okay. From the back seat, Roper grabbed a canteen, took a swig and tossed it to Angus. Macdonald caught the canteen, but didn't open it. Instead, he reached for his back pocket and pulled out a pint.

"I got me own," Angus said, tossing the canteen back. "You want some laddie."

"What is it?"

"Single malt whisky," Angus replied. "Make it meself right here on the Kaiparowits. Double distilled."

"Double distilled?"

"Not like that cheap Kentucky bourbon—that's only once distilled."

"You got a still up here?" Roper asked incredulously. "The Feds will shut you down in a Scottish minute."

"Oh, but they'll never find it," Angus declared, pulling the cork off with his decaying teeth and taking a long pull. "How's he doing?"

"Let's just give him a couple more minutes," Roper answered, sprinkling a little water on Sean's face. "I think he'll come around."

Angus took another drink, then peered down at Sean. "I know that lit'le red headed bastard. He's been up here before."

"Oh," Roper said. "Doing what?"

"Skulking around mainly but right after I saw him, someone put sand in the gas tank of me backhoe. Ruin't me engine, but it's being fixed right now." Angus took one more swallow then offered the bottle to Roper.

"No thanks." Roper waved him off, shaking his head. "I can't believe you had a backhoe up here."

"Yeah and a levered lorry too," Angus said. "Gettin' ready to start minin' me coal."

"And a dump truck—up here?" Roper shook his head again. "You helicopter it in?"

"No, but I was goin' to get me a dozer and blade a better road."

"Won't do you any good," Roper argued. "With the new monument there won't be any mining or road making."

"I've got me leases. It's all perfectly legal and by God I'm goin' to start the minute me backhoe is fixed."

"Angus, you can't. Things have changed." Roper found a place to sit in the shade. "The government will buy back your leases—at a fair price."

"Will they buy back me backhoe, me lorry and all the other equipment I've bought? Will they pay me back for all the money I've spent testin' this coal and what I spent for an environmental impact statement?"

"Probably not."

"Other than this," Angus swept his left hand in a wide arch. "Other than this, I ain't got nothin', not even a wee spot of haggis."

"Like I said, things have changed and they've got the might of the American government behind them."

"Dammit, Roper, I'm an American citizen too."

"Regardless," Roper insisted, "it's a losing battle. You Scots are used to that." After a moment of silence, Roper continued, "monument manager Brisco wants to arrange a meeting."

"Aye, I'll bet the lassie does."

"Will you at least come down and talk to her?"

"I'm a thinkin' them talks would be all one-sided," Angus replied, his face grim. "You got any more water?"

Roper tossed him the canteen and listened to the water gurgle down his throat. What could you say to that? Roper thought sadly. There's no question this monument would create causalities, and not just Angus. They may all be looking for another job in the near future. At least Roper had something he could fall back on—his teaching. But people like Angus or even Ruby, what would they do?

Immersed in their own thoughts, they drifted into gloomy silence. After a few moments, Roper looked up at Angus. "I've been meaning to ask you for some time, are you any distant relation to Flora Macdonald?"

"You mean the wee lassie from the Isle of Skye, who saved bonnie Prince Charlie from that English dog, William Augustus?"

"Yeah, that's the one," Roper replied. "She dressed Charles Edward Stuart, the Young Pretender, as a woman after the Battle of Culloden and rowed him to safety at the Isle of Skye."

"Aye, she was me great, great, great grandmum."

Roper looked sharply at Angus to see if he was joking. "You're not serious?"

"Of course laddie, where'd you think I git all me grit?"

"Did you grow up on the Isle of Skye?" Roper asked, amazed.

"Aye, till I was sixteen, then went to work at Glen Levitt, just a wee bit south of Inverness. Stayed there for four years, then finally worked me way south to coal fields of County Durham. I was part of that bloody coal strike that gave Dame Margaret Thatcher the nickname, the Iron Maiden."

"Then after the strike, you came to America?"

"Aye, but you know, me family's been here before. I should've been given an exemption from taking the citizen's test. Me family fought in the American Revolution."

"As I recall," Roper grinned. "They fought for the other side."

"No matter." Angus also grinned, taking another pull from his bottle.

"Rather than easy citizenship, they should hang you," Roper joked.

"Aye, I cannot explain that one neither, laddie," Angus said woefully, "the fightin' on the side of the redcoats. Who'd believed it?"

"The whole world had gone crazy," Roper agreed.

Sean moaned loudly, holding his head.

Crawling on a mat of pine needles, Roper soaked his black bandana in canteen water and washed the blood off Sean's forehead. The cold water seemed to help. The stirring and moaning increased and he finally opened his eyes.

"What—what the hell happened?" he sputtered.

"We had a little accident," Roper explained. "But other than a dented bumper, some minor front-end damage, a shattered windshield and a flat tire, the Landrover doesn't seem to be hurt too badly."

"Thank God," Sean mumbled.

"Yeah," Roper agreed. "That truck's almost indestructible. What difference will one more dent make?"

"Ohhh," Sean sat up, holding his head as he rested his back against the trunk of the juniper. Then out of the corner of his eye, he noticed Angus peering down. "What's he doing here?"

"Me?" Angus asked fiercely. "Why, I'm the one that missed your head and put that shot in your rubber."

"Forget that for now," Roper interrupted. "You okay, Sean? You're not seeing double or anything, are you?"

"No, just a hellish headache." Sean grabbed for Roper's hand and with effort stood up, then promptly sank back to the ground again. "I want to get the hell out of here."

"Come on, Angus, let's change the tire and see if the Landrover will start," Roper said, standing and walking toward the SUV.

Roper and Angus then removed the bullet-punctured tire and replaced it with the spare. Roper tried to close the sprung passenger's door, but it would only close to the first catch, and not lock. Crawling into the driver's seat, he turned the key. Instantly, the SUV roared to life. He shifted to park then went back for Sean. Half-carrying, half-dragging, he and Angus carefully laid Sean in the back seat. As Angus started to back away, Sean grabbed the front of his wool shirt and pulled him in close.

"Don't think for a minute, Scotty," he whispered through clenched teeth, "that this is over."

"Aye, but you remember, laddie," Angus said without flinching, "he who swims in the Salway Firth, shall end up in the next world."

"You'll be praying for someone to beam you up," Sean hissed.

"Come on," Roper said, "we don't have time for this. Let's get Sean to a hospital."

"You going to Escalante?" Angus asked.

"Kanab."

"But Escalante is closer," Angus said.

"Listen to me," Roper said sternly, "there is no hospital in Escalante, only a clinic."

"Aye," Angus conceded, " I'll drive me own lorry in case this bag-o-bolts don't make it." Snatching his gun from where it leaned against the Landrover, he briskly walked away.

"Fine," Roper barked, "but let's get going."

Roper steered the battered SUV back down off the Kaiparowits, barely able to see through the splintered windshield. He was careful to avoid most of the bone-jarring bumps and potholes, but it was impossible to avoid them all. Staying just back of the dust plume, Angus followed in his old flatbed Mercedes truck. Lying on the back seat, Sean remained silent except for an occasional moan. At Cottonwood Road, Roper turned north for three miles then southwest onto the Skutumpah Road. The first ten miles of Skutumpah were slow and serpentine, but the road perceptibly straightened after that and the going was much faster.

"You okay?" Roper asked after one particularly rough washboard area.

"Just dandy," Sean said tersely.

"Are you going to press charges?"

"I don't know," Sean snarled, as they slowed to cross the bridge over the slot canyon at Willis Creek, "I'm thinking it over."

"Angus is a good man," Roper said, "just a little hot-headed. Going through some tough times."

"He's a murder waiting to happen, is what he is," Sean replied. "If he's that unstable, he shouldn't be carrying a gun."

"Don't worry, I'll get his gun from him," Roper said.

After forty seemingly unending minutes on Skutumpah Road, Roper turned left onto the paved Johnson Canyon Road and after another ten miles they were at US Highway 89. At the highway the little caravan turned right, eventually dropping off the bench and on into Kanab.

The hospital was at the north edge of town, right at the base of the towering Vermillion Cliffs. Ignoring the residential speed limit, Roper roared up to the sienna brick building, then followed the signs to the emergency entrance. As he parked, Angus pulled alongside.

"You stay here with Sean," Roper ordered, "I'll go get help."

A moment later Roper was back.

"A nurse is coming with a wheelchair," Roper said, leaning against the SUV, "she's looking for an orderly to help."

Abruptly, Roper stood up, as if he had just thought of something, and without another word, he walked over to Angus' Mercedes flatbed, jerked open the door and snatched the 30/30.

"I think I'd better take this," he said, "at least for now."

Immediately, Angus rushed over and latched onto the gun. "I think not, laddie. Nobody takes me gun."

As Angus tried to wrench the gun away, a middle-aged nurse arrived with a white-clad orderly in tow. Both instantly froze as they watched, mouths gaping wide, as Roper and Angus fought for the gun.

With a powerful jerk, Roper pulled it away, but Angus lunged forward and once again latched on. Now both had their hands on the gun, wildly grappling for control. Briefly, the gun barrel twisted in the direction of the stunned nurse and orderly, then Roper quickly yanked it back. For a few moments the rifle waved wildly with no one gaining control. Then, gripping on to the barrel, Roper wrenched hard upward and felt Angus' grip slide down the gun.

Ka-boom! The sound waves ricocheted loudly off the Vermillion Cliffs as the discharged bullet whistling harmlessly into the powder blue sky. Startled, both men dropped the gun and it clattered noisily to the pavement. Shocked, the orderly and nurse watched the melodrama unfold in paralytic silence.

Defiantly, Angus looked Roper in the eye, then slowly bent over and picked up the rifle, dusting it off.

"Nobody, takes me gun," he declared fiercely. Then without another word, he climbed into his Mercedes truck and squealed off.

6

THE GRAY CLIFFS

Just southeast of the small town of Escalante are the Straight Cliffs, the most striking example of the Grand Staircase's fourth step, the Gray Cliffs. Forming the cap of Fifty Mile Mountain, the twelve hundred foot high rimrock rises abruptly from Fifty Mile Bench. These Gray Cliffs (Straight Cliffs) run approximately forty miles in a southeasterly direction.

Formed between seventy million and one hundred million years ago during the temperate, wet, and often volcanic Cretaceous Period, the Cliffs are composed of two distinct layers. The gray layer is Tropic shale, the light brown component is the Straight Cliffs formation and the stratified white streaks separating layers are probably laminates of volcanic ash. Together these layers also form the eastern boundary of the Kaiparowits Plateau.

Because of luxuriant, dense plant growth during this period, abundant coal and marine fossils are often found imbedded in these layers.

I t was warm now, as Roper and Moses pushed two cows and a white-faced calf toward Lake Pasture and his only corral on Fifty Mile Mountain. Earlier it had been downright chilly requiring him to don his Levi jacket, but not now. That morning, on the way up from the Bench over the Cliff Trail, he had noted some clumps of scrub oaks were already turning fiery orange and the temperature had turned decidedly cooler, saturating the air with the musty ripe smell of autumn. Here too, on top, the stands of quaking aspens were also beginning to turn, giving the Fifty random splashes of dazzling color. Something about the change of seasons was reassuring to Roper. An eternal cycle you could count on like, but more common, than unconditional love.

Looping the reins over the saddle horn, Roper took off his denim jacket as General Stepper and Moses continued to push the cows forward. Twisting in the saddle, he secured the jacket behind the cantle with the leather tie-down straps.

Stopping abruptly, Moses sniffed then darted into a clump of quakies, scaring up a deer that bounded silently across their path. He was a magnificent animal, a three-point mule deer, with trademark white tail flashing as he disappeared into the thicket of junipers and pinions. Silently, Roper wished him well. In just a couple of weeks it would be deer season.

Roper didn't hunt anymore. He couldn't stand to shoot those beautiful animals, though he felt it was okay that others did. When he has younger and his dad was still alive, they had hunted together. Over the years, it had been a bonding experience, but when his dad had died, Roper lost interest. Almost everyone else he knew did hunt and in a lot of southern Utah homes the deer hunt was without question, one of the major recreational highlights of the year. In fact, public schools usually closed for a day or two for a deer hunt holiday.

Fifty Mile Mountain, being public land, was open for hunting. However, it was so inaccessible that the hunting pressure was usually light, but there were always a hardy few. The last few years a fellow from Abilene, Texas had come out for a week each fall, camped out on top of the Fifty and hunted, usually by himself. With two pack mules and a big bay horse, he lugged his bulky gear up Cliff Trail and set up camp over by Seep Spring. Roper didn't mind. He never caused any trouble.

Leaning in the saddle, Roper opened the pole gate. The dog barked furiously, dashing from side to side until the cows were safely secured in the corral.

Usually Roper corralled about forty head before he drove them down the Cliff Trail onto the Bench. It was hard to take more and a waste of time to take less. Leaning against the quakie-pole fence, Roper counted, using his one remaining index finger. Only twenty-seven head. Not quite enough. Mounting General Stepper, he hollered at Moses then headed south toward Elbow Hollow. He knew there were still cows there.

Usually it would take the better part of two months for Roper to get his three hundred and fifty cows off Fifty Mile Mountain. Though it was hard work, he enjoyed it and he could usually work at his own pace. Most years, there was no real rush. Even if he didn't get all the cows off by winter, the snow would. A foot of snow on the ground, Roper had always maintained, was really the best cowboy. Once the dormant winter grass was covered by even two or three inches, the cows, except for the wild ones, would find their way down Cliff Trail to lower, less covered terrain. By now, most of the cows were trained, knew the way. They'd been doing it for years.

Riding south, Roper and Moses quickly worked their way down to Pool Hollow then climbed the wooded ridge that separated it from Elbow Hollow. As they emerged into the clearing at Elbow Hollow, Roper noticed a charcoal black mare with one white sock and a forehead star tied to a small juniper. That was strange, too early for deer hunters and tourists usually didn't ride horses. Technically, he couldn't keep people off the Fifty, but when he did see strangers, he usually investigated.

"Hello!" he hollered, as he reigned in Stepper beside the black mare.

"Hello, yourself," a man barked, as he stepped from a dense clump of quaking aspens directly behind Roper.

Whirling Stepper around, Roper recognized Monty Coleman dressed in his beige BLM shirt, sleeveless quilted vest and chocolate brown trousers. Nodding, Roper dismounted and tied General Stepper far enough away from Coleman's black mare that they couldn't fight.

"You startled me," Roper said, smiling and thrusting his hand forward. "Don't get many visitors up here."

"Don't imagine so," Monty said, ignoring the offer to shake hands. "It's not exactly freeway up here."

"What you doing up here?" Roper asked, dropping all pretense of friendliness and withdrawing his unclasped hand.

"Don't guess I need a reason," Monty said coldly, "this being government land." He eyed Roper for few moments, then to fill the void he added, "my job, range management."

"You the range con officer for this district?" Roper asked.

"That would be correct," Monty replied.

"Wearing the other hat today, huh?"

"Just checking to see how much feed you got left."

"I've already started moving my cows off onto the Bench," Roper said. "I should be done by mid-November."

"I don't think you've got enough forage till then."

"What you figuring?" Roper asked.

"Seventy percent depletion."

"Seventy percent!" Roper exploded, trying to reign in his emotions. "Not even close. My guess, not more'n fifty percent. Probably more like forty."

"The blue grama grass is completely gone," Monty said curtly, "so is the guyetta. You've got snakeweed everywhere. This range is done."

Looking at the ground, Roper poked through the sagebrush. "What are you talking about? There's clumps of grass everywhere." He brushed back a large sagebrush limb and pointed. "Here—right here there's some rice grass and some squirrel tail."

"You know just as well as I," Monty declared, "cows are lazy. They'll starve before they'll pick through this sagebrush."

"Well, what about these saplings?" Roper asked as he walked over to the quakie grove and forked a tiny aspen shoot through his fingers. "They haven't touched them yet."

Without answering, Monty motioned for Roper to follow and walked about fifty feet due west. There, a two-foot diameter metal cage was anchored into the ground. It obviously protected the grass from the foraging cows. Kneeling, Monty made a show of pulling a measuring tape from his vest pocket and measuring the blades of grass.

"The grass in the cage measures three to four inches with mature heads up to a foot," Monty reported, then quickly stuck the tape in the grass just outside the cage. "Grass here measures an inch or less. Like I said, this range is done."

"You're taking measurements from a high traffic area," Roper argued. "This is the main trail to and from Tank Hollow Spring where they water."

"Random hoop tests show the same," Monty insisted. "Not to mention the windshield test."

"The what?" Roper blurted in disbelief.

"Just eyeballing it," Monty replied, his face as unyielding as his attitude. "What we've got is an emergency situation here."

"That's being a little dramatic. Look at the darn cows," Roper argued, pointing to a rust-colored Hereford in the distance. "They look fine."

"We could debate this all day," Monty said. "But my methods are scientific, yours are emotional."

Faces not six inches apart, they glared at each other.

"So what happens next?" Roper finally asked.

"I'll take my findings back," Monty said tersely, "then the agency will make a decision."

"You know as well as I do," Roper continued, "range depletion calculations are very subjective, open to interpretation. Even your own agency can't agree on one formula."

"That's why we make decisions as a committee."

"What—what if I hire Dr. Waymont—to give a second opinion?"

"Doctor who?"

"Teaches range management for the Ag department at the college in Cedar City," Roper explained. "You know, SUU."

"I can't stop you from hiring whomever you like," Monty said stiffly.

"Will you hold off on any action till I can get you his report?"

"I'm not saying it will make a difference, but we would look at his report."

Without another word, Monty untied the big black, swung into the saddle and headed north toward Cliff Trail.

"In the land of the blind, the one-eyed man wears an eye-patch. And in the land of the Grand Staircase National Monument, the one-eyed man wears Spandex."

"Jesus," Ruby whispered in disgust, quickly making the sign of the cross.

Leaning in closer, Skinner muttered, "What the hell is he talking about?"

"Who knows?" Ruby shot back.

Bucky Lee Eakins droned on. "Ask not what you can do for this land, but rather ask what this land can do for you—"

"—you trying to reverse quote Kennedy?" Ruby groaned out loud.

"Who?" Bucky Lee looked puzzled.

"Oh, hell, forget it," Ruby slumped further into the over-stuffed, faded-green couch. Reaching under her left cheek, she compressed a mound of protruding cotton wadding back through a jagged tear in the threadbare felt, then scooted her bottom more securely over it to keep it from popping out again. In doing so, she inadvertently brushed up against Skinner.

Looking up, he grinned, his most perfect, most disarming smile. With wavy blonde hair wetted and combed straight back, long tapered well-groomed mustache, a tall muscular frame, a pleasingly rugged face with a solid square jaw, he was indeed handsome. And without a doubt, he could sure fill out a pair of Wrangler's nicely.

Bucky rambled on. "Our way of life is threatened by this hippie from the Ozarks. Do youse know he never served his country in Vietnam? Went to England instead. As they say, if youse take the man out of the country, then youse have to take him back again."

"Is there a point to all this?" one of the county commissioners asked sternly, deliberately looking at his wristwatch.

"Sure there is," Bucky rambled, "it's like I'se been a sayin' all along, if'n you pull a camel through the eye of a needle, then youse got a mighty skinny camel."

"So," a cowboy yelled from the back, "nobody's got no friggin' camels."

Inwardly, Ruby was fuming. What was she thinking when she decided to attend this little backwoods melodrama? And where the hell was Roper? Not that he'd promised to come. But still, you'd think since he supposedly represents the—dammit, she chided herself. She was starting to rely entirely too much on Douglas Roper Rehnquist.

"There's some mighty big changes a comin'," Bucky Lee continued, taking a moment to shoot a wad at the plastic spittoon. Missed. "And the answers—the answers, they're a blowin' in the winter."

"What changes?" a rancher shouted from the back.

"Well, fur one thing, they'se gonna shut down all these secondary roads youse guys use to haul your cattle in and out. Now youse guys will have to trail drive 'em on the hoof and a hell-uv-a-lot further," Bucky declared. "They'se goin' to consecrate this land agin and make it holy. That means none of them desecratin' bovines or blasphemin' cowboys."

"Damn 'em, let 'em try," a rancher shot back.

"A place where Adam and Eve can romp in nature agin with their hikin' boots, sunglasses and fig leaf shorts."

Again Ruby's mind began to wander. She'd heard about as many fractured clichés and hillbilly proverbs as she could take for one evening. But Bucky was right about one thing, this monument of Clinton's really could be big trouble. As things were, she was just barely making it. Even before the creation of the Grand Staircase, she could not live solely off her cattle business, particularly in these drought years and having to buy supplemental winter hay. Invariably, she had to augment her dwindling income with creative second jobs.

Big cat hunting and the subsequent selling of the hides to Bucky, she had to admit, had brought in a fair amount of income. But that meant she had to keep three or four hounds around and feeding them wasn't cheap. Also, it required doing business with Bucky, and God only knows how she hated dealing with him, not to mention it was illegal. If she continued down this road, it would only be a matter of time till she was caught, fined or sent to jail.

Also, her big game outfitting and guide service brought in a little money, but that was seasonal, only in the fall, and she was getting damn tired of obnoxious, liquored up greenhorns who shot at everything that moved and grabbed at everyone wearing a bra. One of her best paying customers and one of the few true gentlemen, was a Texan she'd taken deer hunting on the Fifty. After two or three years of guiding, he figured he knew the trails good enough and decided he could make the trek by himself. He continued to hunt on the Fifty, but now without her. Anyway, who knows, the BLM may very well put a stop to hunting as well.

If the drought and the downward spiral of beef prices continued, she would have to find other sources of income. Prostitution, she smiled, was always an option. She'd like to have five dollars for every time she had been hit on or brazenly propositioned. She had resigned herself to the idea that this was the price of working in a man's world. Prostitution aside, realistically that didn't leave much for her to fall back on. In her spare time, she was already filling in as a temporary at the bigger ranches and the last she had checked there were still only twenty-four hours in a day.

So seriously, what about wild bull hunting? Selling permits? Were there enough half-crazy caballeros, or wannabe cowboys running around in the southwest willing to pay for a little excitement? It might just work. The real question, would they be willing to pay three hundred, four hundred, or perhaps even five hundred dollars to kill a wild animal? Maybe, particularly when there was risk involved. Wild bulls were not like wild deer, they would not quickly bounce away into the forest at the first sight of a man. They fiercely defended their territory and when cornered, a wild bull would charge. And believe you me, those horns were no joke. They could easily cut a rider or horse or both to ribbons. Hunting wild bulls could literally be a situation of kill or be killed, and that was the lure of it.

A lot of trophy hunters, back when it was legal of course, paid a hell-uv-a-lot more than that to stalk an African lion or track an Alaskan grizzly bear. No doubt about it, a wild bull would be just as impressive as a trophy, but the successful hunter would pay hell getting it off the Fifty. With no roads into that rugged area, he would have to quarter it then pack it off with horses or mules. By the time he got it off the Fifty, the meat most likely be spoiled and after being quartered, a taxidermist wouldn't play hell trying to do anything with it except for maybe mounting the head. These were small problems, however, that could be dealt with. A lot of hunters wouldn't care one whit about meat or a trophy and would only care about the excitement of the hunt or the thrill of the kill. And Ruby was sure she could offer plenty of that.

In total, she must have twenty to thirty wild cows, maybe more, on her allotment that realistically she'd never be able to get off. So unless she could sell hunting permits, they were worthless to her, part of the high cost of doing business. They still ate her grass and the BLM still counted them toward her total AUMs. Quickly Ruby did the mental math, twenty times five hundred dollars. That was ten thousand dollars!

If Brisco and the BLM did revoke her allotment, she would be dead with absolutely no place to turn. Undoubtedly, she would lose everything, the bottomland on the Escalante River, her cattle, horses, equipment and probably even her trailer house. Everything had been mortgaged.

"We'se needs to diversify," Bucky droned on. "Have an ace-up-a-hole. Something for a raining day. I'se been doin' that, myself."

"Be more specific," Max Yeager hollered. "All we know is the cow business."

"I'se can't say much more," Bucky Lee said confidentially, "'cept there's other ways of makin' money in this heer monument."

"I already got two other jobs, school janitor and grading the county roads, to make ends meet," Pete Goslin yelled.

"I'se know, but all I'm sayin' is there's some big money to be made." Bucky took a moment to expectorate. "Youse just have to look around and smell the cow dung."

"How?" Dell Wallace clowned. "Divorce and marry up?"

"It don't grow on rocks neither," yelled another cowboy.

"It does on some rocks," Bucky muttered under his breath.

"What?" Skinner shouted. "We can't hear you."

"Oh nothin'," Bucky replied more loudly, rubbing the gray stubble of his unshaven chin, "anyhow, now I'm goin' to turn the time over to the rest of youse guys. Give the rest of youse a chance to talk. How bout it, Rube?"

Still lost in her own thoughts, Ruby never heard him.

"How bout it, Rube?" Bucky repeated even louder.

No response. Everyone in the crowded hot cabin turned to look.

Gently, Skinner nudged her in the side, "Rubles, Bucky's talking to you."

"Huh? Whadda you want, Bucky?"

"Youse want to get up and give yer thoughts on this heer situation?"

"No," Ruby stammered. "Let someone else go first. How about Skinner?" She shoved him off the couch and toward the Formica counter. "He loves to talk."

Skinner didn't protest. Without hurrying, he moved behind the kitchen counter, then using it as a podium, he faced the group. In the crowd were almost a dozen ranchers and hands, a prospector, Angus Macdonald of Highland Mining & Mineral, two or three interested citizens from Kanab and believe it or not, two Kane County commissioners.

Looking a little like steers in an auction holding pen, they were all jammed into Bucky's small, littered and sparsely furnished cabin. Most leaned against the bare log walls or stood uncomfortably without support, often shifting their positions. However, two early-arriving cowboys had commandeered the bar stools and a county commissioner instantly snapped up the recently vacated seat on the sofa next to Ruby.

A natural leader, Skinner was also a gifted public speaker. For dramatic effect, he first said nothing, taking a minute to make eye contact with each individual. Finally, he cleared his throat. "Well, I wish't we weren't here, that we had no occasion to be here. But unfortunately, we are here." He paused for a moment for effect then continued. "It's going to do us absolutely no good to sit here and cry, to rehash what an injustice was heaped on our shoulders and how we don't deserve it. Moan about how the democrats, Clinton and Gore, and the BLM has done us dirty. Cry about how our livelihood and lifestyle is being threatened. We already know'd all those things and if that's what this meeting is about then we might just as well go home.

"We need to get over it and move on. And when I say move on, I don't mean fergit it. I mean move on to the next step. And the way I figure it, the next step is the planning phase, constructing a master plan, developing a strategy, a plan of action. The final phase is to carry out that plan of action. Any suggestions on how we ought'ta proceed?" Skinner asked.

"Damn, it's hot in here," Ruby complained, using her hand as a fan. The air was heavy, stale and reeked of a mixture of horse and human perspiration.

The shorter of the two county commissioners stood. Using his most officious voice, Commissioner Noteman said, "we should, and are exploring every legal angle. I'm part of a task force appointed by Governor Leavitt to explore our legal options. In my opinion, the State of Utah will soon file suit against the federal government."

"Filing is one thing," Bucky quipped, "but winnin' is another. Don't ferget what happened to the tortoise."

"What tortoise?" Skinner asked. "You mean the desert turtle over by St. George that they declared an endangered species?"

"No! What tortoise did youse think?" Bucky snapped. "The one whose shot Br'er Rabbit."

Looking perplexed, Skinner shook his head slowly, then continued. "Well anyway, I think we should pursue all angles including legal, though I must confess I'm not very optimistic about that. Any other suggestions?"

"Guerilla warfare," Angus Macdonald fumed from the very back.

"What?" Skinner asked, cupping a hand over his ear.

"Guerilla warfare!" Angus yelled back. "Same way you laddies beat the English in the American War."

"Be more specific," Skinner said.

"Keep hitting 'em, little raids, harassing them till they finally give up. Decide it's not worth it," Angus said, stepping forward.

"Okay, but I still need specifics," Skinner insisted. "How do we hit 'em?"

"Well, for one thing," a rancher in the back interrupted. "Ever damn time they put up a sign closing a road, or any other damn sign for that matter, we could rip it up for kindlin'."

"Aye," Angus said, "and we could destroy their equipment, like they've done mine. There's sand a plenty just waiting to be scooped up into petrol tanks."

"We could sneak into their headquarters in Escalante or Kanab and destroy their telephones, fax machines, records and their computers. Hell, they can't do anything without those damn computers," a prospector growled.

"Or burn the damn place down!" someone shouted, voice shrill.

"Or maybe," Ruby said, sighing in disgust. "We ought to wait a bit. See what their intentions are. Then we can react to whatever they do."

"Rube, that's just plain suicide. Like they say, the best offense is offense and the best defense is to kick some ass," Bucky proclaimed, "an I don't mind using a gun. Anyhow, I heer it's open season on them BLM brown shirts. He who lives by the gun shall inherit the earth."

Ruby glared at Bucky, started to say something then clamped her mouth shut.

"Well," Skinner said, again taking charge. "That might be a little drastic to start with, but it might very well come to that. We need to keep all options on the table. How bout I make a motion for now we all take some time to figure out how we're goin' a do this? How to hit 'em where it hurts most? Then we'll meet back here in a week to go over any proposals and firm up a plan of action. Is that okay with everyone?"

Collectively, the group nodded their assent.

"Okay," Skinner said, "if there's no other business—"

"—Hold on a minute!" Roper yelled as he hurriedly pushed through the open kitchen door and made his way to the Formica counter. "I've got a couple things to say."

"It's a little too late," Skinner said, pivoting to look at Roper. "We're almost done."

"I'm sorry," Roper explained. "I got tied up on Fifty. I wanted to get here sooner."

"Well," Bucky said as nudged Skinner aside. "The whole world's a stage, but now there's no audience. Have at it, Roper."

"As you probably know by now, I'm on the Grand Staircase Advisory Committee."

"One of Arkansas Billy's boys," someone hooted.

"Another damn liberal democrat," another heckled.

"Who elected you?" someone yelled.

A chorus of hisses and boos erupted from the cabin.

Roper patted down the air with both hands. "I just want to let you know, there's another way and that's co-existence. This country's big enough for everyone, hikers, conservationists, ranchers, hunters and just plain tourists."

"What about miners?" Angus yelled. "Is it big enough for miners?"

"It's not that big," Skinner quipped and scattered laughter erupted from the group.

"There's no way to go to bed with the federal government," Bucky declared, "unless, a course, youse asexual."

"They will work with us. Just today, I ran onto Monty Coleman, our range con officer on the Fifty," Roper continued. "We disagreed on forage depletion figures, but he's allowed me to hire an independent expert. Get a second opinion."

"He can't stop you from hiring whomever you want," Skinner argued. "But mark my words, they'll shit-can that report."

"I don't think so," Roper persisted. "We all want the same thing, a good healthy range."

"What you smokin'?" a cowboy shouted.

"What youse gonna a do when they revoke yer allotments, Roper?" Bucky asked.

"Honestly, I don't think it will ever come to that," Roper said, "particularly when we have input right from the beginning."

"I'll take that bet and double it," Skinner said.

"All I'm saying," Roper said patiently, "is let's at least give them a chance."

"Token cowboy," someone from the back snickered.

"Benedict Arnold," another hissed.

"You best be careful out there," Skinner cautioned. "You have no idea what you're getting into."

7

THE PINK CLIFFS

Looming ten thousand feet high and shouldering the mighty Aquarius Plateau are the salmon-colored Pink Cliffs. Adorned by majestic Douglas fir, hardy Englemann spruce and delicate quaking aspen, and gazing out over all the other Staircase terraces, the Pink Cliffs are surely the anointed ones, sitting majestically on their lofty regal throne.

Mere youngsters, therefore occupying the highest step, the Pink Cliffs have their genesis in the Pleistocene Epoch of the Tertiary Period and are a scant fifty to sixty million years old. Making up the entire Claron formation, they are composed of Chablis-pink siltstone cemented with limestone and deposited in a shallow prehistoric lake. Then approximately twenty million years ago, the entire area started uplifting as part of the Colorado Plateau.

Easily eroded, the Pink Cliffs form the magnificent turrets, craggy amphitheaters, delicate minarets, solitary spires and the amazing rippled-walled chasms of Bryce Canyon National Park and Cedar Breaks National Monument.

Sitting on the edge of his bed and holding his throbbing head, Sean Dunn O'Grady silently stared out his window without really seeing the towering, sculpted, red sandstone cliffs just to the north and immediately adjacent to the hospital.

A sienna brick, single story structure with a flat roof, Kane County Hospital was constructed roughly in the shape of an H. The east wing was the doctor's clinic and offices, the west wing contained patient beds and emergency room, the connector wing housed the laboratory and radiology along with patient reception and the business offices.

The hospital was small, but clean. Obviously, they were without the huge collection of technical equipment that crammed large city hospitals nor did they have the full array of white-coated medical specialists, but for the practice of general medicine, they seemed to do pretty well. All things considered, the staff was pleasant and quite professional.

Sean's room was small and painted Navajo white with spotless light beige linoleum squares covering the floor. Arching above the head of the bed was a console that operated everything from the lights to the television. Tubing exited Sean's left hand, abruptly rising to a clear plastic bag of D5LR hanging from a stainless steel I.V. standard.

With his head wrapped with yards of white gauze roll, Sean looked like a meditating, but clearly displaced, Arabian sultan. Sitting cross-legged on the rumpled hospital bed, he gazed out at the immense rampart of rock. He couldn't help but wonder if the shade of red he could see out his window, that of the Wingate sandstone, was the same tint as his hair. Pretty close, he thought.

Starting at the base, he counted three distinct layers. Each stratum had its own bank of red sandstone cliffs. At the foot of each tier's cliffs, a slanting talus slope littered with boulders abruptly dropped to the next level and a new wall of cliffs. Vegetation was sparse, but the top and some of the talus slopes were dotted with pinions, junipers scrub brush and cacti.

Anywhere else in the world these cliffs would be preserved as a national park, but in southern Utah magnificent views like this were commonplace. In fact, Sean knew several red box canyons that had simply been fenced off and used as corrals. Abundance breeds apathy. So in Kanab, these magnificent vermilion buttes, pinnacles and box-canyons only served as a backdrop to Kane County Hospital and the city, and occasionally were useful as corrals or feed lots.

Unfortunately, there were two blemishes on this grand vista. Halfway up the mountain, the city had placed their culinary water storage tank. Though it was painted red, it was still as obvious as a thistle in a melon patch. Also on top of the mountain was the scourge of the twentieth century, the metal pyramids of the communication towers. It continued to amaze Sean, how man managed to trash all his priceless treasures.

Three days before, Roper and that goddamn, bandy-rooster Scotsman had brought him to the E.R. where they had dumped him. The E.R. nurse, excitable and breathless, had called the doctor in from home. After a tedious neurological exam, checking Sean's pupils, sensation, and reflexes, the doc had ordered a CT scan of Sean's head, which surprised Sean. Imagine, a CT scanner in little ole Kanab!

"Nothing." The doc grinned. "Not a thing. Hollow as a dried egg."

Sean had not been in the mood for comedy, but he was relieved there was no skull fracture or subdural hematoma. Thank God!

Not that for one minute did that good report excuse that unbalanced Scotsman for what he'd done. Sean still hadn't decided how to handle it. There were three options as best he could tell. One, he could forget and forgive—not likely. Two, he could do the proper thing and turn it over to Kane County Sheriff, Ivory Jackson. But Jackson was no friend of the monument and was in fact quite vocal about his dislike. And he was not particularly fond of Sean either.

In the past, Ivory had suspected Sean of environmental terrorism, but could never prove it. Before the monument, Jackson had hounded Sean continuously and almost caught him on one or two occasions. Sean suspected the sheriff had no idea how close he'd really been one day about three years ago on the southern Kaiparowits.

Yes, going to Sheriff Jackson would be a dual exercise in futility, mounds of paper work coupled with months of leg-dragging and in the end, nothing would be done. Privately the sheriff would probably feel Sean finally had gotten his just dues.

The last option, however, Sean could handle himself. He was perfectly capable of retribution. Not only capable, but he was damn good at it and furthermore, he would enjoy it.

Covertly or overtly, it didn't really matter. His years as an environmental militant had made him pretty good at both. The more he thought about it, however, the more he favored a face-to-face confrontation. He wanted to look that stubby son-of-a-bitch in the eye and make sure he knew from where it was coming. Watch him sweat, maybe even beg a little. Yes, it would be better if he took care of this himself.

"Morning, Mr. O'Grady," the nurse said brightly, as she waddled into the room.

Startled, Sean flinched. "You ever heard of knocking?"

"My, aren't we the grumpy one?" The nurse smiled. She was surprisingly energetic for such a heavy woman. "How are you feeling today?"

"My head hurts," Sean said irritably. "I could use some Percocet."

"No can do," the nurse said, still broadly grinning. "No narcotics for head injuries. Need to be able to assess any change in your mental status."

"There's already been a big change in my mental status. Write this down, Room one twenty-seven is in a foul mood and needs to be left alone," Sean hissed, then resumed gazing out the window.

"Well anyway, I need to take your vital signs," the nurse explained, unruffled as she stuck the heat sensor thermometer in his ear. Next she strapped the blood pressure cuff to his arm and clipped the pulse oximeter on his right forefinger. "Looks like you'll probably live," she finally pronounced with another meaty grin.

"How surprising," Sean said sullenly.

"You need anything?" the nurse asked as she charted his vital signs.

"No."

"Okay," the nurse replied as she trudged for the door. "I'll be back about noon."

"Don't make any special effort on my account."

"Oh, I almost forgot." The nurse carefully pivoted her bulk around. "Do you want the elders to come by?"

"Who?"

"The Mormon elders."

"Why would I want them?"

"To give you a blessing," the nurse beamed. "Two of them come around every afternoon to bless the sick. I make a list for them."

"For God's sake, I'm an atheist," Sean blurted through slitted teeth. "Do they have a prayer for atheists?"

"Oh," the nurse exclaimed, the perpetual smile suddenly gone. "Well, excuse me. We don't get many of your kind in these parts."

"You don't get many Jews either, I'll bet."

Without another word the nurse closed the door and Sean could hear the heavy thud of her feet receding down the hallway.

"Jesus," Sean mumbled to himself. "I don't have a venereal disease."

It still amazed him, the reaction of people when they learned he was an atheist. Nowadays, it was much more of a social stigma than being gay, at least in Utah. And, Sean thought bitterly, what is it with these Mormons? Always having to lay their hands on someone's head and bless them. Actually, he knew perfectly well what was with them. He used to be one. He had grown up in the Mormon religion and faithfully attended Sunday school, priesthood meetings, young men's meetings and sacrament meetings. All these frequent sessions had accomplished was to bore him. Just once he would have loved to hear an original thought coming from the pulpit, but it was always the same old rhetoric. Members of the church were excommunicated for original thinking.

One year, he'd agreed to read J. R. R. Tolkien's *Lord of the Rings* series to his younger brother (a large Mormon family of nine with his younger brother being ten years his junior). It occurred to Sean, Tolkien's story was about as believable as Joseph Smith's. To Sean they both were great examples of fantasy literature with Tolkien being the better writer. Sometime later he read the *Origin of the Species*. The great naturalist, Charles Darwin and his book were more credible to Sean than the *Book of Mormon* or the *Bible*. The former written by a scheming young man with visions of grandeur, the latter penned by superstitious shepherds who had absolutely no understanding of modern physics, biology or geology. To them, everything they didn't understand was a miracle or an act of God.

Not one to suffer in silence, Sean voiced his opinion on several occasions and was promptly called to repentance by his bishop. It was the bishop's impression that Sean had been possessed by the devil. Another idea that was hard to stomach. If one did not agree with the church, then they were instantly classified as taken by Satan.

Sean, of course, did not repent, but became even more vocal.

Finally, the stake president convened a court of excommunication and Sean was axed, thank God, from the Church. In a way, it was a relief but if he were honest with himself, it was also as if he had lost a part of himself. In a micro-instant, a stroke of the pen, he'd lost his culture, friends and family. Truly, in a way, he was a non-displaced expatriated American or at least an expatriated Utahn.

Sean was flabbergasted this sort of thing could happen in the land of the free. That someone, anyone, could wield this kind of power over another. His only crime was speaking his mind, and that was supposedly protected by the first amendment.

It had been years since he had talked to or seen his family. Through the grapevine he'd learned that some years back his father had died of a heart attack, his Mother had recovered from a total hip operation, his brother just younger than him was now a bishop, two sisters had been married in the temple, he was an uncle times three and his youngest brother was now on a mission to China, of all places.

"Sean," an authoritative female voice called from the hall while simultaneously banging on the partly closed door. "Are you awake?"

Startled, it took Sean a moment to answer. "Yeah, come in."

Monument manager Brisco dressed in her spotless BLM pale green and brown uniform, entered, pulled the extra chair out of the corner, slid it over by Sean, then sat down.

"How you feeling?" she asked, as she smoothed her already impeccable hair.

"Headache, but otherwise I'm fine," Sean answered, still gazing out the window, not making eye contract.

"Nothing broken?"

"Nope," Sean said, finally turning from the window.

"Too hard headed, I guess." Brisco's smile was tight and compact. "I'm glad. Was Doug hurt?"

"Not a scratch." Sean kept his answers short. He didn't feel like talking and didn't want to encourage Brisco to extend her visit.

"You going to press charges?"

"Nope."

"You should," Brisco encouraged. "Need to nip this kind of shoot-from-the-hip, western vigilante behavior in the bud. Bad for business. I heard it was Angus Macdonald."

"Couldn't say," Sean replied curtly. "I was out cold."

"I hope you're not planning some kind of personal vigilante thing," Brisco continued, shifting her weight in the chair. "I will not tolerate that. No Lincoln County style wars here in my monument."

Sean said nothing, but continued to gaze out the window.

"I mean it, Sean."

"I'm sure you do."

In silence, they both looked out the window for a moment.

"I almost forgot to tell you," Brisco said suddenly, "the inter-agency committee will be meeting tomorrow to discuss the condition of the range, focusing on Fifty Mile Mountain."

"Are you going to ban grazing?"

"I don't know for sure," Brisco answered. "but the range is in bad condition. Maybe till the drought improves, but at least it's a start."

"I see," Sean said stoically. "Are you prepared for the backlash?"

"What backlash?"

"You'll see," Sean warned. "You're literally killing the sacred Utah cow. They'll scream like banshees. There'll be a media storm."

"I doubt it," Brisco said, "of the whole state, it's only going to involve a handful of people, none with any financial or political clout. Just twelve families make a full time living off cattle ranching in Kane County, plus anyway, we're on solid ground."

"We're not talking economics here," Sean argued, "we're talking tradition. People will crush their neighbor financially and just call it business, but you start messing with their traditions and they'll die for it."

"Well, I don't think it's that big of a deal."

Sean started to say something, changed his mind and reverted to staring out the window.

"When you get out and feeling better, we still haven't finished with our monument inventory."

"Okay."

"I could use your help," Brisco said. "No one knows this monument like you, Sean."

"Okay, but have you given some thought to my proposal?"

"You mean about a paleontologist?"

"Yes," Sean said, trying not to sound too eager.

"Yes, as soon as I can budget for it," Brisco replied. "I think it's a good idea."

More silence.

"You know," Brisco sighed, still gazing out the window. "I hate deserts, barren rock. No matter how much you sculpt it or paint it, or dress it up, it's still just exposed rock. God, why couldn't I have been assigned somewhere cool and green like Yellowstone or Glacier?"

Sighing again, she loudly slapped her knees then stood up.

"You remember Monty Coleman?"

Sean shook his head slightly.

"You know, Monty, the range conservation officer?"

"Of course."

"Anyway, for now, he doubles as law enforcement officer. I'm sending Monty over to chat with you. I think we should keep this little matter in our organization, not involve Sheriff Jackson. He wouldn't be very sympathetic anyway."

Bending slightly, she looked closely at Sean to see if he was getting any of this. Sean's face was as immobile as the red sandstone mountain in the distance.

"You daydreaming again?"

"No, I heard you," Sean whispered, "but I don't need Monty Coleman."

"Well, you listen to him," Brisco ordered, as she marched for the door. "He's the law enforcement specialist and police matters such as this will be handled by him, at least for the time being. Understood?"

Sean was silent. Brisco sighed, and quickly left the room. For another ten minutes, Sean continued to stare out the window.

One thing for damn sure, he didn't need any help from Judith Brisco's so-called range con man/law enforcement specialist, whichever he was. What was he going to do anyway? Write Angus a severe citation? Make him promise to never do it again, or maybe drag him off to Sheriff Ivory Jackson's jail? A lot of good that would do. There wasn't a thing Monty could do that Sean wasn't perfectly capable of doing.

Rumor had it Monty had been with the Green Berets in Vietnam or the military police. He'd heard both stories. Big deal! Monty was now pushing fifty and even though he may have once been a finely honed, muscular killing machine, he now looked more like an aging Maytag repair man. He didn't look like he was capable of giving a speeding ticket, let alone taking care of attempted murder.

Brisco was right about one thing however, nobody knew the 1.7 million acres of the Grand Staircase National Monument like he did, every mountain, plateau, canyon and spring. And God knows, water could be pretty hard to find in the Grand Staircase. Also, when it came to paleontology, he had a pretty good idea where the best sites could be found. From the high alpine country of the Aquarius Plateau to the slick red rock canyons of the Escalante River drainage, from the immense barren plateau of the Kaiparowits, to the cedar and pinion studded Fifty Mile Mountain, nobody knew or loved this area like Sean O'Grady.

Hell, if it weren't for Sean's hard work, there probably wouldn't be a monument. But the ultimate slap in the face, to bring in an outsider who knew absolutely nothing about the monument, who freely admits she doesn't even like the area, then put her in charge of this massive, yet delicate, jewel. Undoubtedly this is what Jesus meant when he said don't cast your pearls before swine. Thank God, he was a patient man.

Bang! Bang! Sean involuntarily jumped as someone else rapped on the door.

"Enter," Sean growled, then mumbled to himself, "Jesus, I'm popular today."

In trudged Monty Coleman. His haggard face was deeply furrowed, his shoulders narrow and stooped and his gray hair thinning on top. Conspicuous, yet totally incongruous with his patriarchal demeanor, was the cold metallic gleam of a German Sig-Sauer p226 .40 caliber handgun strapped loosely around his right hip.

"Hope, I'm not bothering you," he said softly.

"Would it matter if I said yes?"

"I won't stay long," Monty replied, unruffled.

"Fine."

"Brisco asked me to drop by," Monty said as he sat down on the chair Brisco had just vacated. "You know what happened to you on the Kaiparowits is a felony."

"I suppose it depends on how you look at it," Sean replied vaguely.

"Attempted murder is always a felony," Monty snapped.

"Might've been an accident."

"I might buy that during hunting season," Monty said, his tone leaving no doubt about his attitude, "but not now."

"Whatever."

"Brisco doesn't want this monument to get a bad reputation," Monty continued, ignoring Sean's comment. "She wants to use this as kind of a demonstration case. Catch and punish the perpetrator right away to send a message."

"What kind of message?" Sean asked disinterestedly.

"It's obvious," Monty retorted, "this kind of behavior will not be tolerated on her watch."

"Well, have at it. Go ahead and catch him."

"Going to need some help," Monty said, smiling thinly. "Need to ask a few questions."

"So—go ahead."

"You see who shot your tire out?"

"No," Sean said sarcastically. "I was unconscious. Remember?"

"You didn't see anything?"

"Nope. Maybe you should talk to Roper Rehnquist. He was with me."

"I have talked to Rehnquist," Monty said. "Seems his vision isn't any better than yours."

"Well then, there you have it," Sean replied. " I guess you'll have to go out and do some good old fashioned police work. It's my limited understanding in crime investigation, if you don't have an eye witness then you have to rely on physical evidence."

"No shit," Monty said dryly.

"You found any physical evidence?"

"Some. We have a spent shell casing—thirty/thirty, some footprints and tire tracks."

"Then you have more than me."

Monty scowled, stood and stretched. "You got any enemies Sean?"

"None I can think of," Sean replied sardonically. "I'm pretty universally liked around here, I think. Thank God."

"How about Macdonald?"

"Don't think I know him personally."

"Angus Macdonald of Highland Mining and Mineral," Monty said, eying Sean closely.

"Guess not," Sean answered coolly, meeting his gaze.

"Well, let's get something straight before I go," Monty said quietly, but his eyes were now as flinty as chipped obsidian.

This sudden change startled Sean and sent a chill down his spine, but he still met Monty's gaze evenly.

"I'll make it real simple. Nothing better happen to Angus Macdonald, unless it's me that does it," Coleman said flatly.

Sean didn't reply, but instead stared out the window.

"If you're thinking revenge," Monty continued, "work with me. We can put this guy behind bars."

"I usually work alone," Sean replied. "Eliminates a lot of unknowns—reduces the chances of error."

"Well, give it some thought," Monty said as he shuffled for the door.

Sean turned and watched him leave. Maybe he had too readily dismissed Monty as an aging Maytag repairman. There was something about Monty's eyes that hinted he was no stranger to death and seemed to say, he could still pull the trigger again.

He would have to think about that one. Monty might be a good ally and even though he didn't look it, a formidable opponent.

What the hell, Sean thought. No reason I can't have a headache at home.

Reaching down, he ripped the tape off his hand and plucked out the IV. Blood trickled down his hand from the puncture site and dripped onto the floor creating shocking red pattern on the light beige linoleum. Blood did not bother him, not even his own. Sometimes he even liked the look of it, not only its color but its pasty consistency. By moving his hand back and forth, he made a pattern with the drops that looked roughly like a map of the Grand Staircase. Sighing, he used his thumb to put some pressure on the little wound.

Quickly, he found his clothes in the adjoining closet and with some effort put them on. Then with his hand once again dripping, he slipped out the back door.

Just as he disappeared into the parking lot, he saw the ever-grinning Deputy Manager Ron Sparks heading for the hospital entrance.

8

THE KAIPAROWITS PLATEAU

Roughly saucer-shaped and enclosing one thousand six hundred square miles on top, the plateau's western lip is bounded by the sawtooth spine of the Cockscomb and its eastern brim is bolstered by the massive sheer Straight Cliffs. Its southern rim is markedly gouged and fractured by the deep but tortuous arms of Wahweap Creek and its vein-like tributaries.

From above, the plateau looks flinty gray. Foliage is sparse, consisting of the stunted members of the Pygmy Forest, Utah junipers and pinions, and dotted with blue sage, black brush and Mormon tea.

Formed in lush tropical swamps about one hundred and forty million years ago during the Cretaceous Period, the Kaiparowits Plateau is composed of several layers including the Morrison formation with its priceless treasure of dinosaur fossils, including some newly discovered species, and the John Henry Member which contains rich coal beds up to twenty-nine feet thick in the center, but thinning to less than a foot at the mesa's perimeter.

Towing her horse trailer with her favorite dun and the seemingly ever present parachute cloud of road dust, Ruby pulled her beat up Ford 250 pickup off Hole-In-The-Rock Road just before reaching the massive Dance Hall Rock. Immediately she was engulfed in a suffocating fog of swirling dust. In the surreal light, a combination of morning dawn and powdered clay, she sat back, sneezed and waited for the particles to settle. Absentmindedly, she waited, gazing out the nearly opaque window in the general direction of Fifty Mile Mountain, now temporarily invisible in the circulating vortex.

After a few moments, the dust settled, again restoring visibility and the road. Stepping on the accelerator, she turned west. The track crossed the relatively flat desert floor then abruptly ascended the precipitous slope to Fifty Mile Bench. In the past, she had taken bigger rigs up this road, but this morning she was happy it was just a pickup and a two-horse trailer. The road, at least fifteen percent grade, was serpentine and rough, requiring her undivided attention. Once on the Bench, the road leveled out some and the going was easier.

Finally Ruby pulled the overheated Ford off the road near Cliff Trail. From there, she could see small sections of the path as it snaked its way to the top of Fifty Mile Mountain. As she turned off her hot engine, she noticed that neither Roper's nor Skinner's outfits were here yet. Suddenly, with no wind blowing through the open windows, the cab filled with the boiler-room odors of hot steam and burning oil.

At first it had seemed like a great idea, one of her better ones. Now she couldn't quite shake this nagging sense of foreboding, the growing impression that this day would turn out bad. Once again she rationalized that she really didn't have a choice. Roper's encounter with the range con man on Fifty Mile Mountain the other day had told her one thing, the BLM was considering the closure of grazing on Fifty Mile Mountain. And even if they didn't, she still needed the money and what other way did she have of getting the wild cows off the mountain? For some time now, the BLM had told her, they were also her responsibility. Unfortunately, feral cows could not be simply rounded up and trailed off the Fifty.

Last week she, Roper and Skinner had rounded up what cows they could and had driven them down off the Fifty. It was, as she knew it would be, a harrowing experience. Skinner's palomino was lame if not permanently injured after jumping off a six-foot ledge and sliding down a nearly forty-five-degree vertical slope. The horse was literally covered with a blanket of lacerations and abrasions, and had suffered bowed tendons in both forelegs. She had offered to pay for the horse or at least the vet bills, but fortunately Skinner had declined, saying he was happy to help and the horse would be fine in a month or so. And, he had added with a wink, there were other ways she could reimburse him.

In all, they had recovered sixty head, but that left at least another hundred or so, plus the wild ones which could never be rounded up. They were as much part of the fauna as the deer, mountain lions or coyotes.

Ruby was between the proverbial rock and the hard place, either sell hunting permits or write the feral cows off as a loss. According to the BLM, the wild ones were destroying the fragile eco-system just as much as the domestics. But what irritated Ruby was that Brisco just didn't seem to get it. It was physically impossible to remove the wild ones from Fifty Mile Mountain.

Fortunately, as it turned out, Ruby had no trouble selling the hunting permits. Actually, she had many more requests than she could fill. At a hefty five hundred dollars a piece, it surprised her people had that kind of money to waste on a trophy hunt, but her finances were so bad, she wished she had another twenty-five to sell.

The logistics of it all, however, made for sleepless nights. Twenty-six gun-slinging, half-inebriated cowboys, chasing wild bulls on terrain suited only for billy goats certainly was a disaster waiting to happen. It wasn't that implausible that someone, or one of their horses, could get hurt, maimed or even killed.

Trying to minimize the risk, Ruby had divided the hunt into two separate units, thirteen hunters per section and each section was to hunt on separate weekends. She had conscripted Roper and Skinner, as well as herself, to act as temporary wildlife officers. Their job was to help the hunters in an emergency and make sure no one killed more than one cow. And if possible, keep this little mountain safari from degenerating into drunken, unbridled chaos.

Skinner had been enthusiastic about her plan, Roper more reluctant. Even if she was attempting to sell the Navajos kachina dolls made in Hong Kong, Ruby suspected Skinner would be just as eager. For him, any reason to spend time with her was fine.

Roper, on the other hand, was more skeptical. Immediately, he had sensed the potential danger and worried about possible disaster. Quickly, on the computer, he had designed a basic liability release form and had urged her to make each hunter sign before selling him a permit. Needlessly, she had worried that the form would scare off potential hunters. In the end, it changed about as many minds as prenuptial agreements. Nobody balked.

They had even joked about the potential danger that would make such a document necessary. Not entirely as a joke, Bucky had offered to sell hunt life insurance, but nobody took him up on it.

Much to her chagrin, Bucky Lee had insisted on buying a permit, or at least he had handed Ruby a one-hundred-dollar bill for a down payment. Without cracking a smile, he had said he'd been reading the morning report and it was a bull market. Then after expectorating, he had confessed to Ruby, that he hadn't made wild bull sausage in quite some time, but he was sure it would be quite tasty and if marketed right, there should be a strong demand. Also, regardless of the sausage, everybody he knew loved his homemade wild-bull jerky.

With little success, Roper had tried to convince Bucky that shooting a bull was one thing, getting it off the Fifty was another, but Bucky was confident and could not be dissuaded. He had insisted it was cheap meat and in his profession every corner cut made it more like a circle. For the hunt, he had borrowed two packhorses and enlisted the help of two of his out-of-work and recently out-of-jail nephews. Bucky was proud of his nephews. However, most people thought he liked them hanging around because they made him look good.

Also, against her better judgment, Ruby had sold Angus Macdonald a permit. With their past history, she was not at all sure she wanted him hanging around, but he seemed depressed and down and out. He insisted he needed the meat and he looked so forlorn, she couldn't bring herself to charge him the full five hundred dollars. She had told him the odds of getting useable beef out was pretty slim, but he insisted, "Aye, me bonnie lassie, but I'm not just any man. I'll have ye know I put on a crackin' good show in the nineteen seventy-two clans games at the royal Balmoral. First in tossin' the caper. Second in tossing the spear and second in pushin' the stone." After Angus had assured him he could ride, Roper had lent him a saddle horse and of course, Angus had his own 30/30. By now everyone in the county knew about Angus' legendary gun. Privately Roper had assured her, if Angus were lucky enough to get a cow, he would help him get it off the Fifty.

Though everyone had heard rumors of what happened on the Kaiparowits, the principals involved were keeping mum. Roper, as usual, was a man of few words. He dismissed the incident as, "no big deal." All the irritating redhead had said was, "I don't know what you're talking about." And Angus had simply quoted a Scottish proverb: "Beware of the Scottish reavers, they ride at the black of night and will right all wrongs," whatever that meant.

With a start, Ruby noticed the dust had settled, leaving the air clear, but a silty film on the truck. Cracking open the cab door, she climbed out and stretched. There was an invigorating crispness to the mid-October morning. Not quite freezing yet, but it was certainly light jacket weather. Barely visible in the early light, patches of scrub oak on Fifty Mile Bench were beginning to blaze their brilliant autumn fire.

God, what a beautiful sight! To the east, the sun was just edging above the labyrinthine red rock country of the Escalante Canyons and as if to not be outdone by the scrub oak, wispy rooster clouds overhead suddenly glowed as they were pierced with fiery shafts of sunlight. They blazed a vibrant orange-red, just a shade more brilliant than the more subdued color of the canyons, still shaded from the sun.

Suddenly Ruby felt much better. How could anything go wrong on such a beautiful day? More cheerful now, she opened the horse trailer door, backed out the dun and while still watching the sunrise from the corner of her eye, began to methodically curry her horse.

———————

Alerted by the brief flash of morning sun reflecting off bare metal, Roper spotted Ruby's faded tan and white horse trailer while he was still a full mile and a half away. Frowning, he turned onto the Bench Road. He had a bad feeling about today. Like a chronic backache or toothache, try as he might, he couldn't shake it. Certainly, he could understand Ruby's motivation—money. In Roper's mind, however, money was just money and some things were just not worth it. But that was coming from someone who was not nearly so desperate.

There was no doubt about it, Ruby was hurting. With the drought the range was in bad shape and she was convinced the next step would be for Brisco to begin reducing their AUMs. Unlike Roper, Ruby believed that regardless of the drought, this kind of reduction was part of Brisco's hidden agenda anyway. Being raised in the National Park Service, Brisco had been thoroughly schooled in conservation and even in this new setting, she would naturally continue in that vein.

Most ranchers kept a back up range for emergencies, but Ruby had none. Now with this incessant drought, her own Mudhole allotment was pretty much picked clean and without a back up range, she would either have to buy expensive hay, take the cattle to the auction in Salina or come up with half-baked schemes like this wild cow hunt.

What was she thinking? Mixing guns and alcohol with the primordial frenzy of the hunt. That was like mixing sulfur, charcoal and potassium nitrate and on this day it had the same potential of exploding.

It would solve a lot of her problems if he and Ruby would get together, like Bucky had suggested at the cabin, but something intangible, something not quite palpable, made Roper hold back. Not that he didn't like Ruby. He did. And not that he didn't want to help her. He did. And certainly he could think of a lot worse ways to spend a night than with Ruby Nez. There were, however, several minor nagging concerns.

One, was the religious issue. Not that he was a card-carrying, ultra-pious Mormon, he wasn't. But he had been raised Mormon, his dad had been a bishop and deep down he felt the church was probably true or at least as good, if not better, than any other church. Ruby, on the other hand, was devout Roman Catholic. Not that there weren't good Catholics. There were. But anything fanatical or done for show made him uneasy. This was silly, Roper knew, but with Ruby always making the sign of the cross or saying Hail Mary's, that made him more than just a little uncomfortable. Also, she was not so subtle about her disdain, almost ridicule, for the Book of Mormon, Joseph Smith and polygamy. Not that the Catholic Church had anything to boast about considering its history of inquisitions, black popes and pedophile priests. She, however, would clam up if he dared to broach any of these subjects.

Religion was only part of the problem. The other was her past, or lack thereof. She had told him absolutely nothing about her past and Roper had met none of her family. He knew she was from Texas and that was about it. As for her family, she could be an orphan for all he knew. It was almost as though she was intentionally keeping this a secret. What little he did know about her was what he gleaned through county gossip or innuendo and some of those rumors were not very flattering.

It was him not her, however, that seemed out place. No doubt about it, his years at college had changed his perspective. It was now quite apparent that in a lot of ways he was no longer a fit for the bawdy, provincial ways of Utah's ranching community. Not that he felt superior to his fellow cattlemen but other than cattle, they had almost nothing in common.

Perhaps, if he took up drinking, chewing, cussing, threw his morals out the window and forgot how to think or speak correct English, then none of this would bother him. Though he hated to admit it, and it didn't take a college graduate to see it, Skinner Jacobsen was better suited for Ruby than he. In a lot of ways, they were a perfect match. It was not just that they were both of the same subculture and neither had much education but it was also painfully obvious, they were both beautiful people. And beautiful people belonged together. You certainly wouldn't breed a prize registered heifer to an aging stubby bull.

To his chagrin, he instantly felt the slow burn of jealousy start in the pit of his stomach, rise up in his throat like heartburn, then inflame his cheeks. He'd rather that Ruby end up with almost anyone other than that cocky, self-centered Skinner.

Touching his brakes, Roper began slowing down to a crawl. No point in bringing a cloud of dust with him. Slowly, he pulled off the road next to Ruby's outfit, put his vehicle in park and began unloading General Stepper. Moses, his Catahoula leopard hound, jumped out of the truck and immediately circled the periphery, sniffing for scent. Leading her already saddled and bridled dun, Ruby walked over to Roper. As usual, she was stunning in her tight Levi's and her red and black pattern western shirt with the top two buttons left undone.

"Morning," she smiled. "Glad you could make it."

"Wouldn't miss it for the world," Roper said more cheerfully than he felt.

"You run into Skinner on your way out?"

"Nope," Roper answered curtly, as he threw a saddle blanket on General Stepper.

"Well, I suspect he'll be along," Ruby replied, scanning down the distant Hole-In-The-Rock Road for a telltale signature plume of dust.

"Yeah, I suspect." Roper placed his custom made Carl Darr Saddle on General Stepper's back. "Where's the others?"

"Camped up that draw." Ruby pointed to a wooded ravine that appeared to head straight up to the top of Fifty Mile Mountain. "I checked on them last night before turning in."

"They drinking?"

"What do you think?"

"I think we best go check on them." With one hand, Roper compressed General Stepper's nostrils long enough so that he opened his mouth for air, then he deftly shoved the split bit into his mouth.

"I'm ready," Ruby affirmed, swinging into the saddle with easy grace.

"Lead on." Roper also mounted and nudged General Stepper in behind Ruby's horse, then motioned for Moses to follow.

By the time they approached the camp, the sun was fully up and the clouds had begun to thicken slightly on the far western horizon.

Long before he saw it, Roper could smell the camp. The tangy smoke of a cedar fire greeted them along with the aromas of frying sausage and boiling coffee. On arrival, the camp sounded more like the Buckskin Tavern on a raucous Saturday night than campers just rising. Through the cacophony of noise, Roper could vaguely make out someone cussing.

"Youse men should know that the friggin' highway of life," a raspy voice rang out. "blasts right through the middle of the friggin' rock of ages."

"Oh, God," Ruby said, crossing herself, "it's Bucky Lee."

"Hello, the camp!" Roper called out. Better let them know we're coming, sneaking up on a camp of armed and inebriated rednecks could be dangerous. "Bucky—we're coming in."

"Youse, can come on in, if youse want," Bucky bleated. "We'se all decent."

"That's a matter of opinion," Ruby muttered to herself.

Dismounting, Roper and Ruby walked their horses to the camp periphery, looking for a place to tie them. Scattered through the camp were seven men, rough, unshaven and in various stages of dress. Most looked hung over with bloodshot watery eyes from booze and lack of sleep. Some were still stubbornly nursing unfinished bottles. With two sixteen-inch Dutch ovens, Bucky was bent over by the fire, cooking deer sausage and scrambled eggs on orange crusted coals. The rising smoke smelled of burning cedar pitch.

Off to the right, the flap of an expensive North Face tent opened and Skinner Jacobson made a grand entrance. The only thing missing, Roper couldn't help but think, was the rising crescendo of a drum roll. Looking refreshed, like he had just stepped from the pages of a Sierra West clothing catalogue, his shirt and jeans were clean, wrinkle-free and stylish, his moustache was groomed, his face was clean shaven and his wavy blonde hair was dampened and combed straight back. Skinner was one of those rare men that couldn't look bad if he tried.

"Oh, you're here," Ruby said, seemingly relieved. "I thought you were coming up this morning."

"Nah, thought I'd camp over with the boys," Skinner replied as he walked over to Ruby, "got in late last night. Needed some R and R, cards and drinkin' time."

"Well, let me tie up and I'll come and join you guys," Ruby said.

"I'll help you." Skinner quickly brushed past Roper to help Ruby.

At that moment, another tent flap slowly opened and out crawled Angus Macdonald, bleary eyed, haggard, disheveled and slovenly. Just the exact opposite of Skinner.

"Morning, Angus," Roper greeted, smiling. "That Scotch whisky will get you every time."

"Aye, laddie," Angus mumbled, "this time you be right. In the immortal words of Bobby Burns, the brew of the night has just met the dawn of the day."

"You'd better be careful, that stuff will kill you," Roper chuckled. "That's why I never touch it."

"Aye, aye" Angus said, rubbing his arms to get out the morning chill. "There's another old saying, Scotch whisky makes you old when yer well, and well when yer old. Give you two ticks to decide which applies to me."

Roper smiled then changed the subject. "You think it will rain?" he asked, pointing at the still distant clouds.

"Here, probably not," Angus said. "In Scotland I would say aye."

"Why?" Roper asked. "Clouds are clouds."

"Not so laddie," Angus said, checking out the clouds. "In Scotland we have another old proverb, if ye can't see the mountains, that means it's raining. If ye can, that means it's going to."

"If that's true, I guess it means we're in for a storm."

Momentarily, they lapsed into silence. Roper noticed that Angus seemed to be watching Ruby's every move.

"You never told me you were sweet on her," Roper said, nodding toward Ruby.

"Aye, she's a wee bonnie lass, but she was never sweet on me," Angus said ruefully. "I hope ye have better luck with her."

"Doesn't look like it," Roper replied, nodding toward Skinner.

Finished with securing her horse, Ruby, with Skinner sniffing around her like a bird dog in heat, trudged back to the campfire.

"Sure smells good," Ruby volunteered, as she extended her hands over the fire. "You got any extra, Bucky?"

"Sure," Bucky said. "I'se got plenty. Sausage and eggs is nine bucks a plate and a cup-o-coffee is a dollar extra."

"You're kidding!" Ruby scoffed.

"No, he's not," Skinner said. "The price kind of blow'd us away too."

"Well," Bucky whined, "nobody givin' me sausage an eggs for free and then there's transportation costs." For emphasis, he spat a wad of tobacco juice onto an ember, just missing a Dutch oven. Silently, they all watched it sizzle then slowly disappear.

"What the heck," Roper shrugged, reached for his wallet and pulled out a twenty. "This is for me and Ruby."

Ruby reached over and squeezed Roper's hand. "Thanks."

"Much obliged," Bucky said, loading two sausages and a scoop of scrambled eggs onto a paper plate then handing it to Ruby. "Rome was built by wolves, not charity, you know."

"Jesus," Ruby exclaimed, crossing herself.

Skinner also accepted a plate as did Roper and for a moment they ate in silence.

"Any specific instructions for the day, Rubles?" Skinner asked, finishing his food and tossing the paper plate into the fire. It browned and curled then burst into flames, rapidly turning it into a gray flake of ash.

"Where's the others?" Ruby asked, ignoring Skinner's question. "I thought there would be thirteen."

"Three of the unsociables." Bucky jerked his thumb upwards. "Is camped up there. We didn't see none of 'em last night—not that we cared none."

"Well," Ruby hesitated, looking over the group, "we'll divide this part of my allotment in half. Six will hunt the north half and seven the south. There will be only one cow per person—"

"—but" a lean cowboy interrupted from the other side of the campfire.

"—I know." Ruby cut him off. "I know three of you have two permits and of course, you'll be allowed two cows. You can try hauling the meat off the mountain if you like or you can leave it for the cougars—your choice. Roper, Skinner and myself are not hunting, but will keep an eye on things and will be there to help if anyone needs it. Roper will take the south end, Skinner the north and I'll circulate."

"We've worked out a distress signal," Skinner continued. "If anyone needs help, he should fire two quick shots, count to three then fire one more. Everybody got it?"

Several men nodded their heads, but most ignored him.

Skinner looked the group over one last time, then added, "you best be careful out there. You have no idea what you're getting into."

"Now, unless there's more questions," Ruby concluded, "that's about it."

"I would like to say a quick word," Roper said, tossing his plate onto the fire. "I agree with Skinner. Let's be careful out there. As you know this is billy goat terrain and these bulls can be real mean. Don't shoot at sounds, make sure you can see what you're shooting at."

Roper paused for a moment and looked each in the hunter eye. "You're going to need to have your wits about you today, so why not hold off on the drinking till the hunt is over, then you can have a good party. But for now, leave the bottles in camp."

A chorus of boos erupted around the camp as Bucky Lee dumped a bucket of water on the coals. The fire joined the protest, hissing, popping and issuing a geyser of smoke and ash skyward.

One cowboy muttered, "damn Mormons."

Another mumbled, "token cowboy."

Without another word, Roper walked away, looking for his horse. Grumbling, the rest of the men scattered, gathering up gear and saddling their horses. Roper couldn't help but notice most still tucked a bottle away in their saddlebags. Out of the corner of his eye, he saw Skinner mount his paint and ride north out of camp alongside Ruby.

Mounting General Stepper, Roper rode roughly in a southwesterly direction, angling and picking his way up the precipitous grade of the Cliff Trail. As usual, Moses mostly led the way, his forward progress often interrupted by short detours as he darted into thickets brush or stands of trees investigating promising scents.

As they worked ever upward, Roper had to stop several times to give General Stepper a breather. It was a hard climb, even for a well-trained athlete like Stepper. Covered in lather, the horse's well-defined muscle bundles glistened in the bright morning sun. With any other horse Roper would have been nervous on this trail, but General Stepper was about as sure-footed as a Rocky Mountain bighorn sheep and of course, he knew the path well.

Once on top, the view was unreal. To the north, he could see all the way to the pink ledges of the Aquarius Plateau and the blue-green massive shoulders of the Boulder Mountains. To the south, he could barely make out the crimson sandstone bluffs, domes and pinnacles that marked Lake Powell and Glen Canyon. A little further on to the southwest a seemingly insignificant gash appeared and angled diagonally. That break in the terrain must be the upper reaches of the Grand Canyon, Roper decided, mesmerized by the spectacle. Finally to the distant east, there was a tangle of red rock chasms that made up the canyons of the Escalante River drainage. No matter where he looked, the view was remarkably different, but each scene spectacular. Literally a geologist's paradise.

The top of Fifty Mile Mountain was anything by flat. Numerous arroyos, some fairly deep, carved up the mesa, most of them angling toward the lower western rim. The vegetation was mainly juniper and pinion with occasional dense stands of scrub oak and aspen.

God, how he loved this country. At that moment, Roper had absolutely no regrets about his decision to abandon the classroom. To hell with the others and his nagging doubts that he was a misfit. At this moment, he was a perfect fit. He really did belong to this country.

For the next hour he worked his way across the top of Fifty Mile Mountain to the western brim. Calling this a mountain was a little misleading. Actually, it was roughly a fifty-mile long by five-mile wide mesa. This area, the western rim and just down off the lip of rimrock was where the wild cows usually grazed. Intensely territorial, they considered this their land and would fiercely defend it against intruders. It was a huge area, but Roper suspected the western rim was where most of the hunting would occur.

Getting off General Stepper, Roper securely tied him to a pinion bough then unsheathed his 30/30 and sunk on the ground. He propped his rifle up against one side of the tree trunk and his back against the other. This was as good a place as any to keep an eye on things. From here, he could see most of the southern rim of Ruby's allotment and all the way west to the Burning Hills. Skinner had the area further north.

The sun arched higher in the sky now, burning off the early morning chill. It felt warm and seductively hypnotic. Slowly, the sun seeped inside his denim jacket, through his skin and made its way into his bones. Just for a moment, Roper decided, he would lean his head back against the trunk. He hadn't slept well last night and what sleep he had managed was uneasy and fitful. His eyes burned and his lids felt weighted, like heavy wooden shutters. If he could just close them, if only briefly. With Moses snuggling at his side, Roper shut his eyes and the burning subsided. His mind began to wander like a riderless horse then he dozed, at first lightly then more deeply, like a person succumbing to anesthesia.

It was a fragmented, disjointed dream. Ruby appeared from nowhere scantily clad, waving from a distance, seductively motioning him to come. Breathlessly, he raced toward her, but even as he ran she began receding. Periodically, she would stop, smile provocatively and gesture to him. He would run as fast as he could, but again she retreated just out of reach. Once he caught her briefly, but she pushed him away and kept going.

Even though he became winded, he desperately tried to keep up.

Suddenly, like switching channels, the image changed. It was now Skinner motioning to him but unlike Ruby, he was not smiling. Instead, his face was twisted and taunting and he raised his fists as a pugilistic challenge. When Roper took a swing at him, he grinned, easily dodging and roughly shoving Roper to the ground. Peering down, Skinner started to laugh, at first just a smothered giggle, then uproariously.

Instantly, the image changed again, but now Skinner was not alone. He was joined by the ever beguiling Ruby Nez, also bending at the waist and peering down at him. Now they both began laughing, louder and louder. The clamor was so great Roper's head hurt and he covered his ears. Rolling over, he frantically tried to crawl away, but they blocked his escape and the laughing only intensified.

"Ka-boom!"

Faintly, somewhere deep in the auditory center of his brain, Roper heard the sound and dismissed it.

"Ka-boom!"

This time the sound was louder and the auditory center relayed the signal higher onto the conscious center. Rapidly this site began clearing away the remnants of the dream.

"Ka-boom!"

"It has begun," Roper mumbled tiredly, then struggled to his feet and hobbled with one foot still asleep over to the mesa's edge for a look.

It started as an occasional shot and rare short volley. The shots seemed to be coming from several different directions and it was hard to tell precisely how far away they were. At this altitude sounds could be deceiving. They carried well in the thin mesa air and the echo of a 30/30 sounded like the cannonading of a Howitzer. Damn, Roper thought grimly, this sounds pretty much like the opening day of deer season.

Then for no apparent reason, the shooting seemed to escalate with salvos of gunfire coming in angry bursts and roughly from the same general area. The report of one gun had a slightly different pitch, lower and more prolonged. To Roper's ear, this meant there had to be at least two different rifles firing.

It was beginning to sound more like combat than a bull hunt. Finally with his faculties fully focused, Roper dropped on one knee and listened carefully. Faintly, he thought he heard a shout or cry, but he wasn't sure which. It came from northeast, maybe two miles away. Somehow, this last salvo of shots didn't sound right. Hunting gunfire didn't sound like this, unless there were two hunters positioned on opposite sides of an arroyo, both firing at the same animal running down the wash between them. The other possibility was that two hunters were shooting at each other.

Hopefully, it is nothing, Roper thought grimly, as he quickly untied General Stepper and shoved the 30/30 back in the leather scabbard. Mounting General Stepper, he signaled to Moses, then headed for the gunshots.

As they worked north, Roper noticed his napping sunshine was now almost gone. Like a shroud blanketing Fifty Mile Mountain, the once innocuous clouds had thickened and layered, covering almost the entire visible sky. Rain looked imminent.

It may have only been two miles, but in this terrain it might as well be ten. There was absolutely no way to cover the ground quickly, no way to lope except for very short bursts. A rapid sustainable trot was the best Roper could manage and even then Stepper occasionally slipped and stumbled. The shots continued to guide him. Then suddenly everything became quiet. It was an eerie kind of silence, filled only with the clatter of Stepper's hooves on loose stones and the rhythmic whoosh of air as he breathed. The barely dormant bad feeling of the morning resurfaced and rapidly intensified. Involuntarily, Roper shuddered and quickly looked around. Undoubtedly he was making far more out of this than needs be.

Never leaving the western side of the mesa, Roper's path took him off the lip of Fifty Mile Mountain and down onto the near vertical talus slope towards a deep arroyo. Though there was no water in the wash, both sides had thick undergrowth with knots of pinions and junipers. The going was agonizingly slow. There were enough tangled sagebrush, thick rabbit brush, thorny black brush and house-sized boulders to impede any kind of sustained forward progress.

Impatiently, Roper worked Stepper to the bottom of the arroyo then stopped and took inventory. As best he could tell, this must be pretty close to the area where the shots were fired. A quick survey of the immediate area showed nothing. No horse, cow or human prints. Systematically, he scanned both slopes of the deep ravine. Again nothing. After a moment, he nudged a very nervous General Stepper and they painstakingly worked their way up the wash.

Fifteen minutes later, Roper stopped. Fifty yards ahead, he could see that the wash abruptly ran into a vertical cliff. Undoubtedly, on the rare days it rained, this would produce a spectacular waterfall. At the base of the cliff the water had carved out a splash basin, surrounded by a particularly thick stand of junipers. With Stepper obviously edgy, Roper decided to only go as far as the dry waterfall then turn around and work down the arroyo. He was pretty sure this was the area but then again, he had been at least two miles away.

With nothing turning up, he was beginning to feel a little foolish, over reacting like Ronald Regan did with Grenada. Why did that particular volley trouble him so much? After all this was a hunt and there was supposed to be gunfire. But it was the pattern of the shots and the faint voice that bothered him. Was it a cry for help? A cry of agony? Maybe. But then again, it could just be someone exulting in the excitement of the hunt or thrill of the kill. Or maybe, just the wind in the trees.

As Roper approached the sheer face of the cliff, the walls of the ravine abruptly narrowed to almost the width of a slot canyon, just about enough room for two horses to pass side-by-side. Suddenly, a startled pinion jay cawed loudly, scolded them, then flitted noisily from tree to tree. Stepper flinched, his ears flexed forward and he began nervously fidgeting with his bit. Roper was edgy too, his muscles tense and his nerves wired. Finally the jay quieted down and they inched forward. It was deadly silent.

Oh well, Roper thought, now not more than a hundred feet from the cliff. This is the end of the line; might just as well turn around and head back down the wash.

At that instant, Moses picked up a scent and quickly darted into a thicket adjacent to the waterfall.

Suddenly, out of the corner of his eye, Roper saw a blur, a mass of whirling black as a sixteen-hundred-pound bull crashed out of the thicket and careened down the slot canyon like a bumper car with no brakes.

Caught, with nowhere to go and no time to react, Roper instinctively reached down and whipped out his 30/30. At the same instant, he noticed two disconcerting things: the bull's head was covered in blood and his curved horns looked like drawn sabers.

Roper had the gun about halfway out of the scabbard when the bull hit. The blow knocked General Stepper backwards and sideways. He thudded hard against the right canyon wall just as a razor-sharp horn opened up a huge gash on his left shoulder.

As Stepper crashed into the wall, the downward force of the blow made him bounce and pivot, like a running back hitting and spinning off a tackler. He was then hurled several more yards down the steep wash.

Meanwhile, at impact with the wall, Roper tried to jump clear, but didn't quite make it. For one agonizing minute, his right knee was crushed between the horse and stone wall. Then as Stepper pivoted, Roper lost his support and crashed, still clutching his rifle, to the arroyo floor. Landing on his back, his head bounced off the hard ground, narrowly missing a football-sized rock not more than two inches from his right ear.

For several moments Roper gasped for breath. Then he rolled onto his abdomen just as the bull turned and prepared for a second charge. Quickly, Roper rolled again as the lowered horns raked by him, the pounding hoofs missing his head by inches. Skidding to a stop right in front of the waterfall, the bull whirled for another pass. This time Roper was ready. Lying on his stomach, he propped his elbows in the sand like a tripod, brought the 30/30 to his shoulder and carefully sighted in. The enraged bull snorted, pawed the sand. Then he lowered his head and charged.

Ka-boom! Ka-boom! It took two shots to bring the huge animal down. Slamming to the earth in mid-stride, it ploughed parallel furrows in the sand, skidding to a stop less than two feet from Roper's face.

Exhaling slowly, Roper took a minute to collect himself, then slowly sat up and checked his knee. It had already started to swell and a large purple bruise was forming over the lateral collateral ligament. Gingerly, he tried to stand. A shock wave of pain exploded through the joint, but it did not give way. More optimistically, he tried it again. It was painful, but it appeared stable.

Hobbling, Roper went over to the bull for a closer look. He was a black and white, tall, rangy animal lying on his belly with purple tongue hanging out and body splattered with blood. Roper easily found the two bullet holes in the chest from the shots he'd fired. Then he found another two, one grazing the skull and the other in the left shoulder. Obviously, he wasn't the first to shoot at this bull, but there was no doubt about it, his shots were the ones that had killed him. He was damn lucky to be alive. There was nothing more dangerous than a wounded cornered animal and these wild cows had about the same sweet disposition as desert javelinas.

Quickly, Roper looked around for his horse, but he was nowhere to be seen. Terrified, he had probably continued on down the slope. He would eventually make his way back to the horse trailer, of this Roper was sure, but he would need medical attention. Everything had happened so fast, Roper was not sure how bad Stepper's wound was. He knew he had a nasty shoulder laceration, but prayed no major arteries had been cut.

After walking a few yards, Roper was pretty sure his knee was sound. He called to Moses and slowly started picking his way down the mountain wash, roughly following the horse's path. General Stepper was pretty easy to track. The telltale red splotches more or less led directly down the arroyo and roughly in the direction of the pickup and horse trailer.

Momentarily, Roper lost the trail in the thick brush, but he continued straight downhill. He'd tracked enough wounded deer to know that an injured animal almost never traveled uphill and as he had suspected, in the next clearing he picked up the blood trail again, still heading down the arroyo.

From the size and frequency of the drops, it appeared General Stepper was losing a fair amount of blood. At times, the puddles were alarmingly large, particularly where he'd stopped to rest. If the horse didn't get medical attention soon, he might very well exsanguinate. That thought made Roper shudder. Of course, he had other horses, but none in the same class as General Stepper. Damn, he'd hate to lose that horse.

Off to his left, he heard the rabbit brush rustle, then the clatter of small rocks sliding down the steep slope. Whirling, he aimed the 30/30 in the general direction of the noise and tensely waited. No wild bull was going to catch him off guard a second time. Nothing.

Anxiously, he waited another couple minutes. Still nothing. He tossed a rock in that general direction, but other than the sound of the rock crashing through the brush, there was nothing. Whatever it was, probably rabbit or squirrel, had slipped off into the thick underbrush.

Lowering the rifle, Roper continued on down the wash. Silently he reprimanded himself for his edginess as he struggled to steady his frayed nerves. Ahead, the wash made an acute bend around a huge pillar of gray Tropic shale. As he rounded the curve, Roper abruptly stopped dead in his tracks.

"Holy sweet Jesus!" he mumbled, at the same time wishing he'd mastered Ruby's art of crossing herself—anything to protect him from evil.

Not three feet ahead of him, lying spread-eagle in the coarse blanched sand, was Angus Macdonald, a bullet hole squarely in the middle of his forehead.

9

THE COCKSCOMB

Looking like a double row of jagged sharks teeth, but christened for its uncanny resemblance to the serrated headdress of a rooster, the gray, parallel fins of the Cockscomb begin at the Arizona border on the south, then immediately extend northward, eventually inclining to the nine thousand foot level at Canaan Peak.

Representing a hundred mile rift in the earth's crust, the Comb is the northern most flexure of the East Kaibab Monocline and effectively separates the Grand Staircase to the west from the Kaiparowits Plateau on the east. Millions of years of erosion have exposed its deeper Triassic and Jurassic rocks.

Looking like the teeth of a giant rip saw slicing up through the earth, it is an abrupt and startling rock formation, and one of the most unique and distinctive pieces of natural stone sculpture in the Grand Staircase/ Escalante National Monument.

Roper had seen dead people before, his father and when attending funerals, but never before in his thirty-four years had he seen this, a dead body that had been murdered. Mesmerized, he stared down at Angus for a long time. The bullet had entered in pretty much the geometric center of the forehead, equal distances from both the nose to the hairline and both lateral margins of the skull. The initial bleeding had dried, but it had trailed down both sides of the forehead, pooled in the eye sockets and collected in the ear canals. There, however, was not nearly as much bleeding as Roper would have expected. Blood loss was not the cause of death. The cause of death was glaringly obvious—a gunshot wound to the brain.

He did not see an exit wound, but suspected it was directly at the back of the skull and Angus was lying on it. After taking a moment to contemplate potential ramifications, he decided not to move Angus. Best not disturb things.

For another paralyzing and hypnotic minute, he continued to stare down at Angus, then somewhat shakily searched for a place to sit. Off to the right, he found a large flat chunk of sandstone and sank weakly down. He needed some time to think this through.

Was this murder? At first glance, it did appear to be deliberate. The position of the wound was so perfectly centered on the forehead. Certainly, not only did that made one think the gun was aimed, but also that the shooter was a fairly good shot. To Roper's thinking, it was quite unlikely a shooter could hit a target dead center like this by happenstance but to be honest, not totally impossible. Odds may be one in a thousand or more. But still there was the tiniest chance that an errant bullet could have caused this.

So to be strictly analytical, there were two or three possibilities. One, the most likely, murder. Another possibility and to Roper's thinking less likely, a careless hunting accident. And try as he might, Roper could think of nothing else.

Except, maybe there was a third possibility. How about a self-inflicted gunshot? Suicide? Maybe a person could shoot himself dead center in the forehead with a handgun, but it would be next to impossible with a rifle. An autopsy would undoubtedly clear that up. If fired from a handgun, there would be powder burns on the forehead and of course ballistics, providing the bullet was found, would be able to tell the caliber of bullet, whether handgun or rifle. On superficial inspection, there were no obvious powder burns and there was no handgun in sight. It would be next to impossible to hold up a rifle, aim it at your forehead and pull the trigger. Angus' arms were just not long enough to accomplish that feat.

Furthermore, Roper just couldn't bring himself to believe Angus would commit suicide. He didn't fit the pattern. Yes, he'd had some fairly significant untoward events lately, mainly the revoking of his coal leases, and yes, Roper supposed he was somewhat depressed, but who wouldn't be? When Angus was depressed, however, he was the kind that drank whisky then took action, maybe not necessarily prudent action, like on the Kaiparowits when he shot out Sean's tire. And why would he buy a hunting tag from Ruby if he was planning on suicide? No, that did not seem at all probable.

Mentally, Roper stacked the possibilities in order of probability, first, murder, second, a hunting accident and third, suicide. If it were murder, who would be capable and who would have motive and opportunity to do such a despicable thing? Obviously, Roper did not know everything about Angus' life, business or personal. Certainly, he may have enemies Roper had never even heard of, someone from another life, even from Great Britain. But whoever it was, they would have had to be familiar with the Grand Staircase and know about the wild cow hunt. This imaginary suspect would have had to know that Angus would be out today and where to find him.

The who that would be capable, constituted a very long list. Anybody with a rifle. And God only knows, there were a heck of a lot of rifles in southern Utah.

Try as he might, however, Roper could not come up with a very long list of suspects, but then again, he didn't know Angus all that well. Obviously, Sean Dunn O'Grady, the environmental terrorist, had a grudge and Roper had heard he had been released from the Kane County Hospital. O'Grady didn't look particularly dangerous, but looks could be deceiving. Roper had heard rumors, some fairly well substantiated, about Sean. Certainly, he was no choir boy. And as a secondary motivation, other than the obvious revenge, he wanted no mining of any kind on the Kaiparowits.

Monty Coleman, the range con/law officer of the BLM was the only other one Roper could think of. Certainly, he appeared capable of murder. Roper considered himself a fairly good judge of character and Coleman just plain gave him the willies. Also, if you were partial to conspiracy theories, this all made perfect sense. It might very well be the BLM's way of getting a recalcitrant Macdonald off the Kaiparowits and inactivating his leases. Roper shook his head, amazed at own his loose reasoning, not at all what you'd expect from a college professor. Being realistic, he concluded, both theories seemed a bit thin and a little farfetched.

Perhaps, it was nothing so dramatic. Maybe last night he simply got into a fight over cards with some inebriated cowboy and this was all about a drunken cowboy who couldn't control his anger.

Or perhaps it could have been over a woman. Somewhere Roper had read that love and jealousy were right up there as leading causes for murder. He had to admit, he knew almost nothing about Angus' love life. Had there been a woman in Angus' life? Apparently at one time, he did have the hots for Ruby, although now both claim it was long over. But who knows? Anyhow, being open-minded, there was always the possibility this was a crime of passion. Probably not over Ruby, but there certainly could be other women.

And that was about it. That was all Roper could come up with. In spite of his gruff and blustery ways, the little Scotsman was pretty well liked in these parts.

It had been years since anyone in Kane County had died of a deliberate gunshot wound and coincidentally, the last one Roper could think of, was under quite similar circumstances. Roper didn't know much about it, as it had happened while he was away at school, but Chet Parker, Ruby's ex-husband, had been shot in the head several years ago in what had been ruled a hunting accident. The shooter had never been found, but everyone assumed it had been a careless or novice California hunter with a quick trigger finger. On their first hunt, greenhorn hunters were often jittery and famous for shooting at everything that moved or made a sound.

Well fortunately, it was not up to him to solve this crime and he'd better be careful about disturbing the crime scene. Roper had watched enough television to know not to touch or move things around and he'd better be careful where he walked, there could be crucial footprints or hoof prints that needed preserving. Now more composed, Roper looked around the crime scene one more time and sighed. Perhaps, it was time to get some help.

Clenching his jaw with resolve, Roper stood up, raised his 30/30 to his shoulder, aimed at the clouded gray sky, firing two rapid shots. He counted slowly to three then fired one more. Unless someone just happened to be hunting in the immediate area and considering the terrain, it might be a while before anyone arrived.

While waiting, Roper wandered around the perimeter. Though he knew he shouldn't disrupt the area, the sleuth in him was hard to suppress. He felt he had to do something. Thinking back, it occurred to him that he had heard a noise just before he'd found Angus. At the time he'd thought it was a rabbit or a squirrel in the brush. Backtracking up the arroyo, he circled around the peculiar pillar of Tropic shale then stopped, looking around and trying to remember. No doubt about it, the sound had come from that thicket of rabbit brush off to the right about halfway up the arroyo's western slope.

Carefully, he climbed the steep incline, parted the rabbit brush and looked down at the exposed ground. Usually protected from the elements, the soil was soft and damp, but there was something else. Clustered in the loose soil were tramped multiple boot prints and what appeared to be the rounded concavities of someone's knees. Off to one side, half buried in the dirt, was a single 30/30 casing.

Backing out, Roper decided he best leave this area for the experts. Carefully letting the brush fall back into place, he made his way down the arroyo, past the shale column, to the silent rigid body of Angus Macdonald. Once again he sat down on the flat rock and waited.

So, he'd found a 30/30 shell casing. What did that mean? Probably not much. The 30/30 was probably the single most popular rifle in the entire west, let alone in Kane County. Somewhere Roper had heard, and he had no reason to doubt it, there were more 30/30s in Kane County than there were personal computers. And per capita, there where probably more guns in Kane County than in the whole of East Los Angeles. Instinctively, Roper glanced down at his rifle lying by his side. Even he was carrying a 30/30.

Just because he'd found a casing, did not necessarily mean the shell had housed the bullet that killed the Scotsman. It could just as well have been the bullet that wounded the wild bull before he charged and gored General Stepper. Or, it could have been any other hunter's bullet for that matter even a deer hunter from last year or a poacher.

Roper shivered as a sudden gust of wind whipped through him. It had turned decidedly cooler and the once warm sun was now totally obscured by a thick bank of black clouds.

Suddenly, Roper heard the sound of an approaching horse, the click of metal shod hooves striking hard stone. Within minutes Skinner Jacobson made an appearance, coming in from the south. He saw Angus lying flat on the sand and abruptly reined in his horse. Dismounting, he quickly walked over, bent at the waist for a closer look then whistled softly and removed his Stetson.

"Man, wouldn't ya know'd it. Scotty was dead before he hit the ground."

"Yeah," Roper agreed, rising from the rock, "at least he didn't suffer."

"Damn, that's the crazy thing about hunting accidents," Skinner declared, still staring wide-eyed at Angus. "You just never know when they're going to happen."

Skinner pulled his cell phone out of his front pocket and started dialing. "Shit, no reception this far south," he fumed, putting the phone back.

"What makes you think it's a hunting accident?" Roper asked, slapping the dust off his Wranglers.

"Just one little thing, there's a cow hunt going on," Skinner said sarcastically, "in case you hadn't noticed."

"I think he was murdered," Roper replied softly, ignoring Skinner's barb.

"Murdered?" Skinner eyed Roper more soberly. "Why murdered?"

"Just strikes me that way," Roper explained. "I heard some shots a while back that sounded like two rifles firing at each other, also the entrance wound, it's right in the middle of the forehead. Perfectly centered."

"So?"

"What's the odds of a fortuitous shot ending up dead center?" Roper asked.

"A—a what kind of a shot?" Skinner scoffed. "Speak American, college boy."

"An accidental shot. What are the odds of an accidental shot doing that?"

"Hell, how should I know," Skinner answered disgustedly as he walked a circle around the body, "probably about the same as it hitting anywhere else."

"You see anybody nearby?" Roper asked. "When you came over."

"Nope, just you and now Angus here." Skinner said, shaking his head. "This has just about blow'd me away."

"See any strangers earlier?"

"Nope. None stranger than you."

At that moment, Ruby rode in and jumped off her dun. Talking to Skinner, Roper had not heard her approach. When she saw Angus, she gasped and quickly crossed herself.

"My God! What happened?" she asked, her voice quivering.

"Don't know," Skinner replied. "I think it was a hunting accident. Perry Mason here thinks it was murder."

"What do we need to do?" Ruby exclaimed.

"Are you all right, Rubles?" Skinner asked, concern etched on his face.

With all the attention on Angus, Roper had failed to notice a large purple contusion just below Ruby's left eye. Also, she had a one inch split-cut of her lower lip, now also starting to turn purple. The wound was clotted, but a telltale pattern of dried blood spots had splattered down onto the white collar of her shirt.

"Yeah, I'm all right," Ruby said, waving her hand as a sign of dismissal.

"What happened?" Skinner asked as he gently brushed a little dirt from her face.

"The dun stumbled in the rocks. I fell off and hit my head. It's no big deal."

"You sure?" Roper asked. "I've got a first-aid kit in my saddlebags."

"I said, I'm fine," Ruby insisted. "What do we do about Angus?"

"Somehow, we need to get the law up here," Roper replied.

"Which law?" Skinner asked sarcastically. "The sheriff or the BLM?"

"Whose jurisdiction is it?" Ruby asked as she walked over and stared down at the lifeless Scotsman.

"I'd think it would be the BLM—Monty Coleman," Roper said.

"This here is Kane County, isn't it?" Skinner challenged. "It should be Ivory Jackson. Let's keep the goddamn feds out of it, token cowboy."

With hands on her hips, Ruby whirled and faced them. "For God's sake, will you two knock it off. We'll call them both, let them decide. You try a cell phone?"

"Skinner tried, it didn't do any good," Roper said. "Reception is pretty spotty this far south on the Fifty. We'll have to drive into Escalante."

"Why don't you just go ahead and do that, cowboy?" Skinner said smugly. "Ruby and me'll stay here with Macdonald till you get back."

At that moment there was the distinctive echo of metal striking rock. All eyes looked around just in time to see Bucky Lee Eakins appear, leading his white horse around the vertical column of gray Tropic shale.

"Goddamn big bull up there." He jerked his thumb upstream. "Nobody cut him. Meat's goin' to taste like dried blood. Shit! Friggin' amateurs." Bucky expectorated at a hapless sagebrush to punctuate his displeasure.

"That would be me," Roper said without contrition.

"Me what?" Bucky's speech was slurred, his eyes still red and bleary.

"It was me," Roper repeated, "that killed and didn't cut him."

"Why'd youse do a stupid thing like that?" Bucky asked.

"Self-defense."

"Self-defense!" Ruby echoed with surprise.

"Almost gored me and ripped up General Stepper."

"Might taste like blood, but I can still make sausage outta it," Bucky Lee decided. "You wanna grab you horse and give me a hand?"

"Bucky, we've got bigger problems than saving meat," Roper snapped, gesturing to where Angus lay in the sand.

"Holy shit!" Bucky exclaimed. "You do that too, Roper?"

"Come on, Bucky," Roper replied, shaking his head.

"Roper," Skinner interrupted. "You'd best get going, if you're going to get back afore dark."

"He who lives by the sword," Bucky proclaimed, as he leaned over and stared down at Angus. "He who lives by the sword probably doesn't own a gun."

"Oh, Jesus," Ruby groaned, again crossing herself.

"Well, I'll better be going," Roper said after a moment. "Guess, I'll need to borrow a horse. When General Stepper was gored, he tossed me and took off."

"You can take the dun," Ruby said.

———————————————

Finding Sheriff Ivory Jackson was easy. As usual, he was having afternoon coffee at the Trail's End Café in Kanab. Finding Monty Coleman was a different matter. Nobody had seen him all day.

When he'd come down from the mountain, Roper had found General Stepper waiting for him right next to his Dodge pickup. Fortunately, he was still standing. The bleeding had pretty much stopped, but the wound looked deep and ugly. The bull's horn had ripped right through the skin, the subcutaneous fatty tissue and had lacerated the triceps muscle, exposing a bit of the white bone of the shoulder girdle.

From under the pickup seat, Roper pulled out a first aid kit, found several of rolls of Kerlex and a plastic six ounce bottle of betadine. First, soaking half of the Kerlex in betadine, he packed wet gauze into the wound then using the remaining Kerlex, he dressed it as best he could. Finally, he loaded General Stepper and quickly headed north toward Escalante. As there was no vet in Escalante, he would have to take the horse on to Kanab.

In Escalante, he stopped briefly at the BLM office. Monty wasn't there, but when he told Brisco about the hunting incident, she was furious. First of all she wanted to know why she had not been informed of this moronic, if not illegal, wild cow stunt. Allotments be damned! This was, after all, federal land. No hunts could be sanctioned on federal land without her knowledge and consent. No, it did not matter one damn bit that the Utah Fish and Game did not consider cows wildlife. "You goddamn cowboys behave as if this is your land," she said irately.

Roper had politely reminded her that even though the land may not belong to the rancher's, the cows unquestionably did. This fact only seemed to make her angrier.

"Damn, damn, damn, this just does not look good," she had seethed.

Roper listened patiently as she raged. Just as I'm about to get this national monument up and running—now this. My God, what will they think back in Washington? That she was running some kind of a Wild West show? Or worse yet, that being a woman, she either did not, or could not, control things. They were looking for any excuse to put a man in charge. Now Roper certainly had given them one. Damn it, the monument had only been in existence for a just over a year and she already had one assault with a deadly weapon and now a murder!

And what would this do to tourist visitation? Tourists and travel agencies always talk amongst themselves. Some Asians and Europeans already thought it was a death defying feat just to survive a week holiday in the United States. With something like this, they may not come at all. Already, in their minds, coming to America was akin to visiting a third world country like Mexico where roaming thugs robbed and killed tourists or the Philippines where things were always boiling with political unrest.

"Don't you know," she had asked Roper, "all national parks keep visitation figures? At this point in time, my budget is not solely based on attendance, but I do get to keep all the campground and overnight hiking fees."

She wasn't absolutely sure, but she was willing to bet the Grand Canyon, Zion Canyon or Yellowstone had not accrued two felonies within a year of start up. Finally, as she began to settle down, she conceded she did not know where Monty was but she would track him down and send him out to Fifty Mile Mountain. And yes indeed, this crime was in their jurisdiction.

Somewhat to Roper's surprise, however, Brisco did not offer one word of regret or express one word of condolence for the now deceased Scottish miner, Angus Macdonald. Perhaps, she was just as happy he was gone, though undoubtedly she would have preferred it not be this messy.

So while Brisco was tracking down Monty, Roper had driven on to Kanab. After dropping General Stepper off at the vet and being assured the horse would be all right, he had tracked down Sheriff Jackson at the café. Being on Kane County's search and rescue squad by virtue of his office, Jackson was always ready for an emergency. With the help of the department dispatcher, Deputy Ainsley had been located and had met them at the sheriff's house. Quickly, they had loaded both Jackson and Ainsley's horses, tack and gear, and now the three of them were racing back to Escalante.

Just as they pulled in at the Escalante visitor center, it began to sprinkle lightly and the wind continued to gust from the northwest. Roper wanted to check with Manager Brisco to see if she had located Monty. Sheriff Jackson had not wanted to bother.

Yes, Brisco informed them, she had found Monty on the two-way radio and he was on his way to Fifty Mile Mountain right now. Since he had only been over at Harris Wash, he would probably beat them there. Brisco, however, seemed more than a little irritated that Roper had also enlisted the help of Sheriff Ivory Jackson and his deputy.

"Fifty Mile Mountain is within the Grand Staircase National Monument and that is exclusively the jurisdiction of the BLM," she insisted.

"Well, we'll see about that," Ivory contended, shoving his Stetson way back on his head, while continuing to chew on a toothpick. "The last I checked, unless you bureaucrats have moved it, Fifty Mile Mountain is in Kane County and that's happens to be my territory."

For emphasis, he spat the frayed toothpick on Brisco's floor and marched out the door. Shrugging, Roper joined the two law officers back in the pickup. This was one territorial cat fight he was more than happy to stay out of.

In silence, they drove south out of Escalante on the graded Hole-in-the-Rock Road to Fifty Mile Mountain, eventually parking next to Ruby Nez's Ford.

As they got out, the clouds momentarily parted revealing the afternoon sun quickly sliding toward the western rim of Fifty Mile Mountain. Bathed in the glow of the early evening slanted light, their shadows looked like hinged cartoon figures, ballooning wildly as they walked. Eyeing the angle of the sun, Roper knew they had no time to waste, maybe only a couple of hours before dark. Quickly, the clouds closed again, snuffing out the momentary ray of sunlight.

With a flake of hay to munch on, Roper had left Ruby's horse tied to her horse trailer. While he fetched her, Ivory and Ainsley saddled their horses. As the first sprinkles arrived, the threesome donned rain ponchos, then mounted their horses. With Roper leading the way, they rode easterly up the ravine.

Within minutes, they were at the periphery of the hunter's camp. Several of the hunters had returned and were congregating around a blazing campfire. Ignoring the hunters, they skirted the camp and immediately began climbing Fifty Mile Mountain. By now, the rain was drumming steadily on the plastic ponchos and dripping off the brims of their hats.

An hour later, with the horses lathered in a mixture of sweat and rain, Roper again spied the peculiar Tropic shale pillar projecting from the arroyo wall. As the threesome rounded the huge rock, he could see Brisco had been right about one thing. Monty Coleman was already there, busily interviewing Ruby and Skinner. Shielding his pencil and pad from the rain, he appeared to be taking notes. Not too surprising, Bucky Lee was nowhere to be seen.

After securing the horses, Roper showed Sheriff Jackson where he had found the 30/30 casing. As Jackson poked around, Roper again found his flat rock and tiredly plopped down. He had ridden a lot of miles today. But in spite of the exhaustion, he was fascinated by police work and watched intently as the three law enforcement officers went about their work.

Jackson was moaning about the rain. It was washing away critical evidence, including any horse or foot prints. Monty, as usual, said no more than was absolutely necessary.

As they worked, the officers did not share information, nor did they even talk to each other. Roper thought, there at least might be a few terse words, some bickering over jurisdiction, but there were none. It was as if they'd both decided for the time being to put differences aside and get the work done. Maybe it was the dual urgency of the rain and impending nightfall.

That is not to say they didn't duplicate efforts, obviously they did. Jackson and Monty had both brought flash cameras and in the fading light, they both took multiple pictures of the body, the crime scene and anything else that might potentially be evidence. Individually, they scoured and re-scoured the same area for clues. If they found anything, they did not say or share.

Also, there were no joint interviews. Each officer conducted his own interviews and both interrogated all three of them, Roper, Skinner and Ruby, separately. Jackson had saved Roper for last. Finally, as the sheriff sauntered over, Monty was packing to go. Rain bouncing off his hat and yellow plastic poncho, Roper was still perched on his flat rock.

"You found him, huh—Roper?" Jackson asked, trademark toothpick dangling from the corner of his mouth.

"Yeah, just like he is," Roper confirmed. "Didn't touch anything."

"You say you heard shots, so you came to investigate?" the sheriff asked. "This was a friggin' cow hunt, you'd expect gunshots. What was so peculiar about these shots?"

"I don't know." Roper stood and pooled rain sloshed off his lap. "Guess, it sounded like men shooting at each other. I'd been a little nervous about this hunt anyway."

"You see anyone else?"

"No, not till I fired the signal shots, then Skinner, Ruby and Bucky Lee all showed up."

"Where's Bucky Lee now?"

"Don't know," Roper said. "Said something about trying to haul some meat off the mountain from a cow I shot up the arroyo."

"Angus have any enemies?"

"Not that I know of," Roper replied, "but I really didn't know him all that well."

"Had he had any recent fights or arguments with anyone?"

"Not that I know of," Roper said, wiping the rain from the brim of his hat. "Only conflict I knew of was him losing his coal leases on the Kaiparowits."

"Didn't he used to date that girlfriend of yours?" Sheriff Jackson asked pointedly.

"You talking about Ruby Nez?" Roper responded, sounding a bit defensive.

"Yeah."

"Well, as I understand it, he did date her briefly," Roper replied, frowning, "and no, she's not my girlfriend."

"That's not what I hear," the sheriff said, rolling the toothpick with his tongue. "You two ever argue about Miss Ruby Nez?"

"No!"

"Didn't he take a shot at you the other day," Jackson asked, stopping his chewing long enough to look Roper in the eye, "on the Kaiparowits?"

"Yeah, I suppose so."

"What was that all about?"

"I'm sure I don't know," Roper snapped angrily. "I think it was Sean O'Grady he was angry with, not me."

"Wouldn't you call that a conflict or was that just plain ole horseplay?"

"That was nothing."

"That tick you off, though?" Sheriff Jackson asked. "Him shooting at you like that."

"Nah, I liked Angus. He's been under a lot of pressure."

"Then how do you explain that incident the other day in Kanab?" Jackson asked.

"What incident would that be?"

"The fight you and Angus had on hospital grounds. The one that resulted in the illegal discharging of a firearm within the city limits."

"That wasn't really a fight."

"I wouldn't plan any long trips till this is resolved," the sheriff said firmly, shoving a fresh toothpick in his mouth.

10

GROSVENOR'S ARCH

Looking like a primitive Greek temple perched on the edge of the Acropolis, Grosvenor's Arch majestically looks down on Round Valley and gazes out across the Rush Beds. The uneven dome of the massive arch is held up by three immense, rough-hewn columns. Sculpted from chalk-colored sandstone of adjacent strata, two connected columns support the western arch base, while the east arm has one. Lower down on the two western columns, a small port-hole window looks over the valley. Flanking both bases of these colossal pillars are stately old pinion trees, standing quietly by as perpetual sentinels.

Conceived one hundred and eighty million years ago during the Jurassic period, the arch was carved from enormous three to six hundred foot sand dunes that over the eons were buried, then ossified into Navajo sandstone.

Barely awake, Roper squinted at the clock on the nightstand. It flashed a tardy 8:00 a.m. Groaning, he stretched, then hauled himself out of bed. It had been way after midnight by they time he'd made his way home from the fiasco at Fifty Mile Mountain and even then he hadn't immediately fallen asleep. It had been a very disturbing day.

Surely Sheriff Ivory Jackson did not seriously consider him a suspect in the murder of Angus Macdonald. True, he had been a little peeved at him when he had heard the rumors of him stalking Ruby, but who knows if they were even true. Certainly, Ruby had not confirmed them. Other than that, Roper had liked Angus well enough and even felt sorry for him. It was just unfortunate timing that the Grand Staircase National Monument was created about the same time Angus was due to begin his mining operation.

Circumstantially, he had to admit, it did not look good with Macdonald taking a shot at him and Sean on the Kaiparowits, the gun-wrestling incident at the hospital, then add to that the fact they both were, or at least had been, interested in the same woman. Unfortunately, these events were all taken out of context and if examined more closely, one would have to conclude there was no real enmity between him and Angus. In a way, he would miss the bandy Scotsman, his quaint tales and homey Scottish proverbs, plus he was the only person in the entire monument area as far as Roper knew, who had the slightest idea of what the Battle of Culloden was all about.

Turning the gas stove on to preheat, Roper retrieved the last of Bucky's sausage from the fridge. Molding a patty, he tossed it in the frying pan. After browning the meat on both sides, he cracked open two eggs, adding them to the pan. The aroma of frying sausage made Roper realize how hungry he was. It was so late last night when he'd gotten home, he had just dried off and flopped on the bed. In fact, he hadn't eaten since Bucky's ten dollar breakfast yesterday morning at the hunting camp and that was Bucky's sausage too. Sighing, Roper considered how much had changed in just twenty four hours. Unfortunately, this may not be the end of it. He had an uneasy feeling things had the potential for getting much worse.

By the time he'd finished breakfast it was time to go. His plans were to return to his Lake allotment and drive cows off the mesa down to the Bench. With the increased grazing pressure there, however, the Bench was also rapidly becoming depleted of grass. Roper decided he might have to take the next forty head right on down off the mountain all the way to his Soda Springs allotment.

After dumping the dishes in the sink unwashed, he went to the corral, caught his sorrel mare, Dorey, and loaded her into the horse trailer. General Stepper had been sutured, appeared to be okay and was recovering in the next stall. He gave him a shot of Pen G then calling Moses, they jumped into the cab of pickup and started for the Hole-in-the-Rock Road.

On the way out of town Roper wheeled into the post office. Time to clean out his box. It was only half full, not too bad considering it had been at least two weeks since he'd last collected his mail. Using a wall bench, he quickly sorted through the stack. It consisted of the usual; an assortment of bills, flyers and junk mail. However, right on the bottom was an official blue slip notifying him he had certified mail.

At the customer counter, he signed for the letter. It bore the unmistakable brown, blue and gold logo of the Grand Staircase Escalante National Monument. Tearing open the envelope, he extracted the letter and began to read.

> To: Douglas Rehnquist, permittee Lake allotment, Fifty Mile Mountain
>
> This letter is to inform you of the reduction of animal unit months (AUMs) by fifty percent on this allotment. With the drought, forage depletion estimates are at or approaching a critical seventy percent.
>
> You, of course, will have the standard ten days to comply as allowed by law. If we can be of assistance, let me know. Your cooperation is appreciated.
>
> Sincerely,
>
> Judith Brisco, Monument Manager

Miffed and mystified, Roper stuffed the letter back in the envelope and marched to his pickup. Once in the cab, he pulled his cell phone and personal directory from the glove box, found the number for the Kanab headquarters of the Grand Staircase National Monument, then punched in the digits.

"Grand Staircase National Monument, may I help you," the secretary answered in an officious feminine voice.

"This is Douglas Rehnquist and I would like to talk to Manager Brisco."

"And what may I tell her what you are calling about?"

"The Lake Allotment on Fifty Mile Mountain."

"Just a minute," the secretary said, "and I'll see if she's available."

For a full five minutes, Roper waited on hold. Finally the phone was answered.

"Monument Manager Brisco is out of the office. Would you care to talk to Assistant Manager Sparks?"

"Yeah, sure," Roper said, then waited again.

"Roper, this is Ron Sparks. What can I do for you?" the assistant manager said warmly.

"Ron," Roper replied, "I just got your letter." In his mind, Roper could almost see Sparks grinning affably.

"We sent it a week ago," Sparks replied, "and I've tried to call you a couple of times."

"Well I just got it today," Roper said. "Don't get to the post office that often and I've been out on the Fifty so I haven't been near a phone. Last Monday I ran into Monty Coleman and I thought we had an understanding no action would be taken until we got a second opinion from Dr. Waymont, at Southern Utah University."

"That's news to me," Sparks said. "No such arrangement was ever mentioned to me."

"Do you object to me having Dr. Waymont give a second opinion?"

"Not in the least," Sparks replied cordially. "I can't guarantee it will make any difference, but I can assure you we will look at it."

"You know, you're asking the impossible," Roper continued. "There's no way to get three hundred and fifty cows off the mountain and Bench in ten days."

"We have to go by federal guidelines," Sparks said. "It can be anywhere from thirty days to ten days depending on the urgency."

"You think the range is that depleted that we have an emergency?"

"Yes, we think it's getting critical."

"But ten days!" Roper said.

"Actually, it's now seven."

"How do you figure seven?"

"It was ten, but now it's down to seven," Sparks said. "You need to collect your mail in a more timely manner."

"It—it's absolutely impossible," Roper stuttered.

"You don't need to move but half of them, that's only one hundred and seventy-five," Sparks added, "it's just a fifty percent reduction you know."

"Have you ever been on Fifty Mile Mountain?" Roper asked.

"I've flown over it."

"Have you ever ridden it on horseback?"

"Well, no."

"There's no way on God's green earth that I can trail one hundred and seventy-five cows twenty miles over some of the roughest terrain on this planet in seven days," Roper said through clenched teeth. "I can only take a maximum of forty at a time down that narrow trail. By the time I round them up and push them onto the Bench then on to Soda Springs it's at least a three-day turn around. Do the math, that's twelve to fifteen days at the minimum."

"I'd love to work with you, Doug," Sparks said without rancor, "really I would. But unfortunately we have to go by the rules."

"I'm telling you, it can't be done."

"I'm sorry, Doug," Sparky said. "You'd better get some help. It's a one thousand dollar per cow trespass fee if you don't comply."

"What!"

"It's regulations," Sparky explained, "my hands are tied. I have to go by the guidelines. Only congress can change the rules."

"But you must have some slack," Roper argued. "Can't you at least give me five more days? Otherwise, you might as well get out the calculator and start adding up the fines."

"I would if I could," Sparks said sympathetically, "but as you know, I have to answer to someone else also."

"So this is coming from Judith Brisco?"

There was silence for a moment.

"I can assure you, I will file an official protest."

"Certainly, that's your right," Sparks agreed. "And Roper—"

"—Yes?" he snapped.

"I am truly sorry, but my hands really are tied."

Roper started to lash out, but instead bit his tongue and hung up the phone. It really wasn't Ron Sparks' fault. He was a nice guy and was a lot like Roper. All he really wanted was to find a way to get along. Roper had the feeling if it were just up to him and Sparky, the monument would be just fine, everything would work out.

Trying to control his anger, Roper thumbed through his directory then dialed Southern Utah University and the office of Dr. Bill Waymont. Though not close friends, Roper had known Bill socially from his years at the university. After some negotiating and some pleading, Dr. Waymont agreed to meet Roper at Dance Hall Rock tomorrow, Saturday morning.

Well, he could fume all he wanted, but anger would not pay the one thousand dollar per cow trespass fee. He best get going. Unfortunately, those cows would not move themselves. Still in a bad mood, Roper jammed the Dodge in gear and drove south on the Hole-in-the-Rock Road. Rutted, rough and eroded, it was at most a forty-mile-per-hour road and at that speed it took Roper well over an hour to get to Fifty Mile Mountain.

Parking the truck in his usual place on Fifty Mile Bench, he mounted Dorey and started up the Cliff Trail. Yesterday's clouds had cleared leaving the air crisp and clean. From the rain last night, the ground was damp and there was a slight spicy odor he readily identified as wet sage. However, today Roper had no time to enjoy the sights and smells of the recent rain; he was already getting a late start. Fortunately, at the Lake Pasture corral, he already had forty head penned and ready to go. Not having to round up cows would save him at least half a day.

After reaching the mesa top, Roper rode southwest another half mile to Lake Pasture. Opening the gate, he and Moses immediately began pushing the herd out of the pasture, east over the mesa and down the precipitous Cliff Trail. Initially, the going was slow. After the rain of yesterday, the weather had again turned warm and the cows did not want to leave. If indeed they were starving, Roper thought bitterly, they certainly would not be fighting this move off the mountain. In fact when cows ran out of feed, they often started working their way down off the mesa by themselves. They knew the way.

Once they had reached the Bench, Roper checked his watch, 4:30 p.m. They were still at least four hours away from Soda Springs. Considering the time of year, it would be dark in a couple of hours. He'd herded cattle in the dark before, but it was not easy. Signaling Moses, they kept right on going, driving the cattle southeast down the steep convoluted Bench Road to the flat desert below. From there, it was still another ten miles south to Soda Springs.

It was almost midnight by the time Roper had turned the cows loose on the desert graze and had fed Dorey and Moses. He stuffed down a fistful of Doritos, drank a warm Coke then collapsed onto the bed. Thank God, he and his father had built this cabin and the one on the Fifty. He was just too damn tired to camp out on the cold hard ground tonight.

Nowadays, he thought as he dozed off, it would be impossible to build a cabin like this. Along with the creation of the Grand Staircase came a moratorium on any kind of new construction, including cabins, corrals and roads. Oddly enough, this freeze also included the new land's stewards, the BLM. Their visitor's centers had to be placed outside the boundaries in bordering towns. The thinking, Roper supposed, was to keep the monument as wild and natural as possible.

As usual, in spite of the late night, Roper was up at dawn and after a quick breakfast, spent the morning fixing up things around the cabin, chores that he'd been putting off for way too long. A leaking roof, a window shutter that had lost its hinge and a warped door that wouldn't close tight, occupied his morning.

At noon, he met Dr. Waymont at Dance Hall Rock, just adjacent to Hole-in-the-Rock Road. Dressed in scuffed worn Tony Lama boots and a faded Pendleton shirt and jeans, Waymont looked like anything but a college professor. He was a big-boned man with broad shoulders, big hips, as well as thick graying sandy hair.

When Roper arrived, he was waiting in his pickup, thumbing through a stack of student term papers. Waymont had grown up on a ranch in Wyoming and had never really gotten horses out of his system, so not only did he have his own horse, but he was still a pretty capable rider. In tandem, with Roper leading, they drove their outfits onto the Bench then rode their horses the rest of the way. While Dr. Waymont studied the condition of the range, Moses and Roper began rounding up another forty head of cattle, corralling them in Lake Pasture.

About four o'clock Roper met up with Dr. Waymont as he was preparing to head down the Cliff Trail and back to his rig.

"What do you think?" Roper asked, pushing up his Stetson, exposing a lock of curly auburn hair.

"Well," Dr. Waymont replied as he looped his reins over the saddle horn. "They haven't started eating the saplings yet."

"That's what I told the range con man the other day." Roper nodded with satisfaction.

"However, the blue grama grass and guyetta is down to an inch in high traffic areas and less than two inches most everywhere else."

"With the drought it didn't grow as well last spring," Roper explained, shifting his weight in the saddle. "There's taller clumps in the sagebrush."

"You and I both know cows are basically lazy," Waymont countered. "They'd almost rather starve than work hard for their food."

"So what do you think?"

"I would say somewhere in the fifty percent range." Waymont took off his SUU baseball cap and ran his fingers through his thick hair.

"Monty, the range con man, said seventy percent."

"Well," Waymont hedged, "there's a lot of subjectivity in forage depletion calculations."

"But would you say seventy percent is a bit high?"

"Yeah," Waymont said, gazing upward like he was again doing the calculations in his head, "I would. But even at fifty percent, it's time to start getting them off the range."

"That's what I'm doing," Roper agreed, "but declaring an emergency? They're only giving me ten days. Actually, six now."

"Seems a bit harsh."

"You'll send me a written report?"

"I will," Waymont confirmed. "You'll have it by the middle of next week."

"Thanks," Roper said. "I owe you one."

"Good to see you again, Doug," Waymont as he prepared to go. "You ought to consider coming back to the college."

"Maybe someday, but not now. I like what I'm doing."

"You ready to go down?"

"Go ahead," Roper said. "I've got to move some cows."

"Could you use a hand?" Waymont asked. "I used to know how to drive cattle."

With Moses and Waymont's help Roper drove the herd of forty down the Cliff Trail onto the Bench. There he said goodbye to Waymont, then continued on to the desert and Soda Springs. This time it was well after one in the morning when he reached the cabin and tumbled into bed.

By continuing this punishing routine for another week, Roper and

Moses had managed to drive all one hundred and seventy-five cows from the Fifty to Soda Springs. He had run over two days longer than his allotted time, but as far as he knew no one saw him and anyway, nobody in their right mind should care or complain. What he had accomplished was no mean feat. In reality, the BLM should be congratulating him.

Bone tired, he loaded Dorey in the trailer, Moses onto the front seat and started the forty mile drive back to Escalante. As he was leaving the Bench, he noticed a helicopter circling Fifty Mile Mountain. Then it dropped out of sight to the west over by the Kaiparowits. It may or may not have landed on the plateau, Roper really couldn't tell. It did seem a little curious, however, seeing a helicopter out here, but Roper was too tired to care.

———————

It was another five days before Roper got around to going to the post office again. His only motivation for going back so soon was to see if the letter from Dr. Waymont had arrived. He needed to forward that report to Brisco and Sparks, but there seemed to be less urgency now as he had already complied with their request to reduce his AUMs by fifty percent.

As he had promised, right on top of the stack was the letter from Dr. Waymont, but also mixed in with the pile was another blue slip, notifying him of yet another certified letter.

After signing for the letter, he ripped open the envelope from the Grand Staircase National Monument and read.

> To: Douglas Rehnquist, Permittee of Lake and Soda Springs Allotments
>
> Further forage studies of Fifty Mile Mountain show the range is depleting faster than expected. Estimates now put forage depletion at ninety percent. You are hereby ordered to remove all cattle from these two allotments.
>
> As allowed by law, you will have ten days, then a trespass fine of one thousand dollars per cow will be imposed. If you have any questions, or if we can be of assistance, please call this office.

Sincerely,

Judith Brisco, Monument Manager

Cramming the letter back into the envelope, Roper could barely contain his anger. Rushing back home, he grabbed the phone and punched in the number. After convincing the secretary this was indeed urgent enough to get Brisco out of a meeting, he waited in silent fury.

"Judith Brisco here."

"Judith, you can't be serious," Roper snapped, skipping the salutations.

"You're talking about this last letter?"

"You're damn right, I am," Roper stormed. "I just barely got down to fifty percent."

"I realize that," Judith said, "but Monty was up there in the helicopter the other day continuing to monitor the situation. The grass is gone."

"Right now, I'm holding a letter in my hand from Dr. William Waymont of SUU who estimates fifty to sixty percent."

"We have our own formula and our calculations are ninety percent."

"Why the big discrepancy?"

"We have our standardized formula," Brisco explained coldly. "I have no idea how Dr. Waymont arrived at his figures."

"He's got a Ph.D. in range management."

"We have to go by our figures," Brisco said, not budging.

"There's no way I can get them off the Fifty in ten days."

"You got the first half off in ten days."

"But that was rounding up the easy ones," Roper argued, "the ones closest to the Lake Pasture corral. The rest will be scattered and take three times as long."

"Well then, I suggest you get some help."

"Need I remind you," Roper fumed, "it is a three-day turnaround to get forty head to Soda Springs—"

"—You need to read your notice more closely," Judith interrupted.

"What are you talking about?"

"Soda Springs allotment is now closed too. You must remove all your cattle from both allotments."

"That's all I have," Roper argued, his voice shrill. "I've got nowhere else to go."

"I have to protect the range," Judith replied curtly. "It's public property. As things stand now, it will take years to recover, if ever."

"What this amounts to, is that you're effectively putting me out of business."

"Roper," Judith said without a trace of warmth, "I'm truly sorry."

"Yeah, I'll bet you are."

"And Roper," Judith added, "when we say all cattle that includes the feral ones."

"The wild ones are not mine," Roper protested, "they're unbranded. The law says they are property of the county."

"Your family is responsible for them being there," Judith insisted. "Therefore you are responsible for removing them. They eat grass too, you know."

"You can't be serious!"

"The thousand dollar impound fee applies to all cows."

Stunned, Roper was quiet for a moment, and when he continued, he measured his words. "Can I at least put up a temporary pipe corral down on the desert? My only corral down there is at Soda Springs which you have now closed. Somehow, I have got to load these cows onto semi's so I can truck them to auction in Salina."

"You know the rules, "Brisco chided. "No new construction."

"But the way I figure, the closest existing corrals are another twenty miles away at Red
Well."

"Well, I guess you'll have to go to Red Well."

"By the time I drive forty head off the Fifty to Red Well, then truck them to the auction in Salina, my turnaround time is increased to six or seven days."

"You've got ten days," Brisco said flatly.

"Between the two allotments we're talking three hundred and fifty cows!"

"I'm sorry, Roper."

"It can't be done," Roper declared. "And nobody, and I do mean nobody, is going to round up the wild ones. Shoot them maybe, but drive them off the mountain, no way."

"Roper," Brisco countered, "why do I get the feeling you're trying to stonewall me?"

Swallowing hard, Roper ground his teeth and again lapsed into silence. After taking a minute to think, he continued. "What about Ruby, or am I the only one?"

"That's confidential," Judith insisted. "You'll have to ask her."

Roper slammed down the phone. Ten days to remove the rest of his domestic cows was not only asking the impossible, it was just plain ludicrous. But in those same ten days, to also remove the feral cows was pure unadulterated fantasy. God himself would have trouble with that. Mere mortal men could not accomplish that feat in ten years, ten decades—not ever.

11

CALF CREEK FALLS

Incongruous for a barren land—the cacophony of falling water, the rustling of wind through riparian trees and the loud crack as beaver gnawed trees come crashing down.

Thundering over a near vertical Navajo sandstone rampart, Calf Creek falls through clouds of mist to a blue green gossamer pool some one hundred and twenty-six feet below. Sheer desert varnished canyon walls form a natural amphitheater and gathered at the water's edge, stately river birch and noble box elders silently wait. Dressed in formal wear and perched high above in the box seats, hanging gardens of maidenhair ferns, moss and alcove columbine are continuously bathed in spray as they gaze spellbound at the plunging water.

Downriver, as pan-size rainbow trout swim lazily against the current, energetic beaver section a felled cottonwood hurrying to finish the construction of their seemingly mishmash dam. Next to the red and white marbled canyon walls, gnarly Gambel oak and enormous rabbit brush provide a pleasing green contrast. High above, perched on an unreachable cliff alcove is the ancient mortared brickwork of a Fremont Indian granary.

When Roper had first phoned Ruby, no one answered. It didn't take a college degree for him to realize she was probably doing exactly what he should be doing. Undoubtedly, she was on Fifty Mile Mountain frantically trying to remove her cattle.

Damn her!" Roper silently swore at an invisible Brisco, then instantly regretted it. No point in standing and cussing. Not with a potential thousand dollar per cow trespass fee hanging over his head. Might just as well get going.

On the way out of town, he stopped at the Shell Station for diesel. After putting the nozzle in the tank, he clicked on the automatic stop lever then, went inside the convenience store for a Coke. As he stopped at the cash register to pay, he noticed the usual stack of newspapers on the counter. The Salt Lake Tribune instantly caught his eye. Blazoned across the top of the paper in bold ink was the headline, CATTLE IMBROGLIO—FANNING THE FIRE.

Roper quickly scanned the body of the story. The reporter had briefly explained the history of the monument, how it was created and how BLM's agenda collided with that of the cattlemen. The reporter went on to explain range forage depletion figures and the subsequent closure of the allotments on Fifty Mile Mountain. As Roper continued to read one sentence stopped him cold. Clenching his jaw, he fought to control his rage. Monument Manger, Judith Brisco, was quoted as saying, "I sympathize with the plight of the ranchers, but my job is to protect the range which is nearly devoid of vegetation from dry weather and overgrazing. The harsh conditions are most evident in the cattle themselves. I've never seen cattle in such an emaciated shape."

Though the article continued for a half dozen more paragraphs, Roper slammed the paper down. How dare she! To the best of his knowledge, Judith Brisco had never seen any of his cows. Then to print this trash for the world to see. It was inexcusable. Anyone that knew him also knew he would never let a cow starve to death. Her attempt to justify her actions as rescue mission for the cattle was blatant slander, plain and simple.

Grabbing his change and his Coke, Roper stomped off to his Dodge. He replaced the pump nozzle, started his engine and squealed tires out of the driveway.

As he drove, Roper realized his anger was directly related to his total impotence concerning the problem, his total inability do anything constructive. In a very real way, he was utterly at the whim and mercy of Judith Brisco and the BLM.

Gritting his teeth, Roper resolved he would not go down without a fight. As he had done with Bill Waymont, the range management specialist,

Roper decided he would try to coax Dr. Brian Burgoyne, the vet in Kanab who had sutured Stepper, to come over to Fifty Mile Mountain and inspect his cows, then issue a letter refuting Brisco's disparaging remarks.

By the time he arrived at the Fifty, Roper had calmed down a bit. Mechanically, while still mulling over the latest edict and Brisco's comments, he saddled Dorey, then made his way up Cliff trail. Once on top, instead of turning south to his lease, he headed north toward Ruby's Mudhole allotment. He hadn't seen her in a few days, and to be honest he missed her. As an excuse for the visit, he also wanted to see if she had received the same marching orders from the BLM.

Just after crossing Llewellyn Canyon, he caught sight of her. Wearing a solid red shirt and faded Levis, she was pushing two cows and a calf toward her corral at Mudhole Spring. Riding north and away from him, she did not see him approach. To get her attention, Roper whistled loudly. Turning her horse, she looped the reins over the saddle horn, sat back and waited. Nudging Dorey into a lope, Roper covered the ground in seconds.

"Ruby," he said, removing his hat.

"Roper," she answered. No smile.

"Haven't heard from you for a while," Roper continued. "Thought I'd better check on you."

"Been busy," Ruby said coolly.

"Have you heard any more about the Macdonald investigation?"

"No," Ruby said curtly, "other than I'm a suspect."

"Something bothering you?" Roper asked, eying her closely.

"No, it's nothing," Ruby replied, then snapped, "only, those BLM buddies of yours closed my allotment."

Roper was silent for a moment. "I'm sorry, Ruby. Honestly, neither me nor the Advisory Committee had any input on that. This was purely an internal decision."

"Roper, I'm out of business." Ruby frowned and removed her dusty black Stetson. "I'll have to sell what cattle I can, and it looks like all that money will go to pay trespass fees."

Roper sighed and shook his head. "They did the same to me."

"They did?" Ruby looked surprised.

"Got the letter today."

"But at least you've got two allotments."

"They closed them both," Roper said, shaking his head, "I'm out of business too."

"What're you goin' to do?"

"We've got ten days," Roper replied. "Guess I'll remove as many as I can, then truck them to the auction. Try to get the trespass fees as low as possible. Be glad to take yours too."

"We got to get 'em off the mountain first."

"And all the way to Red Well," Roper added, "they're not allowing us any temporary corrals."

"Damn it, that's what I heard," Ruby agreed, then fell silent for a moment. "With that long of a trail drive, it would help if we could take more cows. Don't you think we could take more'n forty at a time if we had two riders?"

"Tell you what," Roper said. "You spend the rest of the day gathering your cows, maybe forty or so, and I'll do the same. Tomorrow we'll join up herds at the trailhead and try driving them all down all at once. Even with two wranglers, we might lose some, but we got no choice. It's better than a thousand dollar trespass fee."

"Okay." Ruby smiled for the first time. "I never turn down free help even if it ain't very good."

"Who said it was free," Roper grinned.

"Douglas Roper Rehnquist!" Ruby exclaimed with mock indignance. "Are you making a pass at me?"

Blushing, Roper turned away. "Nah, but if you've got no place to stay tonight you can come over to the cabin. I'll cook dinner and give you a place to sleep."

"I might just do that, Roper," Ruby grinned. "What time?"

"Whenever," Roper said, turning Dorey around south toward the Lake allotment. "Whenever you're done here will be fine."

Roper and Moses spent a hard day flushing cows out of scrub oak thickets, deep brushy ravines, dense stands of pinions and junipers, and thick quakie groves usually located in protected canyons. By dusk, they had collected a respectable forty-two head and secured them in the Lake Pasture corral. They'd be ready to move off the mountain tomorrow.

With the shroud of darkness coming on fast, Roper fed the horse and dog, then went into the cabin to clean up and start dinner.

After lighting the gas lanterns, Roper made a fire in the fireplace and another in the wood-burning stove. Next, he put a pot of water on the stove, then glanced at his watch. Ruby could arrive any moment. Not waiting for the water to get hot, he took a cold sponge bath. Shivering and with goose bumps erupting, he quickly toweled off. Why hadn't he plumbed the cabin with running water?

Suddenly, a caustic smell of smoke permeated the room. Roper immediately recognized the problem; he hadn't opened the fireplace damper. Reaching up, he jerked the lever down. Then to ventilate the suffocating smoke he opened the door. With clouds of smoke billowing out the door, he turned to the ice box to see what he could fix for dinner. There wasn't a lot to choose from. It looked like it would have to be ribeye steaks along with fried potatoes and onions. For drinks, he had nothing but water.

Removing the stovetop lid, Roper tossed in a pitch-laden pinion log then sliced potatoes and onions, depositing them into a hot pan. Within minutes, the incense of pitchy pine along with the aroma of sizzling onions replaced the smell of smoke. Now with the potatoes and onions browning nicely, he slapped the steaks on the oven's top grill. Occupied by his chores and the pleasant anticipation of Ruby's arrival, Roper forgot his troubles.

He was shaken out of his reverie by a loud banging on the door.

"It's not locked," he yelled.

He sucked in his breath as the door opened and Ruby walked in. How, he had no idea, but it appeared she had managed to change into a short black pleated skirt with dark nylons. That combined with her cardinal red blouse, her raven hair and her scarlet red lips made Roper feel a little dizzy. Or maybe it was just the stuffy room from the blazing hot stove. For a second, he had to rest a hand on the table for support. She was, without a doubt, the most beautiful woman Roper had ever been associated with. In the past, his usual date was an intelligent bespectacled woman in baggy earth tone corduroys and a loose cardigan sweater.

Smiling, Ruby walked over to the rough-hewn plank table and plunked down a liter bottle of Cabernet Sauvignon.

"I know you don't drink," she said, her dark eyes dancing mischievously. "But I've had this bottle hid away at my camp for some time now, looking for an excuse to drink it. Tonight, I have a good friend along with good food. No point in waiting."

Flashing a smile in Roper's direction, she sat down on the plank and pole chair, crossing her legs and exposing a bit of nylon decorated thigh.

"Well," Roper stammered, still flustered. "I might try a little. It's not like I've never had wine before."

"Fine," Ruby grinned. "I brought my own corkscrew. Didn't think you'd have one."

"How do you like your steaks?" Roper asked. He'd never seen Ruby in this kind of a mood.

"Why don't you surprise me." .

While Ruby worked on the cork, Roper finished preparing the meal, retrieved paper plates and paper towels for napkins from the cupboard, then served up the food. By the time he was done, Ruby had a metal coffee cup half filled with wine positioned on the table directly in front of his plate.

The whole night was intoxicating, the quaint log cabin, the cozy warmth of a wood fire, the pleasure of easy conversation, the subtle seduction of a beautiful woman and the fruity nip of a full-bodied dry red wine. Undoubtedly, this is some kind of ancient conspiracy against men, Roper thought fuzzily.

He knew he was losing control of the evening, but coming to him as somewhat of an epiphany, he realized he really didn't care. This was the closest thing to a miracle he'd ever witnessed. What was wrong with an island moment of happiness in what had otherwise been an endless sea of setbacks? As far as Roper was concerned, it was okay if this evening never ended.

Eventually the conversation lagged, but not uncomfortably, and the wine began to dispense a measure of narcosis. Roper stretched languidly out on the floor in front of the fire and Ruby soon followed, cuddling in close.

After a few minutes, Roper sighed heavily, rolled over and started to get up.

"You can have the bed," he said, nodding toward the only bedroom. "I've got my sleeping bag."

"Not this time, Douglas Roper Rehnquist," Ruby laughed, as she reached up and pulled him back down. "I think we've gone way beyond that."

Softly, Ruby kissed him and her body slowly melted into his. After a moment, she disengaged, stood up, removed her blouse and skirt, and led Roper to the bedroom.

It was a night like no other. Though not overly experienced, Roper was not exactly a virgin either. But this was like nothing he had ever experienced. Mentally and physically, he immersed himself into her completely. For some time now, he'd felt he might be falling in love with Ruby Nez, now there was no doubt.

Exhausted, drained and yet deeply satisfied, he eventually fell asleep in her arms.

It was a night for dreams, wild dreams, sexy dreams, disjointed dreams and terrifying nightmares.

Suddenly, there right in the room was Judith Brisco. She told them they could not cohabitate like this, like a couple of feral cows in heat, and still retain their allotments. Sternly, she demanded they choose now, between their allotments and each other.

Then, as if to save the day, Skinner arrived on a white horse and Ruby suddenly realized she could have Skinner and still keep her allotment. Gallantly, Skinner bent down and pulled her up on the horse behind him and they galloped off with Ruby clinging like plastic wrap.

But Roper followed them to Skinner's cabin and watched through an open window as they had sex. Furious, he looked around for some way to wreak vengeance. Unarmed, he had no knife, no gun and no club, but he did have matches. Quickly, he doused the cabin walls in gasoline, then struck the match. Instantly, the cabin was engulfed in fire. The screams were bone chilling and the smoke was thick and asphyxiating.

Thrashing about and bathed in sweat, Roper struggled for consciousness. It was as if an enormous weight had been placed on his chest. He couldn't draw a breath. The smoke was suffocating and his eyes burned.

"Roper! Wake up!" Someone was shaking him.

With supreme effort he forced his eyes open. Ruby's face was barely six inches from his, but he could hardly make out her features.

"We've got to go. The cabin's on fire!"

Instantly awake, Roper could see huge orange tongues of fire roaring through the rafters and wood-shingled roof. Smoke was everywhere, thick and deadly. Visibility was zero.

"Roll off the bed," Ruby commanded, "onto the floor. Then crawl out of here. I'll follow."

Still stunned, Roper struggled into action. He rolled onto the floor, waited till he felt Ruby next to him, then through the thick opaque smoke headed for the door. At that moment, a blazing rafter came crashing down onto the bed, shooting up a geyser of sparks and instantly setting the sheets and comforter on fire.

Even with his face right next to the floor, Roper could still hardly breathe. His eyes burned and with absolutely no visibility, his claustrophobia was closing in. It took all his inner strength to resist the rising panic. Clenching his jaw, he willed his way through the blinding suffocating shroud. With Ruby holding his left heel with her right hand, they slowly worked toward the door. After what seemed like an eternity, he found it.

Reaching up, he pulled on the handle. It didn't budge. He pulled harder, but it still didn't open. The top casing must have slipped down, he quickly decided. As the upper structural support burned, it had fallen down and wedged against the door.

Standing up in the cloud of smoke, Roper backed up two steps, lowered his shoulder and charged. He bounced off the door like a tennis ball, but the door didn't move. They were trapped! It was either out this door or die. Roper backed up four steps this time and lunged at the door he couldn't see. The rusted old hinges gave way this time and the door burst outward, slamming to the ground. Roper's momentum carried him out with the door and he crashed down on top of it. He was instantly hit with a cold blast of fresh air which he hungrily he sucked in. Where was Ruby?

Whirling, he lunged back into the fiery hell. Like a blind man, he searched with his hands. He found her not ten feet from the door. Quickly, he gathered up her unconscious body in his arms and staggered for the door.

Once outside, Roper laid her on her back then started mouth-to-mouth respirations punctuated with intermittent chest compressions. At first nothing. Choking back a growing sense of desperation, he doggedly continued the CPR. First, only a slight movement of her diaphragm, then a feeble cough. Next, a more violent cough. She was back!

Roper carried Ruby away from the fire and propped her against the trunk of a pinion tree. In stunned silence, they watched the cabin burn.

"Damn it," Roper suddenly vented. "I should've doused the fire before we went to bed."

"I could use some water," Ruby said.

"I've got a spare canteen strapped on my saddle over by the corral," Roper sighed, trying to shrug it off. "I'll go get it."

At the corral, wild-eyed and nervous, the horses, nearly in a state of panic, were pacing at the back of the corral. A quick inspection confirmed they were unharmed. Locating his saddle straddling the pole fence, Roper removed the canteen, slung the strap over his shoulder and headed back to Ruby.

About half way back, he suddenly stumbled over a metal container, reeking of gasoline.

After handing the canteen to Ruby, Roper examined the metal can. It was just what it seemed to be, a two-gallon gasoline can.

"What's that?" Ruby asked, offering the canteen to Roper.

"A gasoline can."

"Yours?"

"Nope," Roper answered. "I've got nothing up here that runs on gasoline."

"So what does that mean?" Ruby asked her eyes wide.

"Arson," Roper replied.

12

DEVIL'S GARDEN

At the base of Straight Cliffs on a westwardly sloping desert bench, rises a bizarre landscape populated with ossified goblins, ghouls, toadstools, and witching towers. Silent, brooding, and frozen in time, some say they were created by the Devil's idle mischief, others by an angry God and even some argue for the simple, but timeless, tools of water, wind and rain.

Sculpted from tri-layered, red, beige and red sandstone, the garden features solitary and clustered hoodoos, mini-domes, porthole arches, pinnacles, corrugated ribbon walls, hour glass columns, balanced rocks and the delicate Mano arch.

If the Aquarius Plateau is an Ansel Adams, then surely the Devil's Garden is a Salvador Dali. Carved from ancient Jurassic sandstone and siltstone, this composition represents Mother Nature at her abstract best.

From high atop the mountain mesa, Roper watched the riders pick their way up the almost perpendicular Cliff Trail. By their slow and sporadic progress, Roper could tell they were not familiar with the terrain. Looking like animated stick figures, he counted them as they struggled upward. There were ten of them and from this height they appeared to be clones, wearing the same clothes: two-tone brown shirts and pants and chocolate brown baseball caps characteristic of the BLM.

Roper was bone tired and though he knew he should be out beating the brush for more cows, he continued to watch from his perch upon Dorey. Resting close by in the warm morning sun, Moses also seemed exhausted and did not appear to be in a hurry either.

Looking back on the last ten days, they were mostly a blur, a fog of long days and hard labor. Roper and Ruby had worked from way before sunup to long after sundown, often till after midnight, to remove their cows from Fifty Mile Mountain. It had been a daunting task. First they had to gather the cattle from the brush, gullies and thickets on the mountain, then drive the stubborn bovine down the almost vertical Cliff Trail to the Bench and on down to the desert. Once on the desert floor, it was another twenty miles northeast to the corrals at Red Well. There they had loaded the cows into semis and hauled them a hundred and fifty miles to the auction in Salina.

During the turbulent week, Roper and Ruby had each lost three cows. They had died from thirst, the physical strain of the forced march or they had slipped off a face on Cliff Trail. Grimly, Roper couldn't help but think if Monument Manager Brisco was really that concerned about the welfare of the cows, she'd never have ordered them to put them through this ordeal.

With the drought and allotment closures, ranchers were panic selling, like the New York Stock Exchange in 1929. Rather than buying expensive feed, they simply dumped their herds at the auction and the price of beef plummeted. Now a full-grown cow would barely bring a hundred and fifty dollars, less than forty cents per pound. As a hedge to selling, Roper had some private land south of Escalante and had put forty head there. Ruby, however, had only twenty acres of bottomland and with the drought it was almost devoid of vegetation. She had been forced to sell everything.

By retaining a small core herd, Roper figured he could probably ride out these bad times, then start over again in a few years. But not so with Ruby. She had no reserve and plenty of debt. Deep down, he was afraid that one day she would simply disappear, probably not even say goodbye, leaving a void in him as large as Fifty Mile Mountain. Of all his growing losses, that would be the hardest to take.

He had fallen in love with Ruby Nez. He had felt it coming on for some time, but ever since that night in the now non-existent cabin, there was no doubt. Then add to that these past ten days, working side-by-side for eighteen hour days and camping together each night, they had grown very close. He enjoyed her spunk, her spontaneity, her mood swings, her sudden laughter, her outbursts of righteous anger and her oft timely advice. They could talk for hours or be silent for an equal amount of time. It didn't really matter. It was comfortable either way. Roper thought he could feel not only their love, but also their friendship grow.

Yes, in some ways they were an odd couple. There were huge differences in education, religion, the way they had been raised and personal wealth, and he still didn't know much about her past. But somehow, these differences seemed to have faded or matured into amusing eccentricities rather than the once annoying character flaws. In his mind, these things no longer presented insurmountable barriers to a long-term relationship. And Roper had to confess, he'd been thinking about that a lot lately.

The cabin had been a total loss and considering the present political climate, there was no way the BLM would ever let him rebuild. Of course, Roper was happy no one was hurt, but he was saddened by its destruction. The cabin had represented more than just shelter. He thought about how he and his father had built it from scratch and that had been no small accomplishment. Most of the timber they had harvested from Fifty Mile Mountain, but any other building materials had to be packed in. It had been a happy time, he and his father working side by side, sharing not only labor, but their lives. The cabin had been like a daily photograph, a tangible memory of their relationship.

There was no question in Roper's mind that it had been arson, but the nagging questions of who and why still troubled him. His list of potential suspects was pretty short. Perhaps some wacko eco-terrorist or environmental activist, Sean O'Grady instantly came to mind, with an axe to grind and a plan to remove all private structures from public property. Or, someone from the BLM, maybe that baneful Monty Coleman executing some agency secret agenda, again to remove all evidence of civilization, however meager, and return the monument to its original and natural Jurassic state. That all sounded, Roper had to admit, a bit paranoid, but paranoid or not, some one did burn the cabin down.

Briefly, he had debated which law enforcement agency he should call. In the end, he ended up calling them both. Sheriff Ivory Jackson had ridden his horse up to meet him. He had agreed it was most likely arson and after scolding Roper for contaminating the gasoline can by handling it, he promptly confiscated it. Also, during the investigation he'd found some partial boot prints and had taken several photographs. There was no way, he had explained, to lug the necessary equipment up on horseback to take print molds.

When he got ready to leave, Jackson had gnawed on his toothpick and stared at Roper for seconds while he thought.

"We've had more crime up here in the last six months than we've had in maybe the last ten years," he had finally said, eyeing Roper closely while working his toothpick. "And I can't help but wonder why you're always in the middle of it?"

"I guess it must be my engaging personality," Roper had said with a smile.

"This drought has hit you ranchers pretty hard," the sheriff had said.

"Not only the drought, but also the allotment closures," Roper had replied bitterly.

"This cabin insured?"

"Yeah, but not for much," Roper had replied then frowned. "You're not suggesting—"

"—I'm not suggesting anything," Jackson had interrupted, "I'm just conducting an investigation."

"I didn't burn my own cabin, Sheriff."

"You're still pretty high on my list of suspects for Angus Macdonald, you know," he had said without smiling. Then he had mounted his horse and headed down the mountain.

Judith Brisco, on the other hand, when she heard about the arson had coldly reminded Roper that there was no way now, with the creation of the sacred monument, that he could rebuild the cabin and if there was any metal or other unburned residue, like appliances or bed springs, it was his personal responsibility to remove them.

At that moment, Roper stirred in the saddle, checked the progress of the riders, then looked back at the rugged mesa behind him.

He and Ruby had not been able to get all their cattle off the mountain in the allotted time. Roper estimated he still had forty or fifty head left. Ruby probably slightly more and neither of them had any idea how many wild ones remained. Unyielding, Brisco had still continued to insist the feral ones were their responsibility. Between the two of them, Ruby had speculated their trespass fees, including the wild cows, could be upwards of a hundred and fifty thousand dollars. Sticking her arms out in front or her, Ruby laughed caustically. "They might just as well cuff and jail me now, cause there ain't no way in hell I can come up with that kind of money."

Though it had sickened him, rather than pay the trespass fee, Roper had shot three old heifers that couldn't keep up and left them on the side of the trail for the coyotes and mountain lions. With the severe time restraints and the exorbitant fines, the government had left him no choice. Bitterly, he suspected more would die the same way.

By now the riders were close enough to make out their features and hair color. Even though it was still early and the November sun was just beginning to chase away the morning chill, the laboring horses were all lathered up like being soaped for a bath. Damn lazy government horses, Roper thought cynically, they're also typical bureaucrats. They aren't used to this kind of hard work and for that matter, the riders probably aren't either.

Nudging Dorey, Roper worked his way over to the trailhead then reined in the horse, hooked his knee around the saddle horn, pushed back his Stetson and patiently waited. After another fifteen minutes, the struggling equine caravan had worked its way to the top. Leading the group, Monty Coleman emerged over the brim, then nudged his charcoal black quarter horse over to Roper, reining in three feet from Dorey. In silence, they glared at each other, waiting for the other to speak.

"Time's up," Monty finally announced, his face immobile and dark eyes cold.

"Excuse me?" Roper said, taken aback by his brusqueness.

"Time's up," Coleman repeated. "We are here to impound your cows."

"And what may I ask," Roper said grimly, "is the legal basis for that?"

"Your cows are officially in trespass," Monty declared, as his horse's chest continued to heave, laboring to catch its breath. "For the safety of the cows and the health of the range we're going to remove them."

"You figure it's that much of an emergency?" Roper asked sarcastically. The horses sniffed each other and thought about fighting.

"You had your chance."

"So you're saying if you don't remove my cows today they will starve by tomorrow."

"Don't be a smart ass, college boy," Monty said, eyes narrowing.

"What are you going to do with them once you get them off the mountain?"

"That's up to Manager Brisco."

"I'd appreciate it if you would return them to me," Roper stated, unhooking his leg from the saddle horn. "Over the years, I've had Ruby Nez's cattle and even some of Skinner Jacobson's wander over, I guess you could call it trespass, onto my allotment. I've always rounded them up and returned them. I would expect nothing less from you."

"Don't hold your breath, cowboy," Monty declared, voice hard. "Likely, these critters will become government property."

"I don't see any government brand on them," Roper contended. "Perhaps you didn't know, in the state of Utah all cattle belong to the brand unless there is an accompanying bill of sale with the appropriate brand inspection. Unbranded cattle, of course, belong to the county, specifically the sheriff's department. Do you have a bill of sale?"

"Well said, backwoods lawyer," Monty sneered, clapping his hands. "But need I remind you, if there is a jurisdiction conflict between state law and the federal government, Washington always trumps."

"Not out here in the West, they don't."

For another moment they glared at each other then Monty spurred his horse forward. "Move aside," he ordered, raising his voice, "or I will arrest you for obstruction of justice."

Lunging forward, Monty's black gelding crashed into Dorey's right shoulder, bulldozing her and Roper off the point and down a sheer slope. Fighting for footing, Dorey frantically staggered in the loose rocks and tangled brush. Though she stumbled to her knees, she regained her balance without sliding more than ten feet down the almost vertical incline.

Smoldering with anger, Roper gathered himself and watched the other nine riders pass silently by. Though he knew some of them, none of them greeted or acknowledged him, or even raised their heads to look him in the eye.

Now effectively excluded from doing his work, Roper shadowed the wranglers off and on for the next two days. It was obvious they were not trained cowboys and they did not have the assistance of the nimble Moses. To say they struggled was an understatement. After forty-eight hours, the BLM cowboys had gathered a paltry fifteen to twenty head of cattle to show for their efforts. By contrast, Roper and Moses usually could round up forty head in a morning. On the third day, the government riders gathered what cows they had and began driving them toward Cliff Trail.

Forging ahead of them, Roper quickly worked Dorey down the trail and onto the Bench, then loaded her into the trailer and gunned the pickup toward Escalante. As he flew past, Roper noted that at the junction of Bench Road and Hole-in-the-Rock Road, the wranglers had already constructed temporary pipe corrals to facilitate loading and shipping of the cows. Roper was livid. These were the very same structures the BLM had denied him, forcing him to make the twenty-mile detour to Red Well.

Ten miles outside of Escalante, he was finally able to pick up a signal on his cell phone. Seething, he punched in the number for the Kane County Sheriff's Department and after going through the usual layers of people, Roper finally had a slightly annoyed Sheriff Ivory Jackson on the phone.

"Ivory," Roper said, through the phone static. "The BLM has spent the last three days rounding up my cows on the Fifty."

"I sympathize with you," Jackson said, pausing with only the sound of him chomping on a toothpick coming through. After a moment, he continued. "Really I do. But there's not a damn thing I can do about it."

"But they're about to load them up in semi trucks and transport them on county roads."

For a few moments, there was silence. "I see," Jackson finally said. "They got a bill of sale?"

"Of course not."

"They got a brand inspection?"

"There's no brand inspectors out here."

"Well then, according to Utah statutes, they can't transport them cows."

"And that's just what they're fixing to do," Roper said.

"Guess it's time for a pissin' contest."

"Guess so."

"I can be in Escalante in about an hour and ten minutes," Jackson said, his voice hard with resolve. "I'll meet you at the Shell Station."

Roper glanced at his watch and noted the time. Might as well go on home and get something to eat. He was almost to Escalante anyhow. On his way home, he again visited the post office. No more certified letters, but there was one from his old Dean at SUU. All was well in Cedar City with the history department, but Dean Sorensen also wrote if Roper was to ever change his mind, there would be a position waiting. Also in the stack was a note from the vet in Kanab confirming his appointment to inspect Roper's cattle two weeks from Monday.

After parking the Dodge in front of the house, Roper trudged tiredly toward the front door. The moment he entered, he sensed something was wrong.

At that instant, he heard the back screen door bang shut and smelled the unmistakable odor of smoke. Following his nose, he raced through the living room and dining room then burst into the kitchen. The smoke was coming from the far corner between the gas range and fridge. Someone had dumped a pile of rags on the floor, doused them with gasoline and set them on fire. From the looks of it, the fire had just been started. The flames were still small and relatively contained.

Pivoting to his left, Roper grabbed a large stewing pot from the cabinet, filled it with water and dumped it in on the fire.

When he was sure it was out, Roper breathed a sigh of relief, then started to investigate. The back door had been locked, but the door jam was splintered and the lock smashed. Outside in the back yard he found a hastily discarded gasoline can by the cedar slat fence. Somewhat unnerved, Roper nudged it with the toe of his boot and turned it over. It was identical to the one he had found up at the Fifty Mile cabin.

This time, Roper picked up the can with a paper towel, placed it into a black plastic garbage bag, then set it on the passenger seat in the Dodge.

Shaken, Roper sat down at the kitchen table. Within a week, he had battled two fires on his property. Obviously, he had been singled out. He was a target. Somebody out there wanted him dead or financially destroyed, or both.

While struggling to make sense of it all, he cleaned up the charred rags then threw a frozen dinner of beef tips and pasta in the microwave. Once it was hot, he picked at it, but he'd lost his appetite. Reaching for the phone, he dialed Ruby's number. No answer, not that he really expected to catch her home and he wasn't disappointed.

Glancing up at the wall clock, he saw it was time to go. Grabbing his Levi jacket, he hustled out to the Dodge.

At the Shell Station, Roper handed Jackson the gas can along with an explanation. Though the Sheriff promised to have it dusted for prints, he wasn't optimistic. The can from Fifty Mile Mountain had yielded nothing. You could buy these cans in almost any of the filling stations in southern Utah.

As they drove south on Hole-in-the-Rock Road in the sheriff's cruiser, the sun began its long slumping arch that would eventually take it behind the Straight Cliffs and Fifty Mile Mountain. Right at the Kane and Garfield county line, near Rat Seep Hollow, the sheriff stopped, parked the cruiser perpendicular across the road, turned on his flashing red lights and they settled back to wait. The desert valley had now settled into the hazy flat light of dusk while Fifty Mile Mountain was still aglow, being spotlighted by the sinking, now invisible, sun.

For two hours, they patiently waited as dusk turned to dark, any moment expecting to see the dual blazing headlights of a semi truck loaded with cows bearing down on them. Finally Sheriff Jackson pulled a fresh toothpick from his shirt pocket, started the car and headed south toward the temporary corrals Roper had seen earlier.

When they arrived thirty minutes later, a half moon had just emerged, suspended over the ghostly labyrinth of the Escalante Canyons. Though the corrals were now empty, there were still plenty of signs they that had been recently used. From the tracks it was obvious the BLM wranglers had corralled, loaded and trucked the cows out, but somehow they did it all without passing them on the Hole-in-the-Rock Road.

There were a number of minor dirt roads the BLM could have used, but none that Roper would have considered suitable for a semi. Three things, however, were abundantly clear. One, apparently the BLM had realized that what they were doing was questionable on legal grounds. Two, they had gone to great pains to avoid the sheriff's roadblock. And three, the fact it played out this way meant they had been tipped off.

It was well after midnight when the Sheriff dropped Roper off to his truck. Cadaver tired, he headed home, mechanically peeled off his clothes and sank into bed.

The next morning he was awakened by a pounding on his front door. Groaning, he rolled over and looked at the alarm clock. Geez, this was becoming a habit, sleeping till after eight o'clock. It had been years since he'd slept in that late. Now it was becoming an annoying pattern, almost as the annoying as that damn pounding on his door. Rolling out of bed, Roper found his Levis and pulled them on, then headed bare-chested for the door as he zipped the fly.

A draft of cold air collided with his exposed chest, making him shiver as Ruby Nez entered. The frosty oblique rays of the morning sun provided brilliant light, but very little heat.

"Geez," he said sheepishly. "I guess I overslept."

"No rush," Ruby said, "we're in trespass now. It's all up to the government."

"We did the best we could," Roper said, running his fingers through his tousled hair.

Don't suppose you have any coffee in the house?" Ruby asked as she settled down on a leather sofa in the living room.

"Actually, I think I do," Roper said. "Dad always kept a little instant when he got older. Kept it around for friends."

Roper disappeared into the kitchen and ten minutes later reappeared with his shirt on, a plate of buttered toast and two steaming mugs.

Ruby grinned. "Have I converted you?" she asked, nodding toward Roper's mug.

"Nah, mine's hot chocolate."

"What's the difference?"

"Not much." Roper smiled. "Taste and indoctrination."

Ruby took a swallow, then sat back holding the warm mug in her hands. "I know where your cows are."

"You mean the ones the BLM wranglers impounded?"

"Yep." Ruby took another swallow. "Believe it or not, they're right here in Escalante, over at the old Carter corrals on the east side."

"You don't say. Are they being guarded?"

"Two federal marshals."

"Give me a minute to shower and get dressed," Roper said, "then I'll go over and try to reason with them."

"I'll join you," Ruby said, putting down her coffee mug.

"Yeah, I'll only be a minute," Roper said as he stood up.

"I mean in the shower."

Instantly, Roper turned a bright crimson.

Ruby laughed, "You're too easy, Roper. I'll go down to the station and fill up my pickup. Be back in fifteen minutes.

It was more like thirty minutes before she returned. This time she let herself in and was helping herself to more coffee when Roper came out of the bedroom, clean clothes on and slicked back wet hair.

"What happened to your floor?" Ruby asked, motioning to the char on the floor.

"Someone tried to burn the place down."

"Like the cabin?"

"Pretty much," Roper replied, then filled in the details.

"I don't like this," Ruby said, her face creased and pinched with worry. "Don't like it one damn bit."

"I've already got the sheriff involved."

"Well that's comforting, considering that he still hasn't solved Angus Macdonald's murder or the cabin fire."

"I think someone is just out to scare me."

"Someone's out to get you! We could've been killed on the mountain," Ruby said angrily, "almost were. Who hates you that much?"

"No one I know of," Roper said. "This has to have something to do with my ranching. Someone's making a statement, either an environmental terrorist or the BLM."

"Either way, you'd better watch your back," Ruby declared, her dark eyes reflecting her anxiety, "till we get this figured out."

"How were things down at the gas station?" Roper asked.

"Well," Ruby said, "there could be big trouble brewing. The boys are talkin' about getting their guns and takin' back your cows. Probably just big talk, but they're getting themselves all lathered up."

"Who's there?"

"The usual morning coffee bunch, Skinner, Pete Goslin, Dell Wallace, Max Yeager and the rest of that crowd."

"You think they're serious?"

"Who knows with that bunch?" Ruby replied, shaking her head. "Probably not."

"We best go check anyway, don't you think?"

Jumping into Roper's Dodge, they headed to the Shell Station. The morning coffee gang had left, but the youthful clerk with braces on his teeth confirmed they had talked of getting their guns and heading for the Carter Corrals. Arming themselves, Roper knew, wouldn't take long. Most of them carried one or more firearms right in their pickup.

When Roper and Ruby arrived at the corrals, one glance told them the situation was labile. The two federal marshals were positioned back-to-back at the south end of the corral near the gate with rifles cocked and ready. Surrounding them was the coffee-bunch, loud, pugnacious and heavily armed. They sported an array of weapons including handguns, shotguns, 30/30 carbines and two assault rifles. Out numbered five-to-one and out gunned ten-to-one, the marshals had fear lacquered all over their faces.

As she climbed out of the pickup, Ruby reached for Roper's 30/30 hanging on the rear window gun rack.

"Ruby, I don't think we'll be needing that."

She met his gaze for a moment. "It could get ugly."

"I hope not," Roper sighed, "but that will only make it worse. Come on, let's try and talk some sense into them."

As they joined the standoff, Skinner, as usual, was doing most of the talking. His voice was loud, cocky and assertive. "Tell me again, by what right you're holding them there cows?"

"They—they're government property," the younger marshal stammered, perspiration beads on his forehead despite the lingering morning chill.

"Is that a government brand I see on them cows?" Max Yeager demanded, his right hand resting lightly on his still holstered .357 Magnum.

Pete Goslin then made a show of walking over to the corral and inspecting the brand on the rust and white colored Hereford heifer. "Skinner, this here looks like Roper Rehnquist's lazy R-brand to me."

"You got a bill of sale for them cows?" one of the coffee crowd challenged.

"Not on me," the older deputy said, barely above a whisper. "They might at the office."

"Well then boys, I'm afraid I'm goin' have to ask you to release them cows," Skinner commanded, his voice hard and threatening.

"That's not possible," the older marshal said firmly, though his eyes darted from man to man and his face was lined with worry.

"You boys is definitely on the wrong side with this one," Dell Wallace asserted, his words choppy and menacing. "In the state of Utah, what you is doin' is called cattle rustling and we don't take kindly to rustlers in these parts."

"These are impounded cows," the younger marshal said, managing to wipe his forehead with the sleeve of his coat and still keep his rifle leveled.

"Taken and impounded illegally," Skinner argued. "Two wrongs don't make no right."

"You're going to have to take them from us," the younger marshal declared, his voice high pitched with false bravado.

"You boys ready to die for them cows?" Skinner asked, flipping the safety button on his 30/30 with his left hand. "Cause by God that's what you're aimin' to do."

"We've got a job to do," the older marshal insisted, "It's nothing personal."

"You're out numbered six to two," Pete Goslin said. "Use your heads."

"You two must not be from Utah," Max Yeager shouted, "cause out here it is personal!"

Neither of the marshals moved.

"I'll give you one last chance," Skinner declared, raising his rifle to his shoulder.

The younger marshal responded by elevating his Remington 870 12-gauge shotgun to his shoulder and the older marshal readied his Colt AR15 .223 caliber assault rifle.

As if on cue, each man of the coffee bunch hoisted his weapon to the firing position. Then nothing—nothing but a lethal edgy silence. Like a deadly game of chicken, each side waited for the other to make the fatal move.

"Hold on!" Roper shouted, walking slowly forward with hands raised high above his head and wedging himself between the leveled guns.

"You best get out of the way," Skinner said, keeping his eye on the forked metal sight of his 30/30.

"This is crazy," Roper said.

"We've got to make a stand somewhere," Pete Goslin said. "This here is as good a place as any."

"But these are my cows," Roper insisted, gesturing at the corral. "Let them have them. They're hardly worth the effort to take them to auction anyway."

"That's not the point, is it?" Skinner hissed. "It's the principal of the thing."

"We got to draw a line in the sand," Dell Wallace asserted.

"I agree," Roper replied, "but not here, not over these cows. This is not our Alamo."

"You give 'em an inch, they'll take a mile," Max Yeager growled.

"Go on home," Roper said, dropping his hands. "

Ruby moved forward and stood at Roper's side.

In the determined silence, Roper and Ruby stood their ground. Finally, one of the coffee-crowd lowered his rifle, then slowly like falling dominos, they all did the same. Roper could hear them grumbling as they broke rank and began to leave.

As he passed by, one burly cowboy muttered, "token cowboy" then continued on toward his truck. "Chicken shit", another scoffed. Skinner grumbled at no one in particular, "I would've shot the son-of-a-bitch if Ruby hadn't been it the way."

The young marshal slowly walked over to Roper and offered him a hand. "Thanks, man," he said, relief mirrored his face like a halo.

"Don't think for a minute," Roper snapped, shaking the extended hand, "that this means, I agree with what you are doing."

13

PARIA MOVIE SET

Frank Sinatra, Dean Martin, Sammy Davis Jr., Clint Eastwood, Robert Taylor and Gregory Peck's boots have all thudded on the plank boardwalk as they swaggered toward the Red Rock Saloon. While in town, they could also see if their mugs were plastered on the wanted posters in the United States Post Office or catch up on much needed sleep at the Lost Lady Hotel. Nowadays, if you listen closely at swinging saloon doors, you can almost hear the ragtime rhythm of a player-piano, stiff poker cards brushing on velvet tabletops or the clinking of ice in crystalline whisky glasses.

To the immediate east of cinema town, rises a towering butte capped by a solid red rock mountain, an isolated island of the receding Vermillion Cliffs. The pedestal, composed of colorful layers of gray, lavender and burgundy banded clay, is actually a laminated shelf of the Jurassic Morrison formation and appropriately christened by early settlers, the Painted Desert. The Indian name, however, is equally fitting, the Land of the Sleeping Rainbows.

Wildly whipping around pinion and juniper branches, the blades of the helicopters also churned autumn leaves and loose soil up into a whirling vortex that snaked erratically across the mesa top. Spiraling upwards like a summer dust devil the funnel of debris twisted a furious course. From the innocent blue sky bellowed a thunderous noise, both rhythmic and chaotic.

Covering her ears, Ruby Nez tried to block out the din, the cyclic beating of the whirling blades, the racket of combustion engines and the bellowing of terrified cows. As the helicopters swooped back and forth, she grabbed her hat to keep it from being ripped from her head, then tried to calm her terrified dun. With the choppers that close, she could feel the sting of airborne granules biting at her exposed neck and cheek.

A week ago, Ruby would have bet the ranch that there was no way to get the rest of her cows off Fifty Mile Mountain, especially the feral ones. Now she was not so sure.

Several weeks ago, with the help of Roper and occasionally Skinner, she had rounded up what cows she could and it wasn't as if she had just given a token effort. For the better part of a week, they worked their butts off and probably permanently crippled Skinner's horse. As proof of their efforts, they were all covered in bruises, scratches and contusions from riding that impossible terrain. Not to mention the thorough shredding of several changes of clothes in the thick brush.

With the wild cow hunt, she had succeeded in removing only another six or seven animals. About half the hunters actually killed a cow. Another had wounded a bull, but had not brought him down. Ruby was not sure if the critter was still alive or dead. With those rugged resilient and almost indestructible animals you never knew. After the tragedy with Angus Macdonald, she had canceled the second week. So by her calculations, that left eighteen or nineteen of her feral cows still on the Fifty. Maybe more. Short of a fleet of surveillance helicopters, there was just no way to know for sure.

Three weeks ago, she had received a certified letter from the BLM, more specifically from new Range Specialist Jess Steinke, stating that her allotment was being closed and any cattle that remained after November 1st would be in trespass. A few days later, Roper had pointed out to her in the *Garfield County News* that the BLM had posted all the allotments that were to be closed and that included her Mudhole piece and his two allotments, Lake and Soda Springs. In fact, every lease on the Fifty, including Skinner's, had been canceled.

Then about two weeks ago to make sure she had gotten the message, Monument Manager Brisco had stopped by Ruby's mobile home in Escalante and insisted she remove the rest of her cows. In her words, Ruby's cows, coupled with this ongoing drought, were single-handedly destroying the entire fragile eco-system of Fifty Mile Mountain. She had one more week, according to Brisco, to remove her offending bovines or by God, they would. Without another word, she had then stomped out of Ruby's mobile trailer and jumped into her green BLM pickup and roared away.

Right after that, perhaps the next day as Ruby recalled, was when the BLM wranglers had rounded up Roper's cattle and impounded them in Escalante. Ruby had expected that the government wranglers would then go back on the Fifty to work on her allotment, but they hadn't. Maybe they had finally realized that kind of work using amateur part time cowboys was futile or very inefficient at best. Hell, it was slow work even when she, Roper and Moses did it and they were experienced hands and knew the terrain better than a U.S. geographical cartographer.

I guess, Ruby thought bitterly as she watched, still mesmerized by the ongoing aerial circus, this is what Brisco meant when she'd said, "or by God, I will." Helicopters! My sweet Jesus, Ruby quickly crossed herself, whoever heard of rounding up cows with helicopters? Vicious murderers or dangerous fugitives or even maverick Yellowstone bears, maybe, but wild cows? This had to be a first, even for the BLM.

For late October, it had turned unseasonably warm as a high pressure system had again camped over southern Utah. Clear and cloudless, the sky was a homogenous powder blue and the air was dry and becoming hazy and smelling of whipped dust. The light rain of almost a month ago, the day of the cow hunt when Angus Macdonald had been shot, amounted to less than a quarter of an inch and was now long gone, leaving no traceable benefit. It had barely made a dent in the six-year-old drought that had strangled southern Utah and had firmly held the entire intermountain west hostage.

Earlier, when she'd tried to ride up Cliff Trail, a helicopter had spied her and swooped over to her as she topped the mesa lip. It had continually buzzed her, low and loud, driving her back down the trail, terrifying her horse and eventually forcing her to turn around. It was obvious that the pilot, undoubtedly following orders, was trying to keep her off Fifty Mile Mountain. Now even more determined, she had simply ridden the north to the far end of Bench Road and sneaked up Rock Garden Trail. Rarely used and not marked on any of the recreational or hiking maps, Rock Garden Trail was even more rugged than Cliff Trail, requiring Ruby to hike most of the way on foot, leading the dun. Once back on top, she had kept to thickets and denser juniper groves, surreptitiously making her way back. It was clear now, why they had not wanted her here.

From the back of her dun, sequestered in a clump of junipers, Ruby watched the operation in jaw-dropping amazement. There were two of them, a MD Hughes 5000 and a Bell 206 Jet Ranger. They worked as a well-coordinated team, even in some ways reminding her of Roper and his hound Moses. The smaller chopper flew low, just above the tree tops, hovering over the draws and thickets, the rotor's wind wildly whipping the branches. The noise was deafening. Panicked cows would bolt from their protective cover only to be chased closely by the nimble smaller helicopter. Once they were out in the open, the larger helicopter would lumber over, hovering above the dazed animals and dropping a huge cargo net. Frenzied, the crazed cows would struggle against the restraining net until completely exhausted.

Then, the larger helicopter would land and the crew would place a broad transport sling around the spent animal or sometimes simply draw the corners of the net up into a hook. With rotary blades laboring, the chopper would take off, lifting the thousand-pound animal off the ground, then flying him down off the mountain. On the adjacent sagebrush flat and right next to the Hole-In-The-Rock Road, the BLM had constructed a temporary five-pipe, panel corral. The animals were dumped and released into the enclosure. When they had a full load, a semi-truck would be brought in to load the captured animals and truck them off.

Ruby had never seen anything like this before. It was a well-timed well-orchestrated event conducted with military precision. Obviously, these guys had done this sort of thing before. Ruby noted that neither chopper bore the BLM insignia. These helicopter wranglers had to be private contractors and they were pretty damn good.

An operation like this had to be expensive. The way they attacked the problem, you'd think they were trying to stamp out something fatal, like colonies of the virulent microbe Anthrax or Ebola, or a pack of rabid hounds or an imbedded cell of mid-eastern terrorists. Apparently, these animals had been judged malignant or contagious or both and had to be eradicated at all costs!

Jesus, Ruby crossed herself again. Was it worth it just to get rid of some somewhat less than lethal, range cows?

Well hell, Ruby thought, shaking her head. There was nothing she could do about it now. Still deeply immersed in thought, she turned her dun and headed toward the Cliff Trail. Surely, they wouldn't buzz her if she was heading off the mesa. Halfway to the trail, she subconsciously detoured, swinging over to the eastern rim. It was a beautiful day, might just as well enjoy the view. By tomorrow, the view might be all that she would have.

Away from the chaos of the helicopters, it was indeed a beautiful autumn day and the magnificent panorama that spread out below made her remember and smile. This was basically the same view she and Roper had last spring as they picnicked after branding. Through the junipers, she caught a glimpse of crimson of the Escalante Canyons far below and to the east. Today in the clear crisp autumn air, they seemed particularly brilliant.

In silence and in spite of the turmoil over on the mesa, she felt a growing sense of harmony as she picked her way toward the Cliff Trail. About a hundred yards from the trailhead, the rimrock jutted out from the mesa wall like a peninsula in the sky. Guiding the dun over to the rock platform, Ruby dismounted and walked to the edge. She never tired of this view. Four thousand feet below, the gray desert sprawled out placidly and unbroken. Hole-in-the-Rock Road was no more than a fine beige ribbon, snaking its way across the valley. Further east, the desert abruptly ended in a confusing maze of red finger canyons that comprised the Escalante River drainage.

Below her and just to the south, something caught her eye, a subtle movement. She lost it and quickly rescanned the area. There it was. Something or someone was coming up the Cliff Trail. Walking over to the dun, she fished her Bushnell binoculars from the saddlebags and trudged back to the rim. Focusing the lenses, she searched up and down the trail. Finally, two hundred yards from the top, she found it. It was a pack train, two mules and one horse, picking their way over the boulder-strewn trail. With panniers bulging and top packs stuffed full, the mules were heavily laden like prospectors' mules and struggling under the weight as they labored up the nearly vertical path. Riding a huge buckskin gelding was a large man wearing a clay brown Stetson and a brilliant hunter's orange jacket. Ruby instantly recognized him. It was the Texan, Ed Hightower. She used to guide him on the Fifty for the deer hunt. Now it appeared, he hunted without her services.

She watched him pick his way up and over the boulder-peppered route toward the top. In his right hand, he was holding the lead-rope of the first mule, the second mule's lead rope tied to the first mule's tail. The going was slow, but he seemed in no hurry as he inched his way upward. Periodically, Ruby trained the binoculars on him and monitored his progress as he slowly made his way toward the top.

Suddenly, just as he had just crested the brim of rimrock, the smaller helicopter came thundering toward the mesa edge. Flying barely fifteen feet off the ground, it swooped directly for the Texan. Then not more than twenty feet away, it abruptly banked up and to the left, roaring on past. Terrified, the buckskin started to buck and rear on the precipitous and narrow trail.

Hightower dropped the mule's lead rope and clutched the saddle horn. In terror, the first mule panicked. Rearing and pivoting, he bolted headlong back down the trail, dragging the second mule with him. He missed the very first turn and soared off the two hundred foot cliff. Instantly, the second mule put on the brakes. With the lead rope still attached to the first mule's tail, the sudden jerk abruptly stopped the airborne animal, then swung him back toward the cliff face like a rapidly falling pendulum. The mule slammed into the cliff, the lead rope pulling free from his tail. Then he plummeted straight down, crashing to the boulder-littered talus slope some two hundred feet below.

Horrified, Ruby gasped, jammed the binoculars back in the saddlebag, then jumped on the dun. When she got there, the helicopter had vanished, but the stunned Texan was peering over the cliff and muttering, his back toward her.

"Hightower?" she said softly, trying not to scare him.

Startled anyway, he flinched, almost losing his footing. "Jesus Christ," he fumed, as he turned around. "Has every one in this God forsaken country gone stark raving mad?"

"It's me, Ruby Nez," she said, tying the dun to a scrub juniper then joining him. "Hope we can salvage some of your gear."

Glancing up, he nodded slightly, then turned and looked over the cliff's edge again. He shook his head slowly in disbelief.

"Do y'all think he's dead, or should I go down there and shoot him, Rube?"

Again Ruby retrieved the binoculars then spent a minute peering down at the mangled mule. "He's dead all right."

"What the hell was that all about?" Hightower asked haltingly. "Y'all trying to keep hunters off your range?"

"You know very well I can't do that. It's public land," Ruby replied, handing the glasses to Hightower. "It's not me, it's the BLM. They're removing all my cows from the Fifty."

"Your cows. Why?'

"They say I'm in trespass," Ruby explained, bitterness in her voice. "It's a long story. Anyway, they tried horse wranglers, couldn't get 'em off. Now they're using helicopters."

"Why the hell did they buzz me?"

"Did it to me earlier," Ruby said. "I guess they were told to expect trouble and ordered to keep everyone off the mountain."

"Goddamn, this is public property and they just killed my favorite mule," Hightower fumed.

"Let's unload your other mule, then go down and see what we can salvage," Ruby said.

"Okay," Hightower said after a minute. "Then I want to talk to those sons-a-bitches."

"Perfectly fine by me," Ruby said, as she unbuckled the pannier strap of Hightower's mule.

With Ruby leading way and Hightower dragging the reluctant surviving mule's lead rope, they headed back down. At the base of the cliff they found the dead mule. Fortunately, he had been packed with mostly durable camping supplies, a folding table and chairs, a tent, a sleeping bag, air mattress and pots and pans. Almost all was salvageable except for the gas lantern, a glass mixing bowl and one of the folding chairs.

Working carefully on the treacherous talus slope, they transferred all the serviceable items to the panniers of the second mule. When they'd finished, Hightower mounted his buckskin, grabbed the lead rope, then turned back to Ruby.

"I can take it from here, Rube," he muttered. "Appreciate your help though."

"I can go back with you and help haul things to your camp."

"No need," Hightower said, "I'll have to make two trips to the camp anyway. Y'all can't carry much in those saddlebags. Go on about your business, but someday I might be needing you to testify in court."

"Just let me know."

"I still have your number at home," he replied

Grasping the mule's lead rope, Hightower spurred the buckskin back up Cliff Trail. Ruby watched his progress for a minute, then shrugged and nudged her dun down the trail toward Fifty Mile Bench. Once there, she trotted the horse down the steep serpentine road to the relatively level desert floor. She then eased the dun into a gentle lope, hoofs leaving paired puffs of dust all the way to Hole-In-The-Rock Road and the BLM's provisional pipe corral.

At the corral, she dismounted, tied the dun to the top pipe rail, then leaned against the fence and began counting. Already they had netted, transported and penned fifteen of her cows, about half of them looked feral. Mentally, she did the math. That amount of money probably wouldn't mean much to the BLM, she decided, particularly after seeing this extravagant air show, but to her that represented a hell-uv-a-lot of money. When you're broke, a little soon becomes a lot.

Monty Coleman was busy completing his own tally on the other side of the corrals. When he saw her he put his notebook in his shirt pocket and trudged on over. He looked gaunt, dusty and tired, and probably his etched scowl was a harbinger of his mood.

"What you doing here?" he demanded, his voice monotone.

"Them's my cows," Ruby declared, pointing a finger at the herd.

"Not anymore, sister," Monty replied coolly, making no effort at civility, "they ain't. You had your chance."

"Some chance. That's like asking a paraplegic to scale Mount Everest in a week."

"Obviously, you didn't try hard enough."

"Well obviously, I didn't have these kind of resources." Ruby arched her arm toward Fifty Mile Mountain.

"Not my problem."

"I'll take 'em from here," Ruby insisted, making a motion to open the gate.

"No, you don't, sister," Monty snapped, applying counter pressure to the gate.

"But they're my cows. They've got my brand," Ruby said, refusing to remove her hand. "Leastways, most of 'em do."

"Don't matter. They're impounded."

"What the hell does that mean?" Ruby asked. "Impounded?"

"Same as if someone impounded your car," Monty explained, a smile as thin as paper. "They're now in the custody of the United States government and to redeem them you have to pay a fine."

"How much of a fine?" Ruby fought hard to check her anger.

"Don't know, not my department. But I suspect that depends on how much these helicopter guys charge." He nodded in the direction of an incoming aircraft. "Can't hold the taxpayers responsible for your transgressions."

"The taxpayers will have to pay for this anyway," Ruby said. "I can't afford even one helicopter for one minute, let alone two for all day."

"You were given your chance, sister."

"You know, I'd call this flat out rustling," Ruby said, evenly meeting Monty's dark eyes.

"Call it what you like," he muttered, forcibly removing Ruby's hand from the gate. "But sister, you and the other ranchers are goin' to find the federal government can do pretty much whatever it wants on its own property."

"In these parts," Ruby hissed, "we either hang or shoot rustlers."

"You'd better be careful with talk like that, sister," Monty said softly, his eyes cold and lethal.

"And you'd better be careful who you call sister," Ruby shot back.

———————

"Forty thousand dollars!" Ruby exclaimed, biting her lower lip. "Forty thousand dollars and I can have my cows back."

A chorus of boos emanated from the back of Bucky Lee's perpetually cluttered cabin.

"And even if I don't buy 'em back," Ruby continued. "Brisco says she is sending me a forty thousand dollar trespass bill that she intends to collect."

"Mighty damn expensive," someone from the group muttered.

"How many cows did they get?" Skinner asked, leaning against the west log wall. All seats were taken, standing room only.

"Twenty-one," Ruby answered from behind Bucky's kitchen counter. "Twenty-one of mine and ten of Roper's."

"They give you a bill yet, Roper?" Skinner asked.

"No. Just a preliminary estimate."

"Mine is only about half of Ruby's—twenty thousand," Roper added as he shifted his weight and turned sideways, trying to create more room. He was sardined on the ragged green couch between two burly ranchers.

"And they killed my prize bull trying to transport it off the mountain," Ruby added bitterly. "Strap broke. Dropped him."

"I shot two cows myself," Roper admitted, "on my Lake allotment. Couldn't get 'em off and considering the thousand-dollar trespass fee, to shoot them was the most economical way."

"I ain't no mathematician," Skinner said, scratching his golden head, "but I did learn't my sums and by my calculations that comes out to about two thousand dollars a head. I thought the trespass fee was a thousand dollars a head."

"Apparently, we have to pay for the helicopters too," Ruby muttered, barely able to contain her anger.

"Well, if you paid the fine, then sold your cattle at the auction, you might come out about right," another rancher from the back quipped sarcastically. "Looks like you'd only go in the hole about fifteen hundred dollars or so per cow."

"More'n that," Ruby said. "Seven of 'em were calves. Probably didn't weigh three hundred pounds apiece, but they're still get a full thousand dollars trespass fee."

"Thirty-seven cents a pound is all we're getting at the auction," Roper said, "that's about seventy dollars per calf and about three hundred dollars per full grown cow. That comes out to less than six thousand dollars for Ruby and about half that for me."

"Jesus, college boy," Bucky cussed, "youse ain't the only one heer that can add."

"Still," Roper persisted, "the point is it will cost Ruby forty thousand dollars to get back six thousand dollars worth of livestock."

"It's forty thousand dollars well spent," a cowboy sneered. "Need to stomp out that dreadful bovine disease afore it spreads."

"What we goin' a do bout this?" a voice shouted harshly from the back. "This here is a goddamn government travesty."

"I'se told youse guys a while back to diversify," Bucky Lee snorted, "like me. Fergit them damn bovines. There's other ways and a hell-uv-a-lot more profitable ways to make a living."

"I don't know what the hell you're talking about, but let me tell you what happened to me," Skinner blurted, his face instantly burning with anger. "Last week I was takin' some salt up to my cows on my Dry Creek lease. Well, I drove up to the watering tank in my pickup, like I always do and commenced to unload my rock salt. Out of nowhere comes this BLM pickup and out jumps this wet-behind-the-ears range management specialist. He gets in my face and tells me I can't do that. I start to get pissed and tell him, I know'd damn well I can, cause I've been puttin' salt down for my cows for twenty years and by God, I'm goin' to keep on doin' it. Cows can't live without salt, you know. He then tells me I can put down as much salt as I like, I just can't drive my pickup off existing roads to do it. Now I am really riled and I say, how in the hell am I supposed get a hundred-pound block of salt, one mile off the road, to this here stock tank?

"It's friggin' unbelievable, but you know what he said? Carry it! There will be no more off-road driving in the Grand Staircase National Monument. No four-wheelers and no pickups. And if you do, I'll write you out a citation. And if you persist, I'll have your lease revoked. A citation on my own lease, and me just for mindin' my own business and takin' care of my own friggin' cows! It nearly blow'd me away."

"You should've shot the little bastard," Pete Goslin shouted.

"Well, I did grab him by the front collar, jerk the little son-of-a-bitch up right in front of me and was just about to physically inform him of my rules when this old geezer jumps out of the pick-up. I didn't even know he was there. Mean eyes. Rested his hand on his revolver, then quietly tells me to back off. He was one scary dude."

"That would be Monty Coleman," Roper volunteered, "monument cop."

"So, what did youse do?" Bucky asked, taking a wad of Skoal and cramming it into his mouth.

"I didn't have no gun on me and I was out numbered," Skinner shrugged. "So I did what any reasonable person would, I did like I was told. Jumped in my truck, drove back to the road, then lugged that salt rock all the way back to the tank. I got blisters in places I've ain't never even seen before."

"If that don't beat all," Max Yeager exclaimed. "We goin' to put up with this shit?"

"Well, I had a similar thing happen to me," a thin, wiry rancher wearing a plaid checkered shirt said. "I took my tractor onto my lease with my front end loader and started building up the banks of my stock tank. Over the years, they'd eroded down some to where they didn't hold all that much water. All of a sudden, I had one of them BLM boys stops and tell me I can't bring a tractor in. I said, shit! Been doing it for forty years. He said, not any more, you don't. I said, just how am I goin' fix my tank? He said, use a shovel."

"Use a shovel!" Pete Goslin shook his head in disgust. "In the blink-of-an-eye that turns a two-hour job into a two-week job."

Bucky stood up spat at the bucket, missed. Then walked around the cluttered Formica counter to join Ruby. "The sword is mightier than the pen," he said slowly, looking the group in the collective eye. "And the pen is mightier than the pencil."

"Jesus," Ruby groaned, then crossed herself. "What is that supposed to mean?"

"You think about it, Rube," Bucky replied, nodding confidentially, as if he had just conveyed a pearl. "It'll come to youse."

"Getting back to Ruby's problem," Skinner said, taking charge. "Roper, did you talk to the cattleman's association?"

"Yes," Roper answered, getting up from the grimy, floral-print couch.

"Where do they stand?"

"Well," Roper hesitated, subconsciously massaging his finger stump. "They said they're not sure this is the hill they want to die on."

"What the hell is that supposed to mean?" shouted Dell Wallace from the back.

"Dell, that's how you talk out of both sides of your mouth," Skinner explained. "Means they won't help."

"I don't think they want to get involved in this one," Roper affirmed. "Federal government is a mighty big foe."

"What a worthless bunch," a cowboy muttered from the pack.

"They can take my membership and shove it," another barked.

"What about the county, Mike?" Skinner turned to County Commissioner Noteman. "What're you guys goin' a do?"

"Personally, I'm behind you all the way," Commissioner Noteman said nervously. "But officially we can't be involved."

"I expected more from you guys." Skinner frowned his disapproval.

"I didn't say we wouldn't help," Commissioner Noteman replied. "It's just that we can't get the office involved in anything illegal."

"What they're doin' is as illegal as hell," Pete Goslin yelled from the back.

"What about the sheriff's office, Ivory?" a leathery cowboy asked, turning to the sheriff.

"Same thing," Sheriff Jackson affirmed. "We'll turn a blind eye as often as we can, but we can't be directly implicated, though by God I wish we could."

"Nobody's got no guts," Bucky vented, then spat at the bucket again. "Pride goeth before the fall and the fall goeth before the winter. And the winter's where youse'll find the young lions."

Ruby shook her head, but remained silent.

"Look what they did to poor Angus Macdonald," someone shouted from the right side of the cabin. "They might do that to any of us."

"Pick us off, one by one," Dell Wallace added.

"Yeah," a cowboy said. "Macdonald was part of this group too."

"Hold on a minute," Roper interrupted, "let's not jump to conclusions. There's no proof they were involved in that."

"If they didn't shoot Macdonald," Skinner said, "who did?"

"They're the only ones who even cared whether he mined in that god forsaken Kaiparowits," Max Yeager said.

"Yeah, it had to be that cold sum-bitch of a ranger or that flower-sniffer—youse know, the little red-heady bastard," Bucky insisted in between chaws on the wad of tobacco, as a little yellow juice seeped down the corner of his mouth and fanned onto his stubbled chin.

"I don't know," Skinner said, smiling ironically. "Gossip has it Roper here is on the short list of suspects."

"You can't be serious," Roper said. "Why would I do something like that?"

"It happens all the time." Bucky grinned, revealing stained teeth. "Youse, him and Ruby had a menagerie. And people that live in glass houses ought'a wear robes."

"Are you talking about Tennessee William's Glass Menagerie?" Roper asked angrily, "or a French ménage a trios?"

"Neither," Bucky said, "I'm talkin' about triangles. Haven't youse ever hurd of love triangles?"

"As usual," Ruby hissed, looking Bucky straight in the eye. "You haven't a clue what you're saying."

"Youse know what I'm talkin' bout," Bucky insisted smugly. "All of youse know."

"Careful," Roper cautioned, clenching jaw muscles "You're treading on dangerous ground."

"Come on," Skinner barked, once again taking charge, "let's get back to business. We'll let Ivory sort that one out. He'll get Macdonald's killer."

"Let me just say one more thing," Roper said, "before we get back to the problem. Listen and listen closely, I did not kill Angus Macdonald."

"Okay, for now," Skinner replied, "like I'se said, we'll let Ivory sort it out. Now what about Ruby? What we goin' a do about that?"

"Well, we gotta do somethin'!" thundered Dell Wallace, most men in the cabin voiced their agreement.

"Where's them cows now?" Skinner asked

"Government impound pens in Salina," Ruby answered, "leastways that what I hear."

"Why Salina?" someone asked.

"I've got one week to come up with the money," Ruby replied grimly, "or they're goin' to auction them."

"Well," Skinner said grinning, "that ain't goin' a happen. How about we all go up to Salina some night and just take 'em back?"

Loud voices of affirmation rose from the back of the cabin.

"Hold on a minute," Roper said, gesturing for them to slow down. "Let's think this through. Do we really want to butt heads with the U.S. government? Let's fight them, but let's be smart about it."

A chorus of boos greeted Roper's comment.

"Hold on a minute!" Ruby yelled. "This is serious business. Let's hear what Roper has to say."

"What you're talking about," Roper continued after the group had quieted down, "is a federal crime. Breaking into a government facility and stealing government property. And eventually the FBI will get involved as well as the U.S. attorney's office."

"Them cows are not government property," Pete Goslin insisted. "Not the way I understand the law."

"Are you now saying you think they legally belong to the government?" Dell Wallace asked.

"No," Roper said. "It's just they have a different interpretation of the law and they have a lot deeper pockets."

"We'se not afraid of 'em," Bucky asserted. "Pigs cain't fly."

"Bring 'em on," a cowboy shouted boisterously.

"You may not like it, but everything they've done may be perfectly legal," Roper said.

"I doubt it," someone bellowed, "and it ain't moral neither."

"What you goin' to do, Roper?" someone shouted from the back. "Just bend over, spread 'em an smile?"

"You best be careful out there, Roper," Skinner cautioned. "You have no idea what you're getting yourself into."

"How about pooling our resources and hiring a good lawyer," Roper said. "That makes a heck of a lot more sense."

"A lot of good that'll do," Pete Goslin shouted in exasperation. "That's like hiring a fox to guard the hen house. You lose money either way."

"Great idea," Bucky Lee mocked. "After youse can pay the trespass fine and the lawyer's fee, then youse surely would get your money's worth from them cows."

"Who's in favor of goin' and gettin' Ruby's cattle back?" Skinner asked loudly, almost stumbling over a burlap bag as he walked to the front of the room, joining Ruby and Bucky at the counter.

"Jesus, Bucky," Skinner exclaimed. "What's this shit?"

"Just some old rocks I found," Bucky Lee answered, quickly picking up the heavy bag and locking it in the closet.

Would it kill you to clean up this dump?" Ruby added.

Ignoring the jab, Bucky returned to the counter next to Skinner and again took charge, "now back to business. We need to stick together. Remember the old sayin', a house divided needs a carpenter." He took a minute and eyed everyone in the room. "Those in favor of helping Rubles get her cows back, say aye."

Everyone in the room shouted an enthusiastic approval. That is everyone except Roper Rehnquist.

14

THE PARIA RIVER

If in the land of the blind, the one-eyed man is king—so it follows, in the dry desiccated desert, even a tiny alkali-encrusted stream, balloons in stature, acquiring an importance way out of proportion to its diminutive size.

Paranoid by nature and bipolar by conduct, the Paria River usually alternates between an anemic surface stream and invisible subterranean ooze. On the rare occasions of sizable rainfall, however, it burgeons to a destructive raging river capable of washing away entire settlements.

With its headwaters high in the Pansaugunt Plateau of Bryce Canyon National Park, this implausible little river single-handedly sustains the communities of Tropic and Cannonville before entering the Grand Staircase National Monument. It then slowly seeps south past Rock Springs Bench and the little ghost town of Pahreah eventually to plunge over a sheer cliff into the Grand Canyon and be swallowed by the mighty Colorado River.

From the deep cover of darkness and the thick knot of pinion trees, Sean watched the cabin, shuffled his cold feet and waited. All he could see from his post was two rectangular beacons, two shafts of light effluxing into the great black void of this late autumn night. From earlier inspection Sean knew one ray was coming from the east window, the other from the open kitchen door. With no moon, at this distance the remainder of the house was not visible, but it had to be in that black hole located between the two beams of light.

It was damn chilly. Sean took off his Gore-Tex gloves, no leather for him, rubbed his hands and slapped the cold and numbness from his arms. The warm Indian summer that had languidly stretched into early November was over. About a week ago they'd received their first snow, mostly melted now, but there were still patches of frozen crust surviving in the shaded areas. Even the daytime air had a decided nip and the nights where just plain damn cold. When he moved into a beam of light he could see his frosty breath.

Inside the cabin, he was certain it was hot and stuffy with a roaring fire in the fireplace and probably one in the stove as well. Undoubtedly that's why they had left the kitchen door wide open. It was too hot. Through the pinion boughs he could almost see the beguiling heat waves wafting through the open door and occasionally he did see fiery sparks belch upward from the chimney. He inched closer. He longed to be warm. He longed to be inside.

Shifting his weight, Sean could hear the frozen snow crunch under his feet, but he couldn't feel it. His toes were too numb. Trying to stimulate circulation, he rocked on his tiptoes then back on his heels, then back to the toes. He repeated the exercise several more times with marginal success. How long had he been hiding here, cowering in the cold like a rabbit hearing the yelp of a coyote? Though he couldn't see his watch, he suspected it had been at least two hours, maybe more.

Just after dark, the pickups had begun to arrive. As they rolled in it was already too dark for Sean to tell who was driving. He had recognized Roper's truck, and of course Bucky Lee's had been sitting there in the driveway when he'd arrived, but that was about it. In the bitter cold they had parked their trucks and immediately headed for the kitchen door. As they stepped over the threshold, their features were momentarily highlighted by the room light, then quickly lost as they disappeared behind log walls.

In addition to Roper and Bucky, Sean had recognized the faces of Commissioner Noteman, Skinner Jacobson, Ruby Nez, Dell Wallace, Pete Goslin, Max Yeager and Sheriff Ivory Jackson. For sure, they were all in the cabin and at least a dozen ranchers and cowboys Sean did not recognize. In disgust, Sean shook his head. If that don't beat all, the county sheriff and county commissioner mixed up in an illegal gathering like this. Yes, it was illegal. This was much more than neighbors getting together to discuss common problems. If it walked like a duck and quacked like a duck, then it was a duck. And this little gathering quacked like a conspiracy and conspiracies were still illegal in the U. S. of A.

Several times in the last two hours Sean had crept over to the cabin, crouched beside the open door and listened, but even if he hadn't bothered, he would have still had a pretty good idea what this meeting was all about. With the BLM unleashing its air power, the sagebrush war had just escalated and the somewhat shell-shocked, opposing war council was now in session.

Not surprising, Monument Manager Brisco's blatant grandstanding, the extraction of cows with helicopters, had attracted national attention. Perhaps that was what she wanted all along but regardless, the media had jumped all over it. First, the *Garfield County News* had headlined with, HELICOPTER ROUNDUP, next the *Salt Lake Tribune* had blazoned, BLM CATTLE GRAB and finally the *St. George Spectrum* joined in the fray with CATTLE BATTLE GOES AIRBORNE. Eventually, with the row exhibiting all the telltale markings of a Wild West showdown, the Associated Press had picked up the story and three of the four national television networks as well.

In Sean's view, the whole thing was being more than a little over dramatized. Not that he didn't agree with the decision to remove the cows, and thank God they were finally gone, at least most of them, though personally Sean doubted they had captured all of them. It just seemed to him Brisco was doing everything possible to attract attention to herself and highlight her take-charge, no-nonsense management style, almost as if she were running for political office. In the past, she had made it abundantly clear she did not like deserts and did not care one whit about this monument, but obviously what she did care about was the appearance of things and the media spotlight.

Helicopters! Were they really necessary? Could the cows have been removed by other less dramatic ways? Or was this just showboating for the Washington politicians and the New York media. Certainly, the ranchers had whined and insisted they couldn't get the cows from the mountain the conventional way, but how hard had they really tried? Who knows? Certainly, Sean had his opinion. Regardless, at least now the majority of the cows were gone, but it would literally take years for the range to recover from the misconduct of those greedy ranchers, if indeed it ever did. Without cows, however, there was a fighting chance.

But talk about grandstanding, Sean shook his head in amazement while changing his train of thought. Ivory Jackson had to be right up there with the very best. The week before this most recent aerial circus and a couple weeks after Sean's release from Kane County Hospital, Sheriff Jackson had showed up late one evening at his modular home in Kanab. Being more gracious than he felt, Sean had invited the sheriff in. Chewing on his trademark toothpick, the sheriff had removed his hat and sat down on the old couch looking sly and relaxed, like he'd just out-foxed the fox.

"How ya doin', Sean?" he'd asked, looking Sean in the eye.

"Fine." Sean kept his answers purposefully short. He wasn't much of a talker under ideal conditions and this house guest was somewhat less than ideal.

"Guess you must be as happy as a pig-in-shit." the sheriff said bluntly, smiling and gnawing the toothpick.

"Excuse me," Sean replied, arching a red eyebrow.

"The monument," Jackson answered. "You must be happy how things turned out."

"Yeah, I've worked on it for years."

"Yes, you have," Jackson agreed, giving Sean a knowing smile. "I've still got some of your work on file in the office. Just couldn't prove it."

"Don't know what you're talking about, sheriff."

"Well, it don't matter now," the sheriff said. "Statute of limitations has run out on most of that stuff anyhow."

Sean remained quiet, feeling that statement needed no comment.

After another moment of silence, Sheriff Jackson continued, "you know Angus Macdonald was killed?"

"Yeah, so I hear."

"Thirty/thirty right through the center of the forehead." The sheriff shifted his weight on the couch then rotated the toothpick to the other side of his mouth. "Happened on Fifty Mile Mountain last week."

"Heard it was a hunting accident."

Jackson ignored him. "There was bad blood between you two, wasn't there?"

"No."

"What about that Kaiparowits incident?

"My tire was shot out," Sean said matter-of-factly. "I have no idea who did it."

"That so?" Jackson asked, eyes narrowing. "Do you own a thirty/thirty?"

"No," Sean lied, "but I suspect I'm the only one in the county who doesn't."

"You mind if I look around?"

"Do you have a warrant?" Sean asked bluntly, meeting Jackson's gaze without flinching.

"I can get one."

"Please do."

Jaws set, muscles clenched, they eyed each other suspiciously.

"Where were you about noon on October tenth?"

"Hiking."

"Where?"

"On Fifty Mile Mountain," Sean smiled thinly, not even disturbing his freckles.

"Did you kill Angus Macdonald?"

"Of course not."

"I think maybe you did." Sheriff Jackson stood up, glaring down at Sean while still working his toothpick.

"You got any evidence?"

"You got an alibi?" the sheriff fired back.

"I always hike by myself."

"May I see your hiking boots?"

"You're blowing smoke," Sean declared. "We both know very well it rained that afternoon."

"It didn't rain till late afternoon," Jackson said slowly. "Macdonald was murdered about noon. How do you know when I got there?"

"I saw you," Sean said, his smile almost insolent.

For another moment, they eyed each other, both defiant and unyielding, then Jackson spat out his toothpick. "Any mud on those boots?"

"There was, but I washed them."

"Well, I wouldn't plan on any trips for a while," Jackson finally said, "not out of the county." He then shook his head and left without another word.

Sean hadn't seen Sheriff Jackson again until tonight though he hadn't tried to leave the county either. Through the grapevine, he had heard he was not the only suspect in the Macdonald murder. Apparently, the sheriff's office had also been investigating that BLM cop, Monty Coleman, who had barged in on Sean in the hospital and made his thinly veiled threats. And somewhat surprisingly, model citizen and eminent advisory committee member, Roper Rehnquist, was also on the short list, presumably a jealousy motive. Rumor had it both Roper and Angus had the hots for Ruby Nez. Sean could understand that. He also wouldn't mind spending some quality time with that little *chicquita*. Finally, Ruby herself was reported to be a suspect. Word had it Macdonald had been stalking her and would not take no for an answer.

Multiple suspects were good, however. Multiple suspects, meant the sheriff's office didn't have a lot of solid evidence, nothing concrete to narrow down the investigation to one person, not that Sean cared.

Philosophically speaking, however, justice had very little to do with legislated law or the state and federal courts, and nothing to do with the Almighty. Justice was severed when someone got what they deserved and that did not necessarily have to come from a formal judicial system or a God. Sean was pretty good at administering justice.

Tonight he would dispense a little justice, but first, he would love to know what they were up to, those insurgents in the cabin. From what little he had heard, he knew they were upset with Brisco's helicopter ploy, but who wasn't? What Sean had not heard, however, is what they were planning to do about it. From the snatches of conversation he did hear, there had been some talk of a raid to recapture the impounded cows, but from the constant bickering, it appeared this was not a consensus.

Even if he did find out, Sean had already decided he would not tell Brisco or Monty Coleman. He'd about had a belly full of those two self-serving bureaucrats. They were totally devoid of any real love or commitment to this land. Anyway, he had always worked better by himself and his methods didn't attract national headlines.

But regardless of the cattlemen's plans, Sean preferred the offense. He always had. Defense could be, and often was, a slow form of suicide. Preemptive strikes made much more sense. Let them at the BLM and those in the cabin debate strategy till they're blue in the face, that wouldn't affect Sean one iota. As a man of action, he would continue his guerrilla warfare. It had served him well in the past and it would serve him well now. Suddenly Sean felt a little warmer. It felt good to be back in action after almost two years of inactivity.

He looked down at his wristwatch. In the dark he couldn't see the hands, but by his calculations, the meeting must have been going on for more than two and a half hours now. Surely, they would be breaking up soon. Inside, he could tell by the increasing clamor, the troops were getting restless. From his experience, the attention span for this kind of a meeting was seldom more than an hour or so and they were well past that. If he was going to mete out any justice tonight, he'd better get on with it.

He tore open the top ear of a ten-pound paper bag of sugar and walked quickly away from the protective pinion grove. He started with Roper's Dodge pickup. Opening the door, he released the gas latch, twisted off the cap, placed a funnel in the receptacle and poured in roughly a cup of sugar. Fumbling in the dark, he inadvertently dropped Roper's gas cap. He dropped down on hands and knees, patting the surrounding area till he found it. Carefully he replaced the cap then stealthily moved to the next truck. Systematically, he repeated the operation until every vehicle had been properly sweetened. That is, every pickup except Bucky Lee's. Sean had stopped at Bucky's GMC, thought about it for a moment then grimly moved on.

Suddenly, there was movement in the shaft of light emanating from the open kitchen door. Sean ducked behind the bed of a Ford pickup. Raising his head slightly, he could see the burly silhouette of Bucky Lee Aiken in the doorway. He stretched, scratched his groin, and spat a wad off to the right of the board steps. Time to go. Sean slipped back into the pinion shadows, then on down the adjacent gravel road to his battered Landrover parked about a half mile away in a juniper thicket.

Roper waited in the darkness inside his pickup. The meeting had ended about fifteen minutes ago, but most of the group still milled about inside Bucky's cabin, venting and discussing strategy. For a few minutes, Roper had stayed with them, but they had mostly avoided him like a contagious disease, so he had trudged out of the cabin, climbed into his truck, started the engine, then turned it off again.

He wanted a chance to talk to Ruby. That's why he waited here in the dark like a fugitive, or probably more precisely, like a plantation slave not welcome up at the big house. If indeed you could call Bucky's hovel the big house. All he wanted was a minute alone with her without the ever increasing presence of Skinner Jacobson. Lately, it seemed he was everywhere, hovering over her like an over-protective parent or even worse, a possessive lover. All Roper needed was just five minutes alone to explain.

It was not as it had appeared in the meeting, that he didn't want to help her. He was sensitive to her plight and understood her predicament very well. Those were her cows the BLM had impounded and considering her financial circumstances, six thousand dollars could make a big difference. Without her Mudhole lease, she had no winter range. What few bales of alfalfa she had harvested from her river bottom piece would be gone in less than a month, then she would have no choice, either sell her remaining cows at the auction or let them starve. The auction money might see her through the winter, but come spring there would be no money left to replenish her herd. Realistically, she was already out of business. Now it was about basic survival.

If Brisco really did try to make her pay the forty thousand dollars trespass/helicopter fees, then it was indeed hopeless. Even he would have to sell some property to raise his twenty thousand dollars, but for her there was no way to get that kind of money. As far as he knew, she had nothing left to sell other than bare necessities, her mobile home, her horse and tack and that little river bottom piece.

Also, Roper had an idea her credit with the bank was stretched to the limit. In fact, if the bank called up the existing note on her lot and mobile home, he was pretty sure she couldn't pay it. That being the case, she would have only one option, petition for bankruptcy. Chapter eleven was out of the question. She could never convince a judge she had a viable way to restructure her business and pay back her creditors. That only left chapter seven and that meant all remaining assets would be sold at bankruptcy auction. After that, what was there to keep her here in southern Utah? With no family in the area, no ranch and no home, Roper suspected she would just quietly disappear some night like a summer shower in the hot desert.

Would this hair-brained scheme they'd cooked up tonight really help? It was certainly dramatic and gave the outward appearance of doing something, but Roper doubted in the long run it would accomplish anything. Even if they did succeed in wresting the cattle away from the marshals at the impound pens, what would they do with them? Surely the FBI would have no trouble figuring out what had happened and who had taken them. And then there was the unique problem of where to hide twenty, one-thousand-pound animals? Hiding stolen cows was not like hiding pilfered VCRs, CD players or color televisions.

So, suppose you couldn't hide them, the next option would be to sell them. Unfortunately, it would be much like trying to sell a piece of stolen art. Where does one sell such a thing? Maybe on the black market. However, there wasn't much of a market for cattle, particularly with the prices being so low. In order to generate a thriving illicit market, the items being sold had to be fairly valuable or rare, like diamonds, fine art or even dinosaur fossils. Beef hardly qualified. Perhaps, one could sell under the table to a few unscrupulous people like Bucky Lee, but he wouldn't even pay market price, thirty-seven cents a pound, and anything less, you might just as well give it away.

Also, the feds would file theft charges. Any small profit obtained from selling the cows would instantly be eaten up in attorney fees, not to mention a distinct possibility of going to jail. Morally, or even legally, the feds may not be right, but they could drag out a court battle for years until the ranchers would beg to be convicted just to get the thing over.

Everything that had transpired in establishing and managing the monument, like it or not, had been by the book, more precisely the Antiquities Act of 1906. Sure the State of Utah had filed a suit challenging the monument's creation, but undoubtedly they would lose. So what chance did a handful of ranchers, barely scratching out a living, have against the might and deep pockets of the United States government? Not much, at least to Roper's way of thinking.

Yes, he did like Ruby a lot. No, that was not entirely correct either. To be strictly honest, he loved her and he would help her most anyway he could, but this ill-conceived cattle raid didn't make any sense at all. To him, this amounted to a long run for a short slide. On the other hand, he didn't want Ruby thinking he didn't support her and that she had to turn to Skinner. More and more, it was beginning to look like a no win situation for both him and her.

At last Roper heard voices approaching the open kitchen door. Finally they were breaking up. The ranchers slowly filed out and made their way to their trucks, jabbering as they went. After a few parting laughs, they climbed in started their engines, then forming an almost continuous single file line, drove slowly down the gravel road, red tail lights flickering in the dark.

It appeared Skinner was walking out with Ruby. Big surprise! When they reached Skinner's truck, he opened the door on the driver's side, instantly spotlighting them in the halo of the dome light. Leaning back against the side of the truck, they talked for a few minutes, heads bowed in earnest conversation.

With his pickup parked about sixty feet behind and to the right of Skinner's, Roper had a good view, but was pretty much invisible to them. As he watched, he felt a surge of guilt, like a teenager spying on a pretty girl and her date. However, when Skinner bent over and kissed Ruby on the lips, another even more powerful emotion instantly surfaced. Jealousy! Had she kissed him back? Smoldering, Roper watched Skinner kiss her again, then climb into his truck and wave goodbye. Gunning his engine, he sprayed a rooster-tail of gravel as he accelerated down the road. What a jerk!

Immediately, Roper was out of the Dodge and heading toward Ruby. By the time he reached her she had already climbed in the truck and closed the door. Suddenly, her headlights flashed on and the engine cranked. With his keys still in hand, he reached up and lightly tapped the window. No response. He rapped again, this time more forcefully. Slowly, the window rolled down and Roper found himself staring squarely down the barrel of a .357 magnum.

"Ruby! It's me," he shouted hoarsely above the clattering diesel.

"Jesus, Roper," Ruby exclaimed, crossing herself with her left hand and cutting the engine. "You scared me."

"Sorry," Roper stammered, reaching through the window and carefully nudging the gun barrel aside.

"What the hell are you doing out here in the dark?" Ruby blurted, as she sheathed the gun in its holster, placing it on the bench seat next to her.

"Waiting for you," Roper said sheepishly.

"Thought you were long gone."

"Nah," Roper replied. "Hoped I'd get a chance to talk to you."

"Well hop in," Ruby invited, "it's too damn cold to talk outside."

As Roper went around and climbed in the passenger's side, Ruby restarted the engine and turned the heater on high.

"Turned cold all of a sudden," Roper observed as he closed the door and window, and blew warm air into his hands. "It could be a long cold winter."

"Yeah," Ruby said, adjusting the fan on the heater, "that's the trouble with this country, it's either too damn hot or too damn cold. There's no in between."

"Any better where you grew up?" Roper asked, shamelessly fishing for information of Ruby's past.

"About the same," Ruby said vaguely. "Not as cold in the winter though."

"Where was that?"

"Here and there," Ruby replied. "You hear what the Farmer's Almanac calls for this winter?

"I don't put much stock in that," Roper said. "The long range meteorological forecast calls for a cold winter, but not much storm."

"So the drought continues," Ruby concluded. "We can't buy a break."

"Looks like it."

Ruby rubbed her hands then held them next to the heater. Turning slightly, she faced Roper. "Come on, Doug, we can do the small talk over a cup of hot coffee tomorrow at the café. It's late, I'm tired, so what did you want to see me about?"

"I—I guess," Roper stuttered. "I just didn't like the way we left things in there. Guess I wanted a chance to explain."

Ruby slumped back in her seat. "Well go ahead."

"It's not that I don't want to help you, it's just that taking on the federal government in a slugging match is not the way to do it."

"Roper," Ruby contended, "I understand what you're saying, but what you've got to understand is I don't have a lot of options."

"Taking your cattle back is not really an option," Roper argued, massaging his finger stump. "I guarantee it will accomplish absolutely nothing except to get you deeper into trouble. It could be dangerous and it is definitely foolish."

"So now you're calling me a fool?"

"That's not what I mean," Roper said, backtracking. "All I'm saying is it won't work."

"There is such a thing as dying for a cause," Ruby said, "sacrificing for the greater good, going down with the ship."

"But there are better alternatives," Roper said quietly, "other than self-destruction."

"Somehow, I fail to see them."

Roper was silent for a minute, then took a deep breath and stumbled on. "Remember last year when we were at Bucky's cabin listening to Clinton's speech?"

"Yes," Ruby replied.

"Most of what Bucky says doesn't make any sense."

"Amen to that."

"Well anyway, Bucky made an off-the-cuff remark," Roper laughed nervously, "that did make some sense and considering all that's happened, maybe it makes a lot more sense now."

"I'm still listening."

"Well, Bucky said, why don't you two join up outfits—less overhead."

Staring straight ahead, Ruby didn't answer right away and slowly an uncomfortable silence settled over the cab.

"Am I supposed to respond to that?" she finally asked.

"Well, it only makes sense," Roper said defensively. "I've got more private land. We can graze our cows together until we can get back on our allotments."

"Where would I live?"

"As you know, dad left me the big house in Escalante," Roper replied, "you've been there before. There's at least two bedrooms I don't use."

"What about my mobile house?"

"Sell it. You could use the money."

"That's obvious," Ruby responded quietly, "but what about your church? And all the gossip?"

"I'll clear it with my bishop," Roper answered. "But other than that, I personally don't care what people say."

"I can see how this might help me." Ruby measured her words carefully. "But what's in it for you? Seems like an uneven merger."

"Well," Roper said. "I just want to help out."

"I don't take charity," Ruby declared flatly without a trace of a smile. "And I don't trade sexual favors."

Roper's cheeks turned crimson. "I wasn't hinting of that at all."

"Well," Ruby continued, "you still haven't answered my question. What's in it for you?"

"I thought," Roper said and took a deep breath. It had been years since he'd been this tongue tied around a woman and he knew he was handling this with all the grace of mud wrestlers. "I thought we could give it a try for a while, platonically of course, and if it works out, then maybe we could get married."

Ruby sat perfectly still, looking straight out the windshield. No way for Roper to read her. She was church silent and her face was immobile as porcelain.

"Does your church and do you consider premarital sex a sin?" Ruby finally asked with some effort.

"I guess so. Why do you ask?"

"Having to clear it with your bishop, that kind of threw me," Ruby conceded. "So what we did at your cabin was a sin? Did you confess or clear that with your bishop?"

"Well," Roper stumbled on, realizing he was now in so deep there was no good way out. "We could have sex or not, whatever you think's best."

"What I think," Ruby said, "is that you haven't really thought this through."

"Since that night at the cabin," Roper plunged ahead, his voice now cracking badly. "I—I've fallen in love with you."

Ruby remained silent for another moment, then reached over and gently patted Roper's hand. "I do appreciate the gesture," she said, "but I have no intention of ever marrying again."

Roper was stunned! In his mind, he had worked out all the possible paths this conversation might take, but no way did he foresee that one coming.

"You can't be serious," he said. "You're still young and beautiful."

"Quite serious."

"But why?" he asked lamely.

"I've had some pretty bad experiences with marriage and with men in general," Ruby said, a trace of bitterness in her voice.

"Would you care to talk about it?"

"No!"

Just then, her engine sputtered, coughed and died.

"Dammit," she said, crossing herself.

15

THE STRAIGHT CLIFFS

Running south-easterly for nearly forty-two miles and soaring to a height of well over two thousand feet, the coyote gray Straight Cliffs look like a massive, though somewhat fractured, barrier dam. The apparent purpose of this stone bulwark, undoubtedly engineered by the Gods, is to restrain, separate and/or isolate the carbonaceous Kaiparowits Plateau from seeping, oozing or otherwise contaminating the delicate red sandstone ribbon canyons that are the trademark of the Escalante/Glen Canyon recreational areas.

Geologically speaking, the Straight Cliffs are an easterly extension of the Grand Staircase's Gray Cliffs. Formed approximately one hundred million years ago in the Cretaceous Period of the Mesozoic Era, the Cliffs are now eroded, exposing a rock face of three distinct sedimentary layers, Tropic shale, the Straight Cliffs formation and the Kaiparowits formation. These layers are very rich in fossils and coal, but from a distance they simply look sheer, stark, silent and imposing.

With almost no traffic, the small caravan snaked through the ebony night, heading mostly north on U.S. Highway 89. The side windows had fogged from the cold, making it difficult to see the witch's moon, hanging overhead and slightly tipped like a gypsy's golden earring. Fortunately, even though it had snowed about an inch early that morning, the roads were now dry and they were making good time.

As planned, just before midnight they had congregated five miles south of the town of Panguitch at the junction of U.S. Highway 89 and Utah

State Highway 12 on the banks of the drought-withered Sevier River. Driving up from Kanab, Dell Wallace, accompanied by Skinner Jacobson and Max Yeager, had brought his flatbed Ford trimmed with eight-foot-high wooden stock racks. Coming in from the west and the town of Escalante, Ruby, Pete Goslin and Bucky were all sardined onto the bench seat of Pete's flatbed GMC with Ruby uncomfortably stuffed in the middle.

Once everyone was accounted for, they had turned right on 89, passing through the small towns of Panguitch, Circleville, Marysvale and the slightly larger Richfield, and were now approaching the tiny farming community of Sigurd. With its auction stockyards huddled on the east side of town in the cedar-dotted foothills just beneath the towering ten thousand foot Musinia Peak, Salina would be next in the series of small farming towns that were strung out along the highway.

Though no trouble was expected, a nervous, jittery excitement permeated the cab. Of course, Sheriff Ivory Jackson had refused to accompany them on the sortie, not wanting to implicate his office, but he had telephoned Sevier County Sheriff Ted "Skinny" Olsen who had promised to look the other way. Sheriff Olsen, like most folks in Utah, sympathized with Ruby's plight, did not appreciate the BLM's heavy-handed Gestapo tactics and felt the monument in general was a slap in the collective face of Utah. In the event of trouble, however unlikely, they had all brought firearms. Hanging in the back window rack was Pete's 30/30. Ruby had her .357 Magnum and though she wasn't positive, she suspected Bucky Lee also had a pistol hidden somewhere in his bulky patchwork fox and muskrat fur coat.

As Pete navigated down the highway, Bucky babbled incessantly, occasionally throwing in one of his nonsensical proverbs. Inwardly, Ruby groaned each time, but she said nothing, preferring to suffer in cramped painful silence. Reeking of animal grease, pinion needles and tobacco juice, Bucky shifted his weight, flopping his left thigh against Ruby. Instinctively, she recoiled, scooting over closer to Pete, which resulted in a quizzical glance from him. But in spite of the stomach-churning odor, occasional hillbilly witticisms and the almost the unbearable closeness, she was grateful for their help, even Bucky Lee's. Without question, these men were risking a lot just being here tonight, the possibility of significant fines or even prison time.

Though she had not expected him, Ruby couldn't help but be a little disappointed that Roper had not come. When she thought about their talk the other night, she immediately had a sharp stab of regret, so she tried not to think about it. Though the way it turned out was probably for the best, she hated hurting Roper. Obviously, he was only trying to help in a clumsy sort of way and he was such a nice guy, a little naive, but nevertheless nice. She had been more tempted than he would ever know. If she were to ever marry again, which was doubtful, it would have to be a different sort of man than the kind she'd been attracted to in the past, that was for sure. And Roper was indeed different.

Even though they had almost nothing in common, with him being a devout Mormon and his college education, she had grown fond of him and over the last few months and had become entirely too dependent on him. It seems he was always there. When she needed an extra hand with the ranch chores, he was always willing to help, never asking anything in return. It was real easy to fall for a man like that. At times, however, like tonight for instance, she questioned his backbone and wondered if she could sustain a strong physical attraction for a man that was a perpetual pacifier. He was definitely more pragmatic than emotional and it seems he'd do most anything to avoid a fight, and that kind of bothered her.

As if to answer the question about physical attraction, her mind rewound to the night of the fire. Instantly, she began replaying the vivid sensual pictures of that implausible night. Even back then she had instinctively known that she needed to keep their relationship friendly and out of the bedroom, but somehow that night she just couldn't help it. Dammit, she had needs too and it wasn't like she jumped in bed with every man she met and it wasn't as if she didn't have strong feelings for him. However that night, though disastrous in most ways, had provided her with a heretofore elusive answer. She also loved him in bed.

Considering the amount of time they'd spent together, she could understand why he had made her that offer of cohabitation or marriage. She still wasn't quite sure which it was. Suddenly she winced from a stabbing pain of guilt. No doubt about it, she had led him on. But it had been nice to have a friend and it had been nice to have a lover, if even for only a night.

Ruby shifted her weight on the seat. Buck up little buckaroo! She'd been down that road before and no plans to travel it again. With Roper, she knew better than to delude herself in thinking there was a way to have a purely physical, detached love affair. And with her past record, she knew damn well it was far better to end it this way.

"Ruby, you ever get your pickup fixed?" Pete Goslin asked as he stared through the windshield at the twin headlights, knifing through the dark night.

"Nah, it's still in the shop. Traded 'em a side of beef to fix it, so they're in no hurry."

"How about you, Bucky?" Pete asked without taking his eyes from the road.

"Damndest thing, for some reason they skipped mine," Bucky said, shaking his shaggy head. "Must'a got spooked and ran away."

"You mean, they got everyone else's but yours?"

"Surely youse heard about the luck of the Chinks—with all them little people they have."

"Jesus Christ!" Ruby exclaimed, making the sign of the cross. "The Chinks? You mean luck of the Irish."

"Nah, I'se mean the Chinks. Nobody's luckier than them," Bucky snorted.

"Got mine out yesterday," Pete continued. "Don't know for sure, but my mechanic thinks someone maybe put sugar down the tank."

"It had'a be sabotage," Bucky grunted. A blast of cold air hit them as he rolled down the window and expectorated. "All of youse breakin' down at the same time, that tweren't no accident."

"Yeah, it's peculiar all right," Pete agreed, wrinkling his brow. "Just can't figure out who would do a thing like that."

"If only all riddles was that easy," Bucky said, rolling the window back up, "I'd be able to 'splain Nostradamus and the Book of Reservations. Just think for a minute who don't want us to have them meetin's."

"Well, it's certainly not the law," Ruby concluded. "Sheriff Jackson was right there."

"No." Bucky nodded, his voice low and conspiratorial. "Leastways, not the Kane County law."

"Who else?" Ruby asked doubtfully. "You saying the BLM vandalized our trucks?"

"Whose else?" Bucky snorted. "Whose else even cares?"

"Could be that damn monument cop," Pete agreed, almost missing a sharp turn in the road. He jerked the steering wheel, throwing Ruby back into Bucky. Then Pete calmly continued on, "He's sure a different one."

"Benefit turn," Bucky declared, giving Ruby's thigh a squeeze.

Instantly choking in fur and the grease stench, Ruby fought hard to extricate herself, sliding back over against Pete. She then wrapped her arms across her chest, clenched her jaw and stared directly out the front window.

"Yep," Bucky continued unfazed, popping the lid off his Skoal and taking a pinch, "that's whose I'm a thinkin' about."

"But if it was the monument cop, how come he skipped over you?" Ruby muttered, still irritated with Bucky.

"Must be my clean livin'." Bucky grinned, exposing yellowed teeth. "And the fact I'se don't run no cows on the monument."

"Could just as well be someone with a personal grudge," Ruby volunteered, "or just kids out on a prank."

"Nah," Bucky argued, as the Skoal can disappeared back into his enormous coat, "too far out. Kids never come by my place."

"This here is Salina," Pete announced, braking down as the highway approached the outskirts of the town. "The place looks dead."

"Fine by me," Ruby said. "The deader, the better."

"The stockyards are on the east side," Pete continued, "from what I hear they're using the old auction corrals."

"Is Dell and them other guys still behind us?" Bucky asked, then turned around and answered his own question. "Yep, like a kite without a tail, bout a half a block back."

"You think they'll have guards?" Ruby asked Pete, trying to ignore Bucky.

"Nah," Pete said, as he turned right off the highway, "leastways, not from the sheriff's department."

"Don't fergit Monty Coleman and the BLM," Bucky said.

"And by now, they could've got federal marshals like over at Escalante," Ruby added.

"I'm a hopin'," Pete said, "this is far enough away they'll think we won't bother."

"Well maybe," Ruby replied, "but them marshals had to go somewhere."

"Yeah, maybe," Pete agreed, as he drove down a residential street, "anything's possible. We best keep our eyes peeled."

"Well, at least we'se got the advantage," Bucky said.

"Why's that?" Pete asked.

Bucky cranked down the window again and spat before he answered. "Haven't youse guys ever hurd the sayin', one if by land and two if by sea?"

"So?" Ruby asked testily.

"Well," Bucky declared, "we'se definitely comin' in by land."

"Jesus," Ruby groaned and crossed herself. "My God, Bucky! Do you ever stop and listen to yourself?"

"You think about it, Rube," Bucky said. "All the great ones speak in parables."

"I hope," Ruby said, gritting her teeth, "you're not comparing yourself to Jesus Christ."

"Been compared to worse."

"Yeah, I'll bet," Ruby groaned.

"I'm goin' to pull over here," Pete said, slowly stepping on the brake. "We're still a couple blocks from the auction, but let's park her and walk over and scout them corrals."

"Fine by me," Ruby said, touching her right hip, making sure the .357 Magnum was still there.

Turning off the pavement, Pete came to a stop directly under an overhanging street light. As they clamored out of the truck, Dell pulled up behind them and killed his headlights. The doors of his Ford creaked opened and the three of them, Dell, Skinner and Max, crawled out and trudged over to join them.

It was a surreal scene, Ruby thought, gathering here after midnight under this frosty street light. With abstract fascination, she watched as they talked. Their hands moved in rhythm with their speech, like a maestro conducting his orchestra, and their sentences were punctuated with exhaled plumes of freezing water vapor.

"How do you want to do this?" Dell asked.

"Thought we'd better stop here," Pete explained, "and scout ahead on foot."

"Well," Bucky replied. "Let's get goin', afore I freeze my ass off."

"How could you be cold in that thing?" Dell asked, wrinkling his nose and nodding at the ankle-length bulky fur coat.

"I agree." Skinner took charge. "Too much noise to drive. Let's send in two scouts, one from the north the other from the south. They can look around for a minute. then come back and report. How about me and Max? I go north, Max you go south."

"We'll wait here then," Pete agreed, working his arms to stimulate circulation, "till you get back."

As quickly as Skinner and Max had disappeared into the night, the rest of them climbed back into their respective trucks to wait out of the bitter cold. Mostly they sat in silence, with just the occasional rolling down of the window accompanied by a draft of cold air and Bucky loudly expectorating. Under the passenger window of Pete's truck, a mustard-yellow stain gathered in the sugary white snow.

After about fifteen minutes, Skinner returned quietly from the shadows followed almost immediately by Max Yeager coming in from the south. Once again they scrambled out of their flatbed trucks and huddled beneath the light pole.

"You see anything?" Skinner asked Max.

"Nah, it's as quiet as sacrament meeting on the opening week of the deer season," Max replied. "You?"

"Same," Skinner answered, small icicles were now hanging from his frozen mustache.

"So how do you want to do this?" Dell queried. "Just drive right up to the pens?"

"Might just as well," Skinner answered. "We got to sooner or later."

"First thing, we need to get them cows in the chute pen," Max added, turning up his collar to the brisk breeze. "So as we can load 'em."

"What about Roper's cows?" Pete asked suddenly, looking at the group.

"Ah, just leave 'em," Bucky muttered. "He ain't scratched our back."

"Maybe we ought'a take 'em," Skinner said, grinning slyly. "Wouldn't mind him havin' to explain that to his BLM friends."

"Leave him be," Ruby said, "he hasn't done us no harm."

"Hasn't helped us none, neither," Bucky replied.

"Well, what do you suggest, Rube?" Max asked, his teeth chattering with the cold.

Looking down at the ground, Ruby was quiet, taking a moment to consider all angles. Finally she looked them in the eye. "Oh for hell's sake, if we've got room, let's take 'em. If he don't want 'em, I'll take 'em."

"That settles it," Skinner said. "Let's get goin'."

They got back into their flatbeds and slowly drove two blocks east to the stockyard. When they'd reached the auction corrals, Pete backed his truck up to the loading dock. Grabbing a flashlight from the glove compartment, Skinner walked over to the pens. Within seconds, the others followed. Skinner opened the gate and everyone except Bucky helped herd the cows to the chute holding pen. From there they would drive them up the loading ramp onto the truck. Tonight this was all accomplished quietly without the usual whooping, hollering and cussing that usually accompanied the herding of cows.

Meanwhile, Bucky refusing to budge from the warmth, chewed, spat and watched the proceedings from the cab of Pete's truck. As he explained, it was too friggin' cold and like Noah of old, he didn't know one damn thing about herdin' cows.

Once all the cows were in the chute holding pen, Max threw open another gate and the cows were then forced up a ramp, fenced high on both sides, and onto Pete's flatbed Ford. Bawling, fighting and complaining every step of the way, fifteen head of protesting cows were crammed, like worms in a bait box, onto Pete's truck. Jumping in the cab with Bucky, Pete moved the truck down the road a bit, making way for Dell's truck to back in.

As Dell thudded up against the loading dock and set the park brake, Pete rejoined the group and they began herding another load of cows toward the loading ramp. Bucky stayed where he was in the heated cab.

Lying apart from the others, one cow was down in the far corner of the holding pen. When nudged, she hung her head, refusing to get up. Flashing her light on the rust-colored cow, Ruby noticed her eyes were dull and that there was an open wound on her left hip. Moving closer, she redirected her light. Apparently an abrasion had gotten infected, abscessed, then ripened until it vented under pressure. A thick creamy pus oozed down her leg. The wound was large and obviously old, covering most of her hip, upper thigh and flank. The cow, Ruby suspected, had been injured during the helicopter roundup. It had been here for several days and obviously no vet had been called. Hell, Ruby thought bitterly, in spite of their claims, the government didn't care a whit about the cows. All that mattered was to get them off the Fifty.

"Hey," she yelled at the group. "We've got a cow down over here."

"If she won't get up," Skinner shouted, "leave her."

"She's got an abscessed leg," Ruby hollered back, "she'll have to be destroyed."

"No shooting!" Skinner yelled.

"Well," Pete said, coming over to look. "You can still get a few steaks off'n her. Let's see if we can get her up."

"I don't know," Ruby said doubtfully. "Meat might be tainted."

"If nothing else, Bucky can take her for sausage," Pete insisted, as he walked over to the cow. "Come on, give me a hand."

With some insistent coaxing and prodding, they finally got the cow up on its feet and it hobbled up on the ramp and onto Dell's truck. With this feat accomplished, they went back for the rest. Unfortunately, there were still five pretty stubborn heifers to load.

Just as they were stuffing the last of the cows onto Dell's flatbed, a spotlight flashed on and flooded the area. Caught off guard, they froze.

"Hey, you over there!" an amplified voice boomed over a loudspeaker. "Stop what you're doing. Don't move a muscle."

As their eyes adjusted to the harsh light, they say that the voice was coming from a sheriff's cruiser just behind Dell's truck and just east of Pete's. Absorbed in their task, they hadn't seen the car sneak into the stockyards.

"I—I mean it," the shaky voice seemed to be coming from the spotlight itself. "Don't move!"

Ruby glanced quickly at the others. Their faces all conveyed the same paralytic mixture of shock and fear. That is, everyone's but Skinner's. Looking like a kid caught with his hand in the cookie jar, he just smiled his most engaging smile, shrugged his shoulders and took a few steps toward the cruiser.

"Ra—raise your hands," the magnified voice thundered. "Halt!"

Skinner stopped and for a moment no one moved. Seemingly paralyzed, they looked at each other waiting for someone to take the lead. Then almost as if cued, they simultaneously raised their hands high above their heads.

Behind the glaring lights, the cruiser door opened and out stepped a uniformed deputy brandishing a Blackhawk .44 pistol. Face flushed with excitement, he appeared to be very young and his hand was visibly quivering as he tried to steady the heavy gun. With haltingly measured steps, he slowly walked toward them. About twenty feet away from the corrals, he stopped and planted his feet.

"Com—come on down from that truck," he commanded, his voice trembling with the same beat as his quaking gun, "but keep your hands where I can see them."

"That's a mighty big gun," Skinner said softly. "Looks like a Clint Eastwood piece."

"It's not regulation," the deputy blushed.

"That's certainly a cannon," Skinner agreed, smiling. "Why don't you put it down afore someone gets blow'd away."

"Wha—what'cha doin' here?" the deputy asked, his oscillating gun still leveled at the group.

"Just as it looks," Skinner replied as he jumped down from the flatbed Ford. "We're loadin' up cows."

"Them's those impounded cows." the deputy declared.

"Well that depends, don't it?" Skinner forked little icicles from his mustache.

"Depends on wh—what?" the deputy asked, walking a little closer.

"On how you look at it." Skinner grinned and reshaped his icicle-free mustache. "The federal government might say they're impounded, but we say they've been rustled."

"Rustled?"

"They've got my brand," Ruby interjected, "and I didn't authorize them being moved here."

"I—I gotta take you in," the deputy said more firmly now, his confidence growing.

"Better check with Sheriff Olsen first," Pete said calmly as walked over to join Skinner and Ruby.

"Sheriff's outta town," the deputy said, "family emergency."

"Yah, I'll bet," Ruby muttered under her breath. "Bet he left so nobody could say this happened on his watch."

"And as always, some dumb son-of-a-bitch never gets the word," Pete growled, nodding at the young deputy.

"What?" the deputy shrilled.

"Oh, nothing," Ruby replied. "Like I said, these are my cows. Got my brand on 'em. You can check."

"These are government property now," the deputy insisted.

"Whose side are you on anyway?" Dell said. "Never met nobody in Utah yet who sided with them friggin' land-grabbin' feds."

"It's my job," the deputy said, dropping his head a little, "got to uphold the law."

Max placed his hand over his heart. "Would somebody please play The Star Spangled Banner?"

"Make fun all you want," the deputy said, "but I got a job to do and I intend on doing it."

"Son, that's very admirable," Skinner said. "but you've also got to be smart."

"I—I'm done talking now," the deputy said, wildly waving the .44. "You guys get on over here now and keep those hands high."

"Just keep your finger off the damn trigger," Dell cautioned.

With the spotlight still blazing, Skinner, Pete, Dell, Max and Ruby slowly congregated, then as a group shuffled toward the deputy. Feeling foolish and vulnerable, they stood in the cold light and faced the young deputy with the big gun.

"If—if any of you got weapons," the deputy commanded in a husky, barely post-pubescence voice, "throw 'em on the ground now."

Nobody moved.

"I mean it!" the deputy shrieked and the gun swayed.

For a second Ruby thought about it, then she slowly unholstered her .357 Magnum and dropped it to the frozen ground. Pete wasn't carrying a handgun and his 30/30 was out of reach in the truck, but the others followed Ruby's lead.

"Okay," the deputy said, tossing his handcuffs to Skinner. "Put those through the pipe fence yonder and cuff one to you and one to the lady."

Skinner looked at the quavering gun for a second, then smiled mischievously. "Anytime, anyplace other than right now, I might like that idea."

"Come on." The deputy turned crimson red. "I'm not foolin'."

Skinner contemplated for another moment, then motioned to Ruby and they did as they were told.

"Now," the deputy commanded gruffly, looking at Pete, Max and Dell. "You three crowd into the front seat." He then pointed the gun at Pete. "You drive. I'll sit in the back seat with a gun aimed at your heads."

No one moved.

"Come on," he shouted a bit hysterically, his eyes wild and frenzied. "I mean it!"

Pete, Dell and Max looked at each other, shrugged and started walking toward the cruiser. Suddenly, the deputy stopped, stiffened and they heard the thud of his heavy .44 as it hit the solid ground.

There was a moment of edgy silence filled only with the sound of breathing and ghostly fog of expelled frozen water vapor.

"In the immoral words of Clint Easton," Bucky said loudly, jabbing his gun harder into the deputy's ribs, then expectorating through a gap in his yellow teeth. "Go ahead, make my bed."

16

PAREAH GHOST TOWN

Established in 1870 on an adjacent sandy plain to the diminutive Paria River, Peter Shurtz could not have predicted what would eventually cause the town's demise. Drought? Indian Wars? Disease? No, water, and lots of it. Providing watershed drainage for nearly 1,570 square miles of the upland Paunsaugunt Plateau, roughly every twenty to thirty years the Paria floods, becoming a raging river, rivaling in magnitude the mighty Colorado.

Colonized as a Mormon farming community, at its height, Pareah boasted forty-seven families, a post office, fertile fields and fragrant orchards. Now only tamarisks, Russian olives, cottonwoods and sagebrush remain on the flood ravaged plain.

Set in the picturesque Paria Canyon, the east wall is composed of vermilion sandstone, spectacularly capped with white Navajo sandstone. The resulting talus slope is created from the Painted Desert formation with brilliant layers of gray, purple, white, vermilion and burgundy. The west wall is constructed of the same layers, except it is more fractured and not as sheer. Once dotted with rough-hewn plank pioneer cabins, no buildings now remain. All have been swept into the Colorado River by the massive floods.

Seated in the conference room of the Kanab field office of the Grand Staircase/Escalante National Monument, Roper stared out the still opaque window. It was dark outside, but that was to be expected. It was barely 6:45 a.m. on December 22, the winter solstice, also the shortest, and to date, the coldest, day of the year. On his right, with his long red tangled hair, dozed Sean O'Grady and directly across the conference table was the ever silent brooding Monty Coleman. Also present were Deputy Monument Manager Ron Sparks, several field officers, range managers and monument specialists. Having just arrived from Salt Lake City, United States Attorney Elliot Mauss was fussing with the contents of briefcase.

Late last night, Monument Manager Brisco had abruptly summoned Roper by telephone. "Be in my office at six-thirty tomorrow," she had commanded. "We've got a major catastrophe!" Without another word, she hung up, leaving Roper to speculate, rather than sleep.

In the conference room this morning, there was very little chatter. It was still early and the attendees either did not know each other very well, or in some cases did not like each other, or were too sleepy for conversation. All except Roper nursed a cup of hot coffee which somehow seemed to require their undivided attention. To occupy himself, Roper glanced at the round clock hanging on opposite wall, then at the seemingly ubiquitous picture of a smiling, but definitely presidential-looking, Bill Clinton. That photograph couldn't help but remind Roper of Clinton's September speech in Bucky's cabin almost two years ago. A lot had changed since then, but no doubt about it, for better or worse, that speech had set all this in motion. Idly, he glanced up at the wall clock again. It was 6:47 a.m. and still no Superintendent Brisco.

Ruby was probably just getting up now and having her first cup of coffee or maybe just getting out of the shower. That thought made Roper smile. That pleasantry instantly vanished as he remembered their last painful encounter. Prior to that, in his mind he had played out every possible scenario. Frankly, he had expected Ruby to not only to accept his proposition, but perhaps with tears in her eyes, be thankful and rush into his arms. Admittedly that was pretty naive, but no way did he expect the grilling about premarital sex and his bishop, followed by a flat unqualified no.

In retrospect, he had been sophomoric, clumsy and probably even condescending. What did he expect? A tearful acknowledgment that he was indeed her savior, her white knight in shining armor. He'd obviously been watching too many Hollywood movies lately.

On the other hand, what did he really know about Ruby Nez? Not much. Nothing about her childhood or background. Just obscure hints of a tumultuous past and that she'd had a tough time with men. And she did have one valid point, he did feel premarital sex, even with her, was a sin and he had confessed the last slip up to his bishop. Those principals had been ingrained in him since childhood and could not be shed as easily as skin from a molting snake. Maybe the religion issue was not as easily bridged as he had previously thought.

At that moment the door opened and in whirled Judith Brisco. Marching straight to the empty chair at the top of the table, she loudly smacked down a stack of manila folders then remained standing, grim-faced and glaring at the group.

Loudly clearing her throat, she looked everyone present in the eye, pausing at Roper, then began. "I suppose," she said slowly, obviously struggling to control her anger, "that by now everyone has heard about what happened in Salina?"

She paused for a moment. Some shook their heads. "Well, the details are still a bit sketchy, but let me tell you what we do know. Apparently last night, some of the ranchers went up to Salina and illegally seized the impounded cows.

"Most of what we know comes from Deputy Sheriff Jimmy Wells of Sevier County. He says about one-thirty a.m., while on routine patrol, he was driving past the stockyards and noticed two flatbed trucks apparently loading cows. When he confronted them, he found they indeed were doing just that. With Sheriff Olsen out of town, he had no back up, but proceeded to try to arrest them himself and probably would have succeeded, but one of the thieves was not with the rest and sneaked up behind Deputy Wells with a gun. They brazenly handcuffed him to a fence, then they finished loading and drove off. Fortunately no one was hurt.

"It was dark and Wells didn't know any of them personally, but he did give us partial descriptions. There were five men and one woman. The woman was about thirty or so, dark long hair and dark eyes, about five-foot-five and in Wells' words, 'real pretty.' Does that remind you of anyone?" Brisco asked bluntly as she glanced at the group then settled on Roper.

"Ruby Nez," Sean blurted, not at all trying to hide the rancor his voice.

"What about the men?" Monty asked, looking down at the table.

"All cowboys," Brisco confirmed. "All wore Stetsons and cowboy boots except the guy who pulled the gun. He wore a fur cap and a dirty fur coat and smelled of tobacco."

"That'd be Bucky Lee Aikens," Monty quietly volunteered.

"And the others would probably be Dell Wallace, Max Yeager, Pete Goslin, Skinner Jacobson or some of their hands," Sean said, scratching his matted red hair.

"How can you be so sure?" Brisco asked.

"I've been keeping an eye on them. They've been having secret meetings."

Suddenly Roper's head jerked up. "What do you mean you've been keeping an eye on them?" he demanded.

"Like I said, they've been having secret meetings at Bucky's," Sean repeated, unflinching. "This little heist was concocted there."

"How do you keep an eye on them?" Roper pressed.

"They always meet at night," Sean answered, smiling smugly at Roper. "I just hang around and see who shows up. Sometimes listen if a window or door's open."

"You happen to be hangin' around on the night of December eighteenth?" Roper asked.

"December eighteenth," Sean answered, frowning as if in deep thought then he grinned. "No, I didn't even knew they were meeting that night."

"So you don't know anything about vandalizing trucks?" Roper demanded, locking eyes with Sean.

"Nah, not a thing," Sean replied coolly.

"What are you two talking about?" Brisco interrupted.

For a moment Sean and Roper glared at each other, saying nothing. Finally, Roper turned to Brisco.

"The ranchers have been having meetings," Roper explained, measuring his words, "I've gone to a couple of them, mostly harmless stuff on how to deal with the cutbacks, recent closures and in general the best way to handle the new monument regs. During this last meeting, someone dumped sugar in everyone's gas tank, ruining their engines including mine."

"So you've been going to their meetings?" Brisco asked, arching an eyebrow at Roper.

"Well, yes," Roper replied, trying not to sound defensive. "After all, I am a rancher."

"Do you tell them what goes on in our meetings?"

"Only things that directly impact them, like allotment closures, road closures, etcetera."

"I see." Brisco frowned. "I don't recall you sharing any information from their meetings."

"Well," Roper stammered, "they never say anything that'll affect us directly. They just mainly react to policies decided on by this committee. And you know—let off steam."

"I see," Brisco repeated, pausing for a moment. "Did they ever discuss their plans for this illegal cow raid?"

"Well." Roper paused, the color drained from his face. "I—I didn't think they were serious."

"Then you knew about the raid," Brisco said quietly, "and yet, you said nothing?"

Roper bit down on his lip, trying to control his temper. It had been years since anyone had talked down to him like that, like a bad little school boy getting a lecture from his principal.

"You knew about a conspiracy to steal government property, yet you did nothing. Elliot, doesn't that make him an accessory to something?" Brisco asked, abruptly turning to the U.S. attorney who now stopped shuffling his papers.

"Technically, it makes him part of the conspiracy," Elliot Mauss confirmed, looking up from his dark leather briefcase.

"Not only did he know about it," Monty Coleman added, his voice a flat monotone, "but he may have participated. From what I hear, not only did they take Ruby's cows, but Roper's are also missing and he fits the general description given by Deputy Wells."

"My cows are gone?" Roper asked, looking confused.

"What a surprise, huh," Monty replied, glaring at Roper. "As if you didn't know."

"Where did they take the cows?" Brisco demanded. "Anybody know?"

"Could be most anywhere," Monty frowned. "My guess is that they're not all still together. Too obvious. I'm thinkin' they've scattered them around in the different rancher's herds. Be a lot of work trackin' 'em down."

"I don't care what it takes," Brisco hissed. "I want them found. This is blatant defiance of my authority!" She slammed her fist on the table.

"Well, one thing it will take," Monty continued, "is a fistful of federal warrants. Those ranchers are not going to let us simply walk in and sift through their herds. Without warrants, they'll probably shoot us."

"They might anyway," Roper muttered.

"That's why we have Elliot Mauss, United States Attorney, here," Brisco snapped.

"Thank God," Sean interjected, smiling sarcastically at Mauss.

"Elliot, give us your take on this whole fiasco," Brisco ordered.

"Getting the federal warrants will be no problem," Mauss said, standing before the group, immaculate in his three-piece olive-green suit. "However, down the road I can see some real legal battles in the offing."

"What kind of legal battles?" Brisco asked.

"Well, for one thing, basic ownership, who has rightful title to those cows?" Elliot Mauss replied, unbuttoning his vest and smoothing his matching green tie.

"That's obvious," Brisco argued. "If they're seized in trespass, they become property of the United States government. It's the law."

"Maybe," Mauss said thoughtfully, "but it is open to some interpretation. In the western states, unless there is a legal bill of sale, ownership is based solely on whose brand is on the animal. That's also part of the Utah State code. A county brand inspector may disagree with you on this one, Judith."

"That's poppycock," Brisco declared, waving a hand in dismissal. "When there is a conflict, federal law always takes precedence over state law."

"Well, at least it's not that clear to me," Mauss continued. "If you arrest a man for trespassing government property, you can try him in court, adjudicate him guilty by due process, then he may have to pay a fine or even do some prison time, but he does not become property of the government."

"For God's sake, Elliot," Brisco barked, "we're talking about cows. They are considered property to begin with. Dammit, don't go PETA on me now."

"All I'm saying is, there is very little precedence for this," Mauss replied. "If it were drugs, that would be a different matter altogether. You get caught selling or distributing drugs and the law is very clear. Federal agents can impound cars, houses, planes, or boats and they become United States government property but even then, they cannot be sold until due process is served. If that person is found not guilty by the courts then he or she may reclaim their impounded property. What I'm trying to say is, it is not so clear with cows grazing on allotments where ranchers have legal leases and have really broken no laws, at least no statutes of the criminal code. Can you can seize, impound and sell their property all without due process?"

"But we have a mandate. We are the guardians of that property and we decide when cows have to be removed." Brisco's face became flushed with anger.

"The real question, after you remove them, whose property do they become?" Mauss questioned.

"Jesus, Elliot," Brisco quipped. "They have due process. They can appeal IBLA. You know, the Interior Board of Land Appeals."

"It's not the same," Mauss insisted. "An appeals board is not a jury of their peers."

"But it is an arbitration forum where their objections can be heard," Judith replied.

"You know very well that can take months, if not years," Mauss said. "So in the meantime, are you allowed to sell their cows?"

"Whose side are you on anyway?" Brisco snapped.

"Yours, of course," Elliot Mauss said evenly. "I just want you to know, legally things are a little fuzzy."

As Brisco stood glaring at Elliot in frustration, someone pounded firmly on the closed conference room door. After a moment, they pounded again, louder.

"Yes!" Brisco bellowed.

The door opened and in walked Sheriff Ivory Jackson, dressed in full uniform with patented toothpick dangling from the corner of his mouth. He removed his cowboy hat and stood quietly beside the open door.

"Yes!" Brisco demanded.

"Don't mean to interrupt your important meetin', Ma'am," Sheriff Jackson said, a bit of sarcasm in his voice, "but perhaps, you'd better come with me and take a look at this."

"Take a look at what?" Brisco retorted, not budging from her post at the head of the table. "Can't you see we're in the middle of a staff meeting?"

"I think this takes precedence," Jackson said, face stoic.

"What the hell is this all about?" Brisco barked. "It's too early to play guessing games."

"Well Ma'am, about an hour ago I got a call from Jarvis Jenkins, you know from across the street," Jackson said. "Anyway, it's kinda hard to explain, maybe it's best if you just come and have a look for yourself."

Hands on her hips, Brisco glared at Sheriff Jackson. Finally, gritting her teeth, she dropped her hands and fell in step behind Jackson. Curious, the others soon followed.

Like the pied piper, Sheriff Jackson led them into the hallway, down to the main foyer, out the front door of the building and onto the sidewalk. To the east the sun was still just below the horizon, but flinging early morning rays upward, silhouetting the eastern bank of the Vermillion Cliffs. Overhead, thin gossamer clouds instantly inflamed, blazing an apricot gold.

Once on the sidewalk, Jackson stopped abruptly, turned to face the group, then waited. After a moment when no one had said anything, he simply pointed to his left at the winter brown dormant lawn. In places, particularly shaded areas, a skiff of crusty snow remained, freezing to form a dazzling lattice of ice crystal.

At first Roper saw nothing, then slowly a bulky, indistinct, dark object began to take shape. As the first rays of sunlight streamed over the Vermillion Cliffs, things suddenly came into focus. Now spotlighted, like a solo actor on an empty stage, the once fuzzy object was apparent, highlighted in the morning sun.

"What the hell?" someone whispered in horror.

"Oh my God!" Sparky exclaimed. His perpetual grin had vanished.

After the initial collective gasp, the group was paralyzed by the macabre sight. Manager Brisco stood rock rigid with hands planted on her hips, mouth gaping open, eyes unblinking. Slowly, she closed her mouth and set her jaw.

Three green metal fencing posts had been sledge-hammered into the frozen lawn in the shape of an equilateral triangle. Impaled on the poles was the bloody head of a cow. The animal's face had been positioned to directly face the front of the BLM building and specifically Brisco's office. Now clearly visible in the bright morning light were the frayed ragged ends of the slashed neck strap muscles with white tendons dangling like severed marionette strings. Congealed blood had stained dark red streaks down the metal posts and where it had dripped to the frozen ground it had formed a clotted puddle of shocking red, vividly contrasted by the underlying bed of sugary white snow and diamond latticed crystals.

With eyes glazed over but still wide open, the cow stared vacantly ahead. Its mouth was agape and a swollen purple tongue flopped out over alabaster teeth, hanging from of the corner of its mouth like a ladle on a punchbowl. Rigor mortis had contracted its facial muscles into permanent contorted sneer.

A handwritten sign had been slung around the massive bloody neck stump: THIS IS A DIRECT RESULT OF MS. BRISCO'S MANAGEMENT POLICIES.

After a few moments, the sheriff cleared his throat. "Jenkins called me about an hour ago, thought he'd heard a coyote in his chicken pen. While he was out investigating, he saw this dark pickup, thinks it was a Ford, pull up in front of the BLM office. He couldn't see real well, but thought he heard a post-hole pounder. The truck left in a hurry, so Jenkins found a flashlight, walked across the street to take a closer peek, then called me."

"Can he identify him?" Monty asked, his voice barely above a whisper.

"Nah," Sheriff Jackson said, "In the dark, he couldn't make 'em out. Not even that sure about the truck."

"Is he positive it was just one man?" Roper asked.

"Not a hundred percent," the sheriff answered.

"How sure is he that it was a man?" Monty Coleman asked, his eyes narrowing.

"Pretty sure," Jackson said, then hesitated. "What do you mean by that?"

"What I'm asking," Coleman clarified, "could it have been a woman?"

"I don't know for sure," Jackson replied. "I didn't ask him that specifically, but I will."

"That head's pretty heavy for a woman to lift," Roper added.

"What do you think they're trying to say by this?" Brisco stammered, still shaken by the grisly scene.

"Well to me, it seems obvious," Jackson said coldly, "someone don't care for your management style."

"I think this is some kind of a gauntlet," Sean volunteered.

"Or a declaration of war," Monty added quietly, turning his back to the spectacle.

"This is definitely," Sheriff Jackson said, turning to face Monty, "and I mean definitely, my jurisdiction, being in town and not in the monument. No loose cannons here."

"Sheriff," Monty said thinly and unsmiling, "just cause it's in town doesn't mean this ain't Monument property. I wouldn't think of infringing on your territory and you needn't worry about mine. I'm going to investigate this. You can do as you wish."

"Yeah, sure" Sheriff Jackson said curtly. "We're still waiting for you to figure out who killed Angus Macdonald."

"I have a pretty good idea about that too," Monty snapped.

"So do I." Jackson spat out his toothpick and stared right at Monty. "It's surprising how many times these things turn up right under your nose."

"Sometimes people can't see their face because of their nose," Monty replied, locking eyes with Jackson.

"What the hell's that supposed to mean?" the Sheriff demanded.

"It means they don't let the facts get in the way of a good investigation."

"Stop!" Brisco interrupted. "Let's end this meeting now. We'll meet again next week, but in the meantime, I want to know where those damn cows are." Then turning to Elliot Mauss, she added, "and I want those damn search warrants."

She wedged herself between Jackson and Coleman. "Monty, I need to know the names of those involved in the raid, then Elliot can officially charge them and you can arrest them. And Monty—"

"—yes, boss," Monty replied.

"Find someone to remove this goddamn thing."

Still scowling, Brisco turned. "And Roper, I need to talk to you in my office. Now."

Not waiting for an answer, she opened the front door and disappeared into the building. Roper hesitated for a moment, surveyed the gory scene on last time, then quickly followed.

"What do you make of all this?" she asked, when they had reached her office. "This barbaric attempt to intimidate me."

Roper didn't answer right away, but gazed out the window at the beheaded animal, now fully visible in the rising sun. To Roper, the bloody head looked like a grisly scene from history books, possibly a William Wallace stunt from an ancient Scottish/English battle where the vanquished heads were piked and displayed as trophies of war.

"You may call it barbaric, and it is, but you've got to understand the ranchers feel they're walking the moral high ground. They feel much like the Polish Jews did in World War two. This is a battle against extermination. This is their Alamo, their Waterloo, their battle of Culloden."

"What they seem to forget," Brisco said, "is this land is not theirs. It belongs to the American citizens and the BLM just happens to be the appointed steward. The last time I checked, this was still a democracy which means the majority rules. And I can tell you right now, the majority do not want their lands over-grazed and cut up with erosion. Nor do they want to hike knee-deep in cow dung. What they want is this land preserved in mint condition for all citizens to enjoy."

"How many citizens, short of the environmental groups, actually visit the monument or even know it is here?" Roper asked then answered his own question. "Not very many. Most of the time there's no one out there. Not one soul in all one point seven million acres. That's some majority."

"That's hardly the point, is it?" Brisco said.

"The west is the only section of the country where the government owns most of the land. It wasn't supposed to be that way," Roper replied. "When territories became states, the federal government was supposed to release all lands to the state."

"We could argue this for days," Brisco said. "You need to read Patricia Limerick's work on colonizing the west. But this is what we have and this is what we will work with. I have a mandate. No one, and I do mean no one, is going to intimidate me!"

Shaking his head, Roper lapsed into a brooding silence. Suddenly everything seemed hopeless. "Then frankly, I don't see an easy way out of this," he said.

"The rancher's will lose," Brisco said. "They can't fight the United States government." She paused for a moment and looked Roper in the eye. "But I had no idea you were burning the candle from both ends, going to their meetings and to ours."

"I wouldn't call it that," Roper said. "More like wearing two hats."

"As it says in the Bible, you can't serve two masters," Judith replied. "This is now a war and I need loyalty."

"Well," Roper said, "I thought I could do more good being neutral. A liaison, a way to keep the lines of communication open."

"You're beginning to look more like a double agent or a snitch," Brisco said. "You are going to have to decide, and damn soon, whose side you're on."

Frowning with forehead furrowed, Roper again fell silent. He then shook his head and glanced up at Brisco. Had she just given him an ultimatum? All he had done was to try to live his life as Jesus had counseled at the Sermon on the Mount, blessed are the peacemakers for they shall be called the children of God. And God only knows he had tried to be a peacemaker. Truly, he had not wanted it to come to this, this mandatory choosing of sides. In the past, he had always felt if they tried hard enough they could find a way to get along, some common ground, but perhaps he was wrong. If compelled, and it certainly looked like he was, he wouldn't have a moment's hesitation deciding where he would pledge his allegiance.

Getting up, he secured his Stetson on his head and looked Brisco straight in the eye. He started to say something, then changed his mind and walked to the door. Placing a hand on the knob, he opened the door and walked out.

"Roper!" Judith yelled, "I mean it."

Roper paused momentarily, then returned to face her. "You'll get this in writing," he said. "But as of now, I officially resign from the Citizen's Advisory Board. Effective immediately."

17

MOLLY'S NIPPLE

At 7,271 feet and located near the monument's southern boundary, Molly's nipple is the area's dominate landmark. An isolated inverted cone of rusty-white Navajo sandstone, it rests on the recumbent massive chest of the Vermillion Cliffs formation and is visible for miles in every direction.

John G. Kitchen, in 1879, established the Nipple Ranch and named the peak in honor of his wife. With abundant subsurface water, Nipple Lake, actually a green pasture, provides the foundation for the ranch that still operates today.

Though from a distance it looks unscalable, there is a reasonable trail that twists its way up black brush peppered hogbacks and boulder-strewn talus slope to reach the summit. From the apex the view is unparalleled. The crest affords a breathtaking view of all the colorful steps of the Grand Staircase. Also visible, to the far north is the drainage of the Paria River and to the east, miles of white Navajo slickrock. To the far east, extends the Kaiparowits Plateau along with the sacred Navajo Mountain and to the distant south, the blue/green Kaibab Plateau and the copper blue waters of Lake Powell.

It was New Year's Day and Judith Brisco stared blankly at the squawking twenty-seven-inch television set. For the last hour or so she had been watching a college football bowl game (normally she never watched television), though she had no idea which game (probably Orange or Sugar or Rose), who was playing (even though the commentators made it sound like a big deal) or what the score was (though someone had just hit a home run). To be honest, she detested football. It was barbaric, senseless and needlessly brutal. Today, she had the TV turned on only for sound. Noise gave the illusion of company, of friends or family and that's the way it was supposed to be on holidays.

Earlier, in desperation, she had called Ron Sparks, intending to ask him and his wife over for dinner. Delores had answered the phone.

"Hi, Delores, is Ron in?" she had asked cheerfully.

"No, sorry. He got a phone call during breakfast and left in kind of a hurry," Delores replied, worry etched in her voice.

"Is everything all right?" Judith had asked.

"Yeah. Yeah, I'm sure it is."

"Did he say where he was going?"

"Something about the Kaiparowits and Ruby something or other."

"Would that have been Ruby Flats?" Judith had asked, trying to be helpful.

"Yeah, probably," Delores agreed. "Something like that. He was in a hurry."

"Did he say when he'd be back?"

"No. He left in too big of a rush."

"Well, have him give me a call when he gets back," Judith had said, glumly returning to the television.

Disinterested, she had then watched a holiday parade (maybe the Rose). About halfway through the parade, with a loud sigh of resignation, she had picked up the phone and punched in Doug Rehnquist's number. Trying to sound cavalier and somewhat festive, she had invited him, of course if he wasn't doing anything, over for a game of chess. To say he had been cool was an understatement. At first he had rattled her by asking, "Who did you say this is?" When she repeated her name, he then had added to the embarrassment by saying, "Oh, hello," with all the warmth that he would have greeted a telemarketer. After a moment of awkward silence, she had repeated her invitation, trying not to grovel. He had completed her mortification by simply saying, "No." That was it, a flat "no" with no offer of a face-saving, truth or not, explanation or charitable excuse. Just plain no. After another moment of humiliating silence, she had blurted, "Maybe some other time," then hurriedly hung up.

Not that she blamed him—especially after literally forcing him to resign from the advisory committee. Her asking Roper to play chess was a bit like George Bush asking Saddam Hussein out to dinner and a movie during a break in Desert Storm. What had she been thinking? Was she cracking up? Was the pressure of this job getting to her? Or, was she just lonely? Maybe, all three. She sighed and changed the channel.

The last three months had been an unqualified descent into the depths of hell. When she had taken this job, no way had she foreseen it degenerating into this—an all out civil war. Naively, she had pictured herself as kind of a benevolent liberator passing through throngs of cheering southern Utah natives, arriving just in time to save their fiscal bacon. Who could have predicted that something so benign, so salubrious as creating a national monument, would be greeted with so much rancor and hostility?

Of course she'd made her share of mistakes along the way, not the least of them, under estimation. Without question, she had completely missed the mark when it came to the passion these ranchers, and Utah people in general, had for the cowboy way of life, even though in Kane County there were not a dozen families that made their entire living off ranching. Some estimates placed ranching income at a paltry one percent of the county's total gross income. Economically speaking, almost no one would miss ranching and soon, if not already, the revenue the monument generated in tourist dollars would greatly outstrip ranching. Nobody ate beef anymore, anyway.

Finally, at long last, and even though she still did not agree with it, Judith realized economic arguments were hardly the point. Call it romanticism, mysticism, heritage or tradition, call it whatever you like but to the people here, the sentimental value of this way of life was priceless.

There was simply no way her years with the National Park Service had prepared her for this situation. At the Park Service, she had been thoroughly grounded in preservation and conservation. Literally, that agency would have had a collective cerebral hemorrhage if someone had suggested they allow cattle grazing. Nothing but native species, plant or animal, were allowed and there was nothing indigenous about a thousand-pound grass eating machine.

If she were perfectly honest, there was no question she had come to this job with preconceived, and maybe even prejudiced, ideas. Though she had implemented the BLM's traditional multiple-use template for land utilization, in principle she had never agreed with it and subconsciously had leaned more toward preservation. Right from the start, she had resolved, if they were going to run their destructive cows on this sacred monument, then it would be strictly by the book, no bending, no amending, no modifying, no exceptions.

Perhaps, in retrospect, this rigid stance had been the wrong approach and perhaps that was another of her failings, inflexibility. Maybe she should have amended the plan to be more user-friendly. Given them more time to remove their cows. Who knows? Certainly, her formula had ruffled a lot feathers and the subsequent fallout had been nothing short of atomic.

Probably, the damage could have been contained, reduced or even prevented if the press had not become involved. Almost like greedy divorce lawyers, they stoked fuel onto an already blazing fire, thereby keeping the opposing parties warring and generating plenty of fresh stories for headlines. Undeniably this crisis, any crisis, sold newspapers, lots of them, but at what price? Now, both sides were so entrenched, so embittered and so blinded that the open window for detente may have already slammed shut and those once solvable issues may now have progressed way beyond any hope of reconciliation.

As things stood now, Monty still had not found the purloined cows and the ranchers remained steadfast in their solidarity and silence. United States Attorney, Elliot Mauss, had continually browbeaten them in the press and dispensed several ultimatums. The last, a ten thousand dollar fine and two years in jail for each participant if they did not come forward and give up the cows. But in spite of all this tough talk, the ranchers had not folded, nor had Elliot actually issued a solitary arrest warrant.

Also, it seems the rash of lawlessness that had inundated the monument remained completely unsolved and growing colder by the day. Despite the efforts of Monty and even the insolent Sheriff Ivory Jackson, no one had any idea who had murdered Angus Macdonald and who had burned down Roper's cabin. Unfortunately, it appeared the Grand Staircase/ Escalante National Monument was becoming a repository for outlaws, much like the infamous Robber's Roost was to Butch Cassidy and The Wild Bunch.

Regrettably, all this crime gave the appearance of anarchy, that no one was in control and this did not speak well for her management style. Already, she'd heard rumblings of discontent coming out of Washington and from the Secretary of Interior. Also, in the last couple of months, she had been visited or telephoned by every member of Utah's congressional delegation. Needless to say, their conversations had varied from mildly disgruntled to openly critical. Not that she had expected praise, not from the group who bitterly opposed the creation of the monument in the first place and were among the first signatories of the pending federal law suit, Utah vs. United States, striving to annul the monument's charter. One senior republican senator had angrily vowed he would have her job, but that was not likely, especially during a democratic administration.

So as a concession to boredom, she watched television and silently took inventory of her life. In the past, most holidays she'd spent with her Mother, but not this year. Her Mother had a cold and didn't like traveling during the holidays.

Sighing again, she reached for the channel-changer and again began surfing the stations. Not much choice. It was either football or old movies. Just as she was about to settle for the *Treasure of the Sierra Madre*, the phone rang. Sparky's finally calling me back, she thought more cheerfully as she picked up the phone. It was still not too late to invite him for dinner.

"Judith?" the man asked, his voice somewhat garbled by the static connection of his cell phone.

"Oh, Sparky," Judith blurted. "The reason I called—"

"Judith, it's Monty," the voice rasped.

"Oh, I'm sorry, Monty," Judith said, a little embarrassed, "I was expecting a call from Ron."

"I need to show you something."

"Today?"

"Yeah, now," Monty answered.

"Can't it wait?"

"It would be better if I showed you now."

"Monty, why does everything with you always have to be so dramatic?"

"Can you meet me at the junction of Cottonwood Road and Highway eighty-nine?" Monty asked.

Judith sighed. What the hell else did she have to do? "Okay, Monty," she said. "Give me an hour."

One hour and fifteen minutes later, Monty and Brisco sped north on Cottonwood Road in Monty's beat up government-issue pickup. Judith did not push him, she knew it was useless. She knew Monty well enough to know he would not bring her out here for something trivial. Certainly, over the years, Monty had always been close-mouthed, but Judith had learned to cope with that and at times actually appreciated it. Government bureaucracies were notorious for backbiting, gossiping and brown-nosing, and the BLM was no exception. So to have someone on your staff that engaged in none of that was at times refreshing. But in spite of his usual economy of speech and his customary reticence, Monty seemed particularly grim today.

In silence Judith watched the now familiar landmarks rush by. For the first twenty minutes the road followed the same canyon as the Paria River, then when the Paria veered to the northwest they continued on up the left fork and Cottonwood Canyon. After another thirty minutes, Monty coaxed the pickup up the steep incline and out of the mouth of the canyon and continued north over almost continuously broken terrain. At Grosvenor's Arch, he turned left off the well-traveled Cottonwood Road. Bypassing the Arch, they drove due west, climbing the steep road to the looming Kaiparowits Plateau. Soon the road narrowed to a barely visible precipitous track that ascended straight up the Gut and at times consisted of no more than a half-tunnel literally carved from the canyon wall. Four inches of snow had fallen, making the going not only slow, but also treacherous. At a blind S-curve, Monty skidded to a stop in the middle of the road, then reaching over he turned the key, killing the engine.

"We'll have to walk from here," he said.

"Not far, I hope," Judith said. "I didn't bring my boots."

"Just around the bend." Monty nodded to the hairpin curve.

Getting out, Judith followed Monty, his boots making almost perfect tracks in the powdery snow. As they rounded the bend, Judith noted another BLM pickup blocking the narrow lane. Up ahead, that green truck completely obstructed the road, which was nothing more than a narrow shelf through the cliff, leaving no place to turn around and no way to get past. Immediately, off to the right, the sheer rock wall rose two hundred feet straight up then off to the left, a dizzying drop of at least three hundred feet straight to the bottom of the canyon floor.

As they approached the truck, Monty stopped, bending to pick something up from the snow. Judith forged on. Through the rear window, she could see someone sitting in the passenger seat. When she got closer, she realized the person was slouching, his head extended back on the seat headrest. Taking off her sunglasses, she walked slowly past the truck's tailgate and bed. She rapped on the window with her sunglasses, then cupping her hands to block the glare, she peered in.

"Oh my God!" she gasped, dropping her sunglasses in the snow.

There, with a bullet hole precisely in the center of his forehead, was Deputy Manager Ron Sparks.

Early that morning Roper had received a call from the Kanab veterinarian, Dr. Brian Burgoyne, explaining that he had an emergency in the Escalante area, a horse with a twisted gut, and while he was there, he might as well inspect Roper's cattle and issue a certificate of health. Roper had assured Burgoyne that this job could wait. He didn't need to use his valuable holiday time doing non-emergences. Stating he had to be Escalante anyway, he really didn't care for football and that his wife was already miffed with him, Burgoyne had insisted it would only take a couple of minutes and would save him another trip from Kanab. When he finished with the sick horse at the Childress Ranch, he would give Roper a call. Probably in a couple of hours.

While he still had the phone in hand, Roper punched in Ruby's number. Maybe she wouldn't mind spending a couple of hours on a holiday socializing. He could fix her a New Year's dinner and perhaps they could talk, and he could once again try to explain. At least she'd be happy to learn he'd resigned from the Citizens' Advisory Committee. After letting the phone ring a dozen times, Roper gave up and flipped on the TV. It was too early for football, but the Rose Parade was in progress. A beautiful multi-colored, multi-flowered schooner from Portland, Oregon was apparently beached on a tropical island populated with scantily-clad, beautiful women. Though it was beautiful, it looked quite out of place for January.

Glancing outside, Roper could see an inch or so of snow on the ground and icicles hanging like stalactites from the eves of his roof. Returning to the parade, he wondered where they got all those flowers this time of year.

About half way through the parade, the phone rang. To his surprise, it was Judith Brisco. Roper was suddenly hit with a pang of guilt. No question about it, the other day when he'd resigned, he had been abrupt, curt and cold, but what did she expect? A man can take only so much. But on the other hand, she had not asked him to reconsider and had even seemed relieved by his decision.

In retrospect, however, Roper was embarrassed by his rude behavior to her on the phone. He would have enjoyed a game of chess, particularly on a day like today. But it was Brisco who had insisted he choose sides and that is just what he had done. Though he felt bad about the way things turned out, first and foremost, he was a rancher.

Before long the phone rang again. Burgoyne was done with the Childress mare and wanted to meet Roper at the Shell Service Station in fifteen minutes. Grabbing his fleece-lined, leather coat, Roper turned up the collar to the wind and headed out into the cold.

Roper got there first and decided to fill the Dodge with diesel. When he went inside to pay, the same teenage girl was working the counter who had been the target of his anger several weeks ago. Sheepishly, he apologized as he pulled out his wallet.

"Mr. Rehnquist." She looked up at him as he counted out thirty-three dollars. "You know Ruby Nez don't you?"

He glanced up. "Yeah, sure."

"That fellow," she whispered, pointing to a man over by the beer cooler, "says he's her brother-in-law and is looking for her."

At that moment the disheveled man, with three-week-old whiskers and shoulder-length, dirty-blond hair walked up and plunked a six-pack of Coors on the counter.

"This three-point-two percent?" he asked.

"I—I don't know," the girl stammered. "I guess."

"Yes, sir, it is" Roper said. "All Utah beer is."

"Damn," the blond man said, smiling. "I should'a brought my Lone Star with me."

Roper studied him for a moment. "I hear you're looking for Ruby Nez."

"Yup. She's my sister-in-law." He grinned a surprisingly pleasant smile for such a rumpled appearance.

"Hi, I'm Douglas Rehnquist," Roper said, extending a hand.

"Sandy Parker." The man vigorously shook Roper's hand.

"Why you after Ruby?"

"Just some old unfinished family business," Sandy explained, still smiling.

"If you're family, how is it you don't know where she lives?" Roper asked.

"I use'ta know, but she's moved."

Just then, Dr. Burgoyne walked in. "You ready to go, Roper?" he asked, blowing warmth into his cupped, bare hands.

"Yeah, Brian," Roper answered, replacing his wallet. "It's not going to get any warmer. Let's go get it over with."

"Wait a minute," Sandy interrupted, still grinning. "You going to tell me where she lives?"

"No," Roper replied, looking him in the eye. "Not until you're square with me why you're really here."

"Perhaps, we better talk," Sandy said after a moment of hesitation.

Roper turned to Burgoyne. "How long do you think this will take, Brian?"

"Not more'n an hour," Burgoyne figured, "probably less."

"All right," Roper said, turning back to Sandy. "If you want to talk, I'll meet you back here in about an hour."

Burgoyne climbed into Roper's Dodge and they headed south out of town on the old airport road. Roper could think of several drawbacks to the recent snow storm, like cold weather and black ice, but there was at least one benefit, other than they obviously needed the moisture, they weren't kicking up the usual cloud of roily dust.

An arm of the Escalante Valley extended for a couple miles south of town and it was in this southerly extension that Roper had his hundred-acre irrigation farm. Here he raised alfalfa to supplement the often sparse forage of his winter range. Almost every winter he trucked bales of hay to Soda Springs and when Brisco closed his allotments, this is where he had brought those few cows he had not auctioned or been impounded. This was his future.

"Sorry, I had to cancel out on you the other day," Burgoyne said as he watched the countryside go by. "I had another emergency. Max Yeager had a colicky horse."

"Seems to happen a lot this time of year," Roper said.

"Yeah," Burgoyne agreed. "They don't drink enough water in the winter."

"Well, with this inspection there is no rush."

While Burgoyne ambled over to inspect the small herd, grousing in the snow on the far side of the field, Roper got out of the truck, leaned against the cab and watched. It was a clear cold day with about an inch of snow on the ground and the air had a hint of smoke from wood-burning stoves. Trapped and compressed by an atmospheric high pressure, this mass of cold Arctic air had camped over southern Utah for over a week. Shifting his gaze, Roper looked across the valley to the west and the snow-blanketed mountains. The sharp contrast created by interfacing arctic-white mountains with a topaz blue sky was stunning. Roper had never seen the sky look quite so brilliant and the cold slanted winter light made imbedded snow crystals dance like rhinestones.

Suddenly, a dark object appeared on the otherwise unblemished sky, coming from the southwest. From this distance there was no noise and it was impossible for Roper to tell exactly what it was. Whatever it was, it was flying approximately two hundred feet off the ground and appeared to be coming right off the Kaiparowits Plateau.

As it moved closer, there was a faint rhythmic whoosh, then it became progressively louder. It was a large helicopter, probably the same kind used by the BLM to transport his cows from Fifty Mile Mountain and by the way the engine was laboring, it was probably carrying a heavy load.

As the craft drew nearer, Roper could see something dangling in a large cargo net. There was no way the BLM could still be rounding up trespass cows this time of year, Roper thought, shaking his head. On the Fifty, the snow was possibly a foot deep, driving the cows off the west side rim into the deep narrow canyons and making it almost impossible to work cows, even from the air.

The chopper's flight path took it over the west end of the valley, just far enough away that Roper couldn't tell for sure what it was transporting. Continuing in a northerly direction, it flew over the airport, then at the last minute veered east and landed about a mile away in a vacant field at the edge of town.

What happened next was surprising. The helicopter immediately lifted off again, then hovered several feet above the valley floor as a flatbed truck came to a stop directly under it.

After a few moments, the helicopter flew south back toward the Kaiparowits and the truck angled north into town. To Roper's thinking, it was a little strange they would go to all this trouble just to transport one cow.

By the time the helicopter was out to a speck on the southern horizon, Burgoyne was plodding through the snow and back to the truck. Slightly out of breath, he leaned back on the pickup cab, next to Roper, sucking air. Taking off his red Kanab High School football cap, he scratched his tousled brown head, leaned back against the cab next to Roper and groaned, "God, I never dreamed I would ever get this out of shape."

"You could still take a few snaps," Roper smiled.

"Thanks," Burgoyne wheezed, "but my football days are long over."

"What do you think, Brian?" Roper asked, still staring out over the valley, the snow crystals flickering in the bright winter sun like dancing polar fireflies.

"They look okay," Burgoyne replied, also following his gaze out and over the valley. "Damn, it's pretty out here. Beats watching football and listening to the wife bitch."

"You know what Brisco said in the newspaper?" Roper asked.

"Yeah, basically."

"To quote her specifically," Roper continued, "she stated she had never seen cattle in such emaciated shape, nothing but skin and bones."

"Well, Roper," Burgoyne shrugged, "they ain't fat."

"No, but they're not skin and bones either."

"Yeah, I agree," Burgoyne replied, replacing his ball cap. "They're no worse than most every other rancher's cows in the area."

"What can you write up for me and still feel good about it?"

"Honestly, I can say these cows have not been mistreated or starved."

"Sounds like condemnation by faint praise."

"Not at all," Burgoyne replied. "You know as well as me, cattle from these arid regions, tend to be less heavy than those from mountain permits. Yours are in no worse shape than any of the others I've checked lately."

"And all livestock drop weight in the winter," Roper added.

"Like I said, they ain't been starved or mistreated."

"That'll be fine," Roper said.

"Sure is pretty out there," Burgoyne commented, after a moment, "like a dusting of diamonds."

"Yeah," Roper said, following his gaze. "I didn't know you were a poet."

"Well, hell." Burgoyne slapped his thighs and stood up. "Guess, I'd better get going, if I want to stay a married man."

"Do you?"

"Depends on the day," Burgoyne said smiling and climbing into the cab. "You ever going to try it?"

"Not from the looks of things." Roper shrugged, trying to keep despair out of his voice.

"Well, it might be just as well," Burgoyne sighed.

When Roper let Burgoyne off at the Shell Station, he noticed that Sandy Parker was still loitering about inside the store. Alerted by the clanging of Roper's diesel engine, Sandy looked up from the magazine he was reading. Quickly stuffing the magazine in the same brown paper bag that contained his six-pack, he limped from the convenience store.

"You ready to talk now?" Sandy asked, grinning at Roper through the truck window.

"Hop in," Roper said. "It's too cold to talk outside."

Hobbling around to the passenger's side, Sandy climbed in. Shifting the transmission to park, Roper left the engine idling, the heat on and settled back into the seat.

"You want a beer?" Sandy asked, tearing into the sack and popping the tab on a can.

"Nah," Roper replied, sizing up Sandy. Other than looking unkempt, he had a pleasant enough face and an engaging smile. A smattering of freckles were scattered on his face and he appeared to be thirtyish. At first glance, he looked honest enough, but these days you could never tell.

"You don't mind if I do?" Sandy asked rhetorically. Not waiting for an answer, he took a big gulp, then smacked his lips. "Not as good as Lone Star but then again, this ain't Texas."

"I noticed you're limping," Roper said, eyeing Sandy.

"Rodeo accident. A mean bronc called Sugar," Sandy said, grinning. "Anyway, I've been meanin' to ask if this brand new Grand Staircase is wheelchair accessible?"

Roper gave Sandy a sharp second glance. "You're not serious?"

"Nah, I'm just funnin' you." Sandy's grin was infectious.

"So, Sandy," Roper began where he'd left off earlier. "If you're a relative of Ruby's, how is it you don't know where she lives?"

"It's kind of a long story," Sandy replied.

"It's not even noon yet," Roper said, looking at his watch. "I've got all day."

Sandy was silent for a moment. Finally he muttered, "might just as well tell you the whole thing."

"Might just as well," Roper agreed.

"It all started about ten years ago in Salado—that's Texas, right on the edge of the hill country and just north of Austin. Chet Parker, my brother, and Ruby, Nez is her maiden name, went and got themselves hitched. Shortly after the weddin' Ruby's daddy up and gets hisself murdered. As you might imagine, Salado being a small town and all, it caused a big commotion and rumors were flying like doublewide trailers in a tornado. Some were sayin', Ruby killed him—payback for years of sexual abuse as a child, but nobody could prove nothing." Sandy stopped long enough to take another swig of beer.

"Do you mind if I ask questions as we go along?"

"Fire away."

"You say Ruby's father was murdered. How did he die?"

"Gunshot wound," Sandy replied.

"Where? What part of the body?"

"To the head."

Instantly, the color drained from Roper's face and he shivered, like he had just seen the Ouija Board's arrow move. "On second thought, maybe, I will have one," he whispered.

Sandy fished a beer out of the bag and handed it to Roper. "Anyways, as I was saying, they couldn't prove nothing, but with small towns being what they are, Chet and Ruby decided it was time to move on. Too much talk. Ruby's dad had left a small spread just outside of town, which they sold, then moved up here to Utah and bought this place in Escalante and the Fifty Mile Mudhole permit." Sandy paused for another swallow.

"Why did they choose here?" Roper asked, not sure he wanted to hear the rest of the story.

"I'm not for sure, but I suspect it's cause this place is so damn remote and nobody had heard of 'em here."

"So, why are you trying to find her now?"

"Hold onto your fishing pole, let me finish the rest of the story," Sandy said, his Adam's apple bobbing as he drained the rest of the can of Coors. "At first, they did fine here. The ranch started making a little money and with them still being newlyweds, the bloom hadn't faded from their blue bonnets yet. Then things began to change.

"Nobody, never said nothing, but I know'd Chet had a bit of a mean streak. I grow'd up with him. One time when I came up to visit, Ruby was pretty beat up. They both laughed it off to being bucked off'n a mean bronc, but I know'd it weren't so." Sandy paused and retrieved another beer for himself.

Roper took another swig. Enjoying the taste of beer must be a learned response. He was beginning to feel sick and hated the taste of beer.

"Anyhow," Sandy continued, "about a year later, Chet goes and gets hisself shot in a deer hunting accident. I'm broke up of course, but other than that, I don't think too much of it. As Chet's only remaining kin, I do my duty and come up for the funeral. Of course, I leave all the arrangements up to Ruby and she decides on a closed casket and a graveside service. Right before the mortuary opens, I go in alone to pay my final respects to my brother. Curiosity gets the best of me and I crack open the casket and take a peek. That's when my jaw hit the floor so hard I was afraid it would wake poor Chet up. After I picked up my teeth off'n the floor I take a closer look. The mortician did as good a job as he could, and you could barely see it, but there really was no mistakin' it," Sandy said, then looked over at Roper. "Give ya'all three guesses of what I saw and the first two don't count?"

18

ESCALANTE PETRIFIED FOREST

Looking like a flood-ravaged and thoroughly scavenged graveyard, half-buried ancient skeletons, now petrified, are littered about at odd angles. Years of erosion have partially exposed them in varying degrees of decomposition.

The decaying silica filled bodies, actually two-hundred-foot primeval conifers, were buried in the Morrison Formation about one hundred and fifty million years ago during the Jurassic Period. At that time, the Colorado Plateau was a wet warm swamp and located much closer to the equator. The massive trees were felled, then ripped away by ancient floods only to be later buried in that river's extensive sand bars. Over millions of years, ossification or petrifaction has occurred as plant cellulose has been slowly replaced by silica sand. Also, annual growth rings have been exchanged for colorful concentric mineralized bands. The red and yellow rings were formed from the iron compounds, probably supplied by local volcanoes and the deep purple layer from manganese.

As an ironic contrast, today this six-thousand-foot arid plateau is some three thousand miles from the equator and present day foliage consists of Utah's pygmy forest, less than ten-foot-high junipers and pinions.

Staring out the window, Roper was silent. He shivered again and rubbed his arms for warmth, but gave no answer.

"You'd never guess what I saw," Sandy repeated.

"What?" Roper finally asked, though he already knew the answer.

When Sandy answered, his voice had suddenly acquired a conspiratorial quality. "A bullet hole square in the center of the forehead!"

"Now for an answer to my question," Roper whispered, as he stared blankly out the windshield, focusing on nothing. "How is it you don't know where she lives? Sounds like you've been here several times."

"After Chet's death, Ruby sold the house in Kanab and moved. Maybe bad memories, maybe economics, who knows?" Sandy said, starting on his third can of Coors. "I just lost track of her, but I know she still has the ranch and still lives in the area."

"You say you have unfinished family business?" Roper asked, measuring his words. "What business?"

"There was a small piece of her father's farm that hadn't sold. Since I still lived in the area, I've been trying to sell it for them—uh—her," Sandy said without blinking. "It finally sold."

"So you want to find her to give her the money?" Roper asked, arching an eyebrow.

"That's about the size of it."

Roper glanced at him for a moment. Sandy looked away and took a swallow from the can. "I don't believe you," Roper declared after a moment. "And, I've got to go."

For emphasis, Roper took the gearshift out of park and started to back up. Sandy grabbed Roper's arm, thought better of it, then let go.

"You're not going to tell me where she lives?" A blast of cold air rushed in as he opened the door.

"Not unless I hear an explanation that makes a lot more sense than what you've just told me."

"You want another beer?" Sandy said as got back in and closed the door.

"No. And you can finish this one," Roper said, handing Sandy the mostly full can of Coors.

"Well," Sandy said, accepting the beer. "It seems the hunter who shot Chet had an attack of the conscience. A couple of months later, after he'd gone home to California, he type wrote an anonymous letter postmarked from Pomona to Ruby apologizing for what he'd done and claiming it was an accident. Indeed, it seemed he was truly sorry for all the grief he had caused, but unfortunately not sorry enough to turn hisself in. Ruby dutifully gave the letter to the Kane County Sheriff on the hope he might get fingerprints for evidence. But other than it came from Pomona, they could never trace it." Sandy paused long enough for a swallow of beer.

"When Kane County finally closed the case and ruled it an accidental homicide, they disbursed all the case evidence. Strange enough or maybe not, but Ruby declined when asked her if she wanted to come and get Chet's belongings, you know the clothes he was wearing, his hunting rifle, wallet with a few dollars and so on. So they contacted me. You can imagine my surprise when I collected his stuff and read the letter. Now I have custody of the letter."

"So?" Roper said, frowning.

"Well, this whole hunting accident thing has never set well with me," Sandy explained, "I mean a bullet hole dead center and all. So after a few years and science got better, I took this here so-called letter of conscience to Baylor Genetics Lab in Houston, just to see if they might be able to get a little DNA from the postage stamp. You know—saliva. I heard someplace they could do that."

"And?" Roper asked, his voice edgy.

"We lucked out. There was just a tiny bit of mitochondrial DNA."

After digesting this for a moment, Roper said. "That's all very interesting, but that still doesn't answer why you are here."

"Sure it does. Just think about it."

"Why don't you enlighten me?" Roper asked, though in the back of his mind he suspected he knew the answer.

"It's really quite simple," Sandy grinned. "I just need to get a sample of DNA from Ruby, blood, saliva, skin or even hair will do. See if it matches."

Roper's mind went running wildly, like water suddenly freed by a ruptured dam. Simultaneously, his brain bolted down several different roads, checking out the ramifications of a dozen different scenarios. What did it all mean? What would this do to Ruby? Was she really a murderer? Where should he go from here? What would this do to their relationship? At a time like this, he knew it was selfish to think about himself, but he also knew that he still loved her. Was Sandy lying? If so, why? Roper knew nothing of Sandy and had no way to corroborate his story. He had to admit, however, Sandy's story did make a certain amount of sense and it did explain his presence here.

Roper wondered where Ruby was right now. Suddenly, it became critical to know. One thing was for certain, there was no way he was going to let Sandy Parker get to her first.

Looking over, Roper studied Sandy carefully. He appeared calm, no fidgeting, no beads of perspiration, no telltale signs of lying.

Finally Sandy asked. "What is she to you anyway? You act like this is personal."

"Nothing, I guess," Roper answered. "Just don't want to see her get hurt."

"You can come with me if you want," Sandy offered.

"No," Roper hesitated for a moment, as though trying to make up his mind, "I've got things to do. She lives in a rented house over in the town of Boulder. Bright yellow and right on Main Street," he said, keeping a straight face. "You can't miss it."

"Where's Boulder?"

"Twenty-five miles east on Highway twelve," Roper said, pointing out the direction. "And you can leave those last two cans of beer with me."

With growing misgiving, Roper watched Sandy limp back over to his white Toyota pickup. As soon as he had disappeared down the road, Roper tossed the unopened beer in the garbage can and gunned the Dodge in the opposite direction toward Ruby's trailer.

For a full five minutes, he pounded on every door and window, front and back. No one stirred. Finally a suspicious neighbor came over to check on all the commotion. She recognized Roper and told him she'd talked to Ruby earlier that morning, invited her over for holiday dinner and drinks, but Ruby had seemed preoccupied. She'd thanked her for the invitation, but declined, saying she had pressing business on the Kaiparowits.

Back in the Dodge, Roper barreled west on state Highway 12 for Cannonville. At Cannonville, he turned south on Cottonwood Road, then east at Grosvenor's Arch. Not giving it a passing glance, he raced past the Arch and headed straight up the narrow road to the Gut. About halfway up, he started to slip on the snow-covered road and shifted the truck into four-wheel-drive. Luckily, someone had been up the road earlier, packing the snow and creating an easy track to follow.

As he approached a blind S-curve, Roper noticed a green BLM pickup pulled off to the side of the track. Barely squeezing past the truck, he proceeded around the hairpin, then quickly slammed on his brakes, sliding a few feet to the left and stopping just inches from a sheer drop-off.

Looming right in front of him and coming his way was a red and white ambulance. Oddly, there were no sirens blaring or flashing red lights.

Jamming the gearshift in reverse, Roper slowly backed around the curve and squeezed off to the side of the road right in front of the BLM truck. Not appearing in much of a hurry, the ambulance lumbered by, then continued down the precipitous grade in first gear. How the hell did they get that vehicle up here anyway, Roper wondered. Fascinated, he watched till it was out of sight, then again put his pickup in gear and started around the bend. Once again, he had to slam on the brakes and back up, this time to let another BLM vehicle pass.

When the second pickup came abreast, the driver stopped and the passenger-side window slowly rolled down. Sitting there in the pickup on New Year's Day was none other than Monty Coleman and Judith Brisco. As Roper lowered his window, he noted that Judith was sitting stiffly in the passenger's seat, looking drained and ashen. Leaning over from the driver's side, Monty did the talking.

"Where you headed, Roper?"

Instantly, Roper sensed something was very wrong. "I got a tip a small herd of my cows, ones you guys missed, had wandered off the Fifty onto the Kaiparowits. Probably due to the deep snow," Roper replied evenly. Inwardly, he smiled. He was getting better at this art of lying.

"Be unusual for them to be over this far," Monty said in his flat monotone.

"They've come this far before."

"Is that so?"

"What do you want?" Roper quipped, not having to fake the irritation. "As far as I know, I don't have to justify my comings and goings to you."

"You got a rifle with you?" Monty asked bluntly.

"My thirty/thirty." Roper nodded to the gun in the rear window rack.

"Been fired recently?"

"Probably not in two or three months," Roper answered, then added bitterly, "last time would've been when I shot a couple of my cows to avoid paying your trespass fees."

"May I see it? Pass the stock end in first."

Roper considered the request for a moment, then leaned back and snatched the gun from the rack, passing it butt end through both truck windows to Judith. Then, like she was handling a live snake, Brisco quickly shuffled it over to Monty. Pulling back on pump action, Monty ejected a bullet from the chamber. Then carefully rotating the gun, he put the barrel to his nose and sniffed, looking a lot like Roper's Catahoula hound Moses. Apparently satisfied, he passed the gun back to Roper.

"Okay?" Roper asked.

"I could cite you for carrying a loaded gun," Monty replied tersely.

"What's going on here anyway?" Roper asked. "You two being out on a holiday, and the ambulance and all."

"Ronnie—Ron Sparks is dead," Judith blurted out, wiping moisture from her eyes.

"How?" Roper exclaimed.

"Gunshot wound to the head," Monty answered reluctantly, giving Judith an irritated glance.

"Accident?" Roper whispered, suddenly feeling cold.

"Right dead center," Monty replied. "What do you think?"

After a few moments of edgy silence, Roper replaced his rifle back on the gun rack, then turned to Judith and Monty.

"Though we've had our professional differences, I was fond of Sparky. He was a good man."

"Have you seen Ruby Nez today?" Monty asked bluntly.

"Why do you ask?" Roper put the truck in gear, starting to inch forward.

"If you know where she is, you'd best say," Monty shouted above the engine noise.

"I have no idea."

"Where you going?"

"On the Kaiparowits to look for lost animals," Roper shouted back, then under his breath, he added, "and lost people too."

"Be careful. It's a tight squeeze getting past Ron's vehicle," Judith shouted.

On the third attempt, Roper did finally round the S-curve and pass Ron's pick up. He continued up the Gut Road and eventually onto the Kaiparowits Plateau. Even on top, away from the activity associated with Sparky's death, a single set of tire tracks continued on. Leaving three inch-deep imprints in the snow, they were easy to follow, like a skier's path in fresh powder. At the junction to Ruby Flats, the tracks turned from the main road, continuing south toward the parking area of the University of Utah's paleontology dig.

Dappled in new snow, with an occasionally clump cascading to the ground, the pygmy forest was dressed in bridal white and bathed in variegated light. It was a stunning sight, but Roper barely noticed.

Sparky dead! And shot precisely in the center of the forehead. Not only was this not accidental, but there appeared to be an emerging *modus operandi*. How many did this make? Shot in this particular fashion. Mentally, Roper began to count. There was Angus Macdonald and now Ron Sparks, but if you went back far enough there was also Ruby's father and her husband Chet. Four in all. Slow down, Roper told himself. Before jumping to conclusions, there were at least two pertinent questions that needed answering. Did Ruby have motive and did she have opportunity?

With her father, her husband, Chet, and Angus Macdonald, the motive would appear to be retribution for some form of sexual or physical abuse or both, but with Sparky, this theory wouldn't hold up. What possible motive could she have for killing Sparky? Perhaps, payback for closing her Mudhole allotment, impounding her cows and destroying her livelihood. That would be enough to enrage almost anyone. And maybe, after a couple of killings, a person could come to believe that murder was a good way to settle most any problem. Undoubtedly, as with almost everything else, with repetition it probably got easier.

How about opportunity? There again, with her father and her husband, opportunity was a given. When Angus was murdered, it had been during the wild cow hunt and there was no doubt Ruby had been on the mountain. After all, it had been her hunt. Finally with Sparky, it was hard to say. Roper didn't know for sure where Ruby was, but he had a hunch she was here on the Kaiparowits. Earlier, a neighbor had suggested that and Roper suspected these tire tracks he was following were hers. So, at least on the surface, it did not look good. One could argue she had both motive and opportunity for all four.

But Ruby Nez, a serial killer! Yes, with four murders, "serial" was an appropriate adjective. However, with Ruby, there was simply no way. Roper had always considered himself a pretty good judge of character and Ruby did not fit the mold, not that he knew all that many killers. Sure, she was tough as reinforced concrete and an excellent marksman, and he could see her being able to kill in self-defense, but cold-blooded, premeditated murder? No way.

Someone, however, was a murderer. There were four bodies to prove it. And even more disconcerting, there was no reason to expect that these would be the last. If the killer was not Ruby, it still had to be someone who was familiar with the area and knew these people. Maybe—probably, even someone Roper knew. Swallowing hard, Roper beat back a growing sense of paranoia, trading it for a sense of urgency. He'd better find out who the murderer was and damn fast.

As he pulled into the relatively flat, but ungraded expanse that served as a parking lot, soupy fog, like a ghostly invader, started bleeding into the area. Through gossamer wisps of shifting clouds, Roper noted without surprise that Ruby's Ford pickup was parked at the far end of the lot, right next to the trailhead leading to the dig. Damn it! She was here.

Dropping to a knee, he examined the petite boot prints stamped in the snow. There was no question where they were headed. Grabbing his 30/30, Roper started down the trail. The going was difficult. Trudging in four inches of new snow and in places two-foot high drifts, not only was the going slow, it was tiring. Silently, Roper wished he had remembered to bring his snowshoes. Seldom used, they were still hanging in his closet.

After about thirty minutes of floundering, Roper arrived at the dig site. Fifty yards straight ahead through the fog was the arroyo and on the far bank, though he couldn't see it, was the partially excavated dinosaur. In the snow and fog things looked different, but there was something else. Something had changed. It took Roper a moment to become aware of it, but on this side of the arroyo there was a complete absence of trees. A roughly sixty-foot circular area had been chain sawed in the pygmy forest. The felled junipers and pinions had been randomly heaped at the periphery of the circle. Inside the enclosure the snow was dirty and tracked with hundreds of boot prints. With so many prints, it was obvious that more than one person had to have been here, but who? And why? The when was easy. It had started snowing last night, so it would've had to have been some time today.

Barely visible in the broken fog was the far side of the arroyo and the dig site. Nothing looked the same as last September. Gone were cordoning ropes and colorful marking flags. Scattered in the new snow were large boulders, looking more like downy pillows on a white satin bed. There was, however, a well-tramped path that led from this bizarre circle, across the arroyo and directly to the dig.

Puzzled, Roper started down the broken path across the arroyo toward the dig. He'd better hurry, he thought glancing up at the sky, with the veiled sun sinking toward the western horizon and the fog still rolling in, visibility was getting worse by the minute. Even now, Roper thought, I might have trouble finding my way back.

Ka—boom! A shot rang out spraying a puff of snow up in front of him.

Roper dropped to the ground. Slowly he exhaled and tried to think. No question about it, that shot had been fired from the far bank, right where he was headed. Holding perfectly still with his 30/30 by his side, he waited for another shot, but all he heard was the pounding of his heart and his own strident breathing. Consciously, he slowed his breathing and fought through the rush of adrenalin, slowly regaining control of his faculties.

"Ruby!" he shouted hoarsely, trying to keep his voice steady.

"That you, Roper?" Ruby shouted back, her words distant and dampened by the fog.

"Don't shoot. I'm coming over."

Getting up, he trudged down the snow-covered bank and up the other side. As he approached, Ruby stepped out from behind a large fluffy boulder. She was wearing a light tan leather coat with fleece lining, her black hair was bound up in a white skier's cap and her jeans were a worn sandy-pecan brown. And as usual, in spite of her usual mishmash clothing, she was beautiful.

"What you doing here, Roper?"

"It's nice to see you too," Roper answered with a trace of sarcasm.

Ruby was silent for a moment. "I'm sorry, Doug," she finally said. "It's been a little crazy lately."

"You can say that again," Roper said, thinking she probably didn't know the half of it. She must have come up here before Sparky was murdered and Sandy Parker arrived.

"I guess, I'm a little surprised to see you, is all," she said.

"How long you been up here?" Roper asked.

"Since about noon."

"You see anybody on the way up?"

"Passed Sparky over on Ruby Flats."

"Was he okay?"

"Don't know. I guess," Ruby replied, her eyes narrowing. "He was going pretty fast, didn't stop to talk. Why?"

"You have any idea why he was in such a hurry?"

"Yeah, I have a pretty good idea—now," Ruby said, placing her hands on her hips and glaring at Roper, "but I'm not answering any more questions, till I know why I'm getting the third degree."

Roper considered this for a moment. What the hell, she'll find out sooner or later anyhow and sometimes you can learn a lot by the way people react to bad news. "Sparky was shot an hour or so ago," he said, watching her closely.

"Dead?"

"Yeah. Murdered."

"Oh, sweet Jesus," Ruby said softly, making the sign of the cross.

Nothing there to hint she might have been involved, Roper thought. For the moment he decided not to mention Sandy Parker. Give it some more time and see how things played out.

"And you think I had something to do with that?" Ruby demanded, her dark eyes fiery.

"Not really. It's just that I was surprised to find you up here."

"How did you find me?"

"Your next door neighbor told me."

She studied Roper for a minute. "Might just as well tell you the whole thing."

"Might just as well."

"Well about ten o'clock this morning, after I told Joann Cripps no to dinner, I was driving south on Smoky Mountain Road wondering if some of my cows that'd escaped the helicopter round up had found their way down off the Fifty to my winter range," Ruby said, quickly adding, "You know I can drive into the Rodgers Canyon area."

Roper nodded.

"Anyway, I was about to Collet Top when I heard this helicopter thundering up the Kaiparowits from the south. I'm a thinking the BLM has really lost it, trying to round up cows this time of year, but nevertheless I keep my eye on it. It passes right over me, then heads over toward Dog Flats or Ruby Flats, right in the heart of the Kaiparowits. Now, I'm really curious, so I turn my truck around and head back to Alvey Wash, then take the Little Valley Road over to Dog Flats and on to Ruby Flats. When, I get to Ruby Flats, I can hear people shouting and the helicopter blades a beatin', so I park my truck and walk through the snow over here." Ruby paused for a moment to see if Roper was keeping up.

"I'm following you so far."

"Just as I get here, the helicopter takes off again. Suspended from it is a huge cargo net and it looks like they are hauling something heavy, but I can't quite make out what. After they've gone, I go snoop around a bit. Whatever it was they took, it seems they took it from right here," Ruby said, pointing at an big empty hole in the bank.

Confused, Roper walked over to the roughly thirty-foot hole and looked down. Gone was Professor Albright's yet to be named Theropod! All of it. All two tons of fossilized rock had simply disappeared. Speechless, Roper sank softly down onto a pillowed-rock and stared blankly at the bare hole. What a loss! There was simply no way to replace something like that. It was priceless. This was one of those rare instances where insurance money was meaningless. Science, specifically paleontology, Professor Albright and the whole human race were the collective losers.

Ruby walked over and put her hand on his shoulder. After a moment,

Roper sighed and pulled himself up off the rock and explained to Ruby about the dig, Professor Albright and the dinosaur.

"What a loss," Ruby agreed, shaking her head.

"Irreplaceable."

"Who do you think took it?"

"I don't know," Roper answered, "but I have an idea that's why Sparky was going so fast when you saw him."

"You think this could be related to Sparky's death?"

"Two major crimes committed on the same day not five miles apart, that's a heck-of-a-lot of circumstance," Roper said. "Especially for an area that averages about one felony every ten years."

"Been much higher this last year."

"That's exactly why I think this recent rash of felonies, murder and arson, are related."

"Certainly makes you wonder," Ruby agreed.

Roper looked up. On the western horizon, the smudge of sun was just setting. Weakly, it beamed through the fog like light from a lighthouse.

"We'd better go," Roper said. "It'll be dark soon."

With Roper leading the way, they headed down the bank of the arroyo to the snow-covered sandy bottom. As they started up the other side, a spotlight suddenly singled them out, harsh and blinding.

"That's far enough!" a voice barked.

"What do you want?" Roper shouted at the light.

"Put those rifles down, then get your hands up and come on up here."

Roper recognized their captors. In the ruddy glow of reflected light their faces appeared gilded, almost ghoulish. It was Monty Coleman, Sheriff Jackson and Deputy Ainsley.

"Ivory!" Roper yelled, turning to face the sheriff. "This is totally uncalled for."

"Don't think so," Jackson said from directly behind Roper. "Not this time."

"Put down the guns, turn the lights out of our eyes and let's talk," Roper said.

No response.

"Are you going to shoot us or arrest us?" Ruby asked staring at the sheriff.

"Not quite sure yet," Monty said in monotone without smiling. "After what you did to Sparky, I could go either way."

"We had nothing to do with that," Ruby replied, her voice not as confident.

"Ainsley, go get them rifles," Jackson ordered, ignoring Ruby. "See if either one of 'em's been fired recently."

"Well," Ruby stammered. "I fired mine just a little bit ago at Roper—by accident."

"Uh, huh," Coleman said.

"We heard from your friend, Sandy, earlier today," the sheriff then said matter-of-factly. "He had some mighty interestin' things to say."

"Who?" Ruby asked, frowning.

"That would be Mr. Sandy Parker, your brother-in-law," Jackson replied scornfully.

"Those are all lies," Ruby said as the color drained from her face.

"Don't matter none," Monty Coleman said, "we got other evidence. Mrs. Sparks knew Ron was coming out here to see you. At first she thought Sparky had said he was going to Ruby Flats, but when she thought about it, she was sure he said he was going to see Ruby Nez."

"Oh, come on, Monty," Roper interrupted, "anyway you slice it, that's pretty thin."

"We haven't even got started yet," Jackson said, rotating the toothpick with his tongue. "There's Angus Macdonald and your conveniently deceased husband, Chet Parker."

Just then, Deputy Ainsley rejoined the group. "This'n been fired recently," Ainsley reported to Jackson.

"Whose gun is this?" the sheriff asked holding the bolt-action Winchester high.

"Mine," Ruby replied, her voice defiant.

"This is plain ridiculous," Roper said.

"Ruby Nez," Jackson interrupted, using his formal voice. "I'm arresting you for the murder of Ron Sparks."

19

ESCALANTE CANYONS

Looming directly to the north, the eleven-thousand foot, volcanic Boulder Mountain provides ample watershed for the Escalante River. Immediately on exiting the Escalante Valley, the river enters its own slickrock canyon which incarcerates it for some eighty miles as it snakes through the desert and eventually into the Escalante Arm of Lake Powell.

On its way the river is joined by some notable tributaries, Death Hollow Creek, Sand Creek, Calf Creek, Boulder Creek, Harris Wash, Silver Falls Creek, Moody Creek, Coyote Gulch, Twenty-five Mile Wash and many others. Each branch proudly arrives with its own deeply carved sandstone gulch, creating a literal maze of red rock canyons.

Even some one hundred and fifty million years ago, this area was still a desert. Howling winds deposited towering dunes of red/white course sand which over the eons solidified into what we now call Navajo sandstone. Resembling the venous structure of a leaf, the Escalante River and its tributaries have chiseled a literal labyrinth of spectacular red ribboned canyons through these ancient ossified dunes, the intricacy and beauty of which is unparalleled.

What started out as a promising drought-buster winter had now fizzled. The weather had moderated back to the warm and dry pattern so characteristic of the last six years. Daytime temperatures soared into the low sixties and nighttime hovered above freezing. Within days, the snow had vanished from Fifty Mile Mountain and the Kaiparowits Plateau. Farmers cast furtive glances at the barren sky and in church they prayed and tithed, hoping to coax a recalcitrant God to send rain. Night after night, Navajos also joined in the supplications with their traditional rain dance ceremony. Neither offering, Christian or Native American, seemed to appease this intractable God. Confounding the faithful, he continued to withhold aqueous favors. Cynical Mormons quipped, if this was how God treated his chosen people, perhaps they would be better off being a little less favored. Mere disciples of meteorology, however, explained the phenomena as a monster high pressure that had drifted in from the coast of California, camping directly over southern Utah and diverting the jet stream with its attendant storms far to the north.

Meanwhile, Roper continued to feed his winter supply of alfalfa hay to what cattle he had left. He'd saved a few of his best young heifers and one prize bull with the idea that he would start another herd when times got better. Realistically, that did not appear to be anytime soon.

Without her permission, he'd quietly rounded up Ruby's cattle, the previously impounded ones that ranchers had been hiding, and mixed them in with his herd in the Escalante fields. Recounting his bales, Roper figured he probably would not have enough hay to make it to April, let alone till late June when his next crop of alfalfa would be ready. When he ran out of hay, he'd privately decided he would sell his cows at auction, but not Ruby's.

As promised, Dr. Brian Burgoyne had sent him a certificate of health. He'd immediately gone to the library and fired off faxes to Judith Brisco, the Utah congressional delegation and almost every newspaper in the state. Several papers had printed the letter with an accompanying editorial note and one, for comparison, had even re-printed that portion of Brisco's original interview claiming his cows were in the worst shape she'd ever seen. It was glaringly obvious that Brisco's appraisal of his cows' health did not mesh with Burgoyne's. As an eye-catching headline, the Salt Lake newspaper had boldly asked, *WHO'S LYING?* Even the county weekly had included a copy of the letter and a companion editorial blasting the BLM for its war of rhetoric and Gestapo tactics. In retrospect, however, Roper was not really sure how much good it did, other than perhaps pull him a little further ahead in the fight for public opinion. And that, he had to admit, did make him feel better. At least his fellow cattlemen and the citizens of southern Utah would not think he'd been callously starving his animals.

On both the television and in the newspapers, U.S. Attorney, Elliot

Mauss, had continually attacked, harangued and otherwise threatened retribution to the midnight cowboys if they did not return the impounded cows. Specifically he had threatened a ten thousand dollar fine and/or two years in jail. So far, other than a lot of bluff and bluster, and the transparent attempt at intimidation, nothing else had been done. Roper could only assume that meant Mauss was really not that sure of his case. If he were, there would have been multiple arrests by now.

Also, Roper had not paid his trespass fee. He figured it was somewhere in the excess of twenty thousand dollars but as of today, he still had not been presented with an accurate accounting from the BLM and he was not sure how to figure in the remaining feral cows. So far, however, the BLM had sent no bill and had made no attempts, legal or otherwise, to collect any money.

Surprisingly, Roper had been visited by all of Utah's congressional delegation. Certainly, it was not because of his political clout or his propensity to make large contributions to political war chests. Roper suspected it was all the media coverage and a chance for photo-ops. Without question, the media had seized on the story with all the zeal of a social crusader.

Other than publicly expressed sympathy, however, the Utah republican delegation seemed powerless to do anything else. With a democratic administration in Washington, loyal democrats chairing every congressional committee and democrats heading every federal agency, their hands were pretty much tied. If the republicans were to gain power in the upcoming national elections, a lot could change and fast.

Also, the Utah State law suit challenging the creation of the monument was going badly and would surely fail. Roper still had mixed feelings. He realized some kind of protection was needed for this unique land, but certainly not at the expense of the ranchers. But regardless of his personal feelings, it looked as though the monument was here to stay, no point in rehashing the past. What was not clear, however, was his long-term personal status. Once the drought was over and the range had recovered, would he get his allotments back?

It had been over two weeks since her arrest, but Ruby was still in jail. Considering the seriousness of the charges and that she had no family in the area, the judge had agreed she might be a flight risk and though he had ruled for bail, he had posted it at one million dollars. Obviously, Ruby didn't have that kind of money.

The one thing that mystified Roper about the arrest was how Sheriff Jackson, Deputy Ainsley and Monty Coleman had all gotten to the paleontology dig so fast. After all, just an hour or so before the arrest Roper had seen Monty and Judith heading down the Gut road. Through the grapevine, Roper had eventually learned the details. When Sandy Parker had arrived at Boulder and realized that Roper had sent him on a snipe hunt, he had gone immediately to the sheriff. Right as he was sitting in Sheriff Jackson's office, Monty, with unprecedented cooperation, had radioed in from the Gut, reporting the murder of Ron Sparks. With that information, plus the details provided by Sandy, Jackson and Coleman had quickly concluded it was Ruby Nez they were after. While Judith had gone on into the main office to co-ordinate things there, Monty waited at the bottom of the Gut road, ostensibly to block any attempt at escape until the Sheriff and Ainsley could get there from Kanab. Together then, as a three-man posse, they went looking for Ruby. The search had not been difficult. They had simply followed the tracks in the snow.

Roper did not think Monty and Ivory realized the significance of what had been taken from the dig. To them it was just ancillary information and probably not pertinent to the case. A separate crime altogether. They had focused on Sandy's theory of the crime and in their minds they had already established method, motivation and opportunity. All that was needed for an airtight case was a little corroborating physical evidence and that was in the works. Along with Sandy's postage-stamp DNA, they had sent a sample of Ruby's court-ordered blood to the genetics lab. It was only a matter of time till the lab confirmed what law enforcement already knew. Ruby Nez was a serial killer.

Presently, their circumstantial evidence was based mainly on opportunity and that she was in some way related to or knew all the victims. Also, they had three other bits of evidence. One, Mrs. Ron Sparks' testimony that on the day of the murder, Sparky had indicated he was going to meet Ruby; two, her 30/30 had recently been fired, though as of yet, a bullet had not been found for ballistics; three, Sandy Parker's oral testimony for whatever that was worth. Though there was no hard physical evidence, no eyewitnesses, no fingerprints, no bullets or casings, rumor had it County Attorney Chick Dunning had boasted he had enough circumstantial evidence to sink the Titanic. Probably didn't realize it had already been sunk, Roper thought bitterly.

From time to time, the sheriff and Monty Coleman had let Roper know he was still a prime suspect, mainly due to his relationship with Ruby. Also they figured he had just as much cause to hate Sparky as Ruby and certainly that kind of hate could lead to murder. In addition, they hadn't ruled out Roper in the Angus Macdonald case. They had openly theorized that he may have killed Macdonald out of jealousy or to protect Ruby. They weren't quite sure which, but it was just a matter of time until they brought him to justice.

On the few times he had attempted to see Ruby, she had either refused or had been cold and uncommunicative. She had refused to give him, or anyone else, her side of the story, stating if he had to ask, that in and of itself spoke volumes. It was all a matter of trust, she had said. When Roper had asked about Sandy Parker, she just snorted, "he's either after sex or money." On those days Roper would leave the jail frustrated, desperate and with a growing sense of hopelessness.

In his mind, Roper had gone over the whole scenario dozens of times. Nothing raised a red flag. Nothing that he could think of needed further investigation. Nothing, other than perhaps the theft at the paleontology dig. Somehow it had to be related. The fact that Ruby had seen Sparky racing away from the site indicated, at least to Roper's way of thinking, that Ron knew about the theft and was probably going for help. From there, it was not much of a leap of logic to assume that was the reason he was murdered. The fossil thieves were trying to stop him. There were other explanations, of course, but none that made much sense to Roper. As the vet Burgoyne had once told Roper when they were puzzling over a sick cow, never look for two separate diagnoses when one will do.

Looking back on New Year's Day, it was strange about that helicopter he had seen while he and Burgoyne were out inspecting cattle. Now he suspected it had been carrying Professor Albright's prize Theropod. A wholly intact dinosaur must be worth a fortune. Add to that a newly discovered yet unnamed species and one could almost name their price. A black market value of well over a million dollars would not out of the question. Maybe more. Certainly, murders had been committed for a lot less.

Mentally, Roper had compiled a short list of potential suspects, but none of them fit the existing evidence very well. For starters, he had always been suspicious of Monty Coleman. Indeed he had shown his cards early. He was no friend of the ranchers and by the looks of him, he knew how to kill. Monty killing Angus Macdonald had a certain perverse logic, getting rid of mining on the Kaiparowits, but try as he might, Roper could not come up with a good reason why he would want to kill Ron Sparks. Of course there might have been internal or personal conflicts of which he did not know.

Then there was that creepy environmental terrorist, Sean O'Grady. Again, he could understand that he might have a motive to kill Angus. Their group despised prospecting and mining and Angus had earlier taken a shot at him. However, Roper had trouble linking O'Grady to Sparky. No reason at all for him to kill Ron. They were on the same side. But then again, there may be personal grudges of which he was not aware. Certainly, Sean had been very vocal about any kind of development of the monument. Sparky, on the other hand, was in favor of limited improvements and closely regulated facility construction. In the past, any advisory committee discussions about turning the monument into another Yosemite had always sent Sean into a rage.

Also, there was Sandy Parker. He just seemed like a con man. But being an apparent flimflam man did not make him a murderer and Roper could not come up with a plausible reason for him to want to kill Sparky or Angus.

And that was about it. Roper had to admit that at least on the surface, Sheriff Jackson and Monty's version of events, those implicating Ruby, made a hell-uv-a-lot more sense than any theory he'd come up with.

Several times, Roper had been back to the paleontology site, but had not uncovered any new evidence. To say it had been discouraging was an understatement.

And again today, Roper was back at the site. With the warmer weather, the snow was all gone and in its place, a pasty wet mud. Without the snow, the chain-sawed circle seemed much more evident. It was an ugly sore that was as apparent as a melanoma on unblemished skin. In the bright sunlight, it was perfectly obvious that right there on the west bank of the arroyo, someone had brazenly chain-sawed a helo-pad.

Shaking his head in disgust, Roper walked across the arroyo to the east bank and the open empty pit that once was the burial place of the ancient Theropod. He looked down at the sticky brown mud. Undeterred, he climbed into the pit and began raking the muck with a forked stick. Starting on the north edge, he systematically worked south. Periodically, he would stop, pick up and inspect anything that might be of significance.

Suddenly the silence was broken.

"You find anything?"

Startled, Roper whirled around, holding his stick like a weapon. With tousled red hair blazing in the winter's beveled sun, Sean O'Grady smiled down at Roper.

"Hold on, cowboy," he said, propping his 30/30 against a gray boulder. "I come in peace."

Roper eyed Sean suspiciously for a moment then lowered his stick. "Thought you tree-huggers didn't believe in guns."

"No," Sean replied. "We don't believe in killing defenseless animals."

"How about humans?"

"Damn shame," Sean said, nodding at the empty hole and ignoring Roper.

"Unbelievable," Roper replied, "and in broad daylight."

"They got away with a fortune."

"I can only imagine."

"Probably more than a million dollars."

"But that's hardly the point," Roper added, "is it?"

"I agree. But how long would it take you to make that kind of money in the cow business?" .

"I'm out of the cow business. Have you seen Lanny?" Roper asked, changing the subject.

"Talked to him yesterday," Sean replied. "He's devastated."

"His life's work, gone in a single afternoon."

"He's a real fighter," Sean said, grabbing Roper's stick. "He'll be back."

"You have any idea who did it?" Roper asked.

"Nah, but I suspect it's the same ones that's took fossils before," Sean replied, pushing the mud into a pile with his boot, then forking through it with the stick. "I know of at least three other sites that have been robbed in the last couple of years."

"This what they usually do? Wait for someone else to dig it up, then sneak in and steal it?" Roper asked, climbing out of the pit.

"No, this is a bit different," Sean explained, raising an eyebrow. "They usually do their own digging, somewhere remote and out of sight."

"That pretty much describes the whole Kaiparowits."

"Yeah, that's why they're so hard to catch."

"You think they'll strike again?" Roper asked.

"No doubt about it," Sean said, giving up with the stick. "I'd bet ten dollars, they've got another dig going right now."

Roper considered this for a moment. "I think it was the fossil robbers that killed Sparky."

"The fuzz don't think so," Sean said, glancing up at Roper. "From what I hear, they're this close," Sean held his thumb and index fingers approximately an inch apart, "to arresting you."

"You think I killed him?" Roper asked, his voice hardening like poured concrete.

"Do you think I did?" Sean asked, ignoring Roper's question.

They glared at each other for a moment.

"Certainly, I've considered you," Roper finally said, "but some things just don't fit."

"I've watched you shoot those wild cows on the Fifty and you're a pretty damn good shot," Sean said. "A dead center shot, so to speak. And if the BLM had done to me what they've done to you, I might just take revenge."

No reply was necessary. It was true, even with only four fingers, he was a good shot and everyone in the county, probably the entire state, knew he was furious with the BLM. Hell, if he were the sheriff, he would also make him a prime suspect.

"Any particular part of the Plateau that you would look?" Roper asked. "If you were going to look for new excavation."

Sean glanced upward, as though searching the sky for revelation. "You might consider Little Escalante Canyon. I've scouted that area before and it looks quite promising for fossils."

Roper took a moment to digest this information. "You mean the eastern part of Headquarters Valley just west of Death Ridge?"

"That's the place," Sean agreed. "Both Death Canyon and the Little Escalante are promising dig sites."

"You want to join forces," Roper asked, instantly wondering if that was a bad idea, "see if we can find them?"

"Maybe," Sean answered. "I was planning on finding them for Lanny anyway."

"Well then, we might just as well do it together."

"This don't mean I trust you," Sean said quietly.

"Nor I, you," Roper replied.

Both were silent for moment.

"How about tomorrow afternoon, say one o'clock?" Roper finally suggested.

Later that evening, Roper decided to visit Ruby again. At the jail he was guided to a small, ten by ten, conference room. A badly scarred oak table sat directly in the middle of the room with two equally mutilated wooden chairs. A bare light bulb hung from the ceiling like a resting pendulum. Other than that the room was totally empty.

Roper stood as Ruby came in. She was dressed in the standard-issue hunter-orange jumpsuit with KANE COUNTY PRISONER stenciled across the back. The outfit didn't do much for her appearance but then again, clothes never mattered to her anyway. Her raven black hair was loose and had that just-washed luster. Her face looked scrubbed and was devoid of makeup or lipstick. Even without the usual female accessories, to Roper she possessed a rare natural grace and beauty. And tonight she seemed a little less aloof.

"Hi, Ruby," he said. "You sure look nice."

"If they're going to keep me in here, they could at least find something in my size," Ruby replied as she tugged at the loose-fitting jumpsuit. Pulling out a chair, she sat down and forced a smile. "How have you been, Doug?"

"Good days and bad," Roper smiled back. "Mostly bad."

"Any news?"

"Well, I've almost got the money put together for your bail."

"How you going to swing that?" Ruby frowned.

"Well, I sold your mobile home, like you asked. Didn't get the twenty thousand you wanted though. Only got ten."

Ruby shrugged. "It wasn't worth twenty anyway. I was being optimistic. Where's the rest coming from?"

"Well, if I sell my fifty head of cows and your forty, that'd bring in another fifteen thousand or so."

"That's a total of twenty-five thousand dollars," Ruby said, quickly calculating. "That's still a far cry from a million."

"We only need ten percent, a hundred thousand, for a bail bondsman to cover the rest."

"Okay, then where do we get the other seventy-five thousand?"

"I've applied for a second mortgage on my house," Roper said. "It's paid for and there's at least sixty, maybe seventy thousand in equity."

"I don't want you to do that," Ruby said, her jaw set.

"Sorry, the wheels are already in motion," Roper replied. "Might even have the money by tomorrow."

"You'll lose your house. Now that we're shut down, you have no way to pay it back."

"There's ways. Don't you worry about it," Roper said.

"What ways?"

"No reason I couldn't go back to teaching."

"But you don't like doing that."

"It wasn't all that bad," Roper grinned, "when you consider what happened to us the last few months in the cattle business. In some ways, I kinda miss it."

"Yah, I'll bet. I flat don't like it."

"Cause you think it will make you indebted to me?" Roper asked. " I just want to help a friend. You'd do the same for me."

Ruby though for a moment, then sighed in resignation. "I do hate this place."

"Don't blame you," Roper said, looking around the stark conference room.

"You have any idea who shot Sparky?"

"Other than you?" Roper laughed, trying to lighten things up.

"Yeah," she smiled wryly, forcing a laugh, "other than me."

"Not really, but I think it had to be the same guys who took the dinosaur bones. Sparky must have seen them and that's why he was killed."

"Well then, I guess we're back to square zero."

"Not exactly," Roper said. "Sean O'Grady and I are going out on the Kaiparowits tomorrow. He thinks this type of theft has been going on for some time and they're still at it."

"Do you trust him?" Ruby asked, frowning.

"Not really, but he knows fossils and he does know the Kaiparowits."

"I suppose, but you know the rumors."

"Yeah," Roper admitted, "but there're rumors about everyone, including us."

"Remember, some rumors are true."

"And some are just good gossip."

"I just don't like it."

"I'll be careful." Roper shrugged.

"Don't turn your back on the little redheaded bastard," Ruby said, her face softening as she grasped Roper's hand.

"Don't worry," Roper replied as the deputy opened the conference room door, indicating time was up. "I won't."

Roper said goodbye, promised to visit again tomorrow and vowed to have her out on bail soon.

By the time he got home, it was late. Nothing much to eat in the refrigerator, so he microwaved a beef tips dinner, washed it down with a diet Seven-up. Thoroughly beat, he struggled out of his clothes and flopped on the queen bed.

Just as he was dozing off, slipping through the deep portals to REM sleep, the telephone rang. It sounded far away, somewhere off in the dark recesses of another cavern. It took him several attempts, groping in the dark, but he finally located the phone on his cluttered nightstand. Without lifting his head from the pillow, he cradled the receiver to his ear.

"Hello," he mumbled, still not quite conscious.

"Mr. Rehnquist?" the muffled voice asked.

"Yeah," Roper muttered.

"Mr. Rehnquist, I hear you might be interested in the goings on out on the Kaiparowits?" The voice sounded slightly garbled, like someone was speaking through a wet bath towel.

"We talking about cows?" Roper asked groggily.

"No. We're talking about digs, paleontology digs," the voice whispered.

"Yeah, I could be," Roper mumbled, instantly becoming more alert.

"Then I might have some information for you."

"Okay," Roper said cautiously. "May I ask who this is?"

"No, you may not," the muffled voice replied curtly.

"How do I know you're telling me the truth?"

"Take it or leave it. Makes no difference to me."

Roper hesitated for a moment. "Okay."

"The Burning Hills could be worth a look," the voice confided, "and maybe Tibbet Canyon."

"Tibbet Canyon?" Roper echoed, surprised. Those two places were in the exact the opposite direction Sean had recommended. "Are you sure?"

"This is not fifty questions," the voice barked. "Like I said, take it or leave it."

"You're talking about the southern part of the Plateau, down beyond Smoky Mountain and in the area of the old Andalex mine?"

"Yeah, down by the coal fires."

"Is there an active dig there now?"

"All I'm saying is, it might be worth a look."

"Thanks for the tip."

"And Mr. Rehnquist."

"Yes."

"You best be careful out there," the voice whispered. "You have no idea what you're getting yourself into."

20

ALVEY WASH

Early morning light illuminates the upper west wall, while the east wall and Alvey Wash itself are still obscured in a gray pre-dawn shroud. Spotlighted high up on the top sandstone layer, just under the volcanic ash hard cap, is a small eroded alcove that obviously has been walled off. Appearing almost inaccessible, the slanted rays reveal this wall is man made with chipped rocks and well mortared joints, the timeless masonry of an ancient Fremont granary.

Providing drainage for the upper Kaiparowits Plateau and Collet's Top of Fifty Mile Mountain, as Alvey Wash descends northward, it chisels deeply into beige-colored cretaceous sedimentary rock, creating an ever deepening gorge. Composed of several layers of fluvial sandstone and christened the Straight Cliffs Formation, the sand was deposited over a hundred million years ago. In the past, its sheer walls and high niches have provided ideal terrain for the ancient Fremont Indians, but this formation also contains abundant prehistoric fossils.

Dry, but when it rains, it quickly becomes impassable. The wash is sparsely vegetated with feathery tamarisks, silvery Russian olives and venerable cottonwood trees. On the slanting talus slopes, junipers and pinions are scattered among house-size boulders.

The next day while waiting for the real estate appraiser, Roper placed a call to Pete Goslin. What he wouldn't give to trade places with Pete, Roper thought idly as he punched in the number. With over a thousand acres of private ground as well as some Forest Service allotments on the Griffin Top, the closure of the monument leases had not affected

Pete that much. So far, the Forest Service had closed no allotments.

"Pete, this is Roper Rehnquist," he said after he'd waited a few seconds for Pete's daughter to fetch him to the phone.

"What can I do for you, Roper?" Pete asked, a trace of hostility in his voice.

"You've heard about Ruby being in jail?"

"Yes," Pete answered cautiously. "Everyone has."

"I want you to know, I think she's innocent," Roper said.

"I've always liked Ruby," Pete replied noncommittally.

"I'm trying to raise money for her bail."

The phone went tomb silent, only the slight crackle of static.

Quickly, Roper forged on, "Pete, I'm not asking for charity, but I still have about fifty head of my cows I'm feeding and about forty of Ruby's. I'd like to sell them along with what hay I have left."

"Why don't you take them to the auction?"

"I will if I have to," Roper said, "but I'd rather not for several reasons. One, I was hoping to get a little better price. Two, I don't have the time right now to transport them. And three, I'd like to sell my hay as well."

"How much hay?"

"Fifty ton."

"That won't feed 'em till summer," Pete said flatly after taking a moment to do the calculations.

"I know," Roper admitted.

"What do you think they're worth?"

"I was hoping to get twenty-five thousand for the cows and five for the hay."

Again, Pete became quiet. In the silence, Roper could almost hear him doing his mental computations.

"I'll give you twenty-five thousand for 'em both."

"Deal," Roper said quickly, "but you're responsible for moving the cows and hauling the hay. And, I'll need the money by tomorrow."

"Tomorrow!" Pete exclaimed. "Why the rush?"

"She's already been in jail for almost three weeks."

"I'll see what I can do."

As Roper hung up the phone, there was a knock on his front door.

Hugh Shelton, the house appraiser sent by the bank, entered and after a few moments of pleasantries, started measuring. Meanwhile Roper finished the bank's application for the loan. In about thirty minutes, Hugh was ready to go.

"Nice house," Hugh said as he headed for the door. "Wasn't it your dad's?"

"I inherited it when dad died."

"Well, he kept it in good shape."

"What do you think it's worth?"

"I've still got to do some calculations, then the bank will get my report. You'll hear from them."

"I need seventy-five thousand. That means the house will have to appraise for a hundred thousand or more," Roper said. "Can you at least tell me if I'm in the ballpark?"

"Is it paid for?"

"Never had a lien."

"Well." Hugh frowned, then huddled with Roper like a co-conspirator. "You might be a little short."

"How short?"

"I don't know. Maybe ten thousand."

"Do what you can," Roper said glumly, "and Hugh, the bank loan committee meets tomorrow. Is there any way you could have the report by early tomorrow morning?"

"For you Roper, that's possible," Hugh replied, nodding.

As soon as Hugh had gone, Roper gathered up his loan application and headed out the door. Where was he going to get another ten thousand?

Sighing, Roper got into the Dodge. Before meeting Sean O'Grady he wanted to drop the loan papers off at the bank, then stop by the jail to let Ruby know he was making progress. At least that would be his excuse. In truth, he just wanted a reason to see her again. The loan officer assured him that if the bank got the home appraisal by early morning, the loan would be processed tomorrow, then it would only take a day or two to prepare the papers and possibly he could have the money later in the week.

By the time Roper had finished, it was 12.30 p.m. Though he only had a few minutes before he was to meet Sean, he decided there was still enough time for a quick visit. As he entered the front door, he could hardly suppress a smile and he had to admit for the first time in a long time, he was in a good mood. At least now he had something good to tell Ruby.

At the reception desk, however, he was told he would have to wait. There was no one to escort him back to the secure area. The jailor had gone to lunch and the receptionist, who also doubled as the dispatcher, had to stay by the phone. Consulting his watch, Roper shrugged and turned to leave. Just then, Deputy Alan Ainsley sauntered in.

"Alan, I need to talk to Ruby. Two minutes."

"So?" Alan replied.

"The jailor's gone to lunch and she," he nodded at the receptionist, "won't let me back without an escort. I only need a couple of minutes."

"Wilson will be back at one."

"I've got another appointment at one," Roper said. "Come on Alan, it's me, Roper. We played high school ball together. Give me a break."

"Oh, all right. No funny stuff, though."

"You have my word, Alan."

Ainsley retrieved a set of keys from the receptionist, then led the way through a locked grated steel door. They turned left down a wide, well-illuminated hall, stopping in front of the cement-walled bunker that doubled as a conference room.

"I'll put you in first," Ainsley said, as he slipped the key in the lock and turned.

"Oh! You've already got a visitor," Ainsley said, a surprised look on his face.

Over Deputy Ainsley's shoulder, Roper caught a quick glimpse inside the small conference room. With her back toward him, Roper immediately recognized the slim frame and black hair of Ruby Nez. Glancing up at him from the other side of the table was the handsome mustached face of Skinner Jacobson.

"I didn't know you already had a visitor," Ainsley said. "I'm sorry."

"Deputy Wilson said we had thirty minutes," Ruby replied.

Ainsley turned to Roper. "Why don't you wait back at the reception area for a few more minutes, then we'll bring you back."

"Don't bother," Roper snapped. "I've got to go."

Like spring weather on the Fifty, Roper's disposition rapidly soured. As he drove to meet O'Grady, his good mood quickly degenerated from contempt to depression and finally to self-pity. What was he thinking? Why the hell was he mortgaging his house? Of the one hundred thousand dollars he was raising for bail, approximately eighty-five thousand was his money. What kind of a fool was she playing him for? Yes, love was blind, but was it was also stupid?

The more he thought about it, the angrier he got. Had his motives been strictly altruistic as he had proclaimed? If he was honest he could not say that he had been raising the money strictly out of compassion with his only desire to help a colleague. Subconsciously, there had always been strings attached. Not only had he expected thanks, he had also expected this would in some way advance their relationship.

Now it appeared she had another option, Skinner Jacobson. Why was he there? Was that why he was so angry?

Deep down he was not very proud of himself. In truth, it seemed this bail project had been anything but a shining example of Christian charity.

But seeing her hunched over the table with Skinner had rattled him. What could they have been talking about? Probably, he was trying to sweet talk her into something.

Was he was making too much of this? Maybe their conversation was about the drought, the price of beef or the allotment closures. So why jump to conclusions? Nowadays two ranchers had plenty to talk about. But somehow the smirk of Skinner's face didn't sit well.

Roper jerked his mind back to the present and checked his watch. As he pulled his pickup over to the curb at the Golden Loop Café, he noted that Sean's Landrover, now fixed and repainted, was parked out front. Climbing out of his Dodge, Roper sauntered over and tapped on the window.

Sean flinched, then rolled down the window. "Didn't see you pull up," he said.

"You want to go in my truck?" Roper asked. "We took yours the last time."

"You mean the time Macdonald shot me?"

"Yeah, but it looks pretty good now," Roper said. "Can't even tell it's been wrecked."

"Still pulls to the right," Sean said.

"Then let's take the Dodge."

"No, we'll take mine. I know where we're going."

"Okay, but I'll buy the gas."

"Better grab your thirty/thirty," Sean said, then nodded toward the back seat. "I've got mine."

"You really think that's necessary?"

"You never know."

After retrieving his rifle, Roper circled to the passenger's side and climbed in. "Where are we going?" he asked, setting the 30/30 on the back seat and securing his seat belt.

"Thought we would take the Smoky Mountain Road down to the Death Ridge and Little Escalante Canyon area. I've heard rumors of digs over there."

"You hear anything about the Tibbet Canyon area or the Burning Hills?"

"Nah—nada," Sean replied, shaking his head. " Why?"

"No reason," Roper said. "Someone told me there might be fossils there."

"Not so far as I know," Sean said, cranking the engine.

"Whatever you think."

Without further comment, Sean put the old SUV in gear and circled back on Highway 12 heading west down Main Street until they reached the Smoky Mountain Road turnoff near the edge of town. At the junction, they turned south and drove for a quarter of an hour in uneasy silence, neither offering any attempt at conversation. Usually Roper didn't mind quiet, but with Sean, it was never a comfortable silence.

Shrugging it off, Roper gazed out the window as the beige canyon walls went flying by. Briefly, he spotted the masonry of an ancient Fremont granary high up in an alcove near the rim just under the dark volcanic ash cap rock. When the Landrover jarred over a deep pothole, Roper quickly re-focused on the road just as Sean, braking hard, pointed the truck down an embankment and onto the sandy wash. When the tires started spinning in the loose sand, he quickly shifted to four-wheel drive and instantly the sand was no longer a problem. After crossing to the other side, O'Grady again shifted to two-wheel drive.

Now on smoother road, Roper again glanced out the window, this time looking for clouds. There were just a few innocuous-looking fluffy ones on the northwest horizon. Even though Smoky Mountain Road was listed on the maps as a graded and improved road, Roper knew from past experience that just a moderate rainstorm could turn the usually dry arroyo into a raging river, washing out the road and making it impassible for days. Today, at least, it did not look that threatening.

After another fifteen minutes of painful silence, Roper loudly cleared his throat. He was still in a nasty mood from that humiliating jail incident and wanted to fight with someone. If it couldn't be with Ruby or Skinner Jacobson, it might just as well be Sean.

"Do you think there is anything to the Whitewater allegations and that whole Susan McDougal thing?" Roper asked.

No answer.

"What about Gennifer Flowers?"

No answer.

"And what about Paula Jones' claim of sexual harassment?"

"Personal life is personal life," Sean said. "Politics ends at the bedroom door."

"Except when you're in the highest office in the land," Roper said. "That position demands a certain amount of dignity. Don't you think?"

"Every president has had his affairs."

"Not every president."

"What is it with you self-righteous Christians?" Sean snapped.

"What do you mean?"

"His personal life has not and will not affect his performance."

"That's debatable," Roper asserted, suppressing a grin. "He's making it very hard for any democrat to be elected in two thousand. He's given the Moral Majority plenty of ammunition."

"Such as?" Sean fired back.

"Such as adultery, lying, his position on abortion, his position on flag burning, his position on school prayer and on and on," Roper maintained.

"I've about had it with the friggin' Moral Majority, the Religious Right or whatever you want to call them hypocrites. They bomb abortion clinics, murder doctors and demand prayer and that creation nonsense in schools. For some reason, I always thought schools were for reading, writing and arithmetic," Sean barked, then paused for a breath. "Personally I see no difference between them and the fundamental Muslims, the Crusaders or perpetrators of the Spanish Inquisition. Religious fanatics are dangerous at any time."

"Faith in God is what made this country great," Roper said. "This has always been a Christian country and most people resent you guys trying to remove God."

"Nobody is trying to take God out of this country," Sean said. "We're just trying to keep him in the churches where he belongs."

"Perhaps a little divine guidance would do this country good."

"Which divine guidance? God, Christ, Allah, Buddha, the Great Spirit or some other God?"

"Does it really matter? They're all the same."

"That so? Why then do countries engaged in war both claim to be doing God's will? You're saying they are both praying to the same God, each asking for his help to annihilate the other? Can't you see the incongruity of it all? Convince the masses you're doing God's work, make it a holy war, then you've got one hell of a soldier."

"Are you trying to tell me God was not on the side of the Allies when they were fighting Nazi Germany and freeing the Jews from extermination camps?"

"What I'm saying is, there is no God!"

"I guess we'll never agree on this subject," Roper said weakly, now wishing he had kept his mouth shut. Perhaps silence was preferable after all.

"My point exactly, it's personal. Keep it out of government and keep it out of schools."

Sean then lapsed into moody silence. Without taking his eyes from the road, he maneuvered the Landrover up Alvey Wash, turning right on the Little Valley Road then south on Horse Mountain Road. To call this track a road was being generous. It was barely one car in width and with enough ascents, descents and curves to make even a veteran roller-coaster rider sick.

Right before the road began its descent to Dog Flat and roughly in the geographic center of the Kaiparowits Plateau, Sean pulled over indicating they would have to walk from here. He pointed out their route through the windshield. Rather than hiking up the relatively easy sandy bottom of the arroyo, they would hike up the west canyon wall that sloped upward steeply, like a multi-fractured hog's back.

Though Roper had lived in southern Utah all his life, he had never been to this particular part of the Kaiparowits. Raising hay and tending cows on the Fifty did not leave a lot of free time for exploring.

Climbing out of the Landrover, Sean hooked his canteen to his belt, then nodded to the jumbled sandstone slope. "If we follow that, it will lead us to Death Ridge."

Slinging the strap of a two-quart canteen over his shoulder, Roper got out and joined Sean.

"You going like that?" Sean asked, arching an eyebrow.

"Like what?" Roper answered defensively.

"In those cowboy boots."

"I do everything in these," Roper said. "They're an all-purpose boot."

"Those leather soles will give you about as much traction as bald tires."

"I've climbed in them before."

"Whatever," Sean said, shrugging and retrieving his 30/30 from the back seat, "but where we're going, you'll probably break your neck."

Silently cursing himself, Roper looked down at his cowboy boots, wishing he owned a pair of hiking boots. Out of habit, he had put on his boots that morning, but his tennis shoes would have been a better choice.

"How far?" Roper asked, eying the broken skyline. A thin carpet of pigeon-gray clouds was visible on the far horizon, but at this distance they did not appear to be particularly ominous.

"Not far," Sean replied, starting up the canyon ridge. "The place I suspect they're digging is just ahead—and don't forget your gun."

"I was hoping I wouldn't be needing it," Roper grumbled, but nevertheless went back for his 30/30.

With Sean leading, they started up the hog's back. Both sides dropped off abruptly into dry gulches that knifed through the mocha colored sandstone. In places, Roper noted, erosion had exposed a thick layer of black coal and the narrow slope was littered with boulders and peppered with thick brush, making the going slow and difficult.

Twenty minutes of strenuous hiking brought them to a semicircular alcove at the base of a beige sandstone cliff. Carved by the forces of erosion, the alcove had been chiseled out of the wall and was roughly a hundred feet in diameter. Over the centuries, wind had blown sand into the natural bowl, creating a thick bed of soil. Taking advantage of any soil, small opportunistic junipers, pinions and sagebrush flourished in the little amphitheater.

At the perimeter next to the cliff, was a twelve by six-foot pit surrounded by piled mounds of excavated dirt. The digging had extended down into the sandstone floor with an irregular three foot area chipped out of the bedrock. The excavated mounds were peppered with slanting radial erosion rivulets and sported new growth, though now winter dead, of June grass and tumbleweeds. Roper was fairly sure this dig had not been worked any time recently.

Without comment, Sean O'Grady propped the 30/30 against a rock, dropped down into the pit and started poking around with his hiking stick.

"This was a paleontology dig, all right," he said.

"Probably," Roper replied, remaining on top of the bank, "but it's not been worked in at least a couple of years, maybe more."

Ignoring his comment, Sean continued to poke about, then reached down and picked up a small fossil fragment. "No question about it, this was an illegal dig."

"How do you know that?"

Sean held up the small fragment. "Experts don't break off and leave fragments like this behind. I know. I've worked a lot of legal digs."

"I don't see how this helps us find Lanny's thieves."

"Probably the same people. There's been an organized ring operating for some time."

"That may be so, but they're not here now and haven't been here in a while," Roper said, taking off his Stetson and wiping the sweat from his forehead with his bandana.

"But they have been here," Sean replied, as he climbed out of the pit. "Let's continue on at least as far as Death Ridge. This is prime fossil territory. There could be more digs."

Again Sean took the lead, hiking in a northerly direction and ever upward. With no obvious trail, the going was slow and tedious. They circled around enormous slabs of eroded rock, picked their way through thick patches of sage and salt brush and slipped as the ground gave way on the steep unstable slopes.

Though technically this was part of the Kaiparowits Plateau, it was hardly flat. They were constantly climbing or descending and with the leather soles and high heels of his cowboy boots, Roper was constantly sliding or stumbling on the slick sandstone. As they worked their way ever north, Roper noted with some chagrin that the carpet of thin clouds appeared to be much closer now and thicker and darker. The cowman in Roper knew they needed moisture, but silently he prayed it wouldn't be today.

Roper longed to sit down, take off his boots and massage his aching feet, but there was no way he was going to give Sean the satisfaction. His soles and heels felt raw and he imagined he had silver-dollar blisters rupturing, leaving raw oozing sores. Oblivious, Sean continued his forced march northward, never slackening the pace.

As they climbed higher on the tumbled ridge, the terrain slowly changed. The lateral walls of the hog's back became more precipitous and the left wall eventually morphed to nothing but sheer cliffs with the right wall almost as bad. The clouds had now thickened, looking like swirling India ink. The oncoming dark shroud, Roper noted, seemed to be dropping lower as it drifted south.

Undeterred, Sean continued on. With Roper limping badly, they eventually reached the summit. Ignoring his painful feet, Roper took in the view. Beneath them to the west was the blue-gray of Dog Flat and the salmon-pink of Ruby Flats. To the far south was the rest of the Kaiparowits Plateau which abruptly ended in a eroded broken horizon carved by numerous drainage canyons. To the immediate north the landscape abruptly changed. Not more than twenty feet away, directly in front of them, plunged a sheer cliff that that formed one wall of a deep gorge. Nodding toward the other side of the canyon, Sean pointed out Death Ridge.

"Where's the site?" Roper gasped, hyperventilating from the climb.

"About half way up Death Ridge," Sean said, again pointing to the far canyon wall.

"There's no one over there," Roper wheezed, sitting down on a flat rock. "If they were, we'd be able see them."

"Well obviously, they're not there now," Sean said testily, "but that doesn't mean they haven't been there. We need to see if there are any signs of recent activity."

"I don't know," Roper said, eying the darkening sky, "looks like we could be in for a storm."

"So what?" Sean said through clenched teeth. "We've got four-wheel drive."

"Doesn't take much storm to wash out Alvey Road."

"It's too cold to rain."

"Even if there was a dig over there, there's no way they could ever get a fossil out," Roper said, thinking his feet couldn't take much more.

"You'd be surprised what they can do with a helicopter," Sean said, then smirked. "Actually, you already know. Don't you?"

As they started down the slope, the dark sky began to spit a few small beady snowballs that stung like silica grains in a sandstorm. To navigate the near vertical drop, they angled obliquely down the gorge wall, eventually reaching the sandy bottom. They then struggled about two-thirds the way up the other side. On the way, they had to circle around several banks of obstructing cliffs as they labored up the boulder-strewn slope.

Sean finally stopped on a large shelf of lead-gray Tropic shale. Like the earlier alcove, scattered evidence of a previous excavation was everywhere, but again nothing appeared to be particularly fresh.

Sean again set his rifle down and poked around with his hiking stick. By the way he systematically worked the site it was obvious to Roper that Sean knew his way around paleontology digs. He finally settled on the northeast corner where the shelf ended and the ridge once again slanted upward. He took a hand rake out of his pack, squatted down and patiently began scraping away the overlying layer of stone and rubble. After a few minutes, he brushed away the debris with a small brush then stood up and stretched.

"This was an illegal dig too."

"Cause you didn't know about it?" Roper asked, sarcasm in his voice.

"Yeah, but this, like the other one, was very sloppy excavation," Sean said, motioning for Roper to come over.

Sean pointed to the area he had been working with his walking stick. "They left an entire forearm, probably a Theropod dinosaur."

Wiping snowflakes out of his eyes, Roper looked down at the partially uncovered fossil. It did appear to be a forearm. "Even if you are right, I don't see how that helps us. This dig hasn't been worked in a very long time."

"At least we know they've been in the area."

"Maybe last year."

"This area is rich in fossils. My guess is they're still working it—somewhere."

"Let's go," Roper said, putting his arm through the shoulder strap of the 30/30. "It's starting to snow hard."

Shrugging, Sean reluctantly climbed out of the pit. Not waiting, Roper had already started down the steep talus slope. Cussing loudly, Sean had to hurry to catch up.

The ground was still warm and the snow instantly melted as it fell on the bare rocks. Ten minutes later, the weather had dramatically changed, degenerating to near blizzard conditions. The wind had picked and visibility was reduced to just a few feet. A skiff of snow had begun to accumulate on the rocks, making the footing treacherous for Roper with his leather soles.

"I forgot my gun," Sean shouted from behind. "Hold on, I'll be right back."

"I'll go slow," Roper yelled back.

As Sean disappeared into the deluge of white, Roper continued to gingerly pick his way down the slope.

Suddenly, Roper's feet skidded forward as his body toppled backward. He began sliding, picking up momentum until he was almost flying down the forty-five-degree slope. His clothes were ripped and shredded as he hurled toward the edge of a fifty-foot drop-off.

Rolling on his abdomen, Roper began frantically clutching at everything, anything that might stop his momentum. He latched onto a gnarly branch of blue sage, but it suddenly tore free. Frantically he grappled with a black brush, angled boulder edges, loose rocks, anything that might impede his progress.

Just as he felt his feet clear the rim and his body soar into space, he grabbed onto the bough of a dwarf juniper. He held on and felt his momentum suddenly come to a jarring stop. Then, like the downward arc of a pendulum, he swung inward, crashing against the cliff wall. As he hit the wall, he heard the branch crack, giving way and abruptly dropping Roper a few heart-stopping inches more. Then it held. Looking like a fish dangling on a line, Roper clutched the fractured branch and tried to calm himself enough to think.

Looking up he noticed that his hands were a good eighteen inches below the rim. Holding the bough with his right hand, he strained upward with his left hand, trying to reach the rimrock. The branch groaned under his weight, separated a little, plunging him down another two inches. On the verge of panic, Roper sucked in a deep breath, calmed himself and waited.

Though it seemed like an eternity, it probably was less than two minutes when Sean poked his head over the edge. Coolly, he looked a down at Roper through the falling snow.

"You take that literally, don't you," he said, smiling.

"What the hell you talking about?" Roper asked as he cautiously extended an arm, trying not to shift his weight.

"That old proverb that cowboys should die with their boots on," Sean replied, then abruptly disappeared.

What an idiot I am, Roper thought bitterly. He should have known better than come out here with an environmental terrorist. What the hell was he thinking?

Now with this stupid stunt, he had unintentionally gift-wrapped a way for Sean to get rid of him and he didn't have to do a thing. Just walk away. No one could prove a thing.

In retrospect, the whole day seemed a colossal farce. It was obvious Sean had known the location of those two digs they'd supposedly happened on and just as apparent, he also knew they were inactive. Now it was clear this whole thing had been staged. The real question was why?

Disgusted with himself, Roper shook his head and immediately the branch groaned. If I ever get out of here, Roper silently promised himself, I'll play a much smarter game.

Roper glanced down past his feet, then sucked in his breath. Because of the clouds, he couldn't see the bottom of the cliff. It was irrational he knew, but that made it even more terrifying. He had no idea how far he would fall or what he would hit at the bottom.

At that moment, the juniper limb cracked again, dropping Roper another three to four inches. Swaying at the end of the string-frayed bough, Roper's heart pounded against his rib cage and even in the bitter cold he was sweating like a hay farmer in July. So this was going to be it, his final hurrah! Silently, he closed his eyes and mumbled his last prayer to God.

"Hey Roper!"

Startled, the voice wrenched Roper from his last communion. Glancing upward, he half-expected to see God, but he didn't, not unless God was a redhead. There was Sean O'Grady reaching over the cliff and shoving the barrel of his 30/30 toward him. Roper flinched. Was Sean going to shoot him right here like a fish in a barrel? He couldn't wait for this fractured branch to break. Perverse bastard.

"Grab hold of the barrel!"

The gun barrel was now about twelve inches from his face. What did he have to lose? Reaching up, he latched onto the barrel, then holding his breath, let go of the juniper limb.

Sean dug in his heels and slowly pulled Roper up to the rim. With one last supreme effort, he was over the top and safely sprawled on top of the ledge.

Exhausted, they both lay on their backs, chests heaving and gulping air. Roper finally rolled over and shakily stood up.

"Thanks, man," Roper mumbled. "I owe you my life."

"You probably do," Sean agreed. "I saw you down there praying and I want to make damn sure we are clear on this, it was me that saved you, not God."

21

THE BURNING HILLS

The moniker, the Burning Hills, is literal, not literary. For as long as anyone can remember, subterranean coal fires have blazed beneath the mounds and hilltops of this multi-fractured southern flank of the Kaiparowits Plateau. Ignited by lightening, the combustion continues unbridled despite repeated and varied attempts to extinguish it. With an apparent life of their own, these fires seemingly will burn until all bituminous coal is consumed. Considering the vastness of this carbonaceous deposit, that won't be any time soon.

Belching like an old railroad steam engine, smoke plumes billow from crater-vents so deep they appear to be bottomless, the veritable mouth of Hades. Producing a chemical reaction with the native adobe-brown rock, the fires oxidize elemental iron, producing a distinctive rust-red halo that circles each vent.

Geologically, the area is composed of the Straight Cliffs Formation, conceived in the wet swampy Cretaceous Period. The upper layers are a mixture of sandstone and siltstone, but under this strata is a massive seam of coal, in some places over forty feet thick Most geologists agree this is one of the largest untapped coal reserves in the world.

The snow had stopped falling by the time Sean and Roper pulled back into Escalante, though the wind was still gusting. What had looked like a major winter blizzard had quickly fizzled. The fast-moving Canadian clipper, a cold front that was mostly bluster with a little moisture, had moved on. Well, not all bluster, Roper thought grimly. It had nearly cost him his life.

It was late, well after 9:00 p.m. when Sean braked the Landrover to a stop in front of the Golden Loop Café. Though he felt guilty, at the same time Roper felt a sense of relief as he glanced at his watch and realized it was too late to visit the jail. The thorny decision of whether to visit Ruby or not had been taken out of his hands. Visiting hours were over.

The ride back from Death Ridge had been mostly in silence. To say that Roper had conflicting feelings about the eclectic day, was putting it mildly. Most confusing, however, was what to make of Sean. Had he been wrong about him all along? Was he really a good guy packaged as an irritating environmentalist? Considering everything that had happened today, perhaps he was going to have to rethink his opinion. On first impression, and even subsequent impressions, he had seemed obnoxious, annoying and maybe dangerous, but there was a reason why impressions were not admissible as evidence in court. They were very often wrong.

There was no arguing the fact that Sean had saved his life when no one would have known the difference if he hadn't. Only Ruby had known he was going out with Sean, but that in and of itself was not particularly damning. If asked why Roper didn't return, Sean could simply claim that he had slipped on the wet slick rocks and gone over a cliff, then crashed to his death on the rocks below. Autopsy evidence would confirm that he had died from multiple trauma as a result of the fall. Likely, no one would even question that finding. So, Roper had no choice but to conclude that O'Grady did not have to save him. Yet he did.

Roper shook his head. As usual, he was probably over-thinking this whole thing. Perhaps, Sean was just as advertised, a dedicated ecologist and a greatly misunderstood human being. At this juncture, Roper was ready to give him the benefit of the doubt.

Roper's head ached from trying to figure everything out. It was way too easy to let emotion, not fact, guide his actions. Deciding to give it a rest, he once again considered the painful conundrum of Ruby and Skinner. Unfortunately, this topic was no better. Did he really want to confront Ruby, like some jealous schoolboy, and demand an explanation? He realized that would be more than presumptuous. With visiting hours over, he knew there was no way to talk to Ruby, but he also knew he was not going to get any sleep tonight if he didn't get some answers.

Sighing, Roper climbed out of the Landrover, again thanking Sean for saving his life. This was one of those situations where mere words seemed lame and insufficient. Sean waved him off, then put the SUV in gear and disappeared down the road. Still feeling unsettled, Roper started the Dodge and headed for home.

Suddenly, in the middle of the block, he wheeled the truck around. If he couldn't see Ruby, then he could talk to Skinner. There were two people involved in that jail scene and there were no visiting hours at Skinner's place. And, the idea of confronting Skinner didn't seem quite so sophomoric.

Though it was almost ten o'clock, there was still a light on in one of front rooms. Jaw clenched in resolve, Roper got out of the pickup, climbed up onto the wooden porch, rang the doorbell and waited. No answer. He rang again. Still no answer. This time he punched the button, holding it down for a few seconds. Shrugging, he turned and as he headed back down the steps he heard the door creak open.

"Whadda you want?"

Partially exposed behind the half-opened screen door was Skinner Jacobson, naked except for leather cowboy chaps, a white terry-cloth towel wrapped around his waist and a black-felt Stetson cowboy hat jauntily positioned on his head.

"Hope, I didn't interrupt anything," Roper said a bit sarcastically.

"Just havin' a shower."

"Water's not that good for leather," Roper observed, nodding at the chaps.

"Whadda you want?" Skinner asked curtly, ignoring Roper's attempt at humor.

Taken aback by Skinner's uninhibited appearance, Roper hesitated. He hadn't thought this through. "Uh, I was wondering how Ruby was doing. I didn't get a chance to see her today."

"How do you expect she is? She's in jail."

"Uh—did she tell you she might get out on bail?"

"Yeah. When?"

"Maybe as early as tomorrow, depends on how fast the bank moves and I'm still a little short," Roper replied, hoping Skinner would take the hint.

"How short?"

"Probably about ten thousand."

"Well good luck," Skinner said, readjusting his slipping towel. "If anyone can get the money, you can."

Small talk with Skinner was never easy and he still hadn't figured out how to ask him what he really wanted to know. "You could help out."

"Love to," Skinner smiled, "but I'm tapped out."

"Yeah, I'll a bet."

"Anyway, Ruby's worried this all comes with some kind of strings attached."

"She's worried, or you're worried?"

"She's not for sale, you know."

"Never thought she was," Roper snapped back, "What were you doing there today?"

"You're not the only one who's single," Skinner said, "though you act like you've cornered the market."

Roper glared at Skinner for a moment. What the hell, he thought bitterly, might as well go all the way. "What were you two talking about?"

"I'm sure it's none of your business," Skinner replied, feigning surprise.

Roper was beginning to feel like a fool. He should have never come over here. What had he been thinking? Had he really expected Skinner to tell him all, like he was a priest and this was a confessional.

"Well, I suppose, when she gets out she'll have to decide," he said lamely.

"Yeah, some competition," Skinner said with a great show of humility. "How could I possibly compete?"

"What do you mean?"

"You with all your money and me with nothing to offer. Nothing, 'cept plain little ole me." He flashed his all-American grin and forked his wet mustache to a point.

"Yoo-hoo, Skinner!" a feminine voice called from inside the house. "Come on cowboy. I'm getting cold."

Glancing knowingly at Roper, Skinner grinned. "Got company. Got to go."

Disgusted, Roper mumbled, "sorry I bothered you, Skinner."

"You best be careful out there," Skinner said as he closed the door. "You have no idea what you're getting yourself into."

Flooded with an assortment of conflicting emotions, Roper climbed back into the Dodge. Wavering between simple confusion and righteous indignation, he gripped the steering wheel and mechanically headed home. There was no doubt about it, Skinner didn't adhere to the same rigid moral code he did, but then again almost no one did. Roper couldn't help but wonder if Ruby really knew what kind of a guy Skinner really was. Somehow he doubted it. Should he tell her? On the other hand, maybe she did know. Maybe, a guy like Skinner was exactly what Ruby was looking for, someone handy for quick companionship but of equal importance, someone who would not try to pin her down to long-term commitments.

After parking the Dodge, Roper trudged into the house, wolfed down a ham sandwich, shed his clothes, examined the blisters on his feet and quickly showered. Tired and discouraged, he turned out the lights and tumbled in bed just as the phone rang.

Damn, Roper thought, why does everyone call just as I go to bed?

"Mr. Rehnquist?" an unfamiliar voice asked.

"Yeah," Roper said, not bothering to hide his irritation.

"This is Ed Hightower. I think I met you a time or two on the Fifty."

"Yeah, the Texas deer hunter," Roper replied, now more cordial. "I remember."

"Sorry to bother y'all at this late hour, but I've been trying to get hold of Ruby Nez for several days. Left messages on her recorder but get no answer. Is she okay?"

"What do you want?" Roper asked, suddenly suspicious.

"Well," the Texan hesitated. "Maybe you heard about my little helicopter fiasco on the Fifty last fall?"

"Yeah, you lost a mule."

"Well, anyway, Ruby was an eyewitness and I need her to testify at the upcoming trial."

"She won't be able to make it," Roper said flatly.

"Why, may I ask?"

"Well," Roper hesitated, "she's in jail."

"In jail?"

Roper rolled to a more comfortable position, then took a few minutes to explain.

"How long will she be in?" Hightower asked. "My trial's not for a month."

"Maybe a long time. I can't seem to raise all the bail money."

"How much you short?"

"Probably, about ten thousand," Roper said.

"I'll wire it tomorrow," Hightower said quickly.

"Why?"

"I've always liked her," Hightower explained. "And, she was always ready to lend me a hand. And, I need her to testify. Where shall I wire the money?"

After making the necessary arrangements, Roper hung up and in spite of the exhaustion, his mind would not slow down. He kept rewinding his conversation with Hightower. It kind of renewed his faith in mankind.

Eventually, Roper's thoughts turned to Skinner Jacobson and the bizarre scene of earlier tonight. What had he said at the end? You best be careful out there. You have no idea what you're getting yourself into. Those two sentences troubled Roper. But why? Where and when had he heard them before?

Finally his mind began to wander aimlessly and he started to doze. It felt good not to concentrate on anything, to just let his mind flow. Abruptly, he sat up and flashed back to the anonymous muffled phone call from last night, the one that asked if he were interested in fossil thieves and told him to look southward toward Tibbet Canyon and the Burning Hills. Roper was sure that's what the caller had said. Could it have been Skinner? With the voice so well disguised, it was hard to tell for sure. Thinking about it, Skinner had often used that expression. It was kind of his signature phrase. If it was Skinner, what could be his motive? Was he trying to help him, decoy him, or trap him? It could be any of these and possibly something he hadn't thought of yet. But somehow, Roper could not bring himself to believe that Skinner was actually trying to help him. It was too out of character.

For the next hour or so Roper tried to analyze all the possibilities and all the facts, but he still could not come up with a single theory that made much sense. However, one thing did ring true, regardless of whether he had been sincere or not, Skinner had been absolutely correct about one thing. Roper had better be careful out there.

Without closing an eye, Roper tossed and chafed till sunrise. Then he got up and fixed a cold breakfast of milk and cereal. What he longed for was a leisurely cup of morning coffee with Ruby. In spite of the taste, the aroma was well worth the trouble to brew it. He was amazed at how open-minded he had become recently. Not only did it not bother him that Ruby drank coffee, but considering the magnitude of the events of the last few days, the whole religious issue seemed inconsequential.

As he ate, Roper planned his day. First, he needed to stop by the circuit court office and see where the bail money needed to be sent. Then he wanted to drop by the bank to see if they had approved his loan and give them the same instructions about where to deposit the money. Next, he needed to transfer the money he'd collected from the sale of his and Ruby's cows, his hay and her mobile home to that same bail account. And lastly, he needed to stop by the Western Union office and pick up the money Hightower had wired.

After the jail scene yesterday and last night's encounter with Skinner, Roper briefly considered dropping the whole thing, but a promise was a promise. He would see it through.

With the rest of the day he would take the mystery caller's advice and explore the Tibbet Canyon and the Burning Hills areas. Briefly, he thought about stopping by the jail before he left town, but he couldn't bring himself to face Ruby.

After he had finished rinsing and drying the dishes, he grabbed a lined denim jacket and stepped outside. It was the complete opposite of yesterday. The front had quickly passed and was replaced by a gathering high pressure, leaving the sky cloudless, but cold. Still surviving was a couple of inches of snow that blanketed the ground and countless ice crystals sparkled on fences, bushes and trees. Randomly bright sunlight beveled through these tiny ice prisms, splitting into a full spectrum of vibrant color. A thin blanket of morning haze had begun to settle over the valley and the air smelled of smoke from wood-burning stoves. Roper sighed, wishing he had more time to enjoy the morning.

By the time Roper had finished with his errands, it was almost ten o'clock. Quickly, he headed back home, hitched the horse trailer to the Dodge, then loaded General Stepper, now all healed, and whistled for Moses. This time he would travel on horseback. Anyway, his feet were too damn sore to do much hiking.

As with Sean yesterday, he headed down Smoky Mountain Road, but this time he bypassed the turnoff to Death Ridge and continued due south. Steadily climbing in elevation, he passed Camp Flat and Collet Top, then as he approached the southern flank of the Kaiparowits, the road began its long gradual decent. At the edge of the mesa the road dropped precipitously, literally zigzagging off the cliff. Shortly after Roper had passed Drip Tank and a mile before the drop-off, the road forked. He took the right hand spur, the Smoky Hollow Road, hardly a road at all. It was a barely visible track that for a good distance consisted of nothing more than the bottom of a sandy arroyo. Fortunately, yesterday's snow squall had caused very little road damage. As the wash carved through the beige sandstone, it had exposed thick bands of black coal.

At the mouth of Tibbet Canyon he pulled the Dodge over and turned off the ignition. From here he would have to go by horseback. Roper climbed out of the pickup and stretched. It was still clear and cloudless, the air was cool and the ground was damp from yesterday's storm, but at this elevation there was no snow.

After saddling up General Stepper, Roper collected his equipment. Today, he would be prepared. He briefly considered taking his 30/30, but he left it hanging in the gun rack, favoring instead his .357 Magnum pistol. The handgun would be less weighty and cumbersome, and anyway he'd forgotten to bring his saddle rifle scabbard. He also retrieved a loop of rope, a canteen, a knife, and a small lunch consisting of a roast beef sandwich and a bag of potato chips. With his gear stowed in the saddlebags, Roper mounted Stepper and sighed contentedly. This was the way God meant for men to travel.

Gently nudging Stepper, they started up Tibbet Canyon. Moses led, periodically darting here and there to check out distinctive scents. Taking a lesson from Sean, Roper did not ride up the sandy arroyo, but instead chose the much more difficult ridge of the west canyon wall. It was like climbing a huge layer cake. They picked their way from one rippled layer of horizontal sandstone up to the next. The advantage was that this route afforded a good view of the canyon and surrounding countryside. As difficult as this terrain was, it was nothing compared to what he and Sean had covered yesterday. For this, Roper was thankful.

The panoramic vista of the lower country to the south became more apparent as they climbed higher. This disheveled and fractured southern flank of the Kaiparowits was a magnificent spectacle. Chiseling deep into the rimrock, intermittent running water had carved an amazing labyrinth of drainage canyons. Roper shaded his eyes and looked even further south. In the distance, he could see a brilliant splash of copper blue—Lake Powell with its amazing red slick rock basin.

After about an hour of steady climbing, Roper had picked his way to the top of Tibbet Canyon. With tongue hanging out, Moses flopped down, panting in the shade of a large boulder; Stepper, with chest heaving, was covered in a foamy lather; and Roper was sore, tired and discouraged. Groaning, he dismounted, stretching his legs.

Other than Moses flushing out a couple of jackrabbits, they hadn't seen anything, no tracks, no digs and no grave robbers. It was beginning to look like another futile day. Perhaps the fossil thieves had made enough money on that last haul and had already retired. Somehow Roper didn't think so. He still had a nagging feeling that they were at work. But where? The mysterious caller had mentioned both Tibbet Canyon and the Burning Hills. Fortunately, they were not far apart, maybe five miles.

Sighing, Roper got back on Stepper, called to Moses and started down the canyon ridge. Glancing at the sun, he figured if they hurried there might be enough time for a quick exploration of the Burning Hills. Sensing they were heading back, Stepper picked up the pace.

After about an hour, Roper was back in his pickup, speeding for the Burning Hills. Not wanting to waste precious time, he wolfed down his sandwich as he drove. First, he went south on Smoky Hollow Road till it intersected with the Smoky Mountain Road, then he headed north where he could see Croton Road branching off toward the northeast. From the map, Roper knew the first couple of miles of Croton Road were actually in the Glen Canyon Recreation Area but as it wound its way north, it entered back into the Grand Staircase National Monument, specifically the Burning Hills area. As with Smoky Hollow, this road was next to impassible when it rained. The first three bone-jarring miles consisted of trying to avoid one deeply eroded gully after another. It was apparent this road had not seen a county grader in a very long time.

After bouncing for about a half hour, Roper knew the minute he entered the Burning Hills. Through the open window, he caught a whiff of coal fire smoke mixed with the rotten-egg smell of burning sulfur.

The hills were a Cretaceous mixture of sandstone and siltstone about the color of aged barn wood except around coal fire vents. Here the iron-rich rocks had oxidized to a brilliant crimson. The land between the hillocks was dissected by hundreds of dry arroyos that occasionally coalesced, creating a slightly larger wash. Further on these washes continued to merge into a deeper canyon that eventually headed south toward Lake Powell. Standing water was rare and when found, it was almost always at the head of a major canyon. As a surface creek it would exist for only a few yards then immediately seep back underground. Vegetation was sparse, consisting of blue sage, black brush, service berry, Mormon tea and buffalo berry. On the higher elevations the pygmy forest flourished and some of the highest slopes sported thick stands of scrub mahogany and oak. Mule deer were common and as a consequence, so were cougars.

As the road wound around the hillocks, Roper could see an occasional plume of smoke, heralding the presence of a coal fire vent. With smoke belching out of the ground, Roper suspected that this would be the perfect setting for a science fiction movie, one depicting an alien planet. As the road wound north, it became less steep and the drainage canyons more shallow.

Suddenly as he rounded a blind curve, Roper slammed on the brakes. The pickup skidded sideways and the horse trailer jackknifed. Directly in front of him was a brown and white paint mare. In the back, Stepper squealed and stomped nervously, rocking the trailer. Spooked by the oncoming Dodge, the paint wheeled and loped off the road, the front bumper narrowly missing her rump by inches.

Shaken, Roper pulled the pickup out of the acute jackknife, then leaving the road, drove a short distance up a sandy arroyo. Parking out of sight around a sharp bend, he turned off the key and sank back into the seat. He slowly took a deep breath, then got out of the truck and walked back down the wash to the road. From here his outfit seemed pretty well concealed. No telltale shinning metal or reflecting mirrors.

The paint had only strayed fifty yards off the road and was now calmly grazing on year-old dead June Grass. Roper noted that the horse was fully saddled and bridled, trailing her reins on the ground. Attached to the saddle was a leather rifle scabbard. It was empty. Also, leather saddlebags tied behind the cantle appeared to be empty.

For a couple of minutes Roper studied the horse. It was a beautiful animal, a brown and white paint of obviously good breeding. She was about fifteen hands high, a broad chest sporting a well-healed scar, muscular hindquarters and in general appeared to be athletic. After a moment, it dawned on him. This was Skinner Jacobson's horse, the one he'd injured that day on the Fifty, the day they'd helped Ruby round up her cows.

Walking slowly and talking softly, Roper approached the horse. He picked up the reins and tied her to a stout juniper limb, then looked her over more closely. Not a wound or scratch on her, but she was crusted with dried lather and looked like she'd been ridden hard recently.

Suspicious of foul play, Roper wondered where Skinner had parked his truck. He certainly hadn't ridden the paint from Escalante. Hobbling down the road on his sore feet made Roper wish he had unloaded Stepper. After rounding the second curve, he spied Skinner's shiny blue GMC pickup and horse trailer parked off to the side of the road. Circling the pickup, it appeared fine, no evidence of accident or foul play. Roper tried the door. It was unlocked. Everything seemed okay. On the seat was a map of the Grand Staircase/Escalante National Monument including secondary roads. In felt-tip pen, two bold X's had been marked on the map, one over the Tibbet Canyon area and the other over the Burning Hills. There was no rifle in the rear window gun rack, but under the seat was a pint of Wild Turkey. Closing the door, he limped back to his own outfit.

From what Roper had observed, it appeared that Skinner was here on precisely the same mission as him. And from the way the map had been marked, it also looked liked Skinner was working with the same information as him. Mentally, Roper crossed off Tibbet Canyon, he'd just been there and there was nothing. That left only the Burning Hills.

Feeling uneasy about Skinner, Roper decided he might as well start his search. Maybe he'd run into Skinner. He tossed Skinner's paint a flake of hay from his truck and left her tied to the tree. After backing the still-saddled General Stepper out of the trailer, he tightened the cinch, mounted and with Moses sniffing air, they headed north.

Glancing over his shoulder, he gauged the time by the sun. If they were lucky, there would be two more hours of sunlight. Settling back in the saddle, he faced north and nudged Stepper deeper into the Burning Hills.

After a few minutes, they came upon a coal fire, its black smoke plume spiraled upward and the smell of burning creosote filled the air. The surrounding rocks were too hot to touch. At the aperture of the vent a sticky black tar residue had puddled in places and was circled by a signature red ring of oxidized iron. For roughly fifty yards in every direction, the area was completely barren. It was an eerie landscape.

Dismounting, Roper looked around. No sign of paleontology digs or of Skinner Jacobsen. At that moment Moses picked up a scent and headed into the thick peripheral brush. Then he abruptly stopped and started baying. Roper hurried over. On the ground, almost hidden in a thicket of black brush, was a reddish brown puddle. Bending down, Roper dipped his middle finger into it. It was congealed, like Jell-O. No doubt about it, it was blood and it had not been there that long.

Roper carefully scouted the area, noticing multiple boot tracks of various sizes in the damp sand. And on the other side of the smoke plume was a set of shallow parallel furrows where it appeared someone had been dragged, boot heels trailing in the sand. With growing alarm, Roper followed the paired ruts. Along the way, more drops of blood were spattered on the beige sand. It didn't take long for Roper to figure out where the tracks were headed—straight to the belching mouth of the coal fire vent.

Standing at the lip, Roper peered into the cavity. The smoke made his eyes water and the heat scorched his face. It was impossible to see the bottom. Picking out a baseball-sized rock that wasn't too hot, he tossed it into the smoky void. It clattered off the side walls several times, but took a full four seconds to thud on the bottom. That was a hell of a long way down, Roper thought.

Shivering in spite of the heat, Roper backed away. He didn't want to jump to conclusions, but it certainly appeared that someone had been murdered and their body tossed into the fiery coal furnace. With Skinner's horse and outfit here, it had to be him. But why? And who put him there?

Maybe Skinner found out something or got too close to something that was supposed to remain secret. The map in Skinner's truck indicated he was searching this area. Why? More than likely, he was here for the same reason as Roper, searching for fossil thieves. Again, why? Perhaps, like Roper, he wanted to help out Ruby. Somehow Roper doubted that. The only other motive that immediately came to mind was money. Maybe he wanted a cut of the action or was trying to collect a recently posted reward for catching the thieves.

Roper knew little about Skinner's personal life other than he was a legendary womanizer. In was conceivable the motive for Skinner's murder may be as simple as an incensed husband or boyfriend. Or maybe he had offended some neighboring rancher, rustling, branding strays or a boundary dispute. Roper had experienced his own problems with Skinner, starting years ago with the bickering over the land his father had purchased. Struggling with his emotions, Roper tried to pull himself together. What should he do now? The answer was obvious. He needed to get to Kanab and report this to Sheriff Ivory Jackson. Yes, he would go to Jackson and not Coleman. Calling for Moses, Roper gathered Stepper's reins and quickly swung up into the saddle.

Ka—boom!

Roper felt a searing pain ripping through his left flank as he was slammed backward off of the horse, landing only inches from the coal fire vent. The fall knocked the breath out of him and as he fought for air, he could felt the heat from the coal fire singeing the hair of his head.
Groaning, he managed to ease his head a foot or so away from the fire. He reached down with his right hand, gingerly exploring the injury. It was a left flank wound, quite far lateral and just beneath the floating ribs. His fingers were covered with pasty red blood. His blood!

Roper struggled to his feet, his eyes blurry. He felt wobbly and lightheaded. Suddenly, there were muscular hands on his chest, violently shoving him back to the ground.

Then someone grabbed his legs, hoisting his butt off the ground and began shoving him toward the brink of the blazing crater. Roper tried to kick his legs free, but his assailant was too strong. Then he twisted and rolled to the right, but all that accomplished was more pain. Like a condemned man, he continued to struggle, but even as he fought, he could feel himself weaken and fade.

"What the hell you doing!" someone suddenly shouted from the fuzzy periphery.

Slowly, Roper felt the man's grip slacken. "Getting rid of this sack-o-shit cowboy."

"Is he dead?"

"No, but give me a minute—."

"—Pull him back. Now!"

Through the fog, Roper thought he heard these words:

Do not go gentle into that good night—
Rage, rage against the dying of the light

Dylan Thomas, he thought, as everything went black.

22

THE BURR TRAIL

Like the rest of the Grand Staircase National Monument, the Burr Trail is no stranger to controversy. To pave, or not to pave, has been the battle anthem for many a bitter skirmish. Progressive county officials foresee their depleted coffers swell from increased tourist travel, while environmentalists champion an unpaved road, thereby preserving the unstained wildness, the uncommon isolation and wild beauty of this vast land. As things stand, a precarious truce teeters. As an uneasy, or unholy, compromise, half the trail is blacktopped.

Regardless of politics, the Burr trail is, one of the most breathtaking scenic byways in America. Leaving the town of Boulder, the road snakes over and around the sheer Navajo sandstone Cliffs, suddenly diving into a deep canyon simply called the Gulch. At the bottom, an unexpected gem, a verdant chattering creek. Moving on, the trail follows Long Canyon as it knifes through a massive bulwark of red Kayenta siltstone, nicknamed the Wall Street of the desert. Chiseled into its precipitous walls are countless niches and alcoves, often veneered with dark desert varnish.

From Long Canyon, the road crosses over to White Canyon Flat, then up White Canyon itself and into the equally magnificent, but unpaved Capitol Reef National Monument.

When Roper came to he realized it was bitter cold and pitch black. The only light came from the crusted orange coals of a dying campfire and the faint speckled light of the Milky Way. There was no moon.

It took a while for the mist to lift from his mind, but chattering of his teeth and violent shivering of his body helped to speed up the process. Roper was sitting upright against a leafless single-leaf ash tree, his hands were tightly bound behind his back and secured to the tree. His ankles were bound with the same nylon cord. Glancing down, he could see his wound had been dressed with white cloth strips that circled his torso. There was a dark irregular stain on the cloth, probably old blood.

On the other side of the dying campfire loomed two dome-tents and off to the right, he could hear the restless shuffling of a large animal, maybe General Stepper. Propped against the trunk of a nearby pinion, was an assortment of excavating tools, picks, shovels and brooms.

Suddenly, Roper was seized with a wave of shivering. Damn, it was cold out here. If he didn't find a way to warm up soon he would be frozen solid way before the morning sun. He lunged forward against the ropes. Nothing gave. He looked around for some way to warm himself. On the ground about two feet away, he spied a heavy woolen blanket lying on the ground. He struggled to free his hands, but to no avail. Somehow, he had to get that blanket before he froze to death. After a few minutes of experimentation, he found if he rolled to his right as far as the rope would allow and flex forward at the waist, he could almost reach the quilt with his teeth.

He gave it a tentative try, but the throbbing from his wound stopped him short. Gritting his teeth, he tried again, fighting through the pain. Bending and straining, his lips finally touched the blanket. Like the jaws of a hand vise-grip, he clamped down on the blanket and as he rolled back, he dragged it partially over his body. By wriggling, he was soon completely covered. Finally, Roper felt himself starting to thaw.

As warmth wormed its way into his body and with his mind now freed from the task of basic survival, he began working on other things. It was amazing how prophetic that anonymous warning had been. It appeared the Burning Hills was the location of the fossil thieves' current excavation and even more disturbing, Roper hadn't had any idea what he was getting himself into. And to his chagrin he realized, he hadn't told anyone where he was going.

Unfortunately, it seems Skinner had paid the ultimate price for being right. However, one question kept resurfacing in Roper's mind, why was

Skinner snooping around here anyway? The only thing that made sense; he must have had an angle on how to make money out of it. Groaning, Roper leaned back and rested his head against the trunk of the tree.

Roper slowly relaxed and his eyelids became weighted and ratcheted closed. More than likely, he concluded as conscious thought began to fade, the same thing would happen to him. It almost already had. Briefly, he had a vision of the blazing coal fire vents. Quickly, he forced his mind to think about something else.

What had happened to Moses? Had they also shot Moses and dumped his body down the coal vent? But Moses was pretty wily. Maybe he'd gotten away, slinking low in the brush, and was still out there somewhere. Roper preferred to believe this.

The constant throbbing of his wound seemed to ease some as his mind began to drift. If he could just change gears and think about something enjoyable, maybe he could sleep. His mind rifled through a series of pictures then settled on one. Once again he was back on the Fifty. He'd just finished a hard day of rounding up cows. Now it was time to head for the cabin. Quickly the scene changed. Now there was the unmistakable aroma of steaks frying and onions sizzling, and he could feel heat wafting from the wood-burning stove. Suddenly the cabin door burst open and there was Ruby in her red dress, waiting for him to fix dinner. Roper's head slumped forward. A smile slowly spread across his face and he slept.

Later, from somewhere deep in the maze of a different dream, Roper felt someone or something nudging his thigh, but it felt insignificant. Moaning, he rolled over as much as his rope constraints would allow, hoping it would go away. However, like the siesta fly, it would not leave. When the poking struck his flank wound, Roper groaned loudly, his eyes still closed.

> *Now is the winter of our discontent,*
> *Made glorious summer by this sun of York.*

"Shakespeare," Roper mumbled, half awake.

"More precisely, the Duke of Gloucester—Richard the Third," a polished voice said.

Sitting up, Roper cocked an eye open. Standing above him was a clean-shaven man immaculately dressed in khaki-brown cargo pants, suede leather hiking boots, a beige long-sleeve shirt, and a chocolate corduroy jacket. Jauntily capping his head was a chestnut-brown, Indiana-Jones, leather hat and dangling from his mouth was an English Dunhill Red Bark pipe with a gold stem band.

"You don't recognize me?" the voice said.

Roper's mind shifted gears and he took a second, more critical look. Gone were the gray stubble and signature wad of tobacco. Absent were the smelly patchwork fur coat and muskrat cap. Completely vanished were the reeking body odor and dirty soiled skin. Departed were the disheveled appearance and shaggy shoulder-length hair.

"Bucky Lee Eakins!" Roper blurted out in astonishment.

"One and the same," Bucky Lee affirmed, "but my Christian name is Bonñet."

"Bonnie?" Roper echoed, his mouth still gapping. "Your parents must've had a very strange sense of humor."

"No, B-o-n-n-e-t—Bonñet," Eakins spelled it out. "Leigh—L-e-i-g-h. My Mother's family name was Bonñet. It's French. My father's mother was a Leigh. Bonñet Leigh is my name.

"That's kind of hard to get your tongue around," Roper said.

"My friends did call me Bonny, but you can call me Bonñet," Bucky said without smiling.

"Wh—what you doing here Buck—Bonñet," Roper choked. "What the hell's going on?"

"*There is a tide in the affairs of men; which, taken at the flood, leads on to fortune*," Eakins answered.

Roper stared in disbelief. Also gone were the fractured proverbs and broken English. Bonñet Leigh was quoting William Shakespeare.

"You want some breakfast?" he asked.

"I want some answers," Roper demanded, nodding at the camp. "What the hell is this?"

"A splendid example of free enterprise. Capitalism at its finest.

"You mean man at his basest, don't you," Roper argued, "robbing paleontology digs."

"I told you chaps a long time ago to branch out," Bonñet stated, puffing on his pipe. "Diversification was the answer, but none of you listened."

"What you working on now?" Roper asked, shifting his back against the tree, "another priceless Theropod—another yet-to-be-discovered species."

"No, I don't suppose we'd be that lucky again," Bonñet chuckled. "That was once in a lifetime."

"So it was you that took Professor Albright's fossil?"

"That was quite an operation. Needed military-type precision, like Nelson at Waterloo."

"So you killed Ron Sparks? And Angus Macdonald?"

"That, you don't need to know," Bonñet snapped.

"And Skinner Jacobson?" Roper said.

"Who?"

"And what happened to my dog?"

"I'm sure I don't know what you are talking about," Bonñet declared, tapping the ash from his pipe.

"And who shot me?"

"Why—that would be me," a familiar voice behind Bonñet joined in.

"And, by God, I'm sorry I'm not a better shot," the redhead declared as he stepped out from behind Eakins. "You should have let me finish him, Doc."

Roper's jaw almost hit the ground. Not only had he not figured out Bucky Lee Eakins, but yesterday he'd elevated Sean from suspect to saint.

"Sean, in this business, as in chess, you need to think several moves ahead," Bonñet Leigh said. "In the future he may come in handy as a bargaining chip."

"Doc?" Roper asked, looking up at Sean. "Why'd you call him Doc?"

"Cause that's what he is," Sean replied, "actually a double doc, twin PhD's. From Yale a degree in English literature and when he couldn't get a job, another degree in paleontology from Berkeley."

"Sean, be careful what you say," Bonñet said. "*Have more than thou showest, speak less than thou knowest.*"

"I suppose that's how you two are connected," Roper said. "Paleontology."

"Yeah," Sean O'Grady replied. "When Bonñet was on the faculty of the University of Utah, he was one of my professors. We worked on a couple of digs together."

"Enough of this!" Bonñet barked. "Sean, why don't you fix some breakfast?"

"Don't matter," Sean said. "He ain't going to tell anyone."

As Sean stoked up the fire and retrieved two Dutch ovens, Bonñet Leigh disappeared into one of the two blue domed tents.

"I just can't believe this," Roper said, shaking his head in amazement. "Bucky Lee is Doctor Bonñet Leigh Eakins."

"Actually, " Sean remarked, cracking a half dozen eggs into the sizzling oven, "he's quite brilliant. He's published at least a dozen scientific papers in professional journals."

"Then why is he doing this?"

"Well, I guess cause now he's got no choice. He was blackballed."

"Why?"

"Well," Sean said as he added Bucky's sausage to the second Dutch oven. "Some say he committed academia's one unforgivable sin—doctoring his research."

"What did he do?" Roper asked, perversely fascinated.

"We, me and Bonñet, were working on this site over in New Mexico's Zuni Basin. Bonñet had this theory that the late Cretaceous dinosaurs were not destroyed by the now famous asteroid, but rather by a massive forest fire. Unfortunately, he couldn't prove it," Sean explained as positioned the ovens on the fire.

"Sounds a bit farfetched," Roper said.

"It's not as crazy as it sounds," Sean replied, heaping glowing coal on top of the ovens. "Those were the latter days of Pangea."

"Pangea?"

"Before the continents separated," Sean explained. "Anyway, one day we hit the bonanza! Some broad bands of charcoal and fossilized briquettes turned up mixed with a large cache of Cretaceous dinosaur bones. It was a remarkable find. Papers were quickly written and published. Many accolades were forthcoming. Regrettably, however, further studies showed the silica contained in mineralized briquettes was found only in Montana, around Butte I think, not from New Mexico, and not from the Cretaceous, but the Jurassic Period."

"So you planted fossilized briquettes?" Roper asked.

"Well—that's what some say."

"It appears, you two have been working this gig for quite a while," Roper said.

"It's worked out good," Sean replied as he lifted the oven lid. The aroma of frying eggs and sausage made Roper realize how hungry he was. "But now we're done."

"Done?"

"With this one we'll have all our orders filled and have more money than we could spend if we were to live through the entire Modern Era," Sean laughed.

"Is it ready yet?" Bonñet shouted, as he reemerged from the tent.

"Almost, Doc," Sean answered.

"What now?" Roper asked, not sure he wanted to hear the answer.

"Well that depends," Sean said.

"Depends on what?"

"On how long it takes us to finish here," Sean replied.

"We should finish by this afternoon," Bonñet said, rejoining the group. "Sean, can you have the helicopter here just before dark?"

"Can do," Sean replied. "Let's eat."

Bonñet Leigh untied Roper's hands then shoved a plate of hash browns, fried eggs and homemade sausage in front of him.

While eating, Roper thought about escape. He had to figure out something before Bonñet Leigh tied him up again. With a growing sense of urgency, he glanced around. All he could see was an obsidian rock about the size of a baseball with sharp edges, lying about two feet off of his left side.

After finishing breakfast, Bonñet Leigh produced a clean white handkerchief and wiped his face, then stood up and tossed the paper plate in the fire. Neatly refolding the handkerchief, he replaced it in his lapel pocket and he sauntered over to Roper.

"I'll take your plate," Bonñet said, reaching for the paper plate, tossing it on the fire and turning to watch it burn. Sean was busy cleaning the Dutch ovens.

Roper quickly tilted to the left, snatched up the rock, hid it between his back, then sat back on it. Not noticing, Bonñet Leigh turned around and retied his hands behind his back, then around the ash tree. Without saying anything, Bonñet went back over to the fire, warmed his hands and watched as Sean scraped out the Dutch ovens. After a moment the two of them began whispering in subdued tones. Roper strained to pick up the conversation.

"You best get going. I can finish up here."

"What we going to do with him?" Sean said, slightly nodding in Roper's direction.

"Just handle it like the other one. That way there's no evidence."

Bonñet Leigh started gathering up the excavating tools as Sean O'Grady headed down the trail.

With fear in his stomach, Roper watched as Bonñet trudged across the shallow arroyo to the dig, about fifty yards to the east. He set down his tools on the far bank, selected a small whisk broom and a hand pick and went to work. Roper could not see the fossil, only Bonñet's head and shoulders above the curvature of the ground. When lying down Roper could not see Bonñet at all and suspected Bonñet could not see him either.

Roper worked the piece of obsidian into position against the tree where he could grate the rope against its sharp edges. It was no easy thing. Every movement brought a stab of pain from his flank and chafed his forearms on the tree bark.

He gritted his teeth and clenched his jaw. Fighting through the pain, he worked his wrists up and down against the rock. After thirty minutes his arms were raw and bleeding, but he pressed on.

Shortly after noon, Sean returned. He glanced Roper's way but other than that, paid him little attention as he prepared to join Bonñet at the dig.

"I could sure use a drink of water," Roper said, getting Sean's attention.

"You better not try anything."

Holding the canteen to Roper's lips, Sean tilted it back and Roper gulped as fast as he could.

"What you going to do with me?" he asked bluntly.

"Well, that depends," Sean replied vaguely.

"On what?"

"On how it goes."

"We're friends. You saved my life," Roper said. "Give it to me straight. That's the least you can do."

Sean looked down at his hiking boots. "You should've learned."

"Well," Roper replied, "I suspect you're right on that one."

"You don't get a second chance," Sean added coldly. "You want it straight, well this is about as straight as it gets. If we get the fossil out without problems and we won't need a hostage, then Doc says I can throw you in the coal vent like the other guy. Then if anyone asks, I'll pretend to be an eyewitness, saying I saw you two fighting and you both fell into the vent. Everyone knows there's bad blood between you two anyway."

"And nobody could prove you wrong."

"Beautiful—huh?"

"Why didn't you get rid of me yesterday?"

"Well," Sean hesitated, "guess it won't hurt none to tell. There were two fellas out here snooping around yesterday. I don't know if they were together or not, but they were here within an hour of each other. One ended up in the vent, but the other guy got away. I didn't recognize him and I'm not sure how much he saw, but if does he come back—anyway, that's partly why Doc's hurrying to finish today."

"So if he does come back with the authorities, then I'll be the bargaining chip?"

"High stakes celebrity poker, "Sean smiled. "Your life for letting us chopper out with a million-dollar fossil."

"Guess it would be better for me if they came," Roper said, glancing up at the sky.

"Let's see your God get you out of this one," Sean laughed as he went to help Bonñet.

One thing was for damn sure, Roper thought. He'd best get free long before the helicopter arrived. With a sense of urgency, he checked the angle of the mid-afternoon sun. It was probably around three o'clock. Ignoring the pain, he went back to work on the chords.

The day wore on faster than he would have liked. But Roper could tell he was making progress. He could now feel frayed fibers with his fingers, but still the rope held fast.

Quickly, Roper checked the sky. The sun was now on the horizon, poised to begin its descent below the western lip of the Kaiparowits Plateau. With growing anxiety, he looked around, hoping for a rescue. But there was no movement, no sound, no helicopter and no posse. Positioning the rock, he redoubled his efforts.

Then before he saw it, he heard it. The rhythmic thumping as huge blades beat the heavy afternoon air. Slowly, the cacophony intensified. There on the horizon, approaching from the north, appeared a magnificent metal bird, briefly illuminated in the slanted rays of the sinking sun. It was a red and white Bell 412 rotorcraft with a hydraulic lift capacity of over five thousand pounds, the draft horse of helicopters. For a few moments, it hovered above the hillock adjacent to the paleontology dig, then slowly descended, landing in the purple shadows of dusk. In the fading light Roper could see Bonñet Leigh holding his hat and bracing against the rotor-wind, waving his arms and giving directions. When the huge craft finally settled, it was less than a hundred feet from the dig.

As the blades slowed, three men carrying rifles jumped out of the cargo hatch and began lugging thick nylon straps toward the dig. Bonñet took charge. Under his direction, they went to work placing the straps under and around the fossil. Roper could see that Bonñet was meticulous and appeared to know what he was doing. Who could blame him for being careful? An intact fossil was worth several hundred thousands dollars more than one reclaimed piecemeal.

With desperate determination, Roper again tackled the rope, giving it all he had. Without warning, it suddenly gave way. His hands were free!

Roper quickly untied his feet. He glanced over at the dig; no one was paying him any attention. Keeping low, he crawled into one of the tents and contemplated his next move. What he needed was a weapon, but he could see none around the camp. Apparently, all were at the dig. His 30/30, however, was still in his truck. He wasn't absolutely sure of the direction to his truck, but he suspected it was directly south, and probably not very far either. Roper doubted that Sean and Bonñet Leigh would lug all that excavating equipment very far.

Stepper was a possibility, but the horse was tethered over by the arroyo and it would be difficult to get him and not be seen. He would simply have to walk. Crawling out, Roper stopped for a moment and looked back. The thieves were still trying to burrow strap channels under the fossil.

Roper stayed to the shadows until the excavators were completely out of sight, then quickly relieved himself and started running, his flank throbbing with every step. In the poor light, the going was slow and difficult, and it took only a few minutes to chafe the blister scabs off his raw feet. Physically, Roper thought, he was a mess. Gritting his teeth, he hobbled on. In the gathering gloom, he stumbled through the cacti, thorny brush and over basketball-size rocks.

After about half a mile, he topped a hillock and suddenly there they were: Sean's Landrover parked at the end of the road along with Bonnet's old GMC pickup. He had not seen those vehicles yesterday. That must mean his Dodge was parked a little further up the road.

With renewed determination, he struggled on down Croton Road. After another quarter-mile or so, he spied the familiar feeder-wash where he'd parked his pickup

At that moment, Moses jumped up from under the pickup and bounded to him with head ducked low, wagging his tail. Damn, he was glad to see that dog. Thankfully, he was fine.

As best Roper could tell, his Dodge had not been touched either. Jerking open the door, he grabbed his 30/30 from the rear window gun rack, then fished a box of shells out of the glove compartment. He quickly took a swig of water from his thermos, poured a lid full for Moses, then slammed the door shut. Then with Moses at his side, he shuffled like an old man escaping a nursing home back toward the dig.

By the time he got back, it was pitch black, but the other side of the arroyo was illuminated like an actor's stage from portable flood lights and hand-held flashlights. Roper could see ghostly figures bobbing about the dig. Then as if by some silent cue all activity ceased and everyone backed away from the dig. One hazy figure separated from the group, heading for the helicopter. Climbing in the Bell-412, he turned on the running lights.

This is it, Roper concluded; they must be ready to move the fossil.

He had to make his move now. Several options flashed through his mind, none of them good.

Glancing skyward, Roper looked for guidance, then quickly made up his mind. Pointing the 30/30 up, he pulled the trigger. The shot thundered in the peaceful evening, sounding more like the salvo of a Howitzer.

"Hey, Bonñet!" Roper yelled as reverberating subsided. "The jig's up. Put down your weapons."

The lights were immediately doused and like ghostly apparitions, the excavators disappeared. Now not being able to see anybody, Roper waited a moment for an answer.

"Put down your weapons and raise your hands," he hollered again.

Suddenly all hell broke loose. Bullets kicked up dirt spray right in front of Roper's face. Some whined overhead and twigs of the single-leaf ash were snapped off, fluttering to the ground like snowflakes. Roper dropped flat and rolled behind a four-foot boulder, then quickly sucked in air. He hadn't thought this through very well.

Then in the darkness, Roper could hear the whine of the helicopter engine and the slow whoosh of the rotor-blades as they struggled against inertia and cut through the heavy night air.

The thieves continued to fire in Roper's direction. Occasionally, he returned their fire, shooting at the brief powder flash produced by their guns. Bitterly Roper thought, they have me right where they want me.

"Hey there token cowboy, you need some help?" a voice said from behind him.

Roper whirled around and stared into the black night. "Skinner?" he whispered. "I—I though you were dead."

"Not that I know'd of," Skinner whispered back, "but I really haven't checked lately."

"I'll be damned," Roper said under his breath. "I saw your outfit and thought—."

"—After scouting the area yesterday, I decided to go for help," Skinner continued. "Unlike you, I ain't no hero."

"So, I guess we just missed each other," Roper said.

"Guess so."

"So where are they?" Roper asked.

"Where's who?" Skinner replied.

"The help you went after."

"Right here," Sheriff Ivory Jackson muttered from the darkness off to Roper's left. "Ainsley's here too."

Roper shivered as he felt a slim arm slide around his shoulders. "And right here," Ruby said, kneeling next to him.

He could feel her warm body next to him. "How did you get out of jail?"

"You ought to know," she answered, squeezing his hand. "You arranged it."

"Well, "Roper asked suddenly, turning back to Skinner. "Who is it they threw down the coal shaft?"

"What you talking about?" the sheriff asked.

Roper quickly explained what had happened and Skinner said with a soft laugh, "I'm almost positive it's not me."

There was a moment of silence, then Sheriff Jackson whispered, "Judith Brisco told me this morning that Monty Coleman has been missing for a day or two."

"Monty Coleman, huh," Roper said with mixed emotions.

"Well, let's not jump to conclusions," the Sheriff added.

"How did you find me?" Roper whispered, still eyeing the helicopter.

"You were just going over that first hill when we pulled up. Looked like you were in a hurry. You didn't see us," Ruby replied, "and we didn't want to make a lot of noise."

"How do you want to do this?" Sheriff Jackson said, suddenly all business.

"They've got the fossil strapped," Roper whispered. "Now they just need to get the chopper in the air."

At that moment, the rotors beat the air more loudly and the huge Bell-412 rose straight up from the hillock.

"On my signal, let's bring her down," Sheriff Jackson said.

Roper watched the big bird toil. As the rotors whipped loudly, it continued its ascent.

"Now!" Jackson ordered.

All five rifles immediately barked, hurling blazing leaden missiles at the aircraft.

Ka—boom!

A flaming fireball illuminated the eastern sky, looking like an A-bomb test at Yucca Flats. The night sky was instantly alive with burning shards of metal and debris that were hurled skyward came then raining down, peppering a thousand-yards in every direction.

The thieves retaliated, spraying a cloud of bullets in their direction. Skinner was hit, but immediately assured it was nothing. After the initial barrage, it quickly settled into a game of shooting at light flashes, then ducking.

After a few more minutes, the night became quiet, abruptly changing from the bedlam of battlefield to an eerie silence. During the lull, Sheriff Jackson whispered to the group. "This could go on all night. Somebody needs to circle around to the other side, so we can get 'em in a crossfire."

"I'll go," Roper whispered back with more courage than he felt.

"Me too," Skinner said. "You lead the way, cowboy."

"Skinner, when you get in position, flick your cigarette lighter twice," Sheriff Jackson said, "then we'll start firing."

"Be like shooting ducks in a barrel, Skinner laughed, forking his mustache.

With firelight coming from the still burning wreckage, Roper and Skinner crawled east, making a wide circle to the far side of the dig. Eventually when they had worked into position, Skinner raised his arm and flicked his lighter. He waited a few seconds and did it again.

Instantly, the sheriff, Ruby and Deputy Ainsley started firing in the general direction of the dig, some thirty yards below Skinner and Roper. When the thieves fired back, Roper and Skinner immediately spotted their positions. With their backs exposed, the thieves were defenseless.

In the darkness, Roper thought he saw Sean. Raising his 30/30, Roper sighted in on his back and slowly tightened his finger around the trigger, then he stopped. He couldn't do it. Sean had saved his life. Moving his aim, he fired into the dirt.

"You're surrounded," Sheriff Jackson yelled out from the other side. "Give it up."

There were several moments of tense silence, then the clatter of metal guns being dropped on the rocks.

"We're unarmed," Sean hollered.

Instantly, four powerful flashlights snapped on as Sheriff Jackson, Deputy Ainsley, Ruby and Skinner trained their beams on the now demoralized thieves.

"Don't move a finger," Sheriff Jackson ordered. "Alan, go handcuff them."

Deputy Ainsley did as he was told, but when he got to Bucky he hesitated. Slowly and unsteadily, Bonnet Leigh Eakins rose from the cold damp earth. He clamped his teeth on his Dunhill pipe and took a couple of puffs. Satisfied it was still lit, he turned to face Douglas Roper Rehnquist.

Et tu, Brute! Then fall, Caesar!

Without missing a beat, Roper added:

Liberty! Freedom! Tyranny is dead!

Run hence, proclaim, cry it about the streets!

EPILOGUE

DANCE HALL ROCK

If you close your eyes and erase the twenty-first century from your mind, you can almost hear a fiddle being plucked, a chorus of laughter and the rhythm of boots a stompin' on the sandstone floor. Dance Hall Rock and its adjacent Forty Mile Spring was a favorite resting spot for early Utah pioneers making their way to Arizona. Up to this point, the road from Escalante had been relatively easy, though uncertain ground lie ahead. Scouts were sent out to survey a route to the Colorado River, while the rest of the company camped, got caught up on chores and rested their animals. Before the scouts returned with sobering news of what lay ahead, spirits were high and many a dance was held in this natural amphitheater.

Constructed from ancient sand dunes deposited in the Jurassic Period, Dance Hall Rock is a solitary bulwark of vermilion Entrada sandstone. Chiseled into this huge rock is a large semicircular amphitheater with a flat floor and a sheer red stone wall as a backdrop. Adorning the entrance is a rock garden composed of spherical sandstone boulders and a small botanical garden containing of one juniper and scattered Brigham tea, snake broom, sagebrush and an assortment of black brush.

After crossing the single-span concrete bridge over the Colorado River, Roper drove through the tourist town, former uranium boom town, of Moab, Utah. Though there was quite a bit of traffic, he suspected this was nothing compared to the peak summer season when tourists flock in droves to see Arches and Canyonlands National Parks, Dead Horse Point State Park, river raft the mighty Colorado or bicycle the red slick rock. Lining the spotless streets were cottonwoods, ashes, box elders and maples, also blazing the full spectrum of autumn colors, pale yellow through fiery red. A brief shower had passed through during the night leaving the air wet, crisp and smelling like newly washed sheets.

Roper had gotten up early, five o'clock, skipped breakfast and headed out. In the dark he had left Escalante, heading down Highway 12 to Boulder, then on to Torrey. At Torrey he took Highway 24 through Hanksville to Interstate 70, then after bypassing Green River he had arrived in Moab via scenic Highway 19 and had stopped for gas.

As he pumped the diesel fuel, he checked his watch. It was still early, barely eight o'clock, and he needed to be in Cortez, Colorado, actually Mesa Verde National Park, by noon. Mentally, he did the calculations. He should just make it, but there was no time for a sit-down breakfast. Instead, as he paid for his gas he grabbed a sweet roll and a cup of hot chocolate from the convenience store and hopped back in the truck.

From Moab, Roper headed south to Monticello, then turned on Highway 666, crossing into the state of Colorado and on into Dove Creek, the self-proclaimed capital of the pinto bean. After another thirty-five miles of hard driving, he entered the picturesque town of Cortez. He was almost there; Mesa Verde was only another ten miles to the east.

Roper paid his entrance fee at the toll booth and asked directions to park headquarters. Fifteen minutes later, he parked his truck in front of the large adobe building and turned off the ignition. He was ten minutes early. Climbing out, he stretched, yawned then went in the main entrance. He spoke briefly with the ranger behind the counter, then picked up a copy of the Mesa Verde National Park newspaper to read while he waited. Settling in, Roper immersed himself in an article about Park visitation. Apparently, this was the slow season, some days there was not more than a hundred to two hundred visitors. This, however, Roper thought, was more than the Grand Staircase National Monument had on a very busy day.

"How are you, Roper?"

Dropping the paper, he looked up. "Just fine. How about you?" He stood up, warmly shaking the extended hand.

"Actually, doing quite well. Did you bring your set?"

"No, I forgot," Roper laughed sheepishly, "but I'm sure you've got one somewhere."

"Several," Judith Brisco replied. "I collect them."

"Sounds like I'm in for a long day."

"Well, I'm a bit rusty," Judith said. "It's hard to find someone who plays."

"With the popularity of video and computer games, it might very well become a thing of the past," Roper agreed.

"Let's go. I've prepared a lunch we can eat while we play."

Getting into her forest-green Park truck, she drove to Chapin Mesa, then after taking the right hand road, stopped at the Navajo Canyon Overlook. They got out and Judith retrieved two aluminum camp chairs and a folding table from the back of the pickup. She positioned them right at the overlook, granting a panoramic view of Navajo Canyon. Slowly, Roper sank into a chair, taking in the vista.

It was a perfect light-jacket day. Not a whisper of air stirred through the burgeoning pinions or towering ponderosa pines. The topaz blue sky overhead was unblemished, clear and cloudless. Cradling his hands behind his head, Roper gazed out at the deep sandstone-carved walls of Navajo Canyon, then off into the distance at the sacred Ute Mountain. It was almost as beautiful as the Grand Staircase, but not quite. It lacked the Staircase's color.

Judith arranged both a picnic basket and a chess set on the table. It was a handsome board, handmade from Cordoba, Spain, Christians versus the Moors. She grabbed a pawn from each side, shuffled them quickly, then extended her closed hands. Shrugging, Roper chose the left hand.

"You're the Moors," Judith announced as she opened her hands.

"That gives you the historical advantage," Roper joked, gathering his pieces.

"I don't, know" Judith said. "The Moors ruled Spain for more than six hundred years."

"I guess that's longer than the Christians," Roper replied, mentally doing the math.

"Do you realize the player with the first move wins sixty percent of the time?"

"I might just as well concede now," Roper said with a smile.

"Okay, I accept your concession," Judith replied, "but let's go through the motions anyway."

There was a moment of silence as they organized their pieces. Without comment, Judith began play by moving her K-pawn to D-4. Roper immediately countered, relocating his K-pawn to D-5.

"How do you like it here?" he asked.

"It's okay. It's good to be back in the National Park Service," Judith replied, moving her knight to C-3. "It's where I belong."

"I'm sorry things didn't work out at the Grand Staircase."

"Me too. I took a demotion by coming here," Judith laughed, then added, "like I had a choice."

"I had nothing to do with that," Roper said quickly, glancing up from the board. "The Utah congressional delegation did that all on their own."

"Oh well. It doesn't matter," Judith replied, "It's your move."

Roper pondered for a moment then moved his pawn to C-6. "You're second in command here, aren't you?"

"Yes."

"It's a beautiful place."

"Yeah , but it's the history that makes it fascinating. Did you know people have lived in this area for about eight hundred years? They first moved in somewhere around the birth of Jesus. That first era was called the Basketmakers. They were mainly farmers. Somewhere around four hundred A.D., the Indians began to hunt, make pottery and construct roofed-dwellings, that era was dubbed Modified Basketmakers. Then roughly around seven fifty A.D. the people started to gather in bands and build villages. That period has been christened Developmental Pueblo. However, the cliff dwellings didn't appear until about eleven hundred A.D. That period of time we know as Classic Pueblo. The fruits of that era are what everyone comes to see."

"What? No Classical Cowboy era?" Roper joked. "Surely there's been cowboy's in the area for some time."

"No. None, and might I say I'm happy to be finished with cowboys," Judith said, but failed to hide a hint of a smile. "Are you back to ranching yet?"

"No. We're still negotiating. Kind of depends on the drought and when the land recovers," Roper said. "It's your move."

"Then what are you doing?" Judith asked, as she moved her bishop to F-4. "Some of us have to work for a living."

"I'm back teaching at SUU. On weekends, I go back to Escalante and farm my private ground—and I'm working on my doctorate." Roper studied the board. After a moment, he angled his Knight to F-6.

"English History or literature?"

"Right—kind of both," Roper replied. "More specifically the Battle of Culloden and the English literature associated that period."

"One of the Scottish battles for independence?"

"Yeah, there were a bunch."

"How about Skinner Jacobsen?" Judith asked, taking two sandwiches from the basket, offering one to Roper.

"Thanks." Roper accepted the ham sandwich. "Like me, he's doing what farming he can. Also, he's finagled a job with the State Highway Department."

"I'll have to admit, Skinner surprised me," Judith remarked, handing Roper a Coke. "He was high on my list of suspects."

"Mine, too," Roper agreed. "As it turned out, he was just trying to help Ruby. Probably infatuated with her."

Judith moved her Knight then looked sharply up at Roper. "He wasn't the only one, now was he? What ever happened to her?"

"Well, it's kind of a long story," Roper said, capturing one of Judith's pawns. "Eventually all the charges were dropped. Sandy Parker's DNA did not match that of Ruby's, meaning she did not kill her husband. Interestingly enough, through a little superb sleuthing on Sheriff Jackson's part, he was able to show that Bonñet Leigh had been in California about the time that confession letter was mailed to Ruby. It's possible he may have been involved in Chet Parker's murder as well."

"What about her father?" Judith asked as she continued play. "I thought she was a suspect in her father's death—some kind of revenge for abuse."

"The abuse was real enough, all right," Roper agreed, "but she was never really a suspect—except in Sandy Parker's mind. The Salado Police

Department was, and is still convinced that it was a self-inflicted gunshot wound, motivated by guilt perhaps."

"So what's she doing now?"

Grinning, he held up his right hand, his ring finger sporting a gold wedding band. "She's living with me now. We're married."

"Congratulations," Judith said, looking up and smiling. "I'm glad something turned out for you."

"She's doing most of the farm work during the week while I'm away. And she just got her real estate license."

"You should have brought her."

"She wanted to come, but she had a closing today. Her first."

By boldly moving his queen from the back row, Roper instantly transformed her into a multi-directional fighting piece. "Check!" he said.

Judith studied her predicament, then after a few moments blocked Roper's check with her knight. "What about Bucky or should I say Bonnet Leigh and Sean O'Grady?"

"Their trial is coming up next month. The thirteenth I think. They've retained two hotshot lawyers from Salt Lake and have pled innocent, but no one believes they will get off."

"What offenses did the county finally charge them with?"

"Three counts of murder, Angus Macdonald, Ron Sparks and Monty Coleman and also with at least two counts of theft of government property, you know—dinosaur fossils."

"Capital murder?"

"Nah, they don't think any of the murders were pre-meditated. As best as anyone can tell, it was a chain of unfortunate events. It looks like these three guys just got in the way of their fossil business, either accidentally or deliberately."

"Which was which?" Judith asked.

"Sheriff Jackson's working theory is that Angus accidentally stumbled onto them. You know he had coal leases on the Kaiparowits. Ron Sparks, he thinks, was tipped off and rushed in too fast, and Monty Coleman had probably been working the case for some time and had simply gotten too close. But, I'm not so sure there wasn't more to it than that."

"Such as?" Judith asked, glancing up from the board.

"Well, I know for a fact Bucky hated Bill Clinton and basically all democrats for creating the monument."

"Why was Bonńet Leigh so against the monument? He had no cattle."

"The monument threatened his fossil business. More tourist traffic and more patrols," Roper explained, reaching for his sandwich. "Whose move is it anyway?"

"Yours. So with Bonńet you think this was all a personal grudge or trying to protect his fossil business?"

"Probably a bit of both. And Sean had a double agenda too, not only the fossil business, but he really was a dedicated environmentalist. Deep down, he wanted absolutely no mining, ranching or any other commercial enterprise on the monument."

"But why poor Ron and Monty? They were all on the same side."

"Yes, but quite different agendas. As you know, you guys wanted to develop the Grand Staircase, more like Yellowstone. Sean definitely did not."

"But Bucky," Judith said, shaking her head. "He certainly had me fooled. He deserves an honorary degree in the theater for that performance."

"I guess in some ways he was a genius, but like a lot of gifted people, he thought society's rules were arbitrary and did not apply to him."

"Apparently not," Judith agreed. "What about the arson? How does that fit in?"

"That was either Sean freelancing, like he did with his sugar-in-the-gas-tank caper or him and Bucky Lee trying to create a diversion. I think, however, that was all Sean, but that's just my opinion."

"And the bloody cow's head planted in front of my office." Judith shuddered. "Who did that?"

"No question about it, that was all Bucky Lee," Roper replied, "trying to intimidate you. Ruby told me they took a sick cow from the pens in Salina and gave it to Bucky."

"Those two," Judith said, shaking her head. "What an unholy alliance."

"They certainly were an odd couple," Roper agreed.

"At the time, it was all pretty scary. Will they be tried in federal court?"

"Yeah, the thefts and murders were all on federal property." Roper's queen brazenly captured one of Judith's knights.

"What about Professor Albright's fossil? Did they every find out what happened to it?"

"Yeah, it took awhile," Roper confirmed. "They eventually traced it to a private museum in Japan and are presently negotiating its return."

"The whole thing was just terrible—a living nightmare."

"I agree," Roper said shaking his head. "And Judith, I'm sorry about your losses, Ron and Monty."

"They were both good men. Everyone knew Ron was, but Monty was very much misunderstood. He was a hard worker, honest and absolutely loyal."

They drifted into silence, both concentrating on the game.

Suddenly, Judith took Roper's queen with her bishop. "Checkmate!"

Roper studied the board for a few moments, then stood up and shook Judith's hand. "Congratulations," he said.

"You want to make it double or nothing?" she asked.

Roper glanced at his watch. "Why not? And don't think I'm going to be so easy on you this time," Roper replied. "And, I'll go first."

AUTHOR'S NOTE AND DISCLAIMER

In fairness to the reader, I should disclose my background—where I came from and where I'm coming from. I grew up in an agrarian family, my father being a parttime farmer/rancher. Thus to this mindset and lifestyle I was thoroughly indoctrinated. Before I began writing the book, I had been following this story very closely for some time, collecting a file not only on the creation of the Grand Staircase/Escalante National Monument, but also the ensuing bitter imbroglio. At first my natural sentiments resided with the ranchers, particularly after interviewing some of them, and I fully intended to make the Bureau of Land Management (BLM) my most deserved and contemptible antagonist.

However, in further researching the book, I also had occasion to interview several of the BLM staff and management and asked for their help on several aspects of this project. This help they freely gave. Subsequently, these men and women unknowingly mollified my point of view.

Now, I honestly feel this conflict was an inevitable clash over culture, ideas and authority. As with a many historical events, right and wrong, moral or immoral, depends on who's telling the story. And the official version is almost always authored by the prevailing party. The Grand Staircase dispute I feel is a classic example of no one being right or wrong, but simply a collision of ideologies. The ranchers were desperately trying to hang onto a way of life that was and is slipping through their fingers. The BLM, on the other hand, was and is honestly trying to discharge their obligations as stewards, a calling they take quite seriously.

What conclusions can be drawn from this, if any? Conflicts are rarely a struggle between good and evil. More often than not, moral labels are not applicable, even foolish. This I feel is especially true of the Staircase feud which when reduced to its basic elements was simply a contest of power and land management. It would be ideal, of course, if life could more closely mimic fiction and all conflicts could be resolved over a friendly game of chess or a cup of coffee. But of this I can assure the reader, time has not dulled, softened nor ameliorated the fierce partisan passions or deep sense of betrayal created by this national monument.

Without question, however, this wild and wonderful land is well worth the trouble to visit, though undeniably it is a park for the hardy. As the reader knows, I began each chapter with a brief description of a unique monument feature. Unfortunately, I ran out of chapters long before I exhausted my caption material. There is so much more I never mentioned.

For the record, some of the events of this novel are completely factual, some are gently embellished and still others are wholly fabricated. Regardless of the final percentages, by definition that makes the finished product a work of fiction. In no way is this book meant to be a precise treatise on monument history, nor should it be construed as a biography for any particular person or persons. Needless to say, the cast of this novel is composed entirely of contrived and imaginary characters.

—Warren J. Stucki